Past Passions

Past Passions

An anthology of erotic fiction by women

Black lace novels are sexual fantasies.
In real life, make sure you practise safe sex.

First published in 1997 by
Black Lace
332 Ladbroke Grove
London W10 5AH

Typeset by CentraCet, Cambridge
Printed and bound by Cox & Wyman Ltd, Reading

ISBN 0 352 33159 3

Contents

Introduction

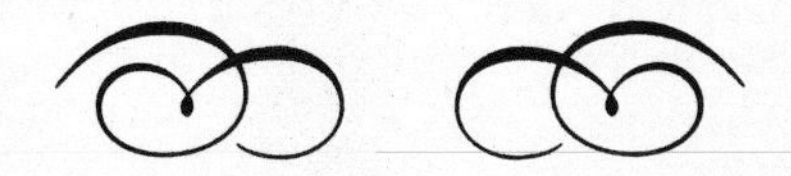

Black Lace is the first series of books to recognise women's erotic fiction as a genre. Before the series was launched in the UK in Summer 1993, there was very little material of this nature which was designed with a female audience in mind. Nancy Friday, author of *My Secret Garden,* was one of the first people to recognise female sexual fantasy as a valid and exciting area for exploration and study. Her work was non-judgmental and legitimised no-holds-barred writing about sex from women's viewpoints. Despite this, erotic *fiction* remained the preserve of men. Friday's book was categorised as non-fiction/sexology and was first published in the early 1970s. Much writing about women and sex in the following two decades took a journalist path; it was where women felt comfortable.

Of course, women writing explicit stories is nothing new; Anais Nin was working in this area 50 years ago and her work continues to sell long after her death. The female erotic imagination is a storehouse of secret treasures whose diversity constitutes a genre in its own right. Men have always been able to access sexually explicit material and have controlled its production and distribution for centuries. At Black Lace, we think women have as much right as men to read blatantly arousing fiction which is their own. Our readers like the fact that Black Lace books guarantee female authorship.

Past Passions brings together extracts from some of the most popular and best-selling Black Lace titles which have historical settings. Whether set in London during the time of the Prince

Regent, a Druid encampment in Roman Britain, India during the days of the Raj or the Australian outback in the 1880s, each story is imbued with a rich and unashamed sense of erotic escapism. Historical fiction has always appealed to women; the details of clothing, custom and courtship being of particular interest. In the Black Lace novel, these things can be explored to their maximum erotic potential; the details of clothing can be fetished and the past can be sexualised. The erotic charge which provided the basis of the subtext in novels such as *Jane Eyre* or *Pride and Prejudice* can be magnified and brought to prominence.

Feedback from our readers tells us that historical and contemporary settings are equally popular. It is important to remember that the free-flowing imagination is not censored by notions of political correctness; any imprint which gives a free rein to explore sexual fantasy is going to encounter writing in which characters challenge notions of 'acceptable' behaviour. Erotic fantasy is an exciting and endlessly fascinating subject. With no shortage of manuscripts from women of all ages and walks of life, we are confident that Black Lace books will continue to reflect the infinite diversity of the female erotic imagination.

Kerri Sharp January 1997

Lord Wraxall's Fancy

Anna Lieff Saxby

The year is 1720 and Lady Celine Fortescue has been summoned by her father to the turbulent Caribbean island of which he is governor. During the long sea voyage to St Cecilia, Celine meets and falls in love with Liam O'Brien, one of the ship's officers. Unfortunately, Celine's father has made other plans for her which involve the arrogant and flamboyant Viscount Odo Wraxall.

Compromised into marriage, Celine is a most reluctant bride. Despite her determination to maintain a distance from her new husband, Celine cannot deny his skills as a lover. This extract sees the new Lady Wraxall brought to Odo's palatial estate and introduced to some of the dastardly man's favourite and most depraved pastimes. Her response to the profane pleasures surprises even herself.

Lord Wraxall's Fancy is Anna Lieff Saxby's first Black Lace book. The historical detail is meticulous and the story dazzles and delights. Wraxall makes an excellent rogue who is used to getting his way in all things. With the Lady Celine, however, he has met his match and is in for an uphill struggle if he wants to bend her to his will. We hope there will be a sequel to *Lord Wraxall's Fancy* some time in 1998.

Lord Wraxall's Fancy

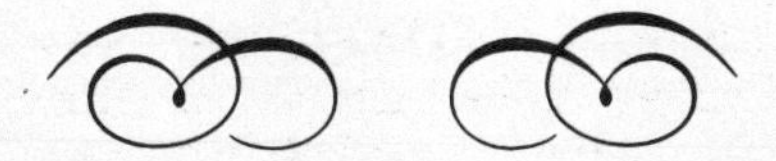

Sir James had spared no expense over the wedding breakfast of his daughter. Celine sat at the centre of the top table, stiffly ignoring the congratulations and bawdy jokes.

Viscount Odo Wraxall was placed at her right. His fingers glittered with rings. He wore cloth of silver embroidered with jet, and the lace at his wrists and throat was black. Long hair, dark as his lace, curled about his shoulders.

They shared a gold goblet and plate. She hardly touched the rich dishes that were offered, and when Odo handed the tall cup of wine to her she turned it, surreptitiously, so that her lips would not rest where his had been.

On her other side, her father was deep in conversation with Mistress Colney. One of his hands was hidden beneath the table, and Celine suspected that it was busy among Sally's petticoats.

The red-headed woman had been out of town for some days, returning just in time to attend the wedding. It was clear from her scornful look that she thought Celine's courage had failed her, or that the lure of a noble name had tempted her; for Sir James was full of claret and self-importance, and was boasting about the alliance in a loud, drunken voice.

'A fine ol' family,' bawled Sir James, leaning close to Sally. 'Not a lot of money, but ver' ol'. Goes back to the Conqueror! Min' you,' he added, lowering his voice to what he thought was a whisper, 'he's a hard bargainer. You'd not believe what the marriage settlements cost me, first an' last.'

Lord Wraxall stirred beside her. He leant forward and raised her chin with one jewelled finger, forcing her to meet his look.

'Do you recall where I saw you first?' he asked, quietly.

It was impossible to misunderstand him. Purchased for her dowry, sold for a great name: she did not need to be so cruelly reminded that she was now as much his property as any slave bought at the barracoon.

Her father lumbered to his feet and began a rambling speech. Odo released her abruptly, and stifled a yawn behind his hand.

Sir James broke off and glared at him.

'Am I boring you?' he asked belligerently.

'Not at all, sir,' said Odo. 'How could it be possible? But – forgive me – to a bridegroom all delay is tiresome.'

Sir James recovered his aplomb and roared with amusement.

'I'll swear it is!' he chuckled. 'Why, where the marriage-bed's concerned, you're as much of a virgin as my daughter. Damme, it must be the only thing you've never tried!'

Lord Odo bowed coldly. His expression of distaste silenced the sniggering of the guests almost before it began. He held out his hand.

'Lady Wraxall,' he said, 'The carriage awaits.'

She started. Lady Wraxall, she thought, with horror. Why, that's me.

Celine allowed herself to be led through a barrage of laughter and jests and handed up into the chaise outside. Lord Odo gave his orders to the coachman and sprang up beside her.

Celine was very aware of her new husband lounging beside her, his body swaying easily as they jolted over the cobbles. He neither spoke, nor touched her. She could not help but be grateful for the unexpected respite.

Twining her hands together in her lap, she looked determinedly out of the window.

The road took them west, and out of town. It plunged into ancient forest, where trees overlaced the way and orchids grew among their dark foliage. Heat lay on Celine's skin, and her clothes stuck to her wherever they touched.

The carriage reached the top of one last hill and started to descend, swaying wildly over the rutted track. Little clearings opened beside the road, each with its tumbledown hut and meagre crops of yam and cassava.

Then the wheels slammed into a pot-hole, and the chaise

lurched wildly. Celine cried out as she was flung from her seat. Moving with that disturbing swiftness that he sometimes showed, Lord Wraxall caught her back to safety.

Startled into speech, she whispered her thanks.

'It'll be easier once we get on to my lands,' he said.

His arm remained around her waist in a gesture of ownership. Celine could feel the warmth of his body through the heavy satin of her gown. She stole a dubious glance at him. His eyes were hooded, but he was watching her: waiting.

'I – I thought this was your land,' she faltered. 'Aren't those your slaves in the fields?'

'Those are small farmers,' said Lord Wraxall disdainfully. 'Free men. I'd be a fool to treat my slaves so poorly: starved animals cannot work. Why this sudden interest in things agricultural?'

Celine looked away. The road was sweeping down towards the sea, and a little way ahead two tall brick pillars marked the entrance to an estate.

'I mean to try to be a good wife, sir. I should know about such matters.'

'Hades! I did not marry you to get a gracious chatelaine!' he said, with a laugh. 'Let us be clear about this, madam. I wanted your person and your fortune. And when I have exhausted the pleasures of both – well, that's for the future. For the present we are at the gates of my plantation. Welcome to Acheron, Lady Wraxall.' His hands slid across the pearly satin of her gown. 'And to your new duties.'

With a final rattle and jerk, they swung to the left and through the pillared entrance on to a smooth paved way. The chaise settled down, swaying slowly through acres of sugar-cane that stretched to the horizon. His touch grew bolder, more demanding, caressing her through the layers of cloth.

'Show me your breasts,' he said, softly.

He cannot mean it, thought Celine. Not here – not now! The carriage blinds were open. Any one of the labourers among the cane could look in and see her.

'Why this hesitation? Must I remind you that I have a husband's right?'

'Wait!' she pleaded. 'My lord, you've been so patient. If you will only give me time, just a little longer . . .'

'What, did you think I was showing gentlemanly forbearance?'

he scoffed. 'How little you know me! If I have spared you until now it is only because I prefer my pleasures undisturbed by the jolting of an ill-made road.'

'I can't,' said Celine. She looked up at him imploringly. 'You must understand. I beg you, don't ask this of me.'

Lord Wraxall met her gaze calmly.

'I have no interest in rape as a pastime, though, now we are married, the concept has no legal foundation. The fact remains that I could force you – ' he said, hooking strong fingers into the low neckline of her bodice ' – if I had to.'

His voice was quiet – he even smiled – but Celine had no doubt that he was serious. When she gave no answer he slowly closed his grip. Her lip trembled, but she met his eyes resolutely.

'Very well,' she said in a bitter voice. 'It's true I made my vows to you, and I'll keep my word – so far as I'm able. But honour, my lord, and love, I'm afraid will be beyond me. You must make do with obedience.'

She thrust his hand away with shaking fingers and jerked at the ribbons fastening the front of her gown. The bodice fell open, exposing the swell of Celine's firm young breasts above her tight-laced stays.

Compelling herself to breathe slowly, she stared at him and tried to make herself as still and cold as a marble stone. But the rocking carriage cheated her. As it swayed, her rosy nipples moved provocatively, now hidden, now displayed to Lord Wraxall's measuring gaze.

'Pretty enough,' he said.

Celine set her teeth as he bore her back against the cushions. She would do her duty, but no more. He leant over her, pushing the wedding dress back from her shoulders and freeing her breasts from the last vestige of covering. He ran his hands over every inch of her pale, exposed flesh.

Celine was a statue.

He caressed her expertly, his touch light but demanding, and dipped his tongue into the hollow at the base of her throat.

She lay rigid, looking up at the quilted lining of the chaise. It was pale fawn leather, held in place by gilded studs bearing the Wraxall crest. Celine counted them: left to right, and then diagonally.

'What, stubborn?' Odo murmured. 'Not for long, I think.'

He bent, and covered her breasts and throat with kisses. His hair trailed ticklingly across her skin. His thin, bejewelled hands moved on her with the skill of a practised seducer. Celine shivered and lost count for a moment.

His tongue flicked out, teasing her nipples. His cheeks hollowed as he sucked at them, nibbling gently.

Celine thought of dull sermons, of Aunt Prudence at her everlasting needlework, of anything but Odo's knowledgeable fondling. She did not want him. She hated him! But his hands held a power over her. It no longer seemed to matter if she cared, what she thought. Despite all her resolution she could feel a sullen excitement growing in her, like a black lily.

He knew her. He was aware of secrets, longings, urgencies that she herself could hardly put a name to. He sensed the flower of eroticism that had its roots in her innermost being. And he fed it, tended it, ruthlessly playing on her awakening body until it turned traitor, fighting against her will.

Hopelessly, Celine felt her nipples respond to his unceasing stimulation, their soft tissue hardening and swelling until they were fully erect. She stifled a groan of despair as she felt an answering tingle between her legs.

Each moment it was harder to remain still and passive: soon, she knew, it would be beyond her power. Celine turned her head away, trying to call up Liam's image, trying to pretend – as she had last night – that the hands caressing her were his. But Lord Wraxall was too quick for her; he forced her back to face him, willing her to meet his eyes.

'Don't think you can escape that way,' he whispered. 'I tolerate no rivals, not even in imagination.'

Lifting her smoothly, until she lay half across his body, he crushed her close. The rough texture of the lace at his breast brushed against her already sensitised nipples, teasing them until they burned and throbbed.

Slowly, he raised her skirts and pushed up the froth of her petticoats. His hand slid along the taut silk of her stockings to the naked skin above.

Her heart fluttered. She dreaded the moment when his lazily questing fingers would reach their goal and learn from the seeping wetness there how much he had aroused her. But even the act of trying to shut him out excited her further. The pressure of her thighs and the swaying of the slow-moving carriage squeezed and massaged her swollen cleft.

He insinuated one hand between her legs, pushing them apart. She felt his fingers moving slowly upwards, sliding easily on her wet skin. He found her pleasure-bud and stroked it repeatedly, delicate as a feather. Celine quivered, unable to prevent herself opening to him.

Lord Wraxall gave a low laugh.

'Did you really think to resist me? Little fool: I knew your mother. I know how the tropic heat calls out to the inheritance in your blood.'

As he spoke, he tantalised the engorged flesh until she writhed and gasped under his expert titillation. She forgot hatred and thrust shame aside. Celine clung to him, past caring for anything but the excitement of his touch.

Gentle no longer, he parted the soft lips of her sex and plunged his fingers deeply within her, again and again. Celine whimpered with enjoyment, thrusting herself against his hand as he bent to kiss her.

She answered his lips with eager desire, feeling the foretaste of ecstasy as he found and teased the pleasure-spot on the wall of her vagina. She abandoned herself, intoxicated with need, pushing herself against him, wantonly encouraging his probing fingers

And then he took his hand away.

'I am master here,' he said, with a mocking smile. 'I could take my pleasure and deny you yours, if I chose. It's no more than many a bride endures. I could tease you and bring you to the brink, and leave you unsatisfied: each time, every time.'

Celine trembled. He could not mean it.

'If you want more,' he said, 'there is a price. Will you pay it?'

Celine sobbed her agreement. She would do anything – anything – if only he'd have mercy on her, satisfy the lust he had so cruelly aroused.

'Not anything: everything. What I demand, you will do. What I order, you will perform. You can hate me, if you want – you would be wise to fear me – but you will obey. Is it agreed?'

His eyes widened. She read unnamable depravities in them. But he already knew that she could deny him nothing. Her desire overwhelmed her fear.

'Is it agreed? Say it!'

'Yes!' cried Celine.

'Then take your reward,' said Lord Wraxall, huskily.

Celine moaned with relief as he kissed her breasts, suckling and tugging greedily at her nipples. His wrist pressed down hard against her clitoris. She could feel the embroidery on his cuff. The black lace of his ruffles, sodden with the juice of her arousal, rubbed fiercely against the sensitive bud.

'You can't imagine what delights your body can yield to you,' breathed Odo against her skin. 'You dream of simple pleasures, candid as the day. But I shall teach you other things. With me you'll take dark paths and hidden ways.'

His thumb thrust deeply into her vagina, pushing and circling. His index finger moved further back, finding and widening the tight ring of her anus, squeezing within. Celine gasped and twisted as he penetrated her, hardly knowing if it was pain or pleasure that she felt.

Her climax was near, she could feel it peaking. Nothing mattered but this growing ecstasy, the nearing moment of release. She surrendered entirely to Lord Wraxall as with cruel, unceasing stimulation he brought her to the edge.

He kept her teetering there a moment, as if to show his power. Then he took mercy, and pushed her over, sending her plunging into an orgasm so exquisite and long-lasting that it felt like a little death.

Celine lay against Lord Wraxall, shaking to the thunder of her heartbeats. Now that her lust was satisfied she felt shame, and horror, and a deep remorse. How could she have surrendered to him so totally, so abjectly?

He pushed her away and busied himself with a handkerchief, drying his hands. The carriage was stationary. She had no idea how long it had been still. Keeping her eyes lowered, she fumbled for the fastenings of her gown.

'What are you doing?' he asked. He flicked her cheek with his fingertips: a light, stinging blow. 'Answer me.'

'I must make myself decent,' she whispered.

Leaning forward, he wrenched the satin bodice out of her hands, dragging it down and off her shoulders, leaving her naked breasts fully displayed.

'I think not,' he said. 'There was a price for your pleasure, my lady, remember? One that you agreed to pay. And now you begin.'

Celine swallowed convulsively and, for the first time, raised her eyes. Lord Wraxall was framed against the carriage window. Behind him, a great plantation house reared its pillars towards the burning sky. On the broad veranda the household staff were gathered, staring and craning.

A footman flung open the carriage door. Odo descended. He held out an imperative hand to her.

She did not stir. No matter what promises he had extorted from her in the heat of passion, she shrank from flaunting herself half-naked before that waiting crowd. But he would certainly have her dragged from the carriage if she continued to resist his will.

'You try my patience, madam,' said Lord Wraxall. 'Come: Acheron waits to greet its new mistress.'

Gathering all her courage, Celine let him help her down from the chaise. Every inch of her exposed flesh was suffused with blushes. She wanted nothing better than to run and hide within the house, but she made herself match his slow pace, sweeping up the shallow steps like a queen.

Formed up in a double line, the domestics flanked the entrance. They did not even pretend to spare her. Whispering together, they looked her over openly, and their eyes were hungry. Celine's nipples tightened involuntarily under their lascivious stares.

Lord Wraxall led her between their ranks, murmuring names: this was Mr Jeffries the steward, and this the cook, François; Charles and Rupert the footmen, the upper-housemaid, the lower-housemaids, the between-stairs maid, the laundress, the gardeners, and half a hundred others.

A foxy fellow in the neat livery of a groom ogled her breasts with insolent desire. His undisguised lust woke dark tremors in her. Looking away hastily, she examined her new home with an interest only partly feigned.

Acheron rose above her, square and white-painted, each of its three storeys surrounded by deep, vine-draped verandas that protected the inner rooms from the direct rays of the sun.

To the west lay a low, circular building, its red-tiled roof supported by massive pillars. It stood apart from the main body of the house, connected to it by a colonnade: a library perhaps, or a music room.

Lord Wraxall caught the direction of her gaze.

'The Rotunda. The design is taken from a temple I visited in Antioch, many years ago. You will see it tonight. Let us go in.'

It was cool and dim inside the plantation house. Green light filtered in through the creepers. Celine freed herself from Lord Wraxall with a jerk and huddled her bodice around her.

'You don't deceive me with these prudish airs, madam wife,' Lord Wraxall said. 'You could feel their desire. You were stimulated by it.'

'No!' cried Celine.

'You're lying,' he said. He brushed her still-taut nipples with one fingertip. 'Do you think I am blind?'

Celine began a fierce rebuttal. Lord Wraxall smiled sardonically, and she found herself faltering into silence. In spite of her shame she could not deny that some part of her had warmed to the response she had drawn from his household. As he had known that it would.

'Do you begin to feel your body's power?' he whispered, leaning closer. 'They want you. They lust for you. And – for the present – you are mine.'

He took her hand, leading her towards the stairs. Celine could not help feeling that to obey so meekly was contemptible. She should resist, rebel somehow against his cool assumption of dominance. And yet it excited her in a way she could not understand.

Celine felt a dart of fear, not unmixed with anticipation. The moment of their union could not be far off now, and she caught herself looking covertly at him, wondering how it would be.

Lord Wraxall led her past the company rooms on the first storey, and up again to the bedroom floor. The house was very quiet. She could hear the susurrus of her gown dragging on the carpet. A trapped fly buzzed against the long window that lit the stairs.

Despite her trepidation Celine could not help staring about her. It was another world: richer, stranger, more corrupt. There were no familiar English appointments: no portraits, or pictures of pink shepherdesses among their laundered flocks. Lord Wraxall had plundered the globe to furnish Acheron.

He seemed gratified by her awe, and broke his silence to draw her attention to Greek statuary and Chinese vases. The carpets were loot from Tangier and Smyrna. That suit of armour was from the hidden land of Japan. Persian miniatures glowed on the walls between scimitars and savage masks.

He did nothing so vulgar as boast, but it was clear that he was proud of his collection. Celine understood with a shock that she, too, was just one more item in his treasure-house. He had not made her expose herself before his servants merely to humiliate her.

Oh, he had enjoyed her shame: it was his nature. But he had displayed her with an owner's pride, like a man who shows off a precious diamond, increasing its value to himself by the envy of others.

Celine's chamber lay at the back of the house, its door guarded by the gigantic figure of a many-armed goddess, poised in a dance step.

'From Rajputana,' said Odo. 'Kali.'

He stroked the smooth metal. Where his hand lay on the statue's thigh the bronze was bright, polished by repeated caresses.

'*Beloved and lovely,*' he recited, softly. '*Deathless, pariah, drinker of blood. Valour in the form of a woman*. She cost nine men's lives to get away.'

The warmth of his tone piqued Celine. It seemed she was not even the most prized among his possessions. Though it brought the inevitable consummation closer, she was glad when Lord Wraxall left the statue and opened the door, standing aside to let her pass.

A pulse fluttering wildly in her throat, Celine crossed the threshold. Lord Wraxall followed close behind her. He closed the door and leant against the panels. With a little smile on his face he watched her look around the bridal chamber.

'I trust you approve my taste,' he said.

The room was high and shadowed, hung with mirrors in ebony frames. It reflected itself endlessly, enclosing her like the heart of a sombre flower.

The furniture was black lacquer, writhing with dragons. A great bed, curtained and canopied with funereal silk, dominated the room's centre. With a lurch of the heart Celine noticed ring-bolts were set into each of its four towering posts. Was he going to tie her down?

The click of the lock startled her. Lord Wraxall twirled the key between long fingers. When he saw her looking, he pocketed it.

'I gave my word,' said Celine in an unsteady voice. 'Is that necessary?'

'I think so,' he replied coolly. 'You have a damnable streak of obstinacy in you, Lady Wraxall. You persist in making me work for every advantage. The day is too sultry for such labours. It's fatiguing, madam.'

He pushed himself away from the door and strolled towards her. In spite of herself, Celine took a step backwards. In the mirrors an infinity of doubles mimicked her actions.

'You see?' said Lord Wraxall.

Celine froze, and clasped her hands together.

'Then what must I do?' she asked helplessly.

Odo circled her slowly.

'You may take off my coat,' he said at last.

With shaking fingers she slipped it from his shoulders. She could smell the musk of his body, running like a base-note under the herbal scent. On his command, she unbuttoned and removed the long-skirted waistcoat, loosened and laid aside the lace at his throat.

His black lawn shirt, damp with heat, clung to the fine musculature of his chest. The tight breeches displayed, almost as much as they hid, his male member, fully erect and lying diagonally across his flat belly. It seemed impossibly huge to her: after one appalled glance, Celine averted her eyes.

Lord Wraxall shook back his hair and stretched luxuriously, crossing to a tall cabinet between the windows. He stood before it, stripping off his rings.

'Remove your gown,' he said, over his shoulder.

'But . . .' she began.

Lord Wraxall sighed.

When the heavy satin lay shimmering about her feet, he signed for her to continue. The tapes of her stiffened outer petticoat were knotted and she had to worry at them with her fingernails. It fell in a flurry of lace.

Lord Wraxall opened the cabinet, and searched through its multiplicity of drawers and pigeonholes.

Celine slipped out of shoes and stockings. She untied the ribbons at her waist and with trembling fingers let the silken underskirt flutter away.

Lord Wraxall turned to face her, weighing a book and a casket in his hands. His hooded eyes ran measuringly up and down her body. The corset pulled her waist in to a tiny compass, emphasising her hips and breasts.

The triangle of curls at her groin was startlingly black against her fair skin. She hid it from him with her hand and a myriad reflected Celines copied the shy gesture.

Seating himself on the edge of the bed, Odo up-ended the casket, spilling its contents on to the covers. Glass chinked against metal, metal against stone: an ivory ball the size of a turtle's egg rolled and fell soundlessly on the thick carpet.

'We will begin your education,' he said, and beckoned.

When she approached, Odo pulled her down beside him, and opened the book for her to see.

'*Aretino's Postures,*' he explained. 'Printed privately, in Geneva. It is your primer. I expect you to study it.'

He turned the pages slowly, so that her eye was forced to linger on the detailed engravings. In infinite variety they catalogued the positions of love. Bending, standing, supported on cushions, the little, stylised figures of men and women left nothing to the imagination.

Celine shifted nervously, the silk coverlet sliding under her naked thighs. What could it feel like to perform such acts? This one, where the woman's legs clasped her lover's hips like a girdle; or this, where she crouched above the man, kneeling over him and taking his upstanding rod of flesh into her mouth? Despite her misgivings Celine could not help but feel a tremor of arousal.

When Lord Wraxall laid the book aside she knew he had sensed it. The moment was surely now. He would throw her back on the black bed and take her. She forced herself to relax, lying slack in his arms, waiting.

Lord Wraxall frowned: it was clear she had misjudged him.

'Virgins bore me,' he said coldly. 'Of late years I have avoided them: they do not know how to please a man of refinement. I am no peasant, requiring only passive flesh to copulate like a hog. Sit up.'

He jerked her upright and with firm hands ordered her position. Celine bit her lip as he made her perch on the very edge of the bed, parting her legs wide, wider still.

'Look in the glass,' he commanded. 'Watch me as I take my pleasure.'

Celine raised her head. The greatest of all the mirrors fronted the fourposter. Tropic heat and dampness had flaked away the silvering, here and there, but its depths were clear.

Her blatant, spread-legged pose showed every secret of her body. Under the fine black curls the outline of her sex stood out strongly, pursed and swollen, a line of dusky rose cleaving its centre.

She stiffened as Lord Wraxall reached down to open her, his darting fingers squeezing and fondling her gently. He parted the inner lips and she glimpsed the entrance to her vagina, pink and glistening, like the throat of a fleshy orchid. His eyes met hers in the mirror and her heart skipped a beat: who could tell what perversities he might demand of her? There were centuries of corruption in that lean, lined face.

It was degrading, vile, to watch herself being caressed so intimately. Ah, but it felt so good. Celine could not prevent herself responding. She flexed her spine, and with a tiny movement pushed against his fingers.

She saw Odo's lips twist in an arrogant smile. He had known she would succumb, she thought bitterly. He was a virtuoso. Over many years he had taken the art of love and made it a science: technical, perfect and cold.

His hand moved between her legs, teasing the bud of her clitoris free of its little hood of flesh. It was timid, shrinking away at first, then growing bolder, swelling, tingling, holding the sensation. He caressed her, leading her by subtle degrees from endurance, to urgency, to overwhelming desire.

Reaching behind him, Odo felt among the items spilt across the bed.

'This,' he said, showing her what he held, 'is an heirloom.'

A slim wand of jade lay in his palm. About six inches long, it was tipped with a rounded knob and inlaid with lilies.

'The Wraxall Fascinum,' Odo murmured. 'The brides of ancient Rome were deflowered with just such an instrument. Of course, my family has a long history, but it cannot be so old. A forgery, I suspect: possibly Arabic in origin, and brought back from the Second Crusade by an ancestor of mine. Still, one does not like to break a tradition.'

He pushed her, so that she fell back across the bed, and knelt beside her rubbing the jade up and down between the lips of her sex, turning it this way and that until the head was coated with wetness. Celine gasped as she felt the tip enter her vagina. It did not hurt, as she had feared, but it was alien: heavy, chill and unyielding.

'Such things had a dual purpose,' continued Lord Wraxall evenly. 'Firstly, they did away with the need to struggle with a reluctant maidenhead, since the hymen had already been broken and the bride prepared – thus.'

He plunged the tool to its full length inside her as he spoke. Celine yelped with shock, but he stifled her cries with a kiss and a velvet thrust of his tongue. He drove the jade wand repeatedly into her, taking her virginity with dispassionate calm.

'So: now we will have less trouble later. And now we come to the second purpose of the fascinum. It is to train you to please a man. Use the strength of your sex on it. Clench down hard on the withdrawal. I shall expect you to clasp me so, when I enter you as a husband. Concentrate, madam. Try it again.'

Celine moaned distractedly. She could not do as he commanded: it was too difficult. Her inner muscles refused to answer to her will. But Lord Wraxall was pitiless. He would accept no imperfection, allow her no rest, until she had proved to him the lesson was well learnt.

The skill he demanded was slow to come. His lips and fingers distracted her as they moved caressingly across her body. Gradually she gained control; as she did so Celine began to take a pleasure in it. The feel of the jade shaft probing between the tightened walls of her sex was no longer repellent. It stimulated. It teased. She gripped it, alternately pulsing and relaxing.

'Yes. Again,' whispered Odo. 'Make me sweat with pleasure as I draw back for the stroke.'

There was no room in her any longer for shame or loathing. She wanted him. She was wet for him. She could smell the salty juices of her readiness, feel them trickling from her sex to wet his fingers. She drew up her knees and rocked her hips, flexing her vaginal muscles on the moving tool. She could feel her pleasure building, knew that if he gave her only a little more time she would reach her climax.

Odo gave a curt nod of satisfaction and sat back on his heels, withdrawing the fascinum. He looked down at Celine who lay open and waiting for him, sobbing for breath, the sodden bedcover bunched beneath her.

'What, surfeited already?' he asked mockingly. 'You disappoint me, madam. My wife should have as great an appetite as myself – and for the same exotic dishes. Shall I leave you to recover?'

Celine reached up to him, clung to him. He had to stay. He had to satisfy the hunger he had roused in her flesh.

'Don't torment me so,' she groaned.

'I confess I am surprised,' said Lord Wraxall, with lazy affability. 'I seem to recall that – compared with another – my person was repugnant to you.'

Celine flinched as if he had struck her. She knew his casual reminder of Liam was meant to hurt – and it did. But it altered nothing. There would be a lifetime for regrets. Now there was only the present – and the needs of her awakened body. The Viscount's practised sensualities were beyond her power to resist. He repelled her – he fascinated her: she had not dreamt that such arousal was possible.

'I have altered my opinion,' she sighed: and in that moment it was true.

Lord Odo took her right hand and carried it to his loins.

'Prove it.'

Trembling at her own daring, Celine let her fingers rove up and down the length of his manhood. She could feel its heat even through the silver cloth. It was hard and straining, ready to press its way out through the flimsy covering, tearing its way through the silks and stitches.

When he released her, to loosen the fastenings of his breeches, Celine did not take her hand away. The thought of penetration no longer terrified her. The fascinum had done its work. She hungered for the feel of a greater tool, warm and resilient, moving vitally within her.

Freed from its tight containment, Lord Wraxall's erection jutted proudly forward, tenting the black lawn shirt. Even now the size of it daunted her a little, but her arousal – and her curiosity – was too strong to let her draw back. She had never really seen a man's genitals before, hardly daring to look at Liam's, and the idea excited her almost beyond bearing.

She clenched the muscles of her sex experimentally. A honey-sweet dart of pleasure pierced her. Celine slipped her fingers into his breeches, pulling his shirt up, seeking for naked flesh. Lord Wraxall drew a hissing breath as she touched him, and she felt his penis throb impatiently.

'Are you so eager to see the sceptre you'll be ruled with?' he asked in a grating voice.

Celine felt herself flush. She nodded.

Lord Wraxall laughed harshly. He pushed her hand away and tugged his shirt off over his head with a single movement.

'Look, then,' he said.

His scarred torso tapered like a wedge from his shoulders to narrow hips. Exposed to the root, his phallus sprang from the bush of curls at his groin, thrusting potently towards her. Blue-veined, and curved like a sabre, its foreskin was fully retracted to expose the swollen, ruddy glans. Celine choked back an exclamation. Her fingers had prepared her for its prodigious size, but not for this.

Odo was pierced.

His cock was pierced. A ring, set with a bead of black opal, ran in through the eye at its tip and out again where the shaft joined the head. Like a second jewel, a drop of clear fluid hung on the gold. The sight was shocking, yet unbearably erotic. A pang of lust, so profound it made her catch her breath, shot through her, and she closed her eyes.

Odo knelt above Celine, watching her reaction with well-concealed surprise. He had not expected her to be so obviously aroused by the sight of his body.

It amused him to find that he felt slightly aggrieved. He had anticipated fright, and squeamish protests. This was almost too easy. He would have to be harsher, testing her limits, pushing her to acts of wantonness that would have her sobbing with shame as much as with lust.

And yet she was damnably beautiful in her abandonment: the tousled hair, the mouth half-opened, her nipples hard with desire for him. Despite his apparent coolness, his own needs were overpowering. He fought to remain calm, breathing deeply, and the scent of her eagerness caught in his throat.

She was more than ready. A lesser man might have been unable to resist. Odo knew even he would not be able to hold back much longer. It irritated him that he must waste his pleasure in Celine with one soon-completed spasm. Such simple gratifications cloyed his palate now: too mawkish, too unsophisticated. He preferred the taste of bitters.

'Use your hands on me,' he said, and was pleased to note his voice betrayed none of the excitement he felt.

When Celine hesitated, he caught her fingers and closed them round the shaft of his cock. He felt her start: they hardly circled it.

With slow enjoyment, Odo guided her hand up the length of his manhood until its head filled her fist, then thrust fiercely downwards so that the ring rotated against her palm. The feel of the gold, moving through and inside the sensitive glans, sent a searing jolt of ecstasy through him.

'Yes,' he whispered through set teeth. 'Like that. Do it like that.'

She did not have to be taught for long what pleased him. Celine was quick to learn, sliding her grip up and down the full length of his velvety shaft, twirling the ring slowly through the swollen cock-tip at each stroke.

Sweat ran on the muscles of Odo's chest as he pushed her other hand between his legs, to cup his testicles. She stroked his balls, teasing them gently, as she masturbated him with a gradually quickening rhythm. Instinctively she found the pad of flesh behind his scrotum, trailing her fingertips along it until Odo could no longer repress a groan of pleasure.

It was a mistake, and he recognised it instantly.

Celine smiled and looked up at him languorously. She moved sinuously on the bed, legs parted wide. He knew she expected him to mount her now, plunge himself to the root in her, give her what she hungered for.

Such childishness diverted him. She thought she had him in her power, that she had conquered him with her unskilled, tyro's caresses. He, who had broached the Grand Turk's own harem, and been served in Delhi by the priestesses of Kama, god of love! No matter: she would learn.

Catching a handful of her hair Odo pulled her head between his thighs. He thrust his prick towards her, nudging her lips with its jewelled tip.

She was stubborn at first, complaining fretfully that he would choke her, and trying to push him away with soft hands. The challenge thrilled him.

Though it cost him much, he shrugged uncaringly and made to withdraw. A momentary flash of dismay lit her dark eyes and he suppressed a chuckle.

Slipping his fingers down to the wet cleft between her legs,

Odo teased the hard nub of her clitoris, calling up all his art until she moaned and thrust against his hand with uncontrollable need. It excited him deeply to be able to override her will, to drive her step by faltering step along the path he had chosen. When he approached her lips a second time she opened for him with a sob, taking the head of his phallus into the warm cave of her mouth.

The feel of her tongue moving on his flesh excited him beyond measure. He wanted nothing better than to thrust his whole length into her throat, but he knew that Celine was not ready for such extremes. She was not yet skilled enough to swallow his manhood without spoiling his diversions by unaesthetic coughs and splutterings.

She was only entering her apprenticeship. There would be time enough to educate her in fellatio, and in his every other caprice. A beginning had been made. Already she was growing bolder, reassured by his caution, stroking her hands up and down the shaft of his cock while she suckled on his glans.

He pumped his hips in tiny movements as she licked the head of his phallus, turning the cock-ring with her tongue. Odo set his jaw, but he could not still the urgency of his need. He knew his crisis was near. He could feel it building, his body hurrying him onward. He thrust two fingers into the slippery depths of Celine's vagina and felt, with exquisite lust, her newly trained muscles clenching greedily on them.

It was too much, even for him.

Odo gave a single, deep, barking cry, and snatched himself out of her mouth. He surrendered totally to his orgasm. His seed spurted out in thick, pulsing jets, spattering Celine's face and breasts.

The intensity of his climax took him unawares. He had not expected Celine's body to yield him such delight. It felt as if his soul was bleeding out of him, drop by drop, to the accompaniment of his racking breath.

Even as he came he heard her cry of despair and knew that her ardour was still unsatisfied. Panting with gratified desire, he looked down at her and smiled slowly; her eyes were dark with loss and pleading.

That he could keep her thus wanting, waiting, set the seal on his enjoyment. Callously, he trailed his hand across her breasts. Her nipples were tight with arousal, and she moaned as he touched her, writhing beneath him. He gathered a drop of semen on one finger tip, and wiped it across her lips.

Then he stood, abruptly, and began to fasten his breeches.

From the corner of his eye he saw Celine push herself into a sitting position.

'You cannot mean to leave me thus! You promised me fulfilment – in the carriage. You promised!'

'Did I?' he said. He shook out his shirt, and pulled it on. 'I don't recall. My memory is somewhat selective, these days. Ah me, the effects of age.'

'Must I beg you to stay?'

'Save your breath, madam. You must learn that your pleasure is in my gift, to be granted or withheld as I choose. Besides, I have made plans for our wedding night. It's my wish that you should spend the intervening hours in anticipation. Your abigail will fetch you to me when all is ready.'

'Is she here yet?' asked Celine.

He smiled at the hope in her voice. Was she looking to find the satisfaction he had denied her at her maid's hands?

'Who do you mean?' he said.

'Bess. Bess Brown, my maid.'

'Not any more,' he said, and flung back his head, laughing at her expression of dismay.

'Did you really think I was going to let you keep your little confidante?' he sneered. 'Your go-between? Oh, yes, I know you have been sending her with messages to your dolt of a lover. No, madam. I have provided a servant for you, of my own choosing.'

He shrugged into his coat and sauntered back across the room to stand above her. Celine's eyes filled with tears.

'I hardly know whether sorrow or indignation shows your beauty to best advantage,' he said meditatively. 'Or perhaps desire. Yes, I think abandonment suits you best, my wife. The half-closed eyes, the wanton movements, the mouth pleading for pleasure – you tempt me. But why spoil the coming banquet? Such feasts are best eaten with a lusty appetite.'

'Stay,' pleaded Celine brokenly. 'Have you no mercy? I – I want you. I starve for you.'

Lord Wraxall looked back at her, his hand on the latch.

'Why, madam, the remedy lies in your own hands,' he said. 'I leave you the fascinum. It should take the edge from your hunger – until tonight.'

Nicole's Revenge

Lisette Allen

France, 1792. Paris is in the grip of revolution. The beautiful young actress Nicole Chabrier has been abandoned by her aristocratic patron and gets caught up in the middle of an angry mob. She is rescued by the mysterious Jacques, who takes her to a secluded mansion which has been deserted by its former occupants. Once there, Jacques offers her every luxury and soon Nicole is consumed with an intense passion for him. Pushed to the limits of her patience, Nicole finds herself enacting darkly erotic rituals of revenge which only serve to further inflame her desire for the obstinate Jacques. In this extract, Nicole is witness to a scene of ribald coupling outside her window and is caught in a state of excitement which, of course, Jacques makes the most of to further embarrass the recalcitrant Nicole.

The second extract by Lisette Allen is from *The Amulet,* set in Britain at the height of the Roman occupation. Catrina has the gift of second sight and is due to be initiated into the Druidic priestesshood by the lecherous Luad. When the pagan tribe captures a Roman legionary and threaten to kill him, Catrina cannot bear the thought that the handsome young warrior will meet an untimely death, and helps to comfort him in the hour of his need. He makes good his escape and Catrina follows him to the decadent city of Eboracum – now known as York – believing he has deceived her. Once there, the debauched Julia takes a keen interest in Catrina and invites her to her pleasure palace where she has created a little bit of Rome in Britain – complete with slaves and handmaidens who are used to pleasuring their demanding mistress.

All of Lisette Allen's Black Lace books have historical settings. In addition to *Nicole's Revenge,* she has written four others which are: *Elena's Conquest,* set in Britain, just after the Norman invasion; *Ace of Hearts,* a tale of card-sharping and sexual intrigue in Regency England, and *Nadja's Quest,* the story of one woman's search for love and adventure in the court of Empress Catherine the Great.

Nicole's Revenge

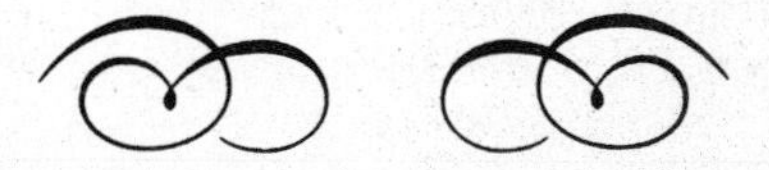

Nicole woke to see the sunlight streaming through the shutters. Climbing sleepily out of her high bed, she yawned and stretched. The cotton nightgown she'd worn scratched her soft, sleep-warm flesh; she pulled it off and wrapped herself instead in the long silk dressing robe she'd worn last night.

Then she went across the room to push back the blinds, throwing the windows wide open.

The fresh, heady scents from the luxuriously overgrown garden, still wet from yesterday's rain, flooded into her room. She breathed in deeply. In the daylight, this great, walled mansion was even more magnificent than she remembered. So it was all true, then, and not some dark dream. Last night, the house, the man Jacques. Especially the man Jacques.

She shivered, remembering her own abandoned wantonness in his strong arms, and the incredible, sensual pleasure he'd aroused in her.

Then, suddenly, an unexpected sound assaulted her ears in the silence: the chilling sound of a woman's scream. Her blood ran cold as she remembered the dreadful scenes on the streets of Paris last night. Her heart thudding, she leant out of the window and saw a dark-haired girl running along the gravel paths towards the house, with a big, roughly-dressed man in pursuit. Nicole gasped, then relaxed as she realised that the girl *wanted* to be caught! Near the wall of the house, almost below Nicole's window, she paused by a great stone urn full of rampant scarlet geraniums, and turned, panting and laughing, to face her pursuer, her hands on her plump hips.

Nicole realised suddenly that this was the ghost-girl she'd seen peeping out from between the shadowy carriages last night. No ghost this, no pale aristocrat, but a beautiful, real young woman with pink cheeks and tousled black hair, in a fresh cotton dress and a maid's white apron.

Then, Nicole gasped again. The big man had caught the girl in his arms and was kissing her roughly, demandingly; at first the girl pushed him off, giggling, but only so she could unlace her bodice and use her cupped hands to lift up her own full, rosy breasts, greedy for his lascivious embrace.

With a shout of gruff laughter, the man bent to guzzle at her dark nipples, while Nicole watched, transfixed, the colour rushing to her cheeks. He was a big, heavily muscular man, with a dark beard; he wore trousers and wooden *sabots*, and looked like some kind of manservant. The blood was pounding in Nicole's veins as she watched the big man's mouth pull and suckle at the girl's ripe teats while he pushed her breasts together with his rough hands. The girl had thrown her head back, her eyes glazed with ecstasy; Nicole felt her own inexorably rising excitement, the melting between her thighs, and gripped the window ledge hard with her fingers, wishing the bearded man's frenzied mouth was licking and pulling at her own aching breasts in that lewd, abandoned way.

Then she had to bite on her lip to stop herself crying out.

Because, below her, the man had sunk to his knees beside the stone urn and was fumbling with his trousers, eventually pulling out an enormous, gnarled penis that thrust quivering into the empty air. The dark-haired girl squealed in delight and knelt down eagerly to face him, clutching her bare breasts and rubbing her hardened nipples against the swollen, purple glans of the man's exposed member in a frenzy of sexual excitement.

The man groaned aloud as her breasts caressed his great phallus; clutching her long, tousled hair, he pulled her flushed face down over his loins, forcing her to take the extremity of that huge knob into her mouth; then he proceeded to finger and squeeze at her thrusting nipples as the girl rapturously began to pleasure him, sliding her soft, moist lips up and down that great, thick stem.

Nicole shut her eyes. Her hand brushed her own swollen,

aching breasts beneath her silken robe. Then, relentlessly, her fingers slipped down across her taut belly to find the soft, melting folds of flesh at the apex of her thighs, to lightly caress her little bud of pleasure. Already it was pulsing hotly, hungrily; with a little groan of need she slid her finger along her honeyed crease, longing with all her being for that huge, primitive organ that the girl was kissing so hungrily to be rammed up inside her.

Too late, she heard the door open quietly behind her. She whirled round to see Jacques leaning against the doorframe, his mouth twisting crookedly.

Nicole pulled her robe across her flushed breasts and hissed furiously, 'Were you never taught to knock at a lady's bedroom door?'

'I see no lady.' He smiled and walked towards her. Nicole saw that already he was shaved and dressed, damn him, as immaculately as ever, in an exquisitely tailored beige coat with dark brown breeches and tan jockey boots. 'I see,' he went on impeturbably, 'a delicious little Parisienne strumpet, waiting, indeed longing, for attention. What was it, my little Nicole, that excited you so? You're certainly finding plenty of entertainment in this house, aren't you?'

She darted swiftly away from the open window, violently ashamed of her own voyeurism. But Jacques calmly seized her wrist, and dragged her back to his side, and looked out into the garden himself.

A slow, fiendish smile lit his face, and his arm encircled Nicole's slender waist, drawing her even closer to him.

'Ah, I see,' he murmured. 'You were watching those two sturdy peasants pleasuring one another. A charming scene, is it not? So refreshingly honest and simple.'

Nicole, hot and sticky and ashamed, looked out again; and again was unable to drag her wide eyes away from what she beheld. The man, hugely engorged, was still on his knees, his trousers down around his muscular, hairy thighs; the young maid was taking as much as she could of his massive appendage between her soft lips, bobbing her head up and down energetically; but so long was his penis that several inches of thick shaft remained unattended, and so she was gripping and stroking the base with one eager hand until his bulky testicles jerked and danced at her busy attentions.

The bearded man's rapt face suddenly began to darken with

the onslaught of approaching climax. Even as Nicole watched, breathless, he threw back his shaggy head and gave a great roar. The girl lifted her head quickly, while her busy hand continued its labours more frantically than ever; the man's swollen, glistening knob began to quiver and shake as his milky semen gouted forth in jet after luxuriant jet, spurting across the girl's ripe breasts. With little guttural moans, the girl bent to rub her nipples against his huge, empurpled glans, writhing in ecstasy at the touch of the firm, velvety flesh on her sensitive buds.

Nicole shuddered and shut her eyes. The man Jacques let his hand slide softly under her silken robe. At the merest touch of his cool palm on her hips, she thought she would faint. Then his fingers slipped down without warning to her hot, honeyed crease; quickly his forefinger found the wet, delicious moistness that dripped from her swollen flesh-folds, and she cried out in stark need. A slow, devilish smile flooded his handsome features.

'Time, I think, Nicole, for your first lesson. A lesson in self-control.'

And before she could even begin to compose herself, he drew his hand away from her quivering vulva, leaving her cold and bereft, and called out through the window, 'Hey, Marianne! And you, Armand! Get yourselves up here to my lady's chamber this instant, you hear me?'

He turned casually back to the horrified Nicole. 'Friends of mine,' he explained lightly. 'Armand is quite splendidly endowed, is he not?'

Nicole blushed wildly; Jacques grinned.

'As I thought. He'll be perfect for our first lesson. Because you, my sweet, as I told you last night, have much to learn in the matter of self-control, and there's no time like the present, is there?'

Nicole dived frenziedly towards the big chest of drawers, rifling through the garments there. 'You insufferable beast. You've told those people to come up here, and I'm not even dressed!'

'No. And you look quite exquisite as you are.'

'Fiend!' she hissed, pulling the silk robe angrily across her breasts. What the hell was this madman talking about? *First lesson? Self control?* He was utterly crazy! But already the dark sweetness of arousal was inflaming her heated blood; her stiffened nipples stood out proudly against the flimsy silk, and she felt wildly, incredibly excited at what might be in store.

They came in together, bowing and scraping; the big man Armand's gaze glittered hotly as he took in Nicole's tantalising figure, then he dropped his eyes swiftly to the ground as Jacques went on easily, 'Citizeness Nicole is the new mistress of the chateau; you understand, Armand and Marianne? You are to obey her, my friends, in every single thing she commands!'

Marianne, plump and pretty in her now laced-up cotton gown, moistened her lips, her blue eyes dancing eagerly. Nicole realised suddenly that the girl had not taken her eyes off Jacques once since she came in the room. The plump little maid was obviously besotted with him. More fool her!

'Yes, monsieur Jacques,' Marianne was saying softly. 'Whatever you say, monsieur Jacques.'

'Not what I say,' corrected Jacques, 'but what Nicole says, Marianne.'

The girl nodded eagerly. She'd agree to anything Jacques said, even if he asked her to throw herself out of that window here and now, thought Nicole sourly.

Jacques, meanwhile, had pulled a chair from the wall and turned it round so he could sit astride it with his arms resting on its back. 'Then it's time to proceed, Nicole.'

She stared at him, bewildered.

'Proceed,' he repeated kindly. 'Give them their orders. They'll do whatever you ask them to, believe me. Now's your chance to practise being my accomplice, *chérie*.'

'I've told you – I don't want to be your damned accomplice!'

'Ah.' He frowned thoughtfully. 'I forgot. You're leaving, aren't you? Never mind, just humour me, this last time. Punish them, my Nicolette. They offended you, didn't they, with their lewd behaviour in the garden below your window just now? Well then, make them do penance. Anything you like.' His dark eyes glinted. 'I assure you; the more wicked your commands, the more they'll like it.'

Nicole swallowed hard. This was absurd, unreal!

Yet wasn't this what she wanted? Power, of the kind that men had. Satisfaction, in whatever way she wanted. Her stomach churned with excitement. Already, the room seemed to be vibrant with arousal, with the sexual heat of these beautiful, expectant people, waiting for her command.

Nicole took a deep, steadying breath. Very well, then – she would humour him! And she would give him something to remember her by before she left!

Drawing herself up proudly, she started to walk slowly across the room, her silk gown swishing against her long, slender legs, and her glorious tawny hair cascading round her shoulders. She noticed with secret delight that Armand couldn't keep his eyes off her. She knew he'd recently climaxed – her legs quaked suddenly at the memory of that magnificent, primitive explosion as his seed jetted across the girl's ripe breasts – so she needed now to build up his arousal anew.

She turned to the watching Jacques with a sweetly innocent smile on her lips.

'Am I to take it,' she purred, 'that you too are to obey my orders?'

His eyes glinted in approval as he gazed up at her from his chair; he bowed his dark head in acknowledgement. 'Absolutely, citizeness.'

'Then I must tell you that I intend to punish this brutal man Armand for his shameful indulgence just now. Fetch me some suitable implements, please, Jacques, from the tower room. I'm sure I can leave the choice to you!'

He bowed again. 'But of course!' Then he rose and left the room.

Nicole turned back to Armand who was watching her again with that hot, hungry look in his eyes. She was really beginning to enjoy this. This was better than being on the stage at the *Comédie Française!*

'Kneel, Armand,' she said coldly, imitating Jacques' dispassionate manner. 'Kneel, before Marianne and myself.' As she spoke, she moved next to the pretty little servant, who looked breathless with excitement.

'Now,' she went on, 'you must prepare to accept your punishment, Armand. You deserve to be chastised, for pursuing Marianne through the garden, for exposing your huge, obscene member to her as you did, for seizing her roughly by the hair, and forcing her to place her hot little lips round your swollen cock, when you know it's far too big for such pleasures. Isn't it?'

'Yes,' he groaned. 'Truly I deserve to be punished, my lady . . .'

'And then,' went on Nicole severely, 'you are to be punished for spurting your lascivious seed all over her juicy breasts, for anointing her pretty nipples until they were wet and glistening with that lewd substance.'

'I'm sorry.' His voice was a whimper now. 'Oh, I'm sorry.'

'Then show us, Armand. Show us how repentant you are, by abasing yourself before Marianne and myself!'

The man moaned and grovelled on the floor, just as Jacques came into the room. He was carrying a whip, and some leather belts; without a word to him, Nicole, her head held high and proud, took the implements from him. She passed them on to Marianne, whose eyes were shining.

'Do what you will with Armand, Marianne. He is yours to punish.'

Marianne moistened her lips eagerly. 'By your leave, mistress, anything?'

Nicole drew a deep breath. 'Anything at all.'

Eagerly Marianne turned on Armand, taking up the big whip in her small, plump hands, assuming a superbly haughty expression. 'Up on your knees, dog! Unfasten yourself and show us your shameful nakedness!'

Fumbling with his trousers, Armand pulled them down over his muscular hips. Already, even though he'd climaxed scarcely ten minutes ago, his huge organ, lying heavily against his hairy thighs, was bulging and stiffening. Marianne raised the whip threateningly. 'Kneel, dog, before me!'

Armand grovelled abjectly, his hairy bottom protruding obscenely from beneath his shirt tails. Jacques, Nicole saw, was watching carefully, leaning with his back against the closed door, his arms folded across his chest and that infuriating secret smile on his face.

Gently, Marianne drew the lash of the whip across Armand's tight buttocks. He groaned aloud. Then Marianne raised the whip, and struck. He shuddered with excitement; Nicole saw his penis thicken and swell, jerking massively up against his belly in his excitement.

'Again!' said Nicole sharply. 'Again!'

And Marianne went on, kissing him softly with the leather lash, stinging him, tantalising him, until his bottom-cheeks were red and shiny. Nicole, her throat dry with excitement, saw the exquisite pulsing of his huge penis at each stroke of the lash, saw how his massive balls jerked and tightened against his groin in his extremity.

Marianne stepped back at last, her cheeks flushed with excitement. 'More?' she whispered to Nicole.

Nicole considered thoughtfully. Then, with an exquisite sense of daring, she bent down to investigate his arousal, and put her own trembling fingers round that huge, hot shaft. The heat of his excitement scorched her palm; she felt the great rod quiver and twitch in her small hand, and was overwhelmed with longing to feel it driving deep, deep inside her. Swallowing hard, she forced herself to let go and stood up again. 'I don't know, Marianne,' she said, frowning. 'He certainly hasn't suffered enough yet. What do you think we should do?'

Jacques, straightening himself, broke in coldly. 'Nicole. Do I have to remind you that you are the one in charge? You are the mistress of this room. It's up to you to devise some devilish torment for Armand, not Marianne. I thought I made that plain earlier.'

Nicole flashed him a look of wild resentment. How dare he speak to her like that, as if she were some stupid child? Putting her hands on her hips defiantly, she said, 'Do I assume, citizen Jacques, that you too are under my command?'

'Absolutely.'

Nicole's amber eyes danced with pure mischief. 'Then I command you to bring out the walnut box of treasures that you saw last night.'

His eyes widened, then he gave a slow grin of approval and went to the drawers to do as she said, bringing out the box of ivory love-aids and placing them meaningfully on the dressing table. Nicole turned back to Marianne.

'Marianne, I command you to tie the wicked Armand's hands behind his back so that he is unable to relieve himself, however great his extremity.' Then she tossed back her hair and glared at Jacques defiantly. 'And you, Jacques, are to pleasure Marianne with the biggest of the ivory penises, while Armand is to watch!'

Armand shuddered in despair, his hands pinioned behind his back as he kneeled on the floor, his huge phallus rearing upwards darkly. Marianne's face was rapt with delight when she heard Nicole's words. 'On the bed? Shall I lie on the bed for monsieur Jacques?'

'On the bed,' commanded Nicole, picking up the big leather whip herself and deliberately letting her robe fall open to display her own ripe breasts and glistening crotch. She was amazed at how much she was enjoying herself. 'On the bed, slut! Lie back, and raise your knees; pull up your skirt to your waist so Jacques can see that you are ready and ripe for him.'

Armand groaned aloud, and Nicole too was almost unbearably excited at the sight of the girl's plump white thighs, the folds of moist, crinkled flesh that peeped from beneath her bush of dark hair. She felt the sudden urge to pay homage herself to the girl's eager sex, to taste, to lick that lascivious, wanton flesh. With an effort, she pulled her gaze away and turned to Jacques.

'Now,' she said with a sweet smile, 'I'm quite sure that *you* need no further instruction on what to do!'

Jacques smiled back equally sweetly, and drew a slender ivory phallus from the box of treasures. Then he walked slowly, purposefully towards the bed, and Marianne gasped, her eyes already glazed with desire as the tall, dark man hovered over her with the weapon of delight grasped in his strong hand.

Nicole frowned. She suddenly realised that she'd made a big mistake. She'd totally forgotten her earlier observation that the serving girl was quite besotted with the handsome Jacques. And now, waiting for his devastating attentions, it looked as if Marianne was on the brink of extremity already.

Jacques looked back at Nicole. 'You're quite sure about this?' He knew, too, that one caress from his lean, sunbrowned fingers would send the luscious little Marianne crashing into orgasm.

But Nicole wasn't going to retreat now. 'Of course I'm sure! Go ahead!' she snapped crossly.

And she watched, biting her lip as Jacques gently inserted the long, smooth piece of ivory between the girl's honeyed flesh lips. Behind her, she heard the crouching Armand's despairing groan as he gazed avidly at the scene.

Nicole wished it was her on the bed. She wished Jacques was pleasuring her with that long, cool ivory shaft, because by now her own loins were churning with exquisite need. Armand was making little guttural noises in his throat, his eyes wide and dark, his rampant penis twitching uncontrollably into the air. The thought of that huge, empurpled phallus, ridged with veins, jerking inside her own yearning love passage made Nicole feel faint with the pain of desire.

She forced her eyes back to the bed, where Jacques was slowly pleasuring Marianne with the ivory penis. Nicole tried to look on, impassive and cool, as she knew Jacques would do. To be fair to him, she thought grudgingly, he was doing his very best to draw out the girl's pleasure. But already, Marianne's plump thighs were trembling, her hips arching; as Jacques slid the sweet ivory softly into her flesh, she threw herself against it with a wild scream, bucking and thrashing in contorted pleasure while Jacques, a grim smile on his face, did his very best to hold the phallus deep within her, to pleasure her fully, to give her all the exquisite satisfaction she so craved.

Marianne fell back at last against the pillows, her face flushed with rapture, her secret flesh still pulsing sweetly around the stem of the ivory penis. Armand had closed his eyes in despair.

Nicole swallowed hard, trying desperately to conceal her own treacherous excitement. She picked up the whip, and trailed the lash across Armand's bulging, muscle-corded thighs. 'Open your eyes, Armand,' she chided him. 'You enjoyed that, did you? You wished it was you, giving such exquisite pleasure to Marianne? Driving your big penis hard inside her sweet flesh, feeling her clutching you deep inside her, hearing her soft moans of delight . . .'

'Yes!' groaned the pinioned Armand, his shaft throbbing unbearably into empty air. 'Oh, yes.'

Then Nicole turned abruptly back to the bed, alerted by a sudden sound. Behind her back, Marianne had pulled Jacques impatiently down to the bed beside her, and with busy, frantic little fingers she was pulling open his shirt, fumbling at his breeches. As Nicole watched, burning with anger, Marianne eased out his strong, fine shaft; fully erect already, it leapt eagerly into her cool palm as she crooned tenderly over it. Jacques, sprawled back on the bed, was shaking his head helplessly as she assaulted him, his dark eyes glinting with laughter. He caught Nicole's furious expression and choked out, 'Wait, my little Marianne, for Nicole's orders.'

But Nicole by now was full of a wild, seething rage. She found it intolerable that Jacques should have let himself become so hugely aroused by this slut of a serving girl, pretty though she was, when he'd rejected her, Nicole, only last night. It was obvious what type of woman *he* was happiest with.

'Please yourself, Jacques,' she said, her voice icy with fury. 'Obviously I'm not the only person in this room who needs a lesson in self-control.'

'Nicole!' he pleaded despairingly, though his eyes were still full of amusement. 'I – oh, Marianne, *chérie* – you know that drives me wild – '

He'd broken off abruptly, because Marianne's little pink tongue was dancing along his beautiful, silken penis, licking teasingly at the swollen glans, and as Nicole watched in cold disdain, Marianne was already opening her eager pink mouth to encircle his hardened flesh, muttering hot little words of endearment as her dark hair spread enticingly over his loins and belly.

Jacques threw himself helplessly back on to the bed, his hands clasped behind his head, his eyes closed with rapture. Marianne wriggled to crouch right over him, her moist mouth working adoringly on his stiffened penis, her fingers caressing the taut, velvety pouch of his exposed testicles, her lips sliding with cataclysmic effect up and down his long, pulsing shaft.

Nicole gritted her teeth. It was quite obviously not the first time that Marianne had attended to him in this way. Self-control, indeed!

She swung round towards Armand, who was almost faint with need. Nicole, her own juices stirring hot and sweet within her aching love channel, muttered to him, 'I think, friend Armand, that you and I deserve our pleasure now. Don't you?'

The man's eyes widened ecstatically. 'My lady.' He gazed hotly at her parted gown, her high, ripe breasts, at the softly curling tawny triangle through which the swollen flesh lips could be glimpsed, moist and ripe. 'For you, anything. Command me, I am yours!'

Almost faint with desire herself at the sight of that huge, obscene rod jerking from his loins, so ready and willing, Nicole bent to unfasten his hands from behind his back.

Then, throwing off her robe, she crouched in front of him on all fours, knowing that the sight of her plump bottom cheeks with the pink, glistening flesh peeping between them would drive him to a wild, animal frenzy.

She was right. With a harsh groan, Armand gripped her bottom with one big hand and used the other to grasp and guide his great penis carefully between her tender lips. She gasped aloud at the feel of him, huge and hot and urgent, forcing her wide open. His big hands reached for her dangling breasts, stroking them, teasing her hard nipples. Then he began to thrust his huge shaft hard into her, sliding his full length against her juicy passage; Nicole, feeling the great, solid penis ravishing her so exquisitely, filling her to delicious extremity, felt the rapturous heat of orgasm begin to envelop her at last.

He clutched fiercely at her nipples with his fingers, squeezing them hard, and Nicole threw her head back, hearing her own little animal moans of ecstasy as his long, bone-hard shaft pumped into her. With a great shout, Armand, sensing her release, pounded to his own climax, jerking deep within her, and Nicole convulsed wildly as the intense waves of pleasure engulfed her entire body, leaving her dazed and exhausted.

With a last, shuddering sigh, Armand was finished, though she could still feel him pulsing deeply within her own sated flesh. Slowly, she pulled herself away from him and rolled on to the floor. He bent over her in silent adoration, and contentedly she let him nuzzle at her breasts, revelling in the sweet rasp of his black, bristling beard against her soft flesh as the melting afterglow spread through her body. 'Well done, my fine Armand,' she whispered.

Smiling softly, she drew herself up and started to pull her robe around herself.

Then she looked at the bed, and all her pleasure died. Because Jacques was still lying there, his shirt and breeches still open, with the little servant wench lying snugly in his arms. They'd been watching it all with evident pleasure; the girl's hand was still cupped lovingly at his groin and Jacques was whispering and chuckling into Marianne's ear, his hand fondling her breasts.

Nicole felt a white, seething shaft of fury shoot through her. Jealousy? No, impossible!

Carefully fastening her robe around her waist, she glared at Jacques and said icily, 'When you've restored yourself to some sort of order, monsieur, perhaps you, the great expert, can give me your considered opinion as to how this first lesson of mine went. Though it might be a little difficult for you to appraise it successfully, seeing as you were so anxious for your own pleasure!'

Slowly, with a secret word in Marianne's ear that made Nicole shake with fury at the intimacy of it, Jacques drew himself up and swung his long legs over the side of the bed. Because his white shirt was still unfastened, she could see the soft, smooth gleam of his suntanned flesh, the flat contours of his belly, the tantalising pelt of silky black hair that swept down to his groin.

She knew, with a sudden, despairing realisation, that it had been *him,* not Armand, that she'd wanted. Him that she'd fantasised about, even as she reached her glorious climax with Armand's shaft pulsing deep inside her.

Jacques was saying lazily as he began to button up his shirt, 'You seemed to achieve a fine level of pleasure yourself, *ma chérie*. Thanks to Armand.'

Nicole struggled for words, but she was speechlessly indignant. Jacques, watching her, stood up with a low laugh.

'You've done well, my Nicolette,' he said. 'Now, I have some business to attend to, and I might be gone for several hours. But I'll be back tonight, never fear. Meanwhile Marianne and Armand will look after you, Nicole, and answer any questions you may have; trust them in everything.'

He pulled on his beige coat and turned to leave the room. Marianne watched him wistfully from the bed; Armand, still busy dressing, nodded his farewell. But Nicole flew after Jacques, catching up with him on the corridor outside, her fists clenched and her small face white with fury. 'I sincerely hope you don't expect me to submit to any more of your games.'

His eyebrows lifted in surprise. 'Submit? But, my Nicolette, you weren't submitting to anything. You were in charge!'

She hissed furiously, 'It didn't feel like it. It certainly didn't take long for you to let pretty little Marianne get her hands on you, did it?'

'Why, my Nicole, I do believe you're jealous. You could have ordered us to stop, you know. But I assumed you were eager to try out friend Armand. I thought I'd give you the chance to enjoy him, which you evidently did.'

She gazed speechlessly up at him. Of course she'd enjoyed being pleasured by the stalwart Armand. It had been a superb experience. But she'd wanted Jacques. He obsessed her, this dark, elusive stranger; tantalised her, drove her mad even now with wanting him. If he knew of her infatuation, how he would laugh at her.

Tossing back her long, tawny hair, she smiled up at him complacently. 'You were right about Armand,' she said in a casual voice. 'He was quite, quite magnificent. In fact, I've never experienced anything like it.'

He threw back his head and laughed, his teeth gleaming. 'You are superb, my little Nicole. A wonderful actress, and I love you.'

To her utter consternation, he bent to kiss her tenderly on the lips.

'Remember, *chérie*. Stay here with us a little longer and soon, I promise you, you will have your chance for revenge.'

'On you?' she muttered, still flustered by his kiss.

He laughed again. 'On whoever you like. Revenge, and much, much pleasure. You did well just now, *chérie*. That little encounter will stand you in good stead for practising on some real live aristocrats tonight. I'll give you your instructions later.' And with that, he turned on his heel and headed off down the corridor towards the great staircase.

'I've told you – I won't be here tonight! I'm leaving!' she screamed after his retreating back.

If he heard her, he made no acknowledgement. She heard his booted feet, light on the stairs; heard his echoing steps in the great hall below, and the final slam of the big front door. She stood there, already missing him. 'I *am* leaving!' she repeated stubbornly to herself, and wondered just who she was trying to convince.

The Amulet

Lisette Allen

The Amulet

Evening had fallen, and Catrina was all alone in the spacious warm chamber to which the maid Nerissa had shown her some time ago. It was all so strange to her, so luxurious after the thatched huts of her tribe; yet somehow it felt familiar, as if she had been here before, in a dream, as if she belonged. Her skin still tingled, moist and deliciously scented, from the ministrations of Julia's maid; the gown of pale-blue silk that lightly clad her body was cool and sensuous where it touched her flesh. This was a place of wonderful mysteries, from the patterned floor tiles that were warm beneath her feet, to the clear, cool water that miraculously spouted from the serpent's head fountain in the centre of the paved, sunlit courtyard. And she had so much yet to learn . . .

Gradually, the light from the setting sun faded away, until she was in a soft, sultry darkness, with only the tinkling music of the fountain in the courtyard outside for company. More than a little hazed by the sweet, strong wine she'd drunk, she stretched her limbs luxuriously on the curved, gilded couch, wondering lazily what to do next. Should she call for someone, or just wait here? The thought of talking to the lady Julia again excited her strangely. She wondered whether she should confide in her, and ask her if she knew anything of a tall, dark-haired soldier called Alexius amongst the thousands of legionaries who inhabited the fortress.

The memory of Alexius, her enemy, disturbed her, as it always did. Pushing him with an effort from her mind, she lay back against her cushions and closed her eyes, feeling the wine singing softly through her veins. And then, she heard a slight, unfamiliar noise from nearby, and tensed.

At the other end of the room was a low, shuttered window, which Catrina had assumed opened out on to the central courtyard. But as she watched, she saw that the shutters were being opened very slowly from the other side, by some unseen hand; they revealed not the courtyard, but another chamber, similar to the one she was in. This other room was softly lit, whereas she was in the seclusion of darkness, and within the golden glow of the luxuriously furnished adjoining chamber two girls were dancing slowly, utterly absorbed in the haunting music of the flute that echoed softly in the still air.

Catrina gasped, shifting her position so that she could gaze at them. They seemed completely unaware of her presence, and as she watched, spellbound, they swayed in time to the music with a graceful, sensuous charm that took Catrina's breath away. In the soft lamplight that bathed them, she could see that the two dancers were darkly skinned, and quite naked except for the short, flimsy skirts that were wrapped around their waists, and the golden bangles that encircled their slender arms. Their long, silky black hair hung in glossy swathes down as far as their breasts, and their beautiful, dusky faces were quite dominated by their huge dark eyes. Each one wore a heavy ivory pendant on a golden chain that bobbed between their pert, high breasts as they moved; Catrina suddenly realised, with a stirring of strange excitement, that their nipples were painted red. They smiled at one another in secret pleasure as they moved, their hands sinuously outstretched, their fingertips curling gracefully. They looked, thought Catrina longingly, as if they were taking great pleasure in one another's beauty.

Then her breath caught raggedly in her throat as she saw what was happening next.

One girl had reached out to stroke the other's firm brown breast lightly, her body still swaying in time to the rippling cadences of the music. As Catrina watched, hypnotised, she cupped her partner's delicious globe of flesh and pulled gently at the tender red nipple until it stiffened and stood out proudly from the swelling flesh around it. The other dancing girl reciprocated, smiling, mirroring the other's actions; then, with both sets of nipples deliciously erect, they glided closer to one another until they were able to rub their breasts lightly together, so that their reddened teats seemed to kiss sweetly with a will of their own.

Catrina watched spellbound, feeling a sudden lick of violent desire deep in her abdomen. At the same time, she felt her own sensitive nipples tingle and harden, poking against the flimsy fabric of her gown. Oh, what would it be like to feel another woman's warm, firm breasts rubbing so tantalisingly against her own hardened crests? At that delicious thought, she was suddenly aware that the delicate folds of flesh that enclosed her own most secret place, the place the Roman had violated, were pulsing with the sweet ache of arousal. Her gaze was wrenched back to the tableau in the adjoining room, because the two beautiful, dusky-skinnned dancing girls had wrapped their arms tenderly round one another, so that the shimmering golden bangles on their arms tinkled like music. And then, they began to kiss, very gently. Catrina, transfixed, could see how their small pink tongues protruded and entwined as their lips met, could see how their darkly painted eyelids closed in rapture, how their stiff-peaked, bouncing breasts rubbed together with even more urgency . . .

Catrina realised that her own breathing had become shallow, almost painful. She was used to the ways of men and women pleasuring one another in the open, lusty ceremonies of her tribe, but this strange, exotic decadence all but overwhelmed her, making her blood race thickly in her veins. If this was an example of the corrupting ways of Rome that Luad had warned her about, then she wanted to know more, much more! As the girls continued to kiss languorously, Catrina realised suddenly that her loose, flimsy silk gown had started to fall apart; her trembling fingers moved distractedly towards her own urgently aroused nipples, stroking and pulling as the sweet shafts of arousal arrowed towards her taut abdomen. At the juncture of her thighs, she could feel that her secret flesh was unexpectedly swollen and moist; instinctively she rubbed her legs together in an effort to assuage her need, desperately conscious all the time of the slick, betraying wetness that gathered in her womanly parts.

Then suddenly, as Catrina watched breathlessly, one of the dancing girls drew back from the kiss and dropped gracefully on to a small couch in the corner of the lamp-lit room. Her partner, smiling happily, knelt swiftly between her companion's legs, gently drawing them apart; then she started to fondle her there with her slim fingers.

The dancing girl on the couch was quite naked beneath her flimsy skirt. Catrina's cheeks flamed with excitement as she glimpsed the intimate folds of her dark, plump sex-lips, glistening with arousal as they peeped from beneath her downy pubic mound. Swallowing hard to ease the sudden dryness in her throat, Catrina saw how the other dancing girl dropped her head and began to dance her pointed pink tongue skilfully up and down her partner's honeyed cleft, so that the reclining girl groaned with sudden, acute pleasure and grasped her own naked breasts, pulling and twisting at the red-painted teats as her excitement mounted.

Catrina, breathing shallowly now, felt her own trembling body racked with urgent need. She thought suddenly, despairingly, of the hateful Alexius, and of that night in the forest when he had bewitched her; she remembered his dark, fiercely rampant phallus as it had nudged at her velvety entrance, ready to dip past her honeyed lips and plunge deep, deep inside her. She shivered, hardly able to bear the hungry, throbbing ache at the pit of her belly. Reaching her hand urgently downwards to find her own slick flesh-folds, the shock of discovery juddered through her as her sensitive fingertips encountered the intricate, swollen petals of her most intimate, most feminine place. Slowly she began to explore.

Luad the priest had warned her that she must never, ever touch herself there, or she would lose her powers. But in that, as in perhaps so many other things, thought Catrina rebelliously, Luad may well have deceived her! Why had he tried to deny her such delicious, forbidden pleasure for so long? She gasped aloud with delight as her fingertip just brushed her hot, plump little bud of pleasure; she felt the fierce excitement leap through her body, and cupped her swollen vulva with her trembling hand, trying in vain to soothe the sweetly agonised ache of longing that engulfed her whole body.

Alexius. Oh, Alexius. My Roman – my enemy.

Then her gaze was drawn once more to the beautiful, erotic spectacle of the two girls pleasuring one another, and she gasped aloud. 'No,' she whispered, half-shocked, half-laughing aloud. 'Dear goddess, no. I must be dreaming!'

For the two dancing girls had shifted again, adjusting their position on the curved couch so that they lay snugly entwined top to toe, curled in an exquisitely erotic tangle of dusky limbs and gleaming dark hair as they gently licked and sucked at one another's lushly exposed femininity. Even as Catrina watched, hardly able to breathe in case the beautiful women stopped, one of them drew her serpent's head pendant from around her neck and used it to probe, very gently, at her partner's secret, tongue-moistened pink flesh.

Catrina thought she would die of need as she gazed at them. Her whole body throbbed with longing; her blood pounded with heavy languor through all her limbs as she watched how skilfully the beautiful dancers pleasured one another by sliding the long, thick serpent heads deep within each other's pouting flesh-lips. They pleasured one another slowly at first, then they started to plunge them in more quickly, with probing, powerful thrusts that ravished every inch of their lush inner flesh as they both started to tremble and writhe in the very throes of delicious orgasm.

Suddenly the shutters slammed across the aperture, leaving Catrina in a state of shocked, trembling arousal in the blackness of her room.

She couldn't believe it. Even the silence was absolute, except for the uneven hammering of her own heart. Her body, clad so sinuously in the pale-blue silk, was finely honed to a state of exquisite arousal, and she needed release, any kind of release, so much!

Then the door opened slowly, and she whirled round to see that there, in the open doorway, stood a man. The dim light from the passageway behind him outlined his massive figure all too plainly; he wore nothing except a scanty linen loincloth, and a glittering, somehow sinister, mask of gold that covered the top part of his face. His black hair was cropped close to his scalp; his smoothly oiled skin gleamed like ebony in the dark shadows.

Catrina shuddered with a helpless spasm of fear as she gazed at his heavily muscled body. And the fear was tinged with a dark, secret excitement as he stepped closer, his bulging arms folded across his broad chest, and she saw that a slight smile curved his full mouth. Who was he? What was he doing here, all on his own, so silent, so strangely menacing in his mysterious golden mask? Helplessly, her eyes were drawn down his powerful, naked torso to his scantily clad loins; she saw the taut bulge of his genitals, and recognised the gleam of pure sexual excitement in those dark eyes that glittered from behind the mask.

Had *he* been watching the beautiful dancers, too? Or – and she felt a hot stab of shame at the thought – had he been watching her, Catrina, as she furtively stroked her own heated body? Perhaps, she surmised wildly, he was some dark, primeval god, who had come in answer to her own surging, sensual need! She suddenly realised that anything, anything at all, was possible in this strange, exotically decadent household.

The man smiled, and said, in a deep, rich voice, 'You wanted something, my lady Catrina?' He reached behind him for the lamp from the passageway and carefully placed it on a small bronze table within the room. Then he shut the door, enclosing them both in the soft pool of light.

'Yes. Oh, yes,' breathed Catrina. Her words emerged in a whisper, because her throat was quite dry with excitement, and her whole body was tingling with wild anticipation.

The man smiled, and pulled casually at the knot of his loincloth, letting the linen garment slide to the floor.

'You perhaps wanted this?' he murmured, in his beautiful slow voice.

Catrina gasped. He had to be some kind of strange, beautiful demon, of the kind that the tribespeople described in their stories of olden times. A demon, or a god!

His massive penis was already erect, and rising like a ramrod from the heavy bag of his testicles. Catrina, transfixed, saw that it was beautifully long and thick, its dusky shaft ridged with veins; the swollen, rounded end seemed to rear hopefully towards her, adorned already with a clear, pearl-like drop of exuded moisture. Slowly, carefully, she saw him cup the pearl drop in his palm and rub all along the hot, quivering length of his phallus, licking his lips as he did so. Then he let his penis go, and it swayed heavily, ripe with virile power.

Catrina felt a heavy, pulsing ache deep within her as she gazed silently up at him, her green eyes dark and sultry. She felt ripe, wanton, ready for the taking. All she could think of, all she wanted, was to feel that delicious, hardened rod of flesh slide up into her tormented vulva, soothing her, filling her, stretching her with its exquisite masculine power.

She sank back breathlessly on to the silk cushions of the couch as if in a dream, her lips parted tremulously, her filmy blue gown slipping back from her shoulders to reveal her tender, luscious breasts in all their pink-tipped arousal. 'Yes, oh yes,' she whispered, holding out her slender arms. 'I want you. Now.'

Slowly the naked and masked god-man moved towards her in the pale golden light of the lamp, his rampant penis swaying heavily as he moved. Catrina reached out to brush it longingly with her fingertips as he knelt beside her, then she put her hand round it, shivering at its throbbing thickness; it was hot and silky, and quivered with a life of its own at her intimate caress. Uttering a little moan of need, she lay back on the couch, instinctively letting her thighs fall apart to reveal the very core of her femininity to her dark, unknown visitor.

'You are sure you are ready for me, my lady?'

Either he was some mysterious god from the world of the spirits, or she was dreaming. Catrina didn't really care which. 'More than ready,' she murmured, smiling dazedly up at his chillingly masked face.

His eyes glittered behind the mask as she spoke. Kneeling beside her, he bent his head to lick her tingling breasts adoringly with long, smooth strokes of his powerful tongue. Languorously he drew the stiffened nubs into the hot moistness of his mouth while circling and nipping with his tongue and teeth until she flung her arms round his massive shoulders, stroking his silken skin and feeling the powerful muscles ripple and tauten beneath her fingers. Uttering low, soothing words in some strange language that she didn't understand, the man gently pulled her churning hips almost to the edge of the couch, parting her legs wide so he could gaze at the dark pink folds of her lush femininity peeping from between the silky tendrils of blonde hair, all the while caressing the sensitive skin of her inner thighs with his big, strong hands. Then swiftly he dipped his head to rasp at her soaking flesh with his long, stiffened tongue, running it up and down her swollen nether lips until they were parted and ready. He let his tongue flicker along the base of her yearning clitoris, and she groaned aloud at the silvery touch and thrust desperately towards him, rubbing her vulva against his face, longing for fulfilment.

Her god-man smiled and lifted his masked head, so she could see that his mouth was smeared with her nectar. Purposefully gripping his rampant member in his fist, he positioned himself on his knees between her thighs so that he could rub the smooth, rounded glans against her glistening sex-lips; then, finally, he slid his penis deep, deep within her, carefully watching her face all the time as Catrina gasped aloud with joy.

Julia, meanwhile, was watching the progress of Catrina and her Numidian house slave with some interest through a cunningly concealed spyhole that linked the two rooms. Julia had listened with careful attention to the barbarian girl's little sighs and gasps as she avidly watched the two Syrian dancers so expertly pleasuring one another. And Julia, well-experienced in such matters, had sensed the exact moment in which to send in the willing Phidias. She'd already told him to put on the gold mask, which was one of the many treasures she'd brought with her from her days in the Roman theatre, and he looked just the part.

'I'm ready, mistress,' he had said, grinning.

Julia eyed him dryly. He certainly was. He too had been watching the Syrian girls avidly, and she could see how his magnificent phallus pushed and swelled already against the restraint of his loincloth. Julia felt her own inevitable surge of scarcely controlled desire. She was almost ready to abandon her plans and let the slave take her now, so she could experience the delight of feeling his dusky, rigid penis slide into her own luscious flesh.

But no. Control was part of the game. The beautiful barbarian girl would soon learn that for herself.

As for Falco, poor, suffering Falco, she felt almost sorry for him, except that it was his own fault. He was with her now, half-naked and in chains, of course, in case he should try to run. Since that first night, when he'd tried to defy her, she'd made him follow her everywhere, because she was determined somehow to make him give way. Getting him to bow down before her household gods was only part of it. She wanted to break him, to make him plead for mercy, to see his beautiful, strong young body totally abased. She wanted him all for herself, with a dark, hungry desire, almost as badly as she wanted Alexius. The thought of the two most desirable men in the fortress, with each other, with her, made her feel quite faint with need. It was one of her favourite fantasies.

Falco was behind her, kneeling and chained, his fair head bowed as the Numidian went into the room where Catrina was.

'Watch,' Julia hissed at him angrily. 'Watch them, gladiator, or I'll make you sorry!'

She could barely restrain her own excitement as she gazed through the secret spyhole and watched it all. Slowly and quietly, just as she'd instructed him, the big masked houseslave stepped towards the stunned Catrina with his lovely throbbing shaft in erotic display and Julia, with a pang of delight, saw how the British girl reached with trembling hands to touch it. She was perfect, this girl: wild, wanton, beautiful, with her silky golden hair and her supple, slender body and high, firm breasts. How eagerly and yet how innocently she responded to the big slave; how exquisitely her lovely body arched with pleasure as the skilful, powerful Numidian began to caress her, his penis throbbing and angry as it reared from his thighs.

Julia was desperate herself. Her nipples were thrusting achingly against the fine wool of her tunic, and her naked labia were swollen, melting with honeyed moisture. Glancing speculatively at Falco's beautiful, despairing profile, at his taut suntanned skin and thick fair hair, she let her eyes rove hungrily over the oiled golden muscles of his naked chest and biceps, taut and straining because of the way he was pinioned. He, too, could see the erotic tableau being enacted in the next room. She knew, because she could see the bulge in the fabric of his loincloth where his phallus strained in helpless arousal.

She wouldn't take him yet. She wanted his lovely body very much; but she wanted him to beg for her first.

She called for her Syrian girls by pulling on a corded bellrope. Julia was very fond of her two dancing girls; they were twins, and she'd bought them four years ago from the household of a bankrupt senator in Rome. Julia had renamed them Lark and Nightingale, because they reminded her of two delicate, graceful songbirds. Training them in the ways of her household had been a pleasure.

When the Syrian girls came in, their red-tipped breasts bobbing enticingly, she told them exactly what she wanted. Lark and Nightingale nodded eagerly and swiftly knelt on either side of her as she leant back against her cushions. Julia sighed and closed her eyes as one of them obediently began to caress and tease her breasts with her hot little mouth, while the other, very gently but with wicked skill, reached to part Julia's soft thighs with her hands and bent her head to lick her there; to savour the warm, hairless, crinkled flesh and breathe in all the musky scent of her sex.

The touch of that hot, velvety little tongue nibbling at her swollen labia and flicking past her clitoris was so sweet that Julia shuddered and arched in delight. Quickly, sensing her mistress's nearness, Lark unlooped the heavy ivory serpent from around her neck and slid it slowly, tantalisingly, into Julia's throbbing vulva, twisting and pulling rhythmically at the delicious instrument of pleasure, tugging it out, slick with Julia's juices, and sliding it back in with blissful slowness while Nightingale continued to suck and lick and pull at the reclining woman's breasts.

Julia moaned in ecstasy and clenched her loins as the hot shafts of pleasure quivered and gathered in her straining abdomen. Her nipples were on fire, burning with exquisite need as the dusky Syrian girl bit and laved, swirling her dancing tongue round each turgid crest in turn. Between her splayed legs Julia could feel the satisfying fatness of the smooth ivory bulging between her vaginal walls, sending wave after wave of excitement through her. She writhed her hips, drawing the solid shaft deep inside herself, imagining that the cunningly carved serpent was alive, menacing, hungry as it plunged deep within her. Almost there, oh, almost there!

And then she heard Falco gasp, and she opened her eyes to see that the sweat was beading on his wide, clear forehead, and his eyes were closed in the agony of his arousal. Julia let her eyes drop, and she saw how his strong phallus strained and bulged beneath his tunic.

Fighting down her own need, she wrenched herself away from her handmaidens' eager attentions, pulling herself off the ivory phallus, and sat up, her face flushed.

'Untie the gladiator,' she said curtly to Lark.

'But, *patrona* . . .'

'Do as I say!'

It was a risk, she knew. But it was one she was prepared to take, because no man would run from this. She settled herself again, back on her cushions, so that she could see the kneeling slave; she watched silently as the girls unchained him, their eyes lowered, and flicked back his tunic, so they could all see how his hot, angry rod leapt up and quivered against his taut belly. Julia caught her breath, and smiled. It was beautiful. Silken, strong, rippled with delicate veins, the swollen plum at the end already ripe to bursting. Some day soon, she would take him. When he had suffered enough . . .

She nodded to the girls to continue with her exactly where they had left off, parting her legs in invitation. Then she glanced again through her spyhole into the neighbouring chamber.

She was glad Phidias had remembered to take a lamp with him. She could see everything clearly in the soft golden light; how the big Numidian was now tenderly ravishing the blonde girl with his massive dark shaft, gently and repeatedly sliding its great thick length juicily into her quivering loins and fondling her breasts with his big hands; she saw how the girl's delicate face was contorted with need, her wide green eyes smoky with desire as she arched herself to meet him and the skilful slave brought her slowly but surely towards certain ecstasy with each stroke of his deliciously lengthy penis.

Julia sighed and closed her eyes briefly with pleasure as the cool ivory serpent slipped welcomely inside her again; her vagina clenched lustfully around it, savouring its intimate caress, and her whole body surged anew with desire as Nightingale nipped and teased obediently at her nipples.

'Look at me, Falco,' Julia whispered huskily, turning her head towards the chained slave. 'Don't you want me? Wouldn't you like to stick your hot, huge penis right up inside me, and feel how ripe I am, how juicy? Wouldn't you like to ride me, to feel me grip and squirm against you, until you can't hold back any more? Wouldn't you like me to push my breasts in your face, gladiator, while you pump yourself deep inside me?'

It was too much for him. She knew it would be. His rampant penis jerked anew at her words, as if it had a life of its own, and its plummy tip was throbbing with desire. With a despairing groan he grasped it in his fist and rubbed and pulled feverishly at the thick shaft, sliding the skin up and down the bone-hard core, until his heavy balls tightened in warning. Then his entire body convulsed as his creamy seed suddenly jetted forth, spurting in great gouts across the tiled floor as he milked himself of every last, luscious drop. At the same moment, Julia, her eyes glazing over with lust as she watched him, began to thrust herself hard against the solid ivory serpent that her handmaiden wielded so cunningly, savouring every delicious inch of it and imagining that it was Falco's great weapon, spurting and thrusting inside her. Then she pushed her hot, aching breasts up into the other girl's face, to have them expertly caressed and licked, until, uttering fierce, high-pitched moans, she shuddered at last into a long, glorious orgasm that left her shaking and weak.

When she'd recovered, the young gladiator was kneeling in silence, his body still trembling with the force of his release as his semen cooled on the floor, his head bowed in an agony of shame. Julia said his name softly, and his grey eyes, bleak and drained, were drawn towards her.

'That was rather decadent of you,' she said silkily, 'to debase yourself like that. I thought you had more self-control, Falco.' She turned to Lark and Nightingale. 'My little songbirds. Put his chains on again. I doubt he'll have the strength to resist you.'

The girls did as they were told, and Julia watched as the cold grey metal bit into the gladiator's smooth golden skin. His penis was somnolent now, a fat, dusky pink snake between his strong thighs; she longed to touch it, to see it surge into life once more. Then, suddenly, Lark was at her shoulder, whispering, '*Patrona.* In the other room. Quickly . . .'

And as Julia swiftly leant forward and gazed through her spyhole, she realised that the barbarian girl, too, was close to her extremity.

Catrina was pressing herself hungrily against the heavy, dusky body of the Numidian, her face flushed and joyous at the pleasure he was bestowing on her. Each time he slid himself into her lush, wanton flesh, she clutched instinctively with her vagina at his gloriously lengthy penis; each time he withdrew, she gave a tiny sigh of disappointment, and dug her small fingers deeply into his broad, powerfully muscled shoulders. Her need gathered, sweet and hard, within her tight belly until she felt ready to split, like some luscious fruit; each time he lightly caressed the nubs of her nipples, or gently stroked her plump, throbbing clitoris, she felt herself gather on the brink in a longing for pleasure that was almost a pain, so acute was her arousal.

Then, at last, when she was a shivering, tremulous mass of need, the masked man smiled and planted his big hands firmly on the couch on either side of her panting body. His sleek, powerful body arched above her like a bow as he withdrew his glistening penis to the very brink of her swollen, pulsing vagina. Then, gazing down tenderly into her rapturous, flushed face, he began to thrust purposefully, almost grimly, with a steady driving force that emptied her mind of everything except pleasure, until she was aware of nothing except the delicious, bone-hard length of male flesh that filled her, stretched her and drove her into sweet, incredible realms of rapture. Gathering all her remaining strength, Catrina arched her trembling hips to meet him and ground her pubic bone against the hardness of his mighty shaft so that her desperately yearning clitoris was pressed and rubbed into ecstasy. Then she exploded into a long, mind-shattering orgasm, so that the lamp-lit room was filled with her whimpering, high-pitched cries of delight as her lover continued to drive his magnificent penis steadily into her spasming vulva.

The big Numidian came to his own climax very quickly after that, groaning aloud in the extremity of his release. Catrina, her own sated flesh still pulsing in sweet afterglow around his gently throbbing shaft, lay back dazed as her mysterious god-man let his velvety mouth drift across her pleasure-engorged breasts. If this was the way the Romans lived, then this was for her!

Then the door opened, letting in a draught of chill air, and Julia glided in.

'Well done, my dear,' she said. 'Full marks, I think, for your first lesson. Don't you agree, Phidias?'

Catrina sprang to her feet, pulling her gown across her flushed breasts in instinctive defence, while the man beside her rose with a satisfied smile on his face.

'She did extremely well, *patrona,*' said the man, carefully pulling the gold mask from his face and bowing his head in deference to Julia.

Catrina gazed from one to the other, speechless. So – the man with the mask was not some god, or spirit, but was a houseslave, under Julia's orders to pleasure her!

'Lesson?' she blurted out, her cheeks burning while her skin was suddenly cold beneath her flimsy gown. 'I don't think I quite understand. You mean you were watching? All of it?'

Julia said, 'My dear, of course I was watching! After all, I arranged it all for you – with the help of my beautiful dancers, Lark and Nightingale, and, of course, Phidias himself! You realised that, surely?' She paused, scanning Catrina's small, anguished face, then went on anxiously, 'You *did* enjoy yourself, didn't you?'

She looked so worried that Catrina found herself almost

laughing. *Enjoy* was not quite an adequate word to describe the utterly sensuous bliss that she'd just experienced! But even so, the thought of them all watching her was more than unnerving; it made her blood race with shame. She caught her breath at the enormity of it. Had Julia laughed at her naivety, just as the hateful Alexius must have laughed to himself when he walked off into the forest that night, leaving her stunned and desolate? His cutting words still lacerated her, even now: *You surely don't think that barbarians are to my taste?*

Struggling to appear calm and collected, she brushed her tousled blonde hair back from her face and said, 'Of course I enjoyed myself. But – forgive me – I didn't realise that I was here to provide entertainment for you all.'

Julia smiled approvingly. The British girl was incredibly beautiful, with her long, silken fair hair and her wide green eyes that were still smoky with sexual fulfilment. And it seemed that she was not without spirit either. Stepping forward to reassuringly touch her hand, Julia said quickly,

'Dear Catrina, please don't be offended! Of course I was watching. I had to observe it all, because you have placed yourself in my care, and it's my duty to assess your needs, your progress!'

She saw that the girl still hesitated, and pressed on, 'Just think for a while, Catrina. You can, of course, leave my house any time that you want to. But perhaps you should cast your mind back a little. What precisely was your situation when I came across you in the streets this afternoon?'

She saw the shadow of fear fall across the girl's small, exquisite face. Good. Catrina had remembered the mob, the hateful, peasant rabble out there in the township, who had been about to tear her to pieces as a sorceress. Julia went on quickly. 'Exactly. Those vile, rough people won't have forgotten you, you know. Stay here with me, I beg you – you'll be quite safe, because no one dares to offend me! And if you really, truly wish to learn our Roman ways, then you have come to the right place, believe me! We shall have such pleasure together!'

The girl's head jerked up at that, and her eyes fastened steadily on Julia's. 'I would like to stay,' she said. 'I would like to learn as much from you as I can about the ways of Rome.' Then she took a deep breath, as if making some kind of decision, and said in a low, yearning voice, 'I want to find a man.'

Julia, misunderstanding, put her hands affectionately on her shoulders. 'So you want to find yourself a wealthy, powerful protector! But, of course, what could be more natural? You are so ravishingly beautiful that you could have any man in the fort at your feet! Oh, we can teach you a little more about adornment, and the art of dressing like a fine lady. Lark and Nightingale will help. And between us, we can instruct you further in the many ways that Roman men like to take their pleasure.'

She'd seized Catrina's hand, and was drawing her out into the dimly lit passageway. Catrina, uneasily aware that perhaps Julia had not quite understood her, tried to pull back as she struggled to find the right words. 'No! I – I don't want just *any* man . . .'

'No, of course not!' broke in Julia abstractedly as they left the room. 'You want someone very special, very rich. Oh, you won't regret your decision to stay with me, I promise you!' Then she broke off, and said, in quite a different tone of voice, 'Falco. What are *you* doing here?'

A young blond slave was standing silently in the shadowy passageway with his hands chained behind his back. Catrina, her own maelstrom of thoughts quite driven from her head by his appearance, stared at him in wonder. He looked so beautiful, and so sad. Why was he chained up? She felt a shiver of unease. What else was going on in this strange, decadent household? Julia, seeing her staring, said, 'So you like my disobedient young gladiator, Catrina?'

Catrina felt the slave's grey eyes burning into her. She asked, 'Why is he chained up?'

'Because Falco has been very wicked. He thinks he's better than everyone else. But you aren't at all, are you, Falco? You're just the same as the rest of us!' She licked her fingertip and drew it down the slave's smooth, lean cheek; Catrina saw how he shuddered and closed his eyes, and felt her heart twist in pity for him.

Then Julia, with a little sigh, turned back to Catrina. 'Some day, you will meet Falco properly. But now, you must be tired. I'll show you to your room, and tomorrow we will make plans. And how very diverting that will be.'

The Intimate Eye

Georgia Angelis

The setting is 18th-century Gloucestershire and Lady Catherine Balfour is despairing of her husband's spendthrift and licentious ways. She is also struggling to quell the passions which arise in her at the sight of so many rugged labourers toiling on her land. But it is when the handsome Joshua Foxe is commissioned to paint the family's portraits that passions begin to escalate out of her control. Foxe, whom Catherine at first believes to be nothing more than a mincing fop, is due to send all the ladies of the house into a spin. In this extract Catherine resorts to desperate measures to gain satisfaction, only to realise she is not the only member of the household indulging in clandestine pleasures.

Georgia has written two other Black Lace books. Her first, *Outlandia,* is set on the mythical South Sea island of Wahwu where the shipwrecked Iona Stanley finds a warm welcome and is initiated into the ways of love. In the second – *Bella's Blade* – the spirited Bella Flowers catches the eye of King Charles II in a theatre in Drury Lane, and embarks on a lusty affair with the merry monarch himself.

The Intimate Eye

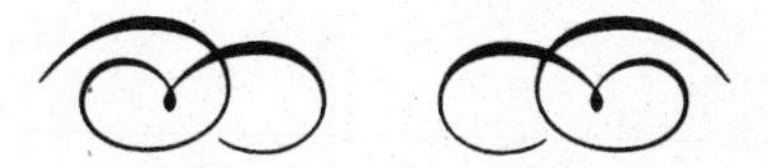

Like a doll Catherine stood, erect, arms outstretched, while her maid, Mary, unlaced her black daydress and coaxed it from her shoulders. It fell heavily to the floor, a dark, suffocating garment of wool and velvet.

Catherine looked on her form in the full-length mirror, but hardly saw herself at all. Rather she looked through her body, her thoughts a million miles beyond. Not even Mary dabbing her neck and shoulders with rosewater on a sponge could rouse her from the trance.

Catherine was thinking of the workmen again. It seemed that every moment her mind wasn't filled with worthy subjects of occupation, she did so. Images of men's bodies swam before her eyes, tormenting her. She mentally shook herself from so discomfiting a stupor, feeling much too warm all of a sudden, and saw then, as if for the first time in a long while, her own body semi-revealed before her.

She wore white silk stockings and buckled red shoes. Panniers of wicker basketwork greatly exaggerated the width of her hips, making her petticoats stand out, thus minimising her waist, which was tightly corseted and gratifyingly trim. Above the corset her breasts swelled, full and seemingly made of pink-tinted alabaster.

Mary stepped up with her fresh evening gown. Catherine held up her arms automatically and it was slipped over her head. It was of an ecclesiastical purple taffeta that shimmered quite superbly as she moved. Its deep square neck and elbow-length sleeves were softened with ruches and froths of ecru lace. With much huffing, puffing and a surprising expenditure of energy, Mary determinedly secured the back laces of the bodice.

Now Catherine, doubly confined, could only breathe in the most shallow of fashions, her breasts rising and falling like plump fruits above the lace edging of the low neckline. Confined and imprisoned, they looked as if they longed for escape. Mary came with a pot of powder and a swan's down puff and dusted them.

'Jewellery, m'lady? Your amethyst necklace and earrings perhaps?'

Catherine gave it some thought, but then shook her head. ''Tis Sunday. I think I shall wear one of the crucifixes . . . the baroque one with the sapphires and pearls.'

Mary nodded her approval, and retrieved it immediately from the small trayed selection of jewellery in the tiny drawer of Catherine's boudoir console. Most of the Balfour jewels were locked away in the strongroom beneath the study, next to Horace's wine cellar. And they could stay there, Catherine had often thought. For the most part they were antique and ugly in their heavy Tudor and Plantagenet gold settings. She'd have long since sold them off to pay some of Horace's debts, but he wouldn't hear of it, and harped on about the ancient name of de Balfour. Yet what good was a name when a family faced the possibility of financial ruin? But Horace would listen to no argument.

The crucifix now hung around Catherine's neck. Gleaming and impressive, it was suspended by a thin ribbon of black velvet. Mary made a few minor adjustments to Catherine's hair and the swallow's tail of lace that decorated its topknot and then the mistress of the house was ready to go below.

She walked sedately, as she was in no hurry to spend a Sunday evening with her family. Indeed sometimes she wished she might escape and never return. God forgive her, what a wicked thought and what a terrible woman she was!

She entered the wainscoted parlour, said good evening to each of them in the same flat manner, then went to sit at the small round table upon which had been placed – as it was every Sunday – the family Bible.

Her son Ralph stood staring out of the window, the slim volume open in his hands, totally ignored. Soon the heavy curtains would close upon the darkening sky, so he devoured the view while he could and also doubtless dreamed of escape.

Horace was hidden behind a close-printed broadsheet. *The Gloucester Gazette* was more than a week out of date, but that didn't bother him.

Sophie and Frances, her other children, sat at a table, embroidery hoops in their hands, though they did precious little sewing. They should have liked to play cards, but on a Sunday such a pastime was forbidden. There could be no gambling, nor anything loosely associated with it, on the Lord's day. So they sat with their embroidery, doing a few stitches of crewel or stumpwork, sighing and yawning often with poorly concealed boredom.

Lucky Uncle Harold had, for the time being, returned to London. He came and went at will. All thoughts of him that evening were decidedly envious.

Catherine took her place, sitting so that all in the room could see her, and so have no excuse for not giving her their full attention. She opened the large and heavy book at the page marked by an elaborate, tasselled marker and, making sure one last time that she was comfortable and ready, began to read the first verse of the new chapter.

She read from the gospel of St John. It really didn't matter to any of those seated or standing dutifully about the candle and firelit room. Once Catherine got underway they automatically switched off, losing themselves in their own individual thoughts: mulling on lovers, new dresses, invitations to parties and the new blacksmith's passably pretty wife. Catherine's reading from the Bible was simply a droning background noise.

This evening even Catherine was not finding it easy to concentrate. She could not capture her usual enthusiasm at all. She mouthed the words but their meaning was quite lost upon her. Her mind was elsewhere. It was filled with naked imagery: burly bathers, rough, muscled and dripping wet. And from there her thoughts jumped, quite unconnected, to the lusty vicar. Would she have been able to resist him quite so steadfastly if he'd been as handsome as the bathing beauty who'd so captivated her? She wanted to be able to say yes but she couldn't. She wasn't sure any longer.

And would she have put up such a struggle if he hadn't taken her so by surprise and frightened her? Again she would have liked to give a mental nod and feel righteous and indignant at his actions, but she could not. If he'd been more handsome, more subtle and gone about her seduction with a little more finesse, how greatly different might have been the outcome.

'Daydreaming's becoming a bit of a habit with you, m'dear,' said Horace, sneering at Catherine amusedly over the top of his newspaper.

She blinked, then flushed at the smirking faces of her husband and offspring. She'd done it again. She couldn't believe it. She was so embarrassed. If only these things would stop plaguing her. If they didn't, she felt she might go mad. She had to get them out of her system somehow. She needed a man!

'Sophie, dear, take over.'

Her eldest daughter declined with disdain. 'I'd rather not, mama. I don't enjoy reading aloud, especially not from the Bible. Ask Frances why don't you?'

Frances narrowed her eyes at Sophie for a malevolent second and then smiled sweetly, reaching for the Bible. 'I'd be happy to.'

Catherine composed herself and sat back to listen, determined to concentrate. Frances read brightly, turning a dreary passage into a holy revelation of crystal clear wisdom. The people on the page came to life, had voices, accents even, and spoke with passion.

The other four people in the room became increasingly attentive, and hung on her every word as if attending a highly commendable play at Bristol's Theatre Royal. There were audible murmurs of disappointment when Frances deemed herself finished and proclaimed, with a rather incongruous bow to her audience, 'Here endeth the lesson.'

They should have liked to clap, though of course, that would have been wholly inappropriate.

'Very nicely read, Frances dear,' complimented her mother.

'Indeed, yes,' said Horace. 'You must read for us next Sunday too. Indeed *every* Sunday.'

Frances beamed and appeared to blush, then closed the Bible once more upon the tasselled marker. 'Did you really enjoy it?'

'Very much so,' insisted Horace.

Sophie compressed her lips, suffering a pang of jealousy. 'I read just as well.'

'Of course you do, dear,' said Catherine, placatingly, though they both knew it wasn't true. 'Now let papa tell us of any interesting items in his gazette. What news makes the front page?'

Horace duly obliged, boring them rigid with the results of a regional by-election.

A light supper was brought in a little later and there was chocolate or wine. Usually Catherine would have stuck to chocolate along with her daughters, but not tonight. Tonight she was behaving uncontrollably out of character, and needed something to ease her troubled mind. Desperately, she decided that drink was the thing. Strong spirits. She matched Horace glass for glass and, when the bottle was finished and he reached for the Genever decanter instead, she asked for a measure before he could neglect to do so.

He raised an eyebrow and went to sit in the Queen-Anne chair by the fireside. 'Not like you, m'dear.'

She tittered, and seated herself opposite him, enjoying the flames too. 'Tonight I feel a little reckless, Horace.'

His eyebrow lifted even higher, an amused smile playing upon his overgenerous, red mouth.

En masse, the children rose to leave as was customary at the hour of nine, the daughters kissing their parents' cheeks, whilst Ralph shook Horace's hand and patted Catherine indulgently upon the head. Goodnights filled the air, then the door closed and the parents were left in silence, staring at the flames.

Catherine felt hot and dreamy, the liquor coursing her veins and making her relax. She gave a luxurious sigh and, when Horace looked up, winked.

He frowned suspiciously. 'Are you drunk, m'dear?'

She laughed gaily. 'I don't think so. My eyes are still focusing, dear. I can see you quite clearly. And what a well-turned-out, handsome devil you are, if I might say so.'

He laughed scoffingly even while he preened. 'Don't talk nonsense, m'dear.'

'I'm not, Horace,' she declared adamantly. 'I really mean it. Perhaps I neglect to look at you properly quite as often as I should. But I'm looking now.'

Immediately Horace sucked in his belly and presented his best profile, positively glowing under such unexpected attention.

She needed a man. And she had one. She need look no further than her own husband, surely? Here was pleasure without guilt or risk. He was not perfect but, given the amount of drink that Catherine had downed, he grew more acceptable with each passing moment.

It was obvious that Horace was pleasantly surprised by this turn of events. It had been a very long time since Catherine had appeared so friendly. But rather than just letting things develop, Horace exhibited his usual impatience in matters of the flesh. Seduction went out the window; he wanted to be up and at it.

He rose from his chair, and said, not very subtly, 'Bed, I think,' Then held out his hand. 'Coming?'

'Already? Won't you sit a while and talk to me . . . or, better still, kiss me?'

'Talk?' He was not enthusiastic. Kissing was different though. That automatically led to other things. Kissing he understood.

Catherine gave a giggly squeal of surprise as her husband dropped to his knees on the rug before her. He shuffled close, his hands on her knees, parting them so that he could get even closer. Soon he was between her legs, amongst her skirts.

He began to kiss her, starting at her forehead, going down over her nose, planting a smacker on her mouth, then travelling on down to her ears, throat and breasts.

She gasped and strained against him. Oh yes, yes. More, her mind screamed delightedly. Her flesh was hot and quivering, all afire. His kisses were ardent, boisterous even, and what they lacked in finesse they made up for in enthusiasm. He nuzzled and teased with his mouth while his hands rummaged beneath her many skirts and petticoats, finding her hidden warmth and softness.

He pulled at her skirts, exposing her legs to above the knees. His watch chain caught in her garter lace and tore it, and his kisses became clumsy as he struggled to unbutton his breeches.

'Slow down, Horace,' she pleaded. 'We've got all night.'

But leisurely lovemaking had never been her husband's forte. He was a man who loved conquest, action and speed. His hard shaft was already prodding at her, following where his fingers probed. She was warm and moist from being in a prolonged state of sexual arousal, so the head of his penis slipped about easily in her folds and found her entrance without trouble, his length plunging into Catherine in one fluid, gratifying leap.

Her body arched and her head went back, a long moan of pleasure issuing from her parted lips.

He kissed her mouth hard as he withdrew his length, then slipped it fully home again. His hands were on Catherine's thighs, holding her open and fully exposed to his delicious battering. He could look down and see where he entered her, hard and glistening, disappearing into her succulent rosiness. He watched his pumping flesh, her tight engulfing cranny and he began to cry out. He thrust, he jerked, stabbing at her wildly and making Catherine call out and clutch at him, her own desire building. But it was too late. He was too soon in coming and then it was all over bar the panting and jerking, his throbbing length softening in her, his sated body relaxing.

Tortured and unfulfilled, she could think of nothing but her throbbing hungry pussy and the despair she now felt instead of delight. It was hard not to let her resentment show.

Horace buttoned up his breeches and gave her a flush-faced wink, slapping her thigh playfully. 'Delightful, m'dear,' he said, gaining his feet and straightening his clothing before moving once more towards the decanter. 'Join me in a nightcap?'

She shook her head and swallowed away the dryness in her throat. 'No, I'm tired. I shall retire. Goodnight.'

'Goodnight.'

He was oblivious to her coolness, oblivious to all concerning Catherine, now that his desire had been quenched. He had ceased to regard her even before she'd left the room, his drink receiving his full and undivided attention.

She lay abed, on her stomach, her nightgown pulled up and a finger stroking her plump bud until at last her unpractised hand brought some relief. Only then could she finally sleep, lulled by a temporary satisfaction and peace. But temporary it certainly was. The next morning she awoke as troubled in mind and body as before, her core vibrant with desire, and crying out for a surfeit of good loving.

Last night had not really helped. Maybe it had even made matters worse. She felt more unfulfilled than ever; so hot and wanton that she was afraid of what she might do.

Catherine's mare carried her across the de Balfour estate. Surreptitiously the labourers watched her, their working movements now automatic. Her tawny hair was not in its usual severe topknot. It hung about her, gently waving, bouncing on her shoulders and streaming down her back. The chill air had brought colour to her pale cheeks. Her small hands in their black leather gauntlets expertly controlled the horse.

She tapped the blond man on the shoulder with her riding crop. 'You, come with me.'

He straightened, eyebrows knitting. 'Milady?'

'I need a man's assistance elsewhere and would borrow you.'

'As you wish.'

His accent was local. Broad and rounded. There was worry in his pale blue eyes for she looked so formidable, wearing that stony, unsmiling expression.

Catherine cantered the mare into the estate copse, riding so fast that the man had to run to try and keep up. By the time he had reached her, Catherine had dismounted. She was pointing a flintlock pistol at him.

He balked, understandably.

'I am a desperate woman,' said Catherine, her hand trembling, her voice faltering. 'Strip.'

'Milady?' His eyebrows shot up. She could not be serious.

'Off with your clothes, man. I . . . I simply have to have you or I shall go mad, I think,' she explained, sounding faintly apologetic even while she tried to intimidate him.

He almost collapsed with relief. She wasn't a madwoman bent on murder after all. Just another wife hungry for a little loving with no strings. There had been several in his life.

He stripped most artistically, happy to please Catherine in whatever manner she wished.

She unbuttoned the first dozen tiny buttons on the bodice of her sage-green velvet riding habit. Her breasts, pale and almost luminous in the shade, beneath the canopy of trees, thrust forward. She watched him intently, moistening at the sight of his rippling arm and chest muscles, and holding her breath as he unbuckled his thick leather belt and let his breeches drop.

He stepped out of them, and stood with his long legs planted wide, a man totally self-assured. His gorgeous length was hardening and rising before Catherine's eyes. A glimmer of a smile at last touched her tense face.

She indicated the leaf-softened ground at his feet with her pistol. 'Down.'

He lay down, smiling, enjoying all this immensely. The pistol aimed at him added a piquancy to the proceedings. He'd never been obliged to take orders from a woman before. Such a novelty was highly stimulating. That and the fact that she was a very beautiful woman. No man in his right mind could have turned down such a pretty, and such a desperate invitation. He watched her approach, hardening all the while. His wondrous length seemed to say, 'Look at me, how could you possibly ignore me?'

And look at it Catherine did as she stood over him, lifting her skirts and lowering herself on to him, her knees either side of his slim hips. Poised there she smoothed his torso and his arms, thrilling at the touch of his warm flesh. Then she claimed his member, running her encircling hand from base to tip, her eyes twinkling.

'I've never seen anything like it,' she purred in praise.

'Handsome, ain't it. Almost a footer when roused.'

'Twelve inches!' gasped Catherine, her fingers trembling with delightful anticipation around the silken sword.

'Aye, just so. I had a lady once who were so impressed she did produce a tape measure from her sewing box and take precise measurements.'

Catherine quivered as she manoeuvred the cumbersome head to her spot and began to lower. Slowly and gently, even a little in awe of the mighty thing, she went down, taking in the man inch by delicious inch.

He reached up and palmed her jutting breasts. Still she lowered, tight and hot about him, her mound at last coming down upon his forest of golden curls. She held her breath, and faintly she shook her head in disbelief. 'So big!'

He felt her quiver and clench about the meaty shaft and his blond eyelashes flickered with the pleasure. He caught her about the hips, and was about to try to wrest Catherine on to her back and take control, but she shook her head vehemently, snatching up the pistol. 'No!'

She wanted to ride him. He was *her* mount, the instrument of her pleasure. She wanted to be in control, wanted to use that glorious shaft as it suited *her*. She didn't want to know the man's name even. All that was irrelevant. He was merely the object to quench her out-of-control desire. She could think no further than that.

With a pistol thrust into his face, the labourer could do naught else but surrender himself to her whims. He did so with commendable bravery and gusto.

Catherine moved slowly, savouring each stroke, trembling

delightedly at the way he filled her to excess. She watched his face – the pleasure in his blue eyes, the tension in his jaw. His nostrils flared as he breathed.

Occasionally he lost control. He couldn't just lie there, an appendage to the hard fleshy pole upon which the lady of the manor took her pleasure. When he could no longer resist, he raised his head, neck cording with the exertion, and fastened his mouth hungrily upon her breasts, teasing the hard nipples and smoothing the silken globes.

Catherine felt the waves of pleasure begin to build, then felt them crash and break almost instantly. Her passion had been so acute that it had taken only the barest minute since her possession to come to climax. She tightened upon him, throbbing, drawing his hard shaft deep within her so that she could feel it at her core. She shuddered and groaned but she didn't stop. She was only partially satisfied. She stroked on gently, her eyes half-closed, her mouth likewise.

His lips fastened on and tugged insistently at her nipples. The sight of her radiant face, and the exquisite feel of being fucked by her, kept the labourer in a heightened state of ecstasy. Several times he felt himself coming near the point of no return and he had to close his eyes to the adorable sight of her, and try to think of something – anything save what she was doing to him.

Her gentle movements soon became more violent, and once more Catherine was stroking deep against him and crying out again.

He waited until she'd calmed for the second time before he begged, 'Please . . .' as he had an urgent need to turn her on to her back and drive into her.

She relaxed upon him and allowed herself to be turned. He was still deeply embedded within her. He sank in deeper, pulling Catherine's legs up and around his back, allowing himself the deepest possible penetration. His flesh pushed in and out, hard and thick, until Catherine gave endless little cries as she felt her depths battered.

There was no one to see them beneath the trees. No witnesses. Only the woodland creatures. What a picture they made, their clothes awry, their pale, intimate flesh exposed. He was sheathed in her tight folds, his flesh piercing her, stretching and rubbing upon her so beautifully that below the waist Catherine felt herself to be one massive, unendurable tingle. Her legs were wrapped tight about him, her stockinged ankles locked behind his back and her arms were snaked about his neck.

The man was grunting now, pumping hard, blowing air down his nostrils. His strokes were measured and hard and made Catherine writhe in pleasure-pain. For the third time her climax approached. So did his. He gripped her about the waist and pumped madly, thrusting himself into her, his cods slapping at her arse. He came with a choking, triumphant gurgle of pleasure.

Neither of them moved until they'd regained some modicum of control over their liquefied limbs and ragged breathing.

She smoothed down the crushed velvet skirts of her riding habit and buttoned her bodice. He pulled on his breeches and woollen stockings, wearing a smug grin. Yes, he looked very pleased with himself.

Catherine mounted her mare and brought the beast alongside. She looked down at him, her face expressionless.

'I hope I can count on your discretion, man,' she told him rather than queried, pistol in hand once more. 'T'would be a crying shame for all the other women in the county if – say I was to hear rumours concerning what took place here this day – you were accidentally shot in a hunting accident. I'm notoriously useless with guns. Such a tragic waste it would be.'

He was quick to reassure her. 'I'd never betray you, milady. Nay. I am your most devoted servant. I knows how t'keep such a precious secret.'

She smiled then. Sensible fellow. 'I thank you. Good day.'

Joshua Foxe's eyes lingered appreciatively upon the age-mellowed limestone of the old manor house. As he rounded a bend in the park's drive, he was next presented with the dazzling, dominating spectacle of Munsey Hall – the de Balfour estate. Its grandeur symbolised wealth and position, from the porticoed, triangular-pedimented entrance, to the shallow rise of honeyed roof tiles behind a classical parapet.

'That be the new hall,' informed Squires, the driver who had picked the young artist Foxe up from Munsey high street. 'A pretty penny been spent on it and all. And the spending ain't stopped yet. No sir. Got some grand ideas do our gent. Very grand indeed.'

'Really?'

'Oh aye. They do say the Lady Catherine despairs of his

extravagance. Not that she's miserly, y'understand,' Squires added quickly in her defence. 'She's a good Christian woman is Lady Catherine. And she do have a great deal t'put up with. He be a philanderer. 'Tis common knowledge.'

Joshua raised his eyebrows and said wryly, 'I am to paint the family's portraits. Is he good for his commission, do you think?'

Squires laughed reassuringly. 'Lady Catherine'll see you paid, sir. She's renowned for making good his debts. Indeed if 'tis monetary matters y'need t'discuss, take yourself to her rather than him. He be all promise promise and then forgets your conversation entirely once you be gone from his presence. Whereas she do listen and do act, most conscientiously too. She truly is the Lady of the Manor.'

The cart swerved around the sweep of gravel, past the main entrance, rumbling upon the flagstones in the immense yard before the purpose-built stable block. Here the equine inhabitants lived far more comfortably than any Balfour tenant in his leaky-roofed cottage.

Joshua Foxe's arrival created quite a stir, especially amongst the female servants. Some hung around the kitchen, laundry and dairy doors, while others stuck their heads out of upstairs windows where they were changing bedlinen and dusting. They in turn called to their workmates, and an army of inquisitive femininity appeared, to witness Foxe's alighting from the cart.

Neither was he oblivious to them. He allowed himself a half smile, especially when one of the laundrymaids, who was watching him so intently, walked, smack, into one of the posts of her washing line and nigh on knocked herself out.

Feet firmly on the ground, he stretched, thankful to use his legs again, after so many hours at the whims of horsepower. He started towards the woman framed by the entrance to the rear of the mansion.

The woman was grave and unsmiling, dressed in a summer-weight shimmering silk gown of amethyst-black. The only relief was a trimming of lace around the low, squared neckline, the elbows and the topknot of her tawny hair.

He was interested, even a trifle disconcerted.

She extended her hand very formally. 'Mister Foxe, how do you do, sir?' Her voice was deep for a female, not simpering and sweet.

'Very well, thank you, milady.'

'Step this way. I will have one of the footmen show you to your room,' said Catherine, thinking that it would be the first real task one of their dozen fancy footmen had actually carried out since being taken on by Horace. Mightn't the shock be too great? She chuckled at the thought.

'Milady?'

She half-turned to the immaculately turned-out Foxe, casting a cynical eye over the way he moved. Or rather minced she thought, noticing his lacy handkerchief.

'Nothing. Just thinking. Here we are. Horace thought a garret. I thought not. I am no artist but I believe it can do little for inspiration to be locked away at the top of some vast house. Much better to be near the ground and near to nature. What say you?'

'I agree entirely,' said Foxe amenably. He smiled winningly, and Catherine cocked an eyebrow. She knew insincerity when she saw it. She opened the door to his room and drew back, allowing him to enter first.

It was a ground floor room at the side of the house, with glass doors that opened out on to the terraces, the vista pleasingly contrived.

Foxe looked about, then turned to Catherine appreciatively. 'The room is spacious. Very nice.'

'You will be spending a great deal of time in it,' pointed out Catherine, 'for it must also double as your studio.'

'I understand. It will be more than adequate.'

Catherine found herself raising an eyebrow again. Was he mocking her? She couldn't tell.

She found him attractive but for some reason he irritated her greatly. Perhaps it was his lazy, indolent manner, a smile that almost-but-not-quite slipped over into a superior sneer. The man was only an artisan, for heaven's sake. She saw no reason for such wry arrogance. She felt that he saw through her; saw the real Catherine, the woman not the lady, and the thought disturbed her greatly.

Flustered, she retreated to the door, wanting to escape. 'I will leave you to settle in. A maid will be along shortly to unpack for you. You will take your meals in the servant's hall. Supper is at seven of the clock.' She closed the door. There, that had shown him; put him in his place.

She went back to her chambers and sat at her walnut writing

desk. She took up her crow quill to write on creamy handmade paper, but as the nib dipped into the dense black ink in its silver well, her hand paused over the paper. It had been her intention to write to her uncle in Bristol, wishing him a happy sixtieth birthday, yet as she tried to think of an opening line her mind refused to cooperate, and began to wander. She stared off dreamily into space, the meeting with Joshua Foxe playing itself over again in her mind. What a handsome man. And didn't he know it. Full of himself. Every female who'd spied him had paused to watch him, mouth agape. Catherine prayed she hadn't done likewise. She couldn't honestly recall her own facial reaction, just an acceleration in her heartbeat. She didn't think she'd made a fool of herself like all the others. She sincerely hoped not. It would be a mistake, she felt sure, to let a man like Foxe know just how disturbing an effect he had on one. How insufferably conceited he would become, how empowered. But she was determined that he shouldn't get the better of her. No. She was a match for that popinjay any day.

She dipped the nib again, wrote *Dearest Uncle,* then paused. He was so handsome. Beautiful almost. Not sharply handsome like young Ralph. Androgynous. Yes. His hair, swept back off his face and secured into a queue with a black ribbon was brown-black. So were his eyes. Dark, intense, smouldering. They burned into one, raked, probed beneath her clothing.

Her breathing grew laboured. Perhaps all artists were like that? Her quill scratched across the paper.

He was tall and slim, a man of restrained fashion. His black frock coat and breeches superbly cut, his cravat fancily tied and profusely lacy. His long legs with trim ankles were snugly encased in black superfine wool, his stockings were dove-grey cotton; his heeled black shoes sported black bows in preference to silver buckles. His clothes were severe compared to her husband's brocade coats and waistcoats with their clutter of braiding and buttons. She liked the simplicity.

She roused herself from her daydreamings and stared down at the paper on the desktop before her. She stared agog. She had written: *Tight buttocks. Cruel mouth. Caress.*

Catherine gasped in horror and frantically tore the paper into many tiny pieces.

* * *

Things were never the same again after the arrival of Joshua Foxe. His very presence was disruptive, even when he wasn't personally responsible. The female servants became lax and unconscientious in their work; they were, Lady Catherine continually scolded them, spending far too much time thinking of things other than their jobs. They were warned to buck up their ideas or else face the possibility of dismissal. It did little good to go on at them though, she knew. Under normal circumstances they functioned efficiently, were good, hard working girls, but just let Foxe walk amongst them or, God forbid, bestow a friendly smile, and their brains seemed to turn to mush.

And Catherine really was no better. She had to avoid him like the plague to maintain any kind of peace of mind. She unsuccessfully tried to lose herself in solitary reading from the Good Book. She couldn't get him out of her mind.

Horace's portrait was well underway. It was a good likeness. Mister Foxe was indeed an accomplished artist; Harold had chosen well. And yet whenever Catherine studied the oil painting she felt she was looking at a caricature. Certainly it had been executed with a frank, even cruel brush hand. But no one else passed comment. Others were apparently impressed. Couldn't they see that Foxe had made Sir Horace look like a jumped-up windbag, a pretentious country bumpkin? Or maybe they did and were just being diplomatic. Perhaps they thought it unwise to comment on something so near to the truth. Catherine decided to do likewise. But it made the prospect of sitting for Foxe something she positively dreaded. Would he expose the real her?

It was Sunday. In half an hour it would be time to leave in the family carriage for morning service at the church. Catherine, perfumed and powdered, and wearing her finest violet silk daydress, left the others at the breakfast table and stepped outside on to the terrace. The urns atop the balustrades had been planted up with stocks, nasturtiums, geraniums and variegated hedera that trailed profusely. She sniffed the stocks, picked one and fastened it into her silver brooch so that the scent would rise later, combating the dank odour of the church.

She rounded the corner to the side of the house and came across one of the upstairs maids very furtively spying in through Foxe's window. The maid must have seen Catherine's approach out the corner of her eye, for she straightened briskly, tried unsuccessfully to adopt an innocent air, and scurried off in the other direction before her mistress could think to call her back.

Catherine cocked an eyebrow, and intrigued, continued at the same pace until she'd come parallel with the floor-length windows into the artist's studio-cum-sleeping quarters. There she paused and peeped, her eyes widening and mouth curling upwards in amusement.

Joshua Foxe was in the process of taking a bath. No wonder the maid had been so illicitly engrossed. Catherine tarried, assured that the man, who had his back half-turned towards her, had no idea of her presence. Leisurely, she admired him. Slim, pale, and lightly muscled, his hair gleamed darkly like a coach's varnish, sleek with the water. It hung down to his shoulders, like sable. Wet, and slightly waving, it made him look a little wild.

In time he rose from the coopered tub, and Catherine drew in her breath. She could see his reflection in a large mirror on the far wall. She observed his tight buttocks and his dormant sex, lying along his leg. He bent, picked up a bath sheet and quickly patted himself all over before securing it around his waist.

He tugged on the bell pull beside the fireplace and two male servants came in to heft the tub of water away between them. A maid arrived after them, her arms full of freshly ironed linen. She bobbed a curtsy to him, and laid out a fresh shirt and cravat upon the bed. Only when she looked up, blushing and smiling, following Foxe with her eyes, did Catherine recognise her as the same maid who had been spying on him from the terrace.

Foxe gave her a coin and Catherine waited for her to quit the room, as she was eager to see him go about the business of getting dressed. But the maid didn't go. Rather she perched her bottom on the edge of his bed and cast him a coquettish grin, saying something that Catherine couldn't even begin to guess at.

Foxe frowned with theatrical severity and wagged a finger at her. She pouted, undeterred, and took her skirts into her hands, raising the hems seductively and slowly. Foxe referred to the time on the mantle clock, nodded and dropped his towel, swift and businesslike.

He stood between her parted legs, smoothing her milky thighs above the black woollen stockings; palming her mound before stroking down through her crease with a gentle finger.

Catherine gasped. She was shocked and disturbed. Absurdly jealous. He was not the man of her dreams, his penis some mythically proportioned instrument of pleasure and terrible dominance. This Foxe was a mere mortal, with a mortal's body. He was still impressive for all that, however. He was beautifully endowed, the stalk that reared from his bush of dark curls being long, and of considerable girth.

The maid's eyes devoured it. He ran the head through her wetness and then inched into her depths, his buttocks clenching; thrusting and jerking.

She wore a happy expression, as she wrapped her legs around him, and she crossed her wrists at the back of his head. He took her swiftly and carelessly, using what had been so freely offered. He pushed up, his hands holding her firmly about the buttocks, keeping her still to accept the force of his powerful strokes.

The girl's face was now gripped by intense emotion. Her teeth were gritted, her glazed eyes raised to the ceiling as she allowed her head to fall back. Catherine could hear nothing, but the maid was undoubtedly making little noises of pleasure each time Foxe filled her with his gorgeous length.

Her crisis evidently arrived, and she clutched at him, her face ecstatic, her mouth open wide to emit her cries. Foxe permitted himself a smug smile and then allowed himself to come.

Catherine watched his expression in the full-length mirror. Then she realised, to her horror, that he was watching her. Her hand flew to her mouth and she leapt sideways out of view of the window. Oh damnation, she could die of the shame! She sped off in mindless panic. Heaven forbid that anyone should see her. And how was she to face the obnoxious Foxe?

The King's Girl

Sylvie Ouellette

Laure has grown up in the wild rural beauty of the French countryside in the early 1600s and, despite the sometimes harsh living conditions, is a person in harmony with her environment; some would say a wild child. As a young woman, she is keen to explore her burgeoning sexuality and has recently taken to spying on René, a stable boy with a god-like physique, who bathes every day in the stream near to where she lives with her father.

In the chosen excerpt, Laure is prepared to be a voyeuse no more and apprehends René on his way back to the stables. An easy seduction ensues, with Laure eager to enjoy every inch of his body. In the ensuing months, however, her life will change beyond measure and René will become a pleasant memory as she is taken into the care of the decadent Monsieur and Madame Lampron who will teach her much in the way of indecent but delightful behaviour.

Syvlie Ouellette is our only French-Canadian author. She has written two other Black Lace books: *Healing Passion,* which is set in an exclusive modern-day hospital where there are lots of kinky goings-on, and *Jasmine Blossoms,* a tale of sexual mystery in contemporary Japan.

The King's Girl

The laurel branch gently bobbed in the wind and grazed Laure's face. With a nonchalant flick of the wrist, she pushed it away and leant forward into the bushes. Above the trees, the pale, late afternoon sun barely pierced the haze of the hot, humid day. The distant rumble of thunder was growing louder and black clouds began to darken the horizon. And, in the meantime, inside Laure's hungry body, a different kind of storm was brewing.

Her emotions encompassed everything from excitement and anticipation, to silliness and even worry, for today was the day she had decided to lose her virginity. Now, all she had to do was wait for the man who would take it.

From her hiding place, she had a perfect view of the narrow creek where René would soon come to wash. Every day for the past few weeks, Laure had ritually spied on her prey, the stable hand. In fact, she had hidden behind these bushes so often, the imprint of her feet remained embedded in the ground.

All day, every day, she would wait for this very moment. And she had never been disappointed. But today she wouldn't silently slip back to her quarters, as she usually did. She would stay and seduce him.

In her mind, success was already a certainty. Judging by the compliments of all the young men who had asked for her hand, Laure knew she was blessed with what people called *'la beauté du diable'* – the devil's beauty.

Her curvaceous figure and sensual, fiery nature attracted men wherever she went, and she revelled in their silent stares. No matter how she dressed, she always felt constricted by her clothes. Her skin longed for freedom. For her, happiness was being naked or wearing the bare minimum.

No one had ever raised an eyebrow when, as a child, she had pranced around clad only in an old shirt, chasing butterflies across the courtyard of the Château de Reyval. In recent years, however, she would be called upon to protect her modesty from prying eyes if she were to so much as remove her bodice. So Laure would tease convention, deliberately allowing her skirt to run up her calves and letting her bodice gape as her generous breasts strained at the ties. Throughout the summer, she even walked around without shoes, unable to tolerate anything between the soles of her feet and the warm, dusty earth.

Strands of untamed hair persistently stuck out from under her bonnet; that is, when she had bothered to wear one in the first place. She much preferred to let her locks cascade freely around her shoulders. Her long, dark-brown mane was just like her late mother's, and the sight of it often brought tears to her father's eyes. But, for others, it was just another reason to despise her.

Juliette, the housekeeper, never missed an occasion to scold Laure on her lax grooming. But the woman's words had no effect on the young maid, who had grown up among the staff at the château and cared little for authority. Almost everybody there had known her since childhood, and through the years Laure had learnt that she could do as she pleased. Roland Lapierre, her father, was the château's blacksmith, as had been his father before him. The staff respected him, some even feared him, and Laure, who had recently started work in the kitchens, took advantage of this as often as she could.

It had not been her choice to become a servant at the château. In fact, she had ranted vehemently in protest. But she had no alternative: her father's meagre wages no longer proved sufficient to provide for his daughter's voracious appetites. For Laure Lapierre enjoyed life and savoured everything it had to offer, down to the last morsel.

And now the old man could barely support the two of them. He had to pay rent on the little maisonette where they lived, unwilling to let his daughter share the servants' quarters. As long as he was around, Laure would have her own home. For now, at least, working in the kitchen meant she would be fed at the master's expense.

At times, her father seemed eager to marry her off. He was finding it increasingly difficult to keep an eye on her now that she had crossed the threshold of womanhood. More and more frequently, cheeky young men took liberties with his beautiful girl: he had interrupted several stolen kisses, and had seen the occasional furtive hand stroking her rounded hips.

Yet he rejected all those who asked for his daughter's hand. For although he was only a simple blacksmith, he thought no one was good enough for his treasure, his beautiful Laure. The man who would have her had to be more than a valet or farm hand; he would have to be wealthy enough to spoil Laure in the way to which she was accustomed.

As time passed, the young woman only grew more eager to appease that yearning which had consumed her since her femininity had blossomed. Fingers brushing her cheek made her weak at the knees and bold kisses stirred even more excitement.

She knew how her body reacted under her own fingers; she had become addicted to the throbbing heat of pleasure she could bring to herself. But now she wanted more than solitary caresses. She hungered for close contact: a man's arms around her; her skin burnt for the soothing touch of a warm body. She didn't want to wait any longer. The time had come, married or not, and she had chosen for herself the man who would be her first lover.

René was just a stable boy but he had the body of a god, with strong arms and square shoulders. His hair was the colour of dirty straw, his eyes the palest blue. Healthy and hard-working, he moved in a way which betrayed great sensuality. His body, strong, tall and defined, was obviously built for rugged, passionate embraces.

He and Laure were opposites, for his hair was just as wispy and fair as hers was thick and dark. His rough, tanned skin also contrasted starkly with her smooth and milk-white complexion. His lips, though full and sensuous, often tightened into the cruellest of smiles whereas Laure's mouth was a hungry furnace that could provide nothing but pleasure and joy. The way they complemented one another made them a perfect match indeed, in Laure's opinion.

René had come to work at the château just a few weeks earlier. Laure knew nothing of him, only that his body was by far the most attractive she had ever seen. They had hardly exchanged a single word. Her day-to-day work rarely took her to the stables, where he worked.

Nevertheless, she had managed to catch his eye. The rest didn't really matter as the mystery only served to excite her even more. Who else was she supposed to choose as her first lover? Certainly not one of the servants she had played with as a child. They held very little interest for her, and the feeling was generally mutual. But René was a different prospect.

She had seen him look at her longingly, whenever he came to the kitchens to fetch food. He always smiled at her and was clearly interested, yet had made no attempt to seduce her.

But Laure was completely taken with him, wanting nothing more in the world than to feel his hard, naked body pressed against her tender skin. She had thought of him so often, imagined them together, sharing a passionate embrace. In her mind, she was already his.

As usual, she watched silently as he appeared in the late afternoon sun, quickly shedding his dirty clothes before entering the stream. On his face she saw a familiar expression of bliss as he gradually sank beneath the cool water. When he emerged, the sight of water trickling down his naked body excited her as never before.

The skin of his bare chest was tanned and velvet-like, offering a sharp contrast to the pale, firm buttocks which had never seen the warming rays of the sun. Standing in water up to mid-thigh, he rubbed a heavy bar of brown soap over his chest, working up lather. The movements of his hands were blunt and powerful as they ran over his body, washing away the sweat and toil of a long day.

René was of peasant stock; his touch would be anything but gentle, as he was probably more used to stroking horses than women. Laure had seen the calluses left by pitchforks on men's palms and fingernails stained after a day spent greasing leather straps. Yet her body craved the contact of those rough hands; her skin yearned for his.

She found it hard to stifle a giggle as she watched his dangling prick moving in all directions, like a feisty fish constantly diving and emerging from the water with great splashes. It surely wouldn't remain flaccid if only she could get a hold of it and caress it. Indeed, it would come alive in her hands. Her own flesh would then join with his and they would become one, like wild rivers that meet and merge under the force of their flow. She knew it would happen. Soon, very soon.

Laure still hadn't decided how to set her plan in motion. Should she disrobe and join him in the cool water? Or surprise him as he walked back to his quarters? She waited a little while longer. The pleasure she took from simply watching the taut muscles move under his bronzed skin was almost unbearable, but she knew this was just a taste of the delights she could expect once she finally got her hands on him.

After washing himself thoroughly, René splashed about in the water, occasionally looking up at the sky; menacing clouds were now drawing overhead. Soon, Laure knew, he would come out and make his way back to the stables.

Halfway between the river and the stables, along the path she had walked so often, was a clearing of soft grass. Time and again she had imagined the scene which would take place there; at that exact spot she would give herself to the man who for so long had been haunting her dreams.

Laure knew of at least three maids who had already been René's lovers, but despite her inexperience, she hoped to be like no other. She had, after all, managed to learn a great deal about lovemaking from what she had seen and heard.

She remembered Martin, the gamekeeper, with Suzanne, the kitchen helper. There had been many other couples who had had no idea she was watching. She had come across them making love in the haystacks behind the barn, in the fields, in the pantry. It was always by accident; she hadn't meant for it to happen. But each time the urge to stay and watch had been overwhelming.

She had seen it all: the men whose engorged members seemed to pierce their partners amidst cries of delight; the temptresses who enticed their man by taking his swollen penis into their mouths. The sounds of moans and gasps still echoed in her ears. And each time Laure had felt jealous. Not that she fancied any of the men, but she just knew she was missing out on something and she now wanted to discover the pleasures of the flesh. But that very first time would be the most important. She wanted her first lover to remember her; she had to impress.

René slowly waded out of the water. One step ahead of him, Laure silently slipped away to wait in the clearing.

With trembling fingers, she quickly undid the laces on the

front of her chemise and drew the edges apart to expose slightly the pink skin of her cleavage. The rays of the sun hadn't taken their toll on her. This summer most of her time had been spent working in the kitchens and she hardly ever went out in the fields as she had done when she was a little girl. Her skin was still pale, soft and delicate, but burning with an ache only a man could soothe.

Her fingers nervously slipped inside the opening, gauged the weight of each breast swollen with the arousal of expectation, and caressed them as René would in just a few minutes. Would he be tempted to suck her taut nipples, or be content to just toy with them?

The thought of his hands on her body drove Laure crazy with anticipation. Already the flesh between her legs was bathed in heady musk and clenched sporadically, impatient to receive its reward.

She left the front of her chemise slightly open, just enough to tease. Not that she was bashful, but she wanted to give her chosen lover an invitation to undress her. The old, brown skirt she had decided to wear had shrunk with the years and now showed her ankles and the lower part of her calves when she walked. The frown on her father's face every time she wore it had almost made her throw it out, but now Laure was glad she had kept it. Today, the old rag was an asset.

Her bonnet conveniently left behind on her bed, Laure quickly undid the pins holding up her hair and combed it with her fingers. She stood silently in the clearing, her heart pounding, as she waited for René to come her way. And she knew he would, and she would welcome him inside her at last.

The day was still hot and heavy as the sun started its descent. The light breeze gradually grew stronger as stormy clouds gathered in the sky. Laure didn't like thunder, but today nothing could make her seek cover, not even the fear of lightning striking her right then and there.

Her man whistled as he approached, the melody buried under the sound of the leaves rustling in the wind. Suddenly he was in front of her, naked. Droplets of water still dripped from his hair and rolled off his shoulders.

Laure's heart beat furiously. There was nothing she could do; the next move was up to him. He looked at her and smiled knowingly, pleasantly surprised, and made no effort to conceal his nudity.

At that moment the storm broke. Laure didn't move when lightning tore through the sky and the wind swept her long brown hair across her face. Thunder crashed above them and rain began to pour down. René didn't utter a word but stared at Laure, relishing her beauty.

In a matter of seconds she was drenched through. Her wet chemise now clung to her breasts, revealing her dark nipples which had stiffened under the wild caress of the wind.

She threw her head back and brought her hands to her neck, stroking her throat with her fingertips. The next bolt of lightning made her close her eyes. She could feel the water trickling down her chest, refreshing, arousing her.

René still hadn't moved. Laure looked at him through half-shut eyes and was pleased to see him feebly run his tongue across his lips. She was also delighted to see his member respond to the sight of her, its bulbous tip jutting upwards, stiff and swollen.

Dropping his bundle of dirty clothes, he took one step towards her. Laure knew at that moment she had won the first battle. She looked at him and smiled in turn. As he advanced towards her, his eyes were fixed on her breasts and she felt her nipples throb and ache in response to his hungry gaze.

Roughly, without kissing her, without even looking her in the eyes, he undid her bodice and skirt. They fell immediately, dragged down by the weight of the water that soaked them.

Laure whimpered. Despite the tempest raging inside her, the coolness of the wind made her shiver. René laughed and pulled her chemise up, slowly revealing the smooth skin of her thighs, her rounded buttocks, the dark triangle of hair at the junction of her legs. The hem was wet through and left a cold, watery trace as it trailed up her body.

René clutched the dripping garment in a tight knot in one hand whilst he slipped the other between her legs. There, amidst the swollen folds of her moist vulva, beat the heart of her femininity. He pushed a long, cold finger inside her and pulled it out slowly, caressing the silken walls of her virgin tunnel, freeing the flow of dew that quickly warmed his hand.

Laure shuddered and threw her arms around his neck, nestling her head under his chin. To feel him so near was a revelation; to have him within reach, a dream come true. Against her cheek she could feel the blood pulsing in his neck. His skin, taut and smooth, felt like fine leather against her lips. His heartbeat strangely echoed the rhythm of her breathing. She tightened her embrace around his neck.

'You little witch,' René said in an amused tone. It was the first time he had really spoken to her. But she didn't want conversation.

'Don't talk,' she yelled above the thunder. 'Just take me.'

She could feel his member nudging at her, its purplish head twitching against her belly. Never before had she been so close to a naked man, although she had seen many of them. And this one was hers for the taking.

In one swift move he grabbed her hips, lifted her and impaled her on his erect penis. She felt his flesh probing into hers; she felt it pierce her. She let out a loud sigh. Now she was a woman.

He held her to him, motionless, for a few seconds. His mouth seized hers and she replied to his kiss ravenously, feeding on his lips and hungrily sucking his tongue.

As her passion mounted, she writhed against him. Her breasts were crushed, her stiff nipples grinding into his hard, muscular chest through the fabric of her chemise. Despite the pouring rain constantly showering him, he exuded a mixed aroma of soapy cleanliness and manly musk. Laure held on tight, only too pleased to give herself over to the strength of his desire.

His thighs were hard and hot against hers, as were his arms and chest. The rain seeped between their bodies but didn't seem to cool them at all. Their passion was too hot to be quelled.

For Laure, things were happening just as she had hoped. At least she had achieved her goal of making him come to her. The rest would surely follow. For the first time in her life, she could enjoy the animal heat of their passion. He was inside her; she could feel him getting harder still.

Without letting her go, he fell to his knees. As she held on to his neck, her face buried in his hair, he grabbed her buttocks and slowly lifted her along the length of his hard shaft. Its rounded head pulsed and teased at her entrance, before he let her slide back down again under her own weight. He repeated the lifting motion time and again. Each thrust was a caress, each stroke a fulfilment.

Against her bare arms she could feel his muscles play under

his skin, strong and frisky like a colt. She felt him alive inside her, sliding in and out. Her pleasure mounted quickly, more intense than she had ever experienced.

Laure didn't mind not having had time to caress him as she had planned. He had taken control, and she was enjoying every moment of it. Gripping his shoulders, she threw her head back, letting her breasts jut out of her open chemise. The rain fell on them, hard and stinging, making her cry out. René bowed his head and took a stiff nipple into his mouth, sucking it roughly until Laure screamed, more in pleasure than in pain, now unable to control all the sounds escaping from her mouth with each breath.

His hands were still under her buttocks, his fingertips digging hard into her flesh and pushing at the entrance of the delicate, puckered rose of her behind. The sensations merged into one, powerful, overwhelming. The fire inside her grew out of control and as she climaxed her strangled groans of pleasure were lost in the uproar of the storm raging around them.

With the next bolt of lightning, he lifted her off him and laid her down on the grass. Still without a word, he ripped her chemise open in one swift motion, exposing her completely, offering her body to the storm and its elements.

She had barely recovered from the peak of her climax when he lay on top of her. His shaft, still hard as iron, was trapped between their rain-soaked bodies. He held her hands above her head and pinned them to the ground. The wet grass stuck to her skin and his grip made her feel like a prisoner. But she didn't complain; she knew she had yet to have her turn with him.

His lips nibbled at her neck, quickly making their way down to her breasts. His mouth wasn't large enough to take in her enormous, dark areolae. He almost choked on them, unable to swallow them, sucking and biting them, almost with a vengeance.

He let go of her arms and grabbed her breasts with both hands, kneading, moulding them like mounds of clay, whilst his mouth continued its assault on them. Laure went wild with the pleasure she took in his touch. He seemed to know her body just as well as she did; he knew how to enhance that exhilarating sensation, that feeling that pleasure was near. He was dominating her, taking her with all his might.

The rain fell harder still, making their bodies slip against each other. Without any effort, he slid down her body, letting his tongue trail across her belly. Just as she had hoped, he drew back until his mouth closed over her wet, excited sex.

She offered herself to the ministrations of the rain whilst her lover buried his tongue in her thick bush, insatiably exploring her. The contrast between the fluid heat of his body between her thighs and the stimulating coolness of the rain on her breasts was intoxicating.

Her pleasure mounted again as his tongue located her bud and teased it expertly. A spasm shook her from head to toe and she dug her fingers into the earth, which was now reduced to silken mud. Suddenly she didn't feel the rain, she didn't hear the thunder, she didn't see the lightning. She could sense nothing but his wet, warm tongue licking the intricate folds of her vulva. It squirmed around, up and down, enhancing her arousal yet not bringing her to fulfilment.

His mouth covered her completely, probing and sucking, tasting and relishing. His lips drew on her bud, extracting all the pleasure from within her. She was oblivious to the world around her, and didn't even notice the rain had now stopped and the storm had passed.

Her second climax was even more violent than the first, and her screams resounded through the forest. René laughed as he let go of her and let his chin rest on her breasts.

The heat of her skin quickly evaporated the few drops of rain still dripping down her body. A ray of sun pierced the horizon and shone between the trees. Laure looked at her new lover and remembered there was still much she wanted to do.

Quickly regaining her strength, she pushed him aside and rolled over on top of him, her thighs straddling his hips, her forearms on either side on his chest. Drops of water glistened on his shoulders. Laure stuck out her tongue playfully and lapped them up. Kneeling in the mud, she set out to do exactly what he had just done to her, to show him she knew how to pleasure a man.

Yet she had to struggle to stop him from moving. It was as if he didn't want to let her have her own way with him. She lay down on top of him, trying to prevent him from pushing her aside as she sealed her mouth around his nipple. But he was stronger than her and their caresses soon turned into a wrestling match, for he was half stroking her, half pushing her away.

They rose to their knees as she tried to get close again. This time she held on tight; her arms locked around his chest, her hands pressing into his back, whilst her mouth seized his nipple, sucking so hard on it that she thought he couldn't make her let go.

But he did. Though he sighed with pleasure, he would not remain passive. Encircling her waist with his leg, he tried to force her off balance and push her head aside.

Laure saw his behaviour as a challenge. She wanted to show him what a good lover she could be, yet he resisted her ministrations. Therefore she would simply have to move on to the next step.

With a grunt, he managed to get up whilst she still held on to him. In front of Laure appeared his swollen shaft, awakened further by their sensuous fight. The sight of it aroused her even more, fuelling her desire to possess him. She seized the opportunity and immediately drew him into her mouth. It was so big she almost gagged, but quickly recovered from the surprise of this new sensation. As she began sucking on it, she felt him ease up.

His hands came to rest on her head, his fingers burrowing into her mass of wet, dirty tresses. Was he giving in? She saw this as a good sign and released her grip around his waist to slowly lower her hands on to his buttocks, digging her fingernails into the pale flesh.

He let out a loud moan, almost a complaint, and she felt the stiff rod pulse violently in her mouth. Laure had finally achieved what she had set out to do earlier that day, only now it seemed like a lifetime ago.

She brought her hands back around his hips and grabbed his shaft greedily. The swollen head responded by letting a few drops of salty liquid seep out of its tiny mouth. Laure's arousal intensified. How intoxicating to feed on him, how mesmerising to have him at her mercy. Once again she forgot where she was, and cared only for the marvel she held in her hands and in her mouth.

Her tongue started a strange dance along the ridge of the purple head, barely touching it and fluttering around it like a butterfly. Next, she tried to engulf all of him, pressing her forehead against his stomach, burying her nose in his forest of curls.

She let one hand slip under his heavy sac, briefly feeling the fullness of his balls before they bunched up. She felt him trembling; she heard him groan. She knew the moment was near. Soon, victory would be hers.

At that very moment, things took a different turn. Grabbing her head forcefully, he pushed her away from him. Laure was baffled. Just when she had thought she was really pleasuring him, he had not been entirely at her mercy.

Seizing her by the shoulders with a devilish laugh, he pulled her to her feet and forced her to turn around to face a large tree near where they stood. Shocked and disorientated, Laure let him push her against the thick trunk and encircled it with her arms.

The bark was cold and wet, slightly crumbly under the tender skin of her arms and chest. Behind her, René bent down and grabbed her ankles. He quickly lifted her legs up and prised them apart. Laure had to hold on to the tree even tighter, pressing her chest and face against it to avoid sliding down its length, the wet wood scraping her breasts.

Despite being in this awkward position, her arousal was just as intense. This was something she had not imagined. What would René do next? The thought filled her with excitement and apprehension.

He nudged at her behind almost immediately, holding her legs against his hips, letting his member find its way between her rounded buttocks, sliding up and down the slick valley. He probed her puckered opening for a little while before impaling her again, this time in a place even she had never explored.

The engorged head slowly made its way inside her, using the dew from her vulva to lubricate the passage. Her delicate hole initially tightened in resistance, but was quickly vanquished by the perseverance of his virility. Eventually he took her completely, to the hilt, his thick shaft spreading her open in a sensation that bordered on pain but generated even more delight.

Still holding on to the tree, Laure felt droplets of rain falling from the leaves and trickling down her face. Against her skin the wet, old bark crumbled away to leave harder bits of wood painfully pricking her breasts. Her right cheek was pressed to the trunk and its musty scent filled her nose as she breathed harder.

Once again, she was on the verge of climax. Her pleasure knew no bounds. She had discovered a new source of joy, continually enhanced by the unusual invasion of her lover. Her encounter with René was turning out to be more than she could ever have hoped for.

The raindrops rolling down her cheeks were soon followed by tears of joy as she reached her peak. Her mouth opened to let out a cry of ecstasy, but no sound came. She held her breath whilst the wave transported her, again a result of the rapturous combination of pleasure and pain.

René screamed behind her, his voice hoarse with exhaustion. His hands held her tight, trembling as he increased the rhythm of his thrusts. He contracted in a spasm, his straining rod finally releasing his seed inside her, surrendering to the violence of their coupling. Yet he continued his motion, the pace subsiding until he could hold her no more and he fell to his knees, letting go of her legs.

Laure let her head fall back and she tasted the saltiness of her tears on her upper lip. Still the bark bit into her tender skin, but her fulfilment was complete.

And it had all been so easy. Somehow she knew that was the key to everything she could ever want: all she had to do was ask.

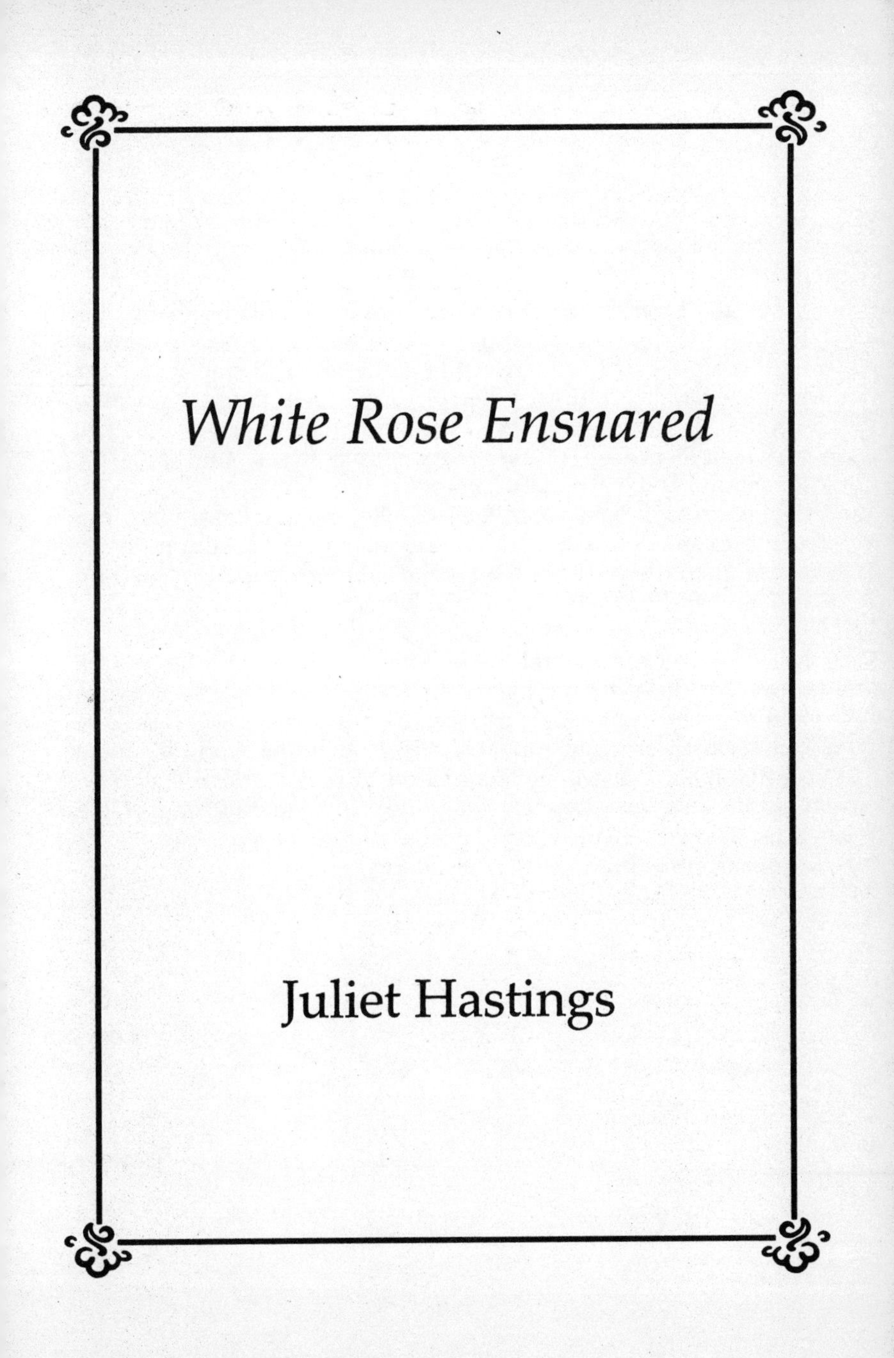

White Rose Ensnared

Juliet Hastings

When the elderly Lionel, Lord de Verney, is killed in battle, his beautiful widow, Rosamund, finds herself at the sudden mercy of Sir Ralph Aycliffe, a powerful knight who will stop at nothing to humiliate her and seize her property. Only the young squire Geoffrey Lymington will risk everything to help her. Against the turbulent backdrop of the Wars of the Roses, the battle for Rosamund and her property unfolds.

This excerpt from *White Rose Ensnared* shows Rosamund in a frame of mind to trust her desires and follow Geoffrey to his sleeping quarters. The response she gets for creeping up on him is not what she expects: it's far, far better than that.

Juliet has written several books for Black Lace. Her first, *Crash Course,* explores the intimate relationships which arise between four very different people on a management training course; *Aria Appassionata* is a contemporary novel set in the world of opera and is about one woman's ambition to play Carmen; *Forbidden Crusade* tells the story of unrequited love in the time of the Crusades; and *The Hand of Amun* explores the powerful mysticism and ritual practices of Ancient Egypt.

White Rose Ensnared

Master Lymington pushed his right hand wearily through his thatch of shining hair, then rubbed his scabbed brow. He was pale and there were long blue streaks under his eyes. 'Well, my lady,' he said with a sigh, 'I believe that we have done all we can to protect the manor. There is no time to build defences here, no time at all. We shall have to face the enemy with what we have. I know your men know what to do and that they will all do their best.' He glanced around the hall and the remnants of Lionel de Verney's household watched him eagerly, nodding. None of them had murmured at taking instruction from a man who could barely be five and twenty. They were all only too pleased to have a soldier of any sort come among them. 'As for me,' said Master Lymington, 'I did not sleep last night, and I am dog-weary. Show me a place where I can lay my head, and I will sleep till the morning and be better for it.'

'Sleep?' repeated Rosamund wretchedly. It was barely six of the clock and she had hoped for his company for a good while yet. Then she registered the strain and fatigue on his white face and shook her head at her own thoughtlessness. 'Of course,' she said, 'of course. I am very sorry not to have thought of it before. A room is prepared for you, Master Lymington.' *Geoffrey*, said her desire. *Geoffrey*. 'Shall I show you there?'

'You are very kind,' he said, and heaved himself to his feet to follow her from the hall and through the corridors to the best guest chamber.

'By the Rood,' he said, looking about him with big eyes, 'here's splendour! I have never had such a fine chamber to myself in my life. I am more used to sleeping at the foot of my lord's bed, or on a pallet in the hall. I shall hardly know what to do with myself.'

'I hope you will be comfortable,' Rosamund said. She wanted now to tell him that she thought he was beautiful, that she desired him, that she had dreamed of him, that he had saved her from the terrors of her own imagination. But she did not know how. Instead she said softly, 'Master Lymington, thank you for coming to help me. I am more grateful than I can say.'

Suddenly his eyes glowed at her. He came forward and caught her hand in his, stooping over it and setting his lips to the tips of her fingers, as chaste a kiss as could be imagined. 'My lady,' he murmured, and just for a second he set the back of her hand to his cheek. She had barely time to feel the velvety stubble beneath her fingers before he had pressed them again to his lips and lowered them, looking into her eyes. 'Good night,' he said softly.

She was dismissed, there could be no mistaking it. She ached to take him in her arms, but his correctness infected her and she merely dropped him a little curtsey and turned away.

Later, in her cold bed, she wept. Margery, her maid, hung over her, little hands clinging to her shoulders, whispering into her ear. 'My lady, my lady, don't weep. If he doesn't fancy you, why in Heaven's name did he come?'

'But what can I do?' Rosamund wept. 'What can I do? Tomorrow Sir Ralph will come and we will all be killed. There is only tonight.'

'Go to him, then,' suggested Margery.

Rosamund suddenly became very still in her arms. She turned and looked up into Margery's face, her eyes wide and dark in the light of the candles. 'Go to him?' she repeated hesitantly.

'Go to him! Go to his chamber! My lady, it is the middle of the night and you have not slept. What man would resist you if you went to him? He will fall at your feet, see if he does not. Go!'

She went, wrapped in a robe of thick wool the colour of curded cream, carrying a candle shielded in her hand, her naked feet silent on the floorboards. Her heavy chestnut-coloured hair was spread over her shoulders like a cloak. It was cold in the corridors of the house, but it was not the cold that made her shiver. She stood outside the closed door of the guest-chamber for some time, listening to the pounding of her heart, wondering if she dared set her fingers to the latch. He would be asleep, his white eyelids lowered over his brilliant eyes, his lips softened with slumber. Rosamund stared into the blue heart of the crocus flame of the candle, her pupils contracting to pinpoints. Behind her, in the shadows of the hall, the striking clock sounded midnight.

The chimes seemed to go on forever. When they had died away into muffled echoes and then into silence Rosamund set her fingers to the latch and lifted it noiselessly, stalking step by delicate step into the chamber where her heart's desire lay.

The candle cast a glowing pool of light around her, but the room was not entirely dark. The banked-down fire burned with a warm, ruddy light, and through the half-closed shutters a pale winter moon was peering. Red and blue light mingled on the white planks of the floor and cast a confusion of coloured shadows on to the damask curtains which hung around the great bed. She seemed now to have passed beyond fear. She walked steadily and in silence to stand beside the pillow and she lowered the candle and placed it soundlessly on the little table by the bed. The light shivered and then burned up with a clear flame, driving back the darkness within the heavy curtains.

He was fast asleep, turned away from her and almost invisible beneath the heavy covers of the bed. She could see his glossy hair and his left hand spread out upon the white pillow. It was a big hand, long-fingered, with strong flat knuckles and blue veins pencilled between fingers and wrist. His other hand and arm were thrust beneath the pillow like a sleeping child's. His slow steady breathing whispered in and out, lifting and lowering the covers as his lungs filled and emptied.

She stood for some time watching him. Her stomach wrung with helpless, empty desire. She longed to hold him, to run her fingers through that heavy mop of hair, to feel his long-fingered hands touching her in return. It seemed almost impossible that he should continue to sleep while waves of emotion flowed from her towards him, but he did not stir. Rosamund imagined herself waking him. He would roll over in the bed and look up at her with wide, sleepy, astonished eyes, then whisper her name and hold out his hands to her. She saw herself sinking into his arms, her face turned up to receive his eager kisses, her eyes closing in rapture.

Under her steady gaze the young squire lay still. He was

dreaming. His breath faltered and he muttered to himself, then let out a heavy sigh. The long fingers on the pillow tensed, gripping at the smooth linen, and then relaxed. Rosamund let out a long breath of decision and slowly stretched out one hand to touch his shoulder.

For a moment he did not move or seem to wake. Then, all at once, he was up from the bed, naked in the candlelight, moving as swiftly and fluidly as a pouncing cat. Something flashed and then strong hands gripped Rosamund's shoulders and dragged them back and she gasped in shock as a sharp point pricked her throat.

For a moment she felt nothing but astonished fear. Then she realised that the brightness at her throat was Geoffrey Lymington's dagger. Then, even as the knowledge filled her brain with cold coiling dread, he released her, pushing her away from him, pulling the naked blade from her throat with an exclamation of horror. She staggered then drew herself upright, clutching the post at the foot of the bed and staring into his face.

He was quite white and the pupils of his eyes were wide and black, so wide that the green iris was no more than a glittering ring. 'Holy Jesu!' he hissed, with the fury of fear. 'God's death, my lady, do you not know better than to creep up on a soldier? I could have hurt you!'

Rosamund was too frightened to reply. She stood shaking her head, breathing raggedly. His face changed, filling with remorse. 'I am sorry,' he said, a little more calmly now. 'I am so sorry, my lady. The room – the place – strange to me – I – '

Still she could not gather her wits sufficiently to reply. She put her hand to her throat, feeling the place where the dagger had touched her skin. A sting of pain made her wince and she drew her hand away and stared in disbelief at a single bead of bright blood, like a ruby.

'I have hurt you! My lady, in the Virgin's name, you know I – '

He fell silent. She lifted her eyes to look at him and for the first time registered his nakedness. Her eyes flashed up and down his body, in one glance seeing all of his beauty, hesitating infinitesimally as they rested on the dark arrowhead of curling hair in his groin where his penis hung softly over the dangling pouch of his testicles. She looked back at his face. Her breathing slowed and very slowly her hand clenched into a fist. Geoffrey stood for a moment puzzled and staring, then he took a quick shocked breath and grabbed for the cover of the bed. He pulled the glossy fabric across him to hide his groin and flushed scarlet as he did so.

Still his torso was naked and Rosamund felt desire begin to return, stalking into her as her eyes passed slowly over his bare broad shoulders, gracefully clothed with strong muscle, the lifting cage of his lean ribs, his taut, ridged abdomen. The flat plane of his diaphragm below his ribs rose and fell, catching the light as he breathed. Her throat tightened and a shiver ran between her shoulder-blades, chilling her with icy yearning. But what could she say to him? She gazed, and was silent.

Geoffrey caught his lower lip between his teeth, shifting his feet awkwardly on the bare floorboards. 'My lady,' he said at last, 'why are you here? What is the matter? Is the enemy coming?'

With a question to answer she could speak. 'No,' she said. 'No, there is no danger.'

'So,' he insisted, 'why are you here?'

His arched brows were drawn down tightly over his glittering eyes. He frowned as if he could not believe why any lady should come all alone to a gentleman's room. Surely, surely to God, he must want her? Why was he making her ask? Rosamund had not considered the possibility that explanations might be necessary. She had not thought of what she could say. In her imagination he had opened his arms to her wordlessly and their kisses were their eloquence.

He was still looking at her in helpless confusion, he really wanted an answer. She sought her vocabulary and found no inspiration. 'I wanted,' she began, hesitated, and then blurted out, 'I wanted you to swive me.'

The moment the word was past her lips she knew it was wrong: crude, coarse, inappropriate. She clamped her hand at once across her offending mouth as if her fingers could snatch the word back out of the air, but it was too late. The damage was done. She gazed at Geoffrey over her smothering hand, appalled.

His face changed at once. The nervousness and apprehension left it and it hardened, becoming cold and severe. He set his jaw and his nostrils flared as if he winded some unpleasant odour. There was no hint of tenderness left in his expression. He flung back his head and laughed, a cold, unpleasant laugh. 'Is that all?'

he asked the rafters. 'Is that all you want?' He flung aside the bedcover and walked naked towards her, smiling bitterly. 'My Lady de Verney, as I have said, I am your most humble and obedient servant.'

Rosamund took a step back, afraid of his sudden chilly energy. Not even his splendid nakedness attracted her now. She opened her mouth to explain that she had not meant it, not that word, that she had meant – But before the first sound escaped her he pounced, catching her by her arms and pulling her towards him. She gasped and he caught hold of the fronts of her robe and made as if he would tug it open. 'No!' Rosamund cried, not understanding his sudden violence, and she caught the robe from his hands and tore herself away.

'Come, come, my lady,' he said through his teeth, 'don't be coy. That won't get you what you *want.*' And he reached out again and seized the creamy wool and dragged it apart to reveal Rosamund's full white breasts.

She hung from his hands, trembling, her eyes tightly shut. He stared down at her naked flesh, his lips parted, breathing shallowly. Before his eyes her coral nipples erected, stiff with cold and shame. 'Christ Jesu,' he whispered, as if the treasures of the Orient were suddenly poured into his hands. He was still for so long that at last Rosamund opened her eyes, risking a glance at him. His chest was rising and falling with his breathing and in his loins, in the dark triangle of his groin, his phallus was rearing into proud, eager life. Rosamund watched, fascinated, as the pillar of flesh lifted and grew and swelled, the pale skin darkening with the rush of blood and drawing back and back from the purpling tip. It was beautiful. Even in her fear she yearned for it.

'Please,' she whispered, licking her dry lips with the tip of her tongue. 'Geoffrey, please.'

His eyes lifted to her face and he seemed suddenly furious. 'Please?' he repeated mockingly. 'Please? Oh, forgive me, my lady, if I am slow to obey you!'

'No,' she protested, 'I didn't mean – ' But he dragged her towards him, pushing the sleeves of her gown fiercely down her white arms so that they were pinned behind her, her naked breasts jutting lustfully forward. He laughed and put one big hand over her breast, trapping the hard nipple beneath his palm and chafing it roughly. 'No,' Rosamund tried again, writhing, 'no, please – '

'It is too late to change your mind,' he hissed into her face, and then his mouth descended on hers. His lips should have been soft, but they delivered his kiss with such controlled ferocity that they might have been made of steel. She gasped as his hot tongue probed her mouth, thrusting without compunction between her lips. The plush roughness of his three days' beard scrubbed at her tender cheek, hurting her and stinging her with pleasure. She gave one desperate heave, trying to free herself from his iron grip, and then moaned and submitted, hanging limply in his grasp as he consumed her with his hungry mouth and crushed her aching breast beneath his hand.

He tugged her roughly to the bed and flung her on to it. Before she could find her balance and push herself up he hurled himself on her, pinning her down with his strong, lean body. One hand caught at her thigh, pulling it to one side, opening her to his assault. She whimpered, 'No,' and tried to drag herself away, but he drove his hips between her open thighs and caught at her wrists, pulling them above her head. She tried to pull free, tried again, but he was too strong for her. She gave a little whimper of desperation and he smiled and held her helpless.

There was a long moment of stillness. Rosamund lay gasping, staring up into Geoffrey's bright, fierce eyes, and as her breath heaved in and out so her breasts lifted and fell, rubbing her tight nipples against the hard plane of his chest. Between her legs his swollen penis waited, hard and ready, nudging against the moist lips of her sex.

He took one hand from her wrists, holding her securely with the other. His hand moved down to her body and cupped one full breast, weighing and approving it. He caught the dark tip between finger and thumb and squeezed experimentally. Rosamund winced and turned her head aside, closing her eyes as cold tendrils of sensation radiated from the little point of flesh. He squeezed again, watching her reaction, and then his hand continued unhurriedly down her body, stroking the soft swell of her belly, and his long agile fingers began to explore the dark curls of hair that clothed her pubis. She gave a little cry, not knowing herself whether she was petrified with fear or with lust.

His fingers slipped between her thighs and gently, softly, traced the lips of her wet, swollen sex. A long sigh escaped

Rosamund's loosened lips and the muscles of her vagina clenched tight with sudden want. Her head fell back, exposing her long white throat. Now his weight above her was not frightening but wondrous, his strong hands were tools of her delight, she lay powerless and desperate and aching for him.

'You are wet,' he murmured. His voice was thick with lust. 'Wet as a river. You are ready for me.'

And he took her. He placed the hot swollen head of his cock precisely between the moist, eager lips. Then he reached up and caught hold of her white wrists and pulled her arms wide apart, holding them there like one crucified so that her breasts were lifted high and offered to his gaze. He stared down into her face as his tight flanks hollowed and he thrust slow and firm and pushed the whole length of his stiff, rampant penis into her snug, aching tunnel.

Rosamund's eyes opened wide and her lips parted and she breathed in great gasps as if she was smothering. He was penetrating her, possessing her, and it was bliss such as she had never imagined. She could not move; her wrists were pinioned by his strong hands and her body was trapped beneath his delicious male weight, and there was nothing but ecstasy.

'You wanted me to swive you,' he hissed, withdrawing from her and thrusting again, harder this time. The thick shaft slid back into her all at once, making her grunt with shock and pleasure. 'You wanted to be swived, my *lady*.' Again he thrust and filled her, and this time a moan escaped her shaking lips. Even the bitterness of his words could not detract from her pleasure. 'Your wish is my command. I will swive you until you beg for mercy.' And he began a steady, driving rhythm, breathing in hot pants as he pushed himself in and out of her. Sensation pooled in her loins and began to spread, cold between her shoulders and on the points of her breasts, hot on her throat and in her belly. Her body juddered as he rammed her. The hard, hairy base of his penis rubbed against her clitoris and it swelled and flushed, and as the stimulus went on and on so she began to groan in time with his movements. Her eyes were still open, gazing up at his face. He was frowning, concentrating on the approaching moment, his eyes closed tightly and his lips drawn back from his teeth. He looked beautiful and remote and angry. Her lips were dry with her panting and she was crying out now with urgency, trying to lift her round hips to accept his thrusts, gasping as he shafted her remorselessly. Every time he withdrew from her she whimpered with grief, then cried out in joy and triumph as his thick rod filled her again.

'Oh,' she cried, writhing under his restraining hands, 'oh, oh, Jesu have mercy.'

'Only I can have mercy on you,' he hissed, never slackening the pace of his urgent movements. 'And I will not, my *lady*, I will not spare you, I will swive you until I see you die beneath me.' He thrust harder still, more sharply, and she groaned with the pleasure and the pain. 'Do you feel me?' he demanded. 'Do you?'

'I feel you,' she moaned, her head thrashing from side to side. The sensation was growing, mounting within her in a crescent wave of bliss. 'My lord, my lord, I feel you, oh God in Heaven, I feel you.' Her hips bucked beneath him as if she would draw him into the very centre of her. Hot red pleasure possessed her and she writhed as her whole body succumbed to the throes of orgasm. 'Oh God, oh, oh – '

Her eyes rolled back and a long, wavering cry of ecstasy hung on her lips. Geoffrey made a noise like a beast in pain and gave one last, convulsive thrust, forcing himself up into the very heart of her. He let go of her wrists and fell on her, his heaving chest crushing her breasts, his hot breath scalding the hollow of her shoulder. They lay together very still, breathing in quick shallow gasps, sweat shining on their exhausted limbs.

Then, suddenly, Geoffrey withdrew and pulled away, sitting upright on the bed with his back turned to her. She lifted her head and made a little sound of protest, narrowing her eyes to peer through the mist of pleasure that hazed them. His back was beautiful, tapering from broad shoulders to narrow waist, the deep furrow of his spine like a line drawn in snow. His head was bowed. She said softly, 'Geoffrey?'

He did not lift his head. 'And do you welcome all guests to de Verney manor so warmly?' he asked, and his voice was thin and cold.

She was still with shock. Then, without a word, she slipped from the high bed to the floor. Her legs were shaky, but she stood firm as she pulled her gown back around herself. After a moment he lifted his head and looked at her, a wary, puzzled look.

'You take me for a whore,' Rosamund said evenly. He flinched, but he did not deny it. She felt very weary and old, as if all her illusions had been stripped from her with her modesty. Soon she would weep – but not before him. 'You are mistaken,' she said, and her voice sounded tired. 'I expressed myself badly. A whore would have had more subtlety, do you not think?'

He did not speak, only frowned. Rosamund drew a long, deep breath and said, 'Sir, I swear to you that no man has known me before except my husband.' Then she turned and went towards the door. She felt quite empty. She had known physical rapture, but his coldness had turned it to bitterness. She suddenly hoped that she would die on the morrow, rather than live with memories so blighted.

Before she reached the door his footsteps were behind her, quick and quiet. He caught her shoulders in his hands, holding her back, and turned her to face him. She allowed it, and stood still with her eyes closed and her heart aching. From behind the screen of her closed lids she heard his voice, hesitant, trembling a little. 'My lady, I – ' He broke off. 'Tell me your name,' he said, and his voice shook.

She opened her eyes and looked into his face. He looked like a boy, young and defenceless, as if she had hurt him rather than he her. His beauty robbed her of words. She clenched her hand before her breast and made herself speak. 'Rosamund,' she whispered.

'Rosamund,' he breathed. He lifted one shaking hand and touched her cheek, then laid his fingers briefly to the tiny scab on her white neck where his dagger had touched her. His face contracted in a spasm of regret and shame. 'I am so sorry,' he said, soft as a breath, his eyes lowered. 'I have done everything wrong.' He lifted his eyes to hers. They were glittering and bright in the faint light of the candle, of the smouldering fire and the winter moon. 'I, I wanted you so much. You know I did, we both felt it. But I thought you were a virtuous lady. I came back to help you, not to lie with you. It would have been wrong to suggest anything . . .' He shook his head, gazing into her face with transparent earnestness. 'It was so difficult,' he went on uncertainly. 'I made myself cold. I didn't want to shock you, to shame you. And then, then, to hear you say that, that word – I thought I had been mistaken in you. I thought you had made a fool of me. I was angry.' He looked once more into her eyes, and then his head fell. 'I'm sorry,' he repeated. 'I don't expect you to forgive me.'

Her anger melted at the sight of his contrition. She managed a wan smile. 'It's not all your fault,' she offered. 'I surprised you; and then I used the wrong word, did I not?'

He nodded, still looking into her eyes. She was very conscious of his closeness, of the warmth emanating from his naked skin. 'But I was angry,' he said. 'I was so rough with you. I must have hurt you. And I meant to be chivalrous!' He gave a little bitter laugh and shook his head. '*A verray parfit gentil knight,*' he quoted ironically. 'You may be an apprentice in the art of love, my lady, but I am not. I should have known better.'

Rosamund lowered her head. He sounded as if all was lost. 'Well,' she said at last, 'you did not hurt me. I do forgive you, Master Lymington.'

'Geoffrey,' he said softly. 'Geoffrey, my lady. You used my name before, don't stop.' His voice was suddenly warm, caressing and tender, and Rosamund felt a tiny glow of hope warming her heart. She looked up into his face and her stomach curled and softened as if the brightness of her eyes were melting her like warm honey. He lifted his hand to her cheek again, a touch of feathery lightness. 'Don't go,' he whispered. 'Don't go yet.'

She leant her cheek into his palm, closing her eyes and letting out her breath in a soft sigh of bliss. For a moment he stroked her white skin with his strong fingers. Then he cupped her chin in his hand and turned it towards him. She opened her eyes and looked at his beautiful face hanging above her, gazing down at her, and an overwhelming sense of peace and contentment possessed her as she realised that he was about to kiss her and that his eyes were glowing with desire. She parted her lips and stretched her long throat up and he lowered his head and placed his mouth on hers, gently, so gently.

Her dream was true. His lips were softer than rose petals, sweeter than wine, and his strong searching tongue was smooth as cream. The hot, dark pleasure that had consumed her as he took her retreated, shrinking into insignificance beneath the delicate, sensual rapture of their kiss. She sighed with bliss and opened herself to him, savouring the exquisite sensation as he explored her mouth, tasting the inside of her soft lips, inviting her hesitant tongue to twine around his, stabbing deeply into her throat so that she gasped. She lifted her hands and placed them around his back, sweeping them across his silken skin, feeling the hard bone and the strong muscle beneath it, the points of his shoulders, the delicious hollow of his spine. Her robe fell open and their naked bodies pressed together, breast to breast. He wrapped his arms around her, his big, strong hands pressing between her shoulders and cupping the swell of her buttocks, holding her close.

They kissed until she lost all sense of time, until her head was spinning and her knees were weak with ecstasy. At some point he lifted his mouth from hers and kissed her closed eyelids, her cheeks, the point of her jaw. Her head fell back and his lips fastened to the white column of her neck. She felt his teeth then, biting into her soft flesh as he would bite into an apple, and a feverish clutch of pleasure made her body jerk against his. He set his teeth into her neck, lashing her skin with his tongue until she cried out in sweet pain. Then he released her and kissed the dark mark and stooped to catch her behind the knees and around her shoulders and he lifted her into his arms. She lay limp and unprotesting, her heavy hair trailing down and sweeping against his thighs as he carried her towards the rug of white sheepskin that lay before the glowing fire.

He laid her down on the soft white wool and crouched over her, his strong lean thighs straddling her legs. He leant forward so that he could kiss her again and as he kissed her he ran his hands down her shoulders to the swell of her full breasts. His fingers traced the outside of her breast, the smooth heavy curve up to the nipple, and then he held the white globes in his hands, squeezing them, kneading them. Rosamund let out a sigh of pleasure and arched her back, inviting him to caress her more strongly. For answer he moved a little further down and kissed her throat, her collar-bone, her breastbone, so that she whimpered with anticipation. Then he took her breasts in his hands and lowered his lips to her nipples, suckling each in turn, drawing out the darkening tips into stiff buds of sensation, and Rosamund's sighs became moans of delight. For long moments he worshipped her swollen, sensitive breasts, lapping at them, rubbing the taut nipples with his thumb, while her head turned from side to side in helpless bliss. Then he moved again, lifting himself lightly above her. She felt his hand on the tender skin of her flank and automatically she parted her legs, offering herself to him.

'Beautiful,' he whispered, and his breath stirred the soft curls of her mound. She drew in a sharp breath, astonished and disbelieving. Then he placed the palms of his hands on the inner surface of her white thighs and gently, firmly, pushed them apart. She spread her legs wide, knowing that his glittering eyes were devouring the sight of her open sex. She was slippery and shining with desire, and between the moist lips the pale pearl of her clitoris was engorged and exposed, protruding from its hood of flesh, begging for his touch.

His hands moved again, encircling the soft mound, and his long fingers very gently spread the damp folds of flesh apart. Rosamund shivered and her stomach jerked, forcing out gasps of need. Geoffrey leant forward and parted his lips and placed his warm mouth over her sex. She whimpered as his breath sighed against her skin. Then, very delicately, his tongue lapped at her, running in one movement from the bottom to the top of her labia, making her shake with the promise of pleasure. He began to lick at her, the point of his strong tongue worming its way through the whorls of flesh. She moaned and shifted her hips, trying to make him lick her at her epicentre, at the place where she ached and yearned for him. But he teased her, concentrating on the lips of her sex. After a moment he caught hold of her thighs and held her still while he thrust his tongue up inside her, as far into her as he could, making it move within her like a tiny penis.

'Oh,' Rosamund whispered, 'please, my lord, please.' She tried to move so that his tongue would caress her where she most desired, but he held her firmly, still thrusting inside her. She relaxed and lay limp, accepting what he did to her, and by subtle degrees her pleasure grew.

Then, suddenly, he had stopped. She lifted her head and made a little noise of protest. He was kneeling over her, his mouth glistening with her juices. Quickly he kissed her and she tasted herself on his lips and tongue, salt and sweet, with a musky tang of woman. He took her hands in his and placed her palms on her breasts. 'Stroke yourself,' he whispered. 'Touch yourself, sweetheart.' And he was gone, sliding back towards her spread thighs. She hesitated, then gingerly ran her hands over her breasts, flickering her nails over her turgid nipples. Quick jets of pleasure ran through her, flashing like lightning through her spine. She gasped and caught her lip in her teeth.

He kissed her belly, kissed the soft fleece of her mound. Then he lay again between her legs, and this time he did not tease her.

His dexterous tongue began to lap moistly against her swollen pearl of pleasure, flicking against it, rubbing at it. She cried out and her searching fingers involuntarily seized her hard nipples, pinching them until they ached and stung with sharp delicious pain. He continued to lick at her clitoris and she moaned deep in her throat as beneath his working tongue his strong fingers began to search the damp folds, probing and exploring. His hand slipped below the entrance to her vagina, drawing moisture back to the dark, secret place behind, spreading her juices there until she was slippery and tender. His thick thumb slipped into her sex and began to move in and out. Her gasps and moans instantly adjusted to match the rhythm of his thrusts and her hips began to lift and lower as if waves were rocking her. The pleasure built and built within her: her cries became sharper and more urgent. Then she let out a squeal of shock as his forefinger slid along the juicy furrow between her buttocks and found her tight, puckered hole and began to penetrate her there. For a moment she tensed against him. But then his hot tongue lashed against the quivering stem of her clitoris and her cry of protest became a groan of delight. He drew in the little shaft of flesh between his lips, working at it mercilessly as he pushed his finger and thumb into her moist orifices. She felt shame and embarrassment that he could touch her in that shameful spot, but the rich, dark, heavy pleasure that it gave her was undeniable. Her crisis was approaching, swelling up from her deliciously filled sex and anus, glowing white-hot in the shivering bud of her clitoris, tipped with icy delight in the tormented peaks of her breasts. Rosamund flung back her head and cried out and her body arched and stiffened and Geoffrey held her there, the tip of his tongue just flickering against her, his finger and thumb squeezing gently within her, keeping her balanced on the fulcrum of ecstasy so that her rigid body quaked and shook for long, convulsive seconds.

At last he released her and kneeled upright, drawing her into his arms. She lay shuddering, her eyes wide and dark with shock, looking up at him as if he were a sorcerer. He smiled down into her face and said nothing. The warmth of the fire glowed on their naked flanks, casting a ruddy flush over pale skin.

'What did you *do* to me?' she whispered at last. 'You touched me – Holy Jesu, it must be wicked to touch a woman there!'

Geoffrey chuckled gently. 'Sweetheart,' he said softly, 'last night I saw a friend of mine take a woman there, and she seemed to get nothing but pleasure from it.'

'Take her?' Rosamund repeated in disbelief. 'In her, her fundament?'

'He put his cock in her arse and swived her there,' Geoffrey said with relish, grinning as Rosamund turned her head aside in confusion at his coarseness. 'Shall I do that to you, Rosamund?'

'No!' Rosamund exclaimed, putting her palms against his chest as if she would push him away. 'No, never!' For a moment she was stiff with tension; then the memory of pleasure softened her limbs. She looked up at his knowing, teasing face and felt suddenly naive and unsophisticated. 'You have had so many women,' she whispered sadly. 'Have you not, Geoffrey?'

'Many times many,' he agreed, still looking down at her with a smile.

'I am sure I must seem boring to you,' she said, closing her eyes. She remembered her description of Edmund Bigod. 'Insipid,' she suggested.

'Rosamund,' Geoffrey said softly. Reluctantly she opened her eyes and looked into his face. He had ceased to smile. 'My lady, believe me. I have never in my life lain with a woman as lovely as you. I have never in my life desired a woman as much as I desired you, the moment I saw you.' He traced his fingers down her nose. 'You remember,' he said, 'how you touched me, and you felt I was hard already. I longed for you so much, just looking at your face.'

Rosamund reached up impulsively and put her arms around his neck, hugging him close to her. They kissed, a long, sensuous kiss. His mouth tasted of her sex. The movement of his tongue between her lips made her bowels coil and writhe again with desire for him. Very hesitantly she put her hand on his thigh and began to slide it upwards towards his loins. She expected to find his phallus there soft and weary, since it had worked so hard earlier. Instead she let out a little gasp of surprise and pleasure as her fingers touched a hot, iron-hard length of flesh, taut and throbbing with eagerness. Her lips were suddenly dry and she ran her tongue around them to moisten them, swallowed hard, and looked down.

Her fingers barely met around the dark, straining shaft. She moved her hand experimentally, gently drawing the satiny skin up and down. Geoffrey took a quick, deep breath and let it out in a long hiss of pleasure. Rosamund delicately trailed her fingertips over the tight, close-drawn pouch of his balls, feeling how the skin was tense and the heavy stones swollen with seed. She explored a little further back and touched that strange place behind the soft sac where the skin was surprisingly smooth and taut and hairless. Curiosity tempted her to probe further, but shame prevented her. She returned her hand to his magnificent, jutting phallus and slowly stroked it up and down, imitating the movement of a woman's sex around it and listening to his breathing shake. The tip of his cock swelled still further, becoming a broad, glistening dome, and a single clear tear appeared in the tiny slit. She ran her thumb over it, smearing the fluid over the purple glans.

Geoffrey shivered. 'My lady,' he said thickly, running his hands over her white shoulders, 'I would have you again.'

She looked up at him eagerly. Her loins felt hollow with need. 'Oh, yes,' she breathed, and began to lie back again on the soft fleece.

'No,' he said, 'no, sweetheart, before I took you. Now we should give pleasure to each other.' He drew her back up and kissed her, then knelt upright on the rug, his proud erect cock thrusting upwards from his groin. 'Come,' he said, 'kneel over me. Take me as you will.'

Rosamund had never imagined that there might be more than one way of doing the deed, and for a moment she stared in incomprehension. Geoffrey smiled and gently tugged her towards him, spreading her thighs so that she straddled him, her wet sex hovering open and inviting over his tumescent penis. He put his hands on her breasts, rubbing at the dark nipples. 'Come,' he whispered.

The head of his cock was hot and expectant between the parted lips of her sex. The sensation was so strange, so piquant: she was in control, and yet what she controlled was the possession of herself. She hung above him for a moment, relishing the tension that filled them both, and then she began to sink down upon him.

His long, thick shaft slid easily between her silken walls. She lowered herself slowly, inch by inch, savouring each moment as she felt herself penetrated, opened, filled. Then he was fully inside her and her swollen clitoris rubbed against his body. She moaned with pleasure and her eyes closed. Her hips moved in little circles, stimulating herself against him until she thought she would die of ecstasy then and there. She lifted herself up again and sank down again, again, again, writhing with pleasure as she impaled herself upon his hot, throbbing cock.

Gradually, as her rapture grew, she lost control. Her head rolled from side to side and she moved in jerks. Geoffrey released her breasts and instead took hold of her full white haunches, gripping the rich orbs in his strong hands and wresting supremacy from her. Now he lifted her up and down on his eager penis, tautening and thrusting with his firm buttocks as he lowered her, shoving himself up into her as she groaned and shuddered. She leant back, resting her hands on the floor, her back and her white throat arched and her breasts jutting wantonly towards the rafters. He reached eagerly forward with his lips to suck at her stiffened nipples and as she felt his mouth on her her sensitised body lurched instantly into orgasm. She spasmed around him, her body heaving, her inner muscles clutching frantically at his body as it slid in and out. His face tensed with ecstasy. He drove himself into her, ramming furiously upwards, gasping her name on each thrust, until he cried out and pulled her soft body close to his and shook as he spent himself inside her, rigid with tension as his seed pumped from him.

She pushed closer to him, hiding her head in his shoulder. Their arms were wrapped around each other, around shoulder and waist. Rosamund's hand stirred faintly in Geoffrey's thick, shining mop of hair. Their hearts pounded, gradually slowing as the waves of pleasure receded.

Beneath them the hall clock coughed and chimed, a single melancholy stroke. Rosamund turned her head on Geoffrey's shoulder. One hour: only one hour. Tears prickled at her closed eyelids. She clutched his bare skin more tightly, feeling his hands squeezing her in answer. 'I must go,' she whispered.

'Don't go. Stay here with me.'

'I must go. What would they think? And you must sleep, you are tired.'

'I would waken all night to give you pleasure.'

'No, I must go.' She drew back slowly, fighting tears. The sensation of loss as his body slipped out of hers was overwhelming. He clung to her, pulling her close, blindly seeking her lips with his.

'One day,' he whispered, 'one day I will lie with you in the morning, and at noon, and in the afternoon, and in the evening, and all through the night. I shall have you at Matins and Prime and Terce and Sext. We shall have a Holy Office of wantonness.'

She wanted to believe him, but she knew that when the dawn broke it would signal the approach of Sir Ralph, coming to take the manor by force and punish her for her insult to him. Against his power they would be helpless, although Geoffrey were braver than a lion at bay. She could not make him promises knowing that the morning might bring them suffering and death. She pulled away from him and got to her feet, catching up her robe and drawing it on. He knelt on the rug, looking up at her, the firelight illuminating the fine bones of his face with red and gold.

'Thank you,' she said softly. She reached out and touched her fingers to the scab on his brow, the bruise on his cheekbone, smiling sadly.

'I am sorry about the first time,' he said. Perhaps he, too, felt their doom approaching, for he spoke no more words of love or desire.

She shook her head. 'That gave me pleasure too,' she told him, and as she looked back she realised how true that was. The dark consuming passion of his violence had set her blood burning: a different pleasure to the second, as different as the squeal of a trumpet is different to the soft music of a flute; but still music.

She went to the door and he did not pursue her. The latch resisted her hand, as if it too wanted her to stay, but she forced it and at last it let her go. The door opened and she stepped out into the cold of the corridor.

She turned back to take a last look at him, naked and beautiful in the firelight. 'Good night,' she whispered.

'Good night,' he replied, soft as a breath.

She closed the door and went away. A little way down the corridor she stopped and looked out of the mullioned window on to the dark garden. The moon's pale face was hidden behind a swathe of thick cloud, and countless small flakes of snow were spiralling down from the blank sky.

Western Star

Roxanne Carr

It's 1851 and a flood of settlers is pouring westward through Missouri into the new state of California. Maribel Harker is a wilful young woman determined to experience the Wild West. Dan Cutter is the rugged frontiersman in charge of the wagon train passing through Maribel's home town. Her intention to seduce the rugged Dan into coupling with her meets with his natural resistance to get involved with someone half his age. He's known Maribel's father a long while and it just wouldn't seem right. But she's grown into a fine young woman and Dan knows it's going to take all his willpower to resist her. This extract shows Dan weakening to her charms and slaking his lust with the dusky Perdita while Maribel seeks out some fun of her own.

Roxanne Carr is a prolific Black Lace author who has written the best-selling Black Lace trilogy. The three books: *Black Orchid, A Bouquet of Black Orchids* and *The Black Orchid Hotel* follow the fortunes of Maggie who becomes the proprietor of an exclusive club and hotel where giving and receiving pleasure takes top priority. Roxanne's other books are: *Jewel of Xanadu,* set in the time of Kublai Khan; and *Avenging Angels,* set in a Spanish holiday resort where women get even with the men who work in and run the nightclubs and bars.

Western Star

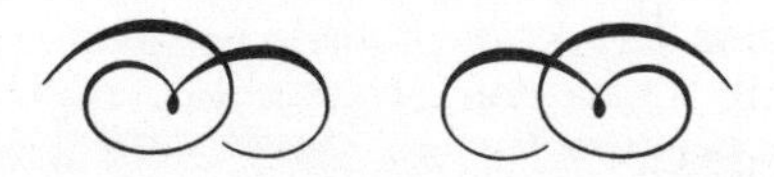

Maribel was like a desert flower in bloom among the cacti. Pretty as a picture in her blue, floral sprigged dress with her hair done up like a ten-year-old child. Dan watched her surreptitiously as she held court at the far end of the table, keeping the young men either side of her in thrall.

Jim and Leslie Johnson were brothers from the neighbouring ranch. It was quite clear to Dan that both were in love with Maribel, for they hung on her every word, falling over themselves to beat the other to perform every little service for her.

It would have been quite comical if Dan hadn't felt quite so attracted to her himself. But he was a grown man, damn it, not a fawning young pup. He felt quite sorry for the Johnson boys – Maribel could easily chew them up for breakfast and spit them out, one after the other.

What she needed was a real man, someone who could take her in hand and tame that wild sexuality which, it seemed to him, was already running out of control.

Just then, Maribel looked up and their eyes met. She did not look childlike now. Dan sucked in his breath as he recognised the look she was giving him. Hunger, pure, unadulterated sexual hunger. And recognition. Damn her, she knew he was attracted to her!

His cock leapt up in his trousers, aching as his eyes fell to the proud thrust of her breasts beneath the high-necked dress. Picturing the silky path between them, he imagined sliding himself back and forth between those perfect globes, his fingers pinching her hard, pink nipples, rolling them in his palms until her back arched in ecstasy, and words of surrender poured from her soft, red lips . . .

'Can I get you anything, señor?'

He jumped as Perdita appeared at his elbow. Looking up at her, he saw her features soften, her eyes widening in acceptance, and he realised that his face must reflect his thoughts. It did not matter that Perdita had mistaken the object of his lust, he was only grateful that she was willing to accommodate it.

Discreetly, he ran his hand up under her skirt and stroked the naked skin behind her knee. Perdita leant forward to refill his plate and her soft, black hair caressed his cheek. She smelled of a strange, sweet perfume he had never encountered on any other woman, and remembering how she had come to him before, he was suddenly eager for the meal to be over.

'The usual place?' he whispered close to her ear as she made to move away.

She nodded slightly and moved on.

'When will you be riding out again, Dan?'

Cutter started as he realised that John was speaking to him and all eyes were now on him. Including the bright blue, intelligent eyes of the woman-child at the end of the table.

'The next batch of settlers is due to arrive in Independence in two weeks, John. As soon as they're ready we'll be off. I want to be in California before winter sets in.'

'Do you have many women in your wagon trains, Mr Cutter?'

It was Maribel who had spoken. Was it only he who detected an underlying purpose to her question?

'Some men take their wives, yes.'

'But . . . no lone women?'

There was a ripple of laughter around the table, though neither Maribel nor Cutter joined in. Dan had the uncomfortable feeling that Maribel's enquiry was not as casual as everyone else thought and he knew he had to treat it seriously.

'The Oregon Trail is long and hard, Miss Maribel. The physical hardship is bad enough; you all know what happened to the Donner party.'

There was a general murmuring round the table at the mention of the poor unfortunates who had perished en route to California. Maribel held Cutter's eye without flinching and he continued,

'There are also other dangers. Though most of the natives are friendly enough, there are some hostiles who find the wagon trains easy pickings. It's no place for a woman, especially not a woman alone.'

Maribel's lips curved slightly in a smile as she held his eye steadily. Cutter had the uncomfortable sensation that she was laughing at him. The conversation restarted around them and he turned to John gratefully as the other man began to tell him about his cattle problems.

Dan ate the rest of his meal quickly, careful not to catch Maribel's eye again. He could hear her sweet voice, and felt her eyes on him more than once, but he refused to respond.

Let Maribel play her flirtatious games with the Johnson boys – he would far rather meet Perdita in the barn for some good, healthy, straightforward carnal fun. As soon as was polite, he excused himself and left the table.

Catching Perdita's eye, he strode out of the dining room, conscious of Maribel's eyes burning into his back.

It was warm in the barn. Dan walked into the shadows and waited for Perdita. The sweet smell of dry straw tickled his nostrils as he pressed himself against the wooden walls beneath the hay loft.

Hearing Perdita's soft footfall, he waited until she had stepped into the barn before making a playful grab for her. Squealing, she fell down with him and rolled on to the prickly bed of hay, laughing as his lips fastened on the long, brown expanse of her throat.

'Mmm! You smell good!'

Raising himself up on his elbows, he gazed down at the girl affectionately. Her dark hair was spread out around her head, contrasting dramatically with the pale gold of the hay. Moonlight streamed through the glassless window, milky pale, spotlighting the girl who waited expectantly for him to begin.

'Have you missed me?' he asked her teasingly as he began to unlace the front of her dress.

She laughed, a rich, throaty chuckle which set his blood on fire.

'A little,' she admitted, sitting up so that he could pull her dress over her head.

'Still walking out with José?' he asked conversationally as he worked at the fastening to her chemise.

'Si, señor, we are to be married soon.'

Dan stopped what he was doing, looking at Perdita in surprise. 'Married? Are you sure, then? About this?'

Perdita giggled, pressing the upper half of her body against him and rubbing her small breasts suggestively against the front of his shirt.

'José will not mind – he has great respect for Señor Cutter. And we are not married yet!'

Dan looked down into her laughing brown eyes and gave a mental shrug. It was none of his business. Perdita's olive-toned skin was warm and smooth under his fingers as he pushed the chemise over her shoulders, revealing the brown-tipped peaks of her breasts.

They were smooth and hard beneath his palms as he caressed them, pushing Perdita gently back on to the hay. His cock pressed painfully against the front of his trousers and he knelt up to remove them. Perdita stopped him with a glance.

'Let me señor,' she whispered huskily.

Rising up on to her knees, Perdita motioned him to stand. Her fingers worked nimbly on his belt and buttons and in no time he stood naked before her. It gave him a potent sense of power to find himself towering over her. Perdita knelt like a supplicant at his feet, her sensitive fingers roving at will up the hair-roughened expanse of his legs.

He was very aroused, his cock jutting from his belly in readiness and Dan could already feel the pre-orgasmic gathering of sensation in his balls. Standing with his feet planted firmly, shoulder width apart, he allowed Perdita to kiss and caress his lower body, his frustration building as she touched him everywhere but on the rigid shaft that craved it most.

Impatient, he nudged her cheek with the tip of his cock, smearing the clear fluid of pre-emission in a glistening stripe across her smooth skin. Perdita smiled. Her small, pink tongue darted out and dabbed at the tiny mouth of his cock, pressing gently into the slit so that it jerked involuntarily with delight.

Gazing coquettishly up at him through her lashes, Perdita spread her lips wide and enclosed the bulbous head of his shaft in her hot, willing mouth. Tangling his fingers in her hair, Dan closed his eyes and gave himself over to her.

She had a clever, knowing touch, her lips and tongue working in unison to bring him the greatest pleasure. Unerringly finding the sensitive spot where his cock and balls met, she alternately licked and sucked until the sweat broke out all over his body and his limbs began to tremble.

Within the private world behind his closed eyelids, Dan saw Maribel again as he had seen her masturbating in the water of the mountain pool. In his mind's eye, he imagined himself swimming out to her, replacing her questing fingers with his firm, strong cock, sliding it into her unsuspecting body . . .

Her eyes would open in shock to find him between her legs, pushing past the momentary resistance of her maidenhead, filling her, making her his. And, as in his imagination he pumped his seed into Maribel's reluctantly welcoming body, he came in Perdita's hot, wet mouth.

Crying out, he flooded her, collapsing to his knees beside her and reaching blindly for the comfort of her arms. Opening his eyes, he was momentarily disorientated to find himself drowning, not in bright blue eyes, but in Perdita's dark gaze.

He instantly felt ashamed. Cupping his hands around her face, he rained kisses over her soft skin, tasting himself at the corners of her generous mouth. Though she murmured and clung to him, Dan sensed that she had noticed his preoccupation and he immediately set about making it up to her.

Urging her to lie back down on the hay, he quickly dispensed with her drawers and the soft moccasins she still wore. Running his hand possessively over the thick, black hair of her mons, he dipped his head and nibbled gently at her navel.

There was a rustling in the straw nearby and Dan raised his head, immediately on the alert. Perdita might be confident that her fiancé would not object to her generosity, but Dan had no wish to be found by him bare-assed in the barn.

Unless . . . no, Maribel would not dream of following them out here. His thinking about her could not conjure her up. His sharp eyes raked the dark corners surrounding them. Perdita stirred restlessly and Dan shook his head. It must have been a rat, nothing more.

Smiling, he ran his hands tenderly along Perdita's body. Her skin was soft and smooth and he pressed his lips against her waist, darting out his tongue to lick at the moist pearls of sweat that were pushing through her pores.

Salt and musk blended on his tongue and in his nostrils as his lips worked their way inch by painstaking inch across her belly, his fingertips playing with the crisp, dark hair which shielded her secret places from view.

Perdita moaned restlessly and Cutter raised his head to smile at her. Coaxing her to bend her knees, he placed one hand on each and gently pressed them apart.

Above them, in the hay loft, Maribel lay rigid, certain she would be discovered. Trembling, her mind went over the glorious, unexpected sight that had confronted her when she crept into the hay loft.

Cutter must have forgotten that it was possible to enter the hay loft from the outside of the barn, if he had ever known it. From her vantage point, mere feet above his head, she had watched, wide-eyed, as Perdita had undressed him.

The stab of jealousy had taken her by surprise. She wanted to be in the other girl's place, wanted to touch and hold him, to pay homage to that marvellous tool which stood proudly against his belly, pointing towards his heart.

Maribel had never seen a cock like it. The boys she had stroked and brought off in her hand had been childlike in comparison. From her overhead view, she had had a perfect view of the veiny shaft, her eyes widening at the sight of the purplish, bulbous head with its potent, glistening tip.

What had it tasted like? Maribel licked her lips as she imagined taking that rigid shaft into her mouth, sucking the juice from it like a calf at its mother's teat. The white, milky fluid had clung to Perdita's lips, running in viscous rivulets down her chin as Cutter had withdrawn from her mouth. The girl seemed to enjoy the taste, for her pink tongue had darted out to catch what she could and the slender, brown column of her throat had rippled as she swallowed greedily.

There were sounds coming from below now, urgent, breathy noises which made Maribel risk rolling over on to her stomach and pressing her eye against the crack in the hay loft floor. What she saw almost made her gasp aloud.

Cutter was kneeling between Perdita's smooth-skinned thighs and was supporting her bottom with his large hands. Her legs were hooked over his naked shoulders and his face was buried in the soft cleft of her sex.

Maribel had never seen a woman's private parts in such detail before and she stared in fascination. In dramatic contrast to the pale red-gold fleece between her own legs, Perdita's pubic hair was thick and black. As she watched, Cutter buried his tongue deeply into the woman's body, leaving the deep pink folds of skin above exposed to Maribel's avid gaze.

Perdita's eyes were closed, her head thrown back and her mouth open wide. Strange, animal noises were coming from her throat as Cutter used his rigid tongue like a miniature penis to probe and poke at her gaping vagina. Her sex lips were swollen and glistening with the clear fluid of her own arousal. Maribel was fascinated to be able to actually see the hard nub of flesh which she so enjoyed touching between her own legs, standing clear of the surrounding skin, pulsing with independent life.

The smell of sex was heavy on the air, acting like a potent drug on the senses. Maribel was conscious of her own fluids soaking through her drawers and she longed to hitch up her skirts and relieve the mounting pressure in her bud. Yet the scene being enacted below kept her transfixed.

Cutter's tongue was moving higher now, his lips nibbling the swollen folds of skin so that Perdita began to moan louder. To Maribel's frustration, his head now obscured her view. She knew, though, the exact moment when his lips enclosed Perdita's quivering bud, for the woman went wild. Her head thrashed from side to side, her legs scissoring round Cutter's shoulders so that Maribel feared she would throttle him.

A voluble stream of Spanish poured from her lips and her hands clawed at the man who had raised his head and was watching her, relishing her enjoyment.

'Oh, God, God, let that be me!' Maribel whispered fervently as she watched his hands pinch at Perdita's nipples, his fingers dipping into her soaking sex and tweaking the deep pink nub which still quivered wantonly.

Cutter was hard again. Maribel held her breath as she watched him spread Perdita's legs still wider, so that the entrance to her body gaped lewdly. Maribel's eyes widened as he positioned the tip of his cock against her. Surely he was too big, even for that dark, moist hole?

Perdita cried out as he suddenly thrust into her body, burying his shaft inside her until his balls touched her bottom cleft. At first Maribel was dismayed, thinking that the girl was in pain. Then she saw Perdita's face and knew that she was mistaken.

Her eyes were glazed, her skin bathed in sweat, but it clearly was not pain which had caused her to cry out. It seemed to Maribel that Perdita had been transported to a level of ecstasy that she could only guess at.

Suddenly, Maribel could stand it no longer. She had to have something inside her, she had to be filled, stretched as Perdita was being stretched by Cutter's marauding cock.

Casting her eyes about frantically, Maribel saw her bull whip lying on the straw beside her. She had brought it for protection, as she always did when beyond the safety of the house walls. Smiling, she picked it up and stroked it.

The leather was warm and pliable under her fingers and she brought it up to her face. Closing her eyes, she rubbed it against her cheek, breathing in the warm, pungent scent of well-handled leather. Impatiently, Maribel bunched her skirts around her waist and pulled off her drawers. Sitting with her back supported by the wall, she bent her knees and opened her legs as wide as they would go.

Her sex was hot and very, very wet as she pressed her hand against it. Her fingers sank lovingly into the silky, swollen flesh as she began to move them back and forth.

Below her, Cutter's groans were mingling with Perdita's as their love-making became more frenzied. Glancing down, Maribel watched his hips pumping up and down, faster and faster as he raced towards his moment of crisis.

The handle of the bull whip was hard and unyielding as she positioned it, working it gently between the fleshy folds of her sex lips. Yearning for a real, living column of flesh, she gritted her teeth and twisted it from side to side, stretching the entrance to her body so that she could slide the handle inside her.

The silken walls of her vagina closed around the intruder, drawing it in and bathing it in juices. Maribel felt the sweat break out over her body as she moved the handle experimentally back and forth.

Razor-sharp needles of sensation zig-zagged through her body and she almost cried out. Never before had she experienced this curious pleasure-pain and she knew she was teetering on the precipice of something powerful, something which she would seek out again and again. Taking a deep breath, she pushed the handle deeper into her body.

Maribel sat very still. The movement from below had stilled now and she guessed that Cutter and Perdita now dozed, sated in each other's arms. She felt stuffed, the walls of her vagina expanding and contracting as they alternately tried to welcome and expel the intruding object.

Closing her eyes, Maribel allowed the scenes she had just witnessed to replay across her mind. Only now it was she who was suckling at Cutter's cock, it was her throat which was flooded by his creamy ejaculate, her face that was smeared and besmirched by his climax.

Slowly pulling the handle of the bull whip halfway from her body, Maribel imagined his teeth nibbling at her breasts. Slipping one hand inside her bodice, she pinched one nipple hard through her chemise, rolling the hard button of flesh rhythmically as she plunged the slippery leather back in again.

Stretching her legs yet wider, she pictured Cutter's wet tongue lapping at her most intimate flesh, imagined him tasting her, violating her body with his mouth.

By pulling the handle closer to her body, Maribel discovered that she could tease and torment her straining bud as she moved the bull whip back and forth inside her body. Burying it to the hilt again, she looked down to see the long, thin thong of the whip protruding from her tender flesh, like a sinister black snake coiling on the hay.

Imagining Cutter's weight bearing down on her, she substituted his cock for the handle in her mind's eye and began to move it faster, back and forth, back and forth, stimulating her pebble-hard bud with every movement.

Maribel was hot, so hot. Her lips and throat felt parched, her arms and legs as heavy as lead. Her hair lay in wet strands on her forehead as her breath came in short, painful gasps. It was building, building . . .

'Cutter!'

His name formed silently on her dry lips, the smell of him filling her nostrils, the imagined taste of him coating her tongue.

Suddenly, without warning, a kaleidoscope of colour exploded behind her eyelids and heat seared through her body. Wave after wave of white-hot sensation overwhelmed her and she had to stuff her fist into her mouth to muffle the cries she could not contain.

The bull whip slipped out of her and Maribel sank down on the straw, exhausted. Pleasurable after-shocks chased through her sweat-slicked body as she lay still, waiting for her heartbeat to slow and her temperature to return to normal. She felt dizzy, yet exhilarated, sure that this was but a fraction of the pleasure she would experience at Cutter's hands.

She had to have him, she *had* to! And as she drifted into a pleasurable half-doze, her mind turned on the problem of how she was going to seduce him.

Below her, Cutter thought he heard a sigh and stirred. Lifting himself up on one elbow, he listened intently, unable to shake off the feeling that they were not alone. He was getting jumpy, he decided, when nothing but silence greeted him. Maybe he had read too much into Maribel's teasing.

Angry with himself for allowing her to invade his thoughts again, he turned to the woman who lay in his arms. Perdita was asleep, her long, black lashes shadowing her cheek. Her lips, still swollen from his kisses, lay slightly open and she was snoring softly. He smiled.

Content to watch her as she slept, Cutter felt a small stirring of regret. He had a feeling that this was probably the last time he and Perdita would enjoy each other. No matter what she said, he had no taste for other men's wives.

Slapping her playfully on the rump, he woke her.

'Come on, time to get back,' he said firmly.

Perdita pouted sleepily at him, dressing quickly when she saw he was not in the mood to linger. When they were both dressed, she leant over and kissed him on the lips before slipping quietly out of the barn.

Cutter stayed in the barn for a few moments more, listening. His mind reluctantly went over the conversation he had had at the dinner table with Maribel. Surely he had been mistaken to think she was seriously considering joining the wagon train?

He chuckled to himself. John would never allow such a thing. A woman in charge of her own rig? It was unthinkable. No, Maribel Harker was no more than a tease. No doubt if he made advances to her, she'd take fright and run a mile.

He grinned. Maybe that's what he should do! As he rose, his eye was caught by the hay loft above him. There was something odd about it, though he couldn't for the life of him think what it was. Then it struck him. There was no ladder.

Dan's blood ran cold as he realised that that must mean there was an entrance to the hay loft outside the barn. Sure enough, when he went outside he saw it.

Climbing up the ladder, he couldn't shake off the feeling of premonition. He cursed under his breath when he saw Maribel curled up on the straw bed. How long had she been there? More to the point, how much had she seen?

The tooled leather bull whip lay curled against her body, like a lover. Cutter bent down and caught the unmistakable woman smell of her. Touching the handle of the bull whip, he realised it was warm and moist. Bringing it to his face, he passed it under his nose, breathing in the heavy, honeyed scent which overlaid the smell of the leather.

Realising it had recently been inside her body, his hand clutched convulsively round it. Despite his recent exertions, his cock responded to the stimulus and he found his eyes roaming at will over the sleeping girl.

Her arms and legs were akimbo, and for the first time he noticed that her legs were bare. A few feet away, her drawers lay abandoned and Cutter had an instant vision of what had taken place up here while he was making love with Perdita.

Not knowing whether to be angry or aroused, Cutter watched Maribel sleep, much as he had Perdita a few minutes before. Her face was flushed, her full lips curved in a soft, satisfied smile. He wondered how she would look when she came, whether her mouth would open wide, whether she would close her eyes, or let him share it with her . . .

He could find out. All he had to do was lean across and kiss her full, soft lips, let his fingers creep beneath her skirt and discover the delights hidden beneath. He guessed she would still be wet and warm . . . would she welcome his advances?

Dan smiled to himself and quietly backed away. He was in no hurry. The girl needed a firm hand and now he wasn't so sure that he wasn't the man to provide it.

He bared his teeth in a grin as he strolled back to the house. If, as he guessed she would, Maribel made enquiries about joining the wagon train, he wouldn't try to stop her, not immediately. Let her come along and find out what life was really like beyond the frontier. That should soon dampen her ardour!

And when she realised she had bitten off more than she could chew, he would send her back to the homestead and her father, suitably chastened. He grinned again. Though he didn't usually consider himself a cruel man, he had to admit he rather like the idea of taming Maribel Harker.

And he had a strong suspicion that Maribel would like it just as much as he.

Dance of Obsession

Olivia Christie

Paris 1935. Georgia D'Essange is an exotic dancer, married to the proprietor of *Fleur's* – an exclusive club where women of means can indulge their every whim. When Georgia is suddenly widowed, her stepson Dominic inherits the business and demands Georgia's help in running it. He is also eager to take his father's place in her bed and passions and tempers are running high. Men as well as women perform at *Fleur's,* and this extract finds Georgia and Dominic in the port of Marseilles, recruiting dancers for a daring new act.

Olivia Christie's second Black Lace book, *French Manners,* is due for publication in October and chooses France at the time of the Second Empire as its setting.

Dance of Obsession

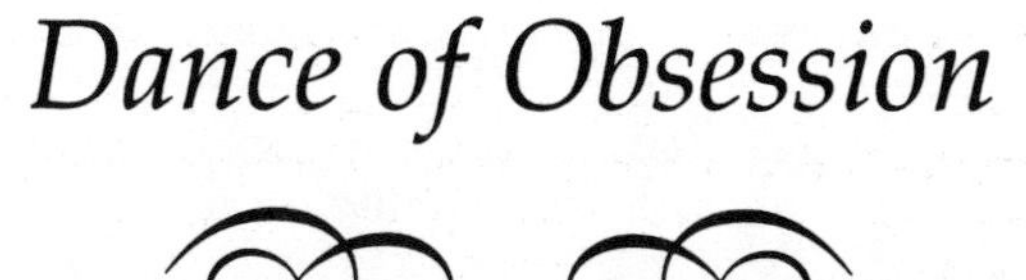

Late in the afternoon, the downtown area of Marseilles was hot and steamy, smelling of sweat and rotting fish. Narrow streets leading to the harbour front swarmed with sailors who had come ashore to drink and buy themselves a woman for the night.

Georgia was relieved to be out of Paris. Her leisurely drive down to the south with Marc, Dominic, and Natasha had been successful and relaxing, and, although Marseilles was unpleasant in the summer, they would not be here long. So far they had done well in their search for a new team. Stefan, Christophe, Pierre and Philippe had already been sent to their villa at Cap d'Antibes, and would be joined there by the others they had picked out during the past week. They had only two more to find.

Georgia was glad that Marc was able to accompany them. This was his home town, and his tall, powerful body discouraged unwelcome attention. Every year she had come to Marseilles with Olivier on their way to the villa. Together they had checked out the harbour bars for fresh talent, looking for men with raw, untamed energy, who would provide a contrast to the beautiful boys they had already selected. It had proved to be a successful formula in the past – she only hoped it would be as successful without Oliver.

Dominic looked uncomfortably out of place. His easy grace seemed to desert him as they pushed past the rough crowds, and he gave a snort of disapproval when Marc led them through a shabby, green-painted door, and down a narrow staircase into a dark, smoky bar.

'Marc!' A tall man, unshaven, with a ballooning belly and a crumpled cigarette dangling from his mouth, hurried forward and embraced him. 'I have kept a table for you.' He shook Georgia's hand respectfully. 'Madame, a pleasure as always. You are still caring for my friend here? He looks well.'

The man's eyes rested admiringly on Georgia before he shifted his gaze to Natasha. 'Mademoiselle.' He smiled at her, and then at Dominic. 'So you are the son of Monsieur Olivier. I am pleased to meet you,' he said, pumping Dominic's hand up and down. 'Your father was a great man, a great lover. And you – he would be proud of you. Here . . .' he swept some plates and glasses on to a tray. 'Please – sit down.'

The four of them perched on bare wooden chairs. The bar was packed with sailors, eager to forget their hard lives in a haze of alcohol. They looked rough and dirty.

Georgia knew that this would be the most difficult part of their selection. Olivier had taught her that the addition of one or two rough sailors or fishermen gave an edge to their act. Even after training they kept a raw, male magnetism that thrilled their clients. They needed Marc's local knowledge to help them to avoid any real villains.

Tomorrow night, if all went well, they would drive to the villa where they could settle down to the serious work of training their new team. In the meantime, however, there were two more to choose.

The proprietor came over to them, placed a couple of *pichets* of red Bordeaux on the table with some tumblers, and sat down beside Marc. 'There are a few you could look at,' he said. 'And many you should not go near. See that man over there? The one by the stairs? He killed his girl last week. The police have no evidence, but he won't be around for long.' He shrugged. 'She had a couple of brothers.'

Georgia watched Dominic look around the bar in disgust. She understood how he felt. She, too, had been horrified on her first visit here. She grinned at Marc, remembering the ruffian he had been then. Who would have expected him to become such a good friend? She hoped that Dominic would think about that and realise that this part of their work was worthwhile.

Natasha looked striking in a straight, black cotton skirt, slit high on her thigh. A low-necked, violet jumper stretched over her breasts which, though small, were well rounded with high, pointed nipples. Her hair shone in a straight streak down her back and her eyes were outlined with a thick line of kohl. She had been so discreetly dressed and so demure since they had left Paris that Georgia was surprised to see her like this, but she felt pleased that the girl had made an effort to fit in here. In the short time they had been together, Natasha had begun working with the men they had already chosen, and had learnt a few of Georgia's routines.

Georgia pointed out the men recommended by Marc's friend. 'What do you think?' she asked.

Natasha seemed unsure. 'Can we talk to them?'

Georgia shook her head. 'Watch them first. Take a careful look, and then decide whether you think you could work with them or not. Marc can explain to them what we want.'

'Maybe Natasha has the right idea. Maybe she should talk to them.' Dominic grimaced as he tasted the rough red wine. 'This looks like her sort of place.'

Georgia looked at him sharply. He had been less trouble than she had expected during their trip down here. This was the final stage, and she hoped that he would not make their task any more difficult.

'Let me see what I can do.' Marc stood up and crossed over to the bar. He spoke briefly to the proprietor, then took a jug of wine over to a corner table and offered a drink to a young man sitting there alone.

'What do you think?' asked Georgia, discreetly watching Marc's companion.

Dominic shrugged. 'He'll do,' he said, without enthusiasm.

Georgia saw Natasha glance at a dark-haired man slumped over a drink at the bar. He was powerfully built and looked young enough, but his swarthy face had a badly healed scar that ran from his jaw to the corner of his eye.

He seemed to interest Natasha. 'That one is exciting,' she said. 'What about him?'

'He's hideous. You'll never make anything of him,' Dominic sneered.

Natasha looked up at him. 'I thought we needed a contrast to your perfect good looks,' she said quietly.

'So you choose a monster?' Dominic bit his lip. 'That's going too far.' He gestured towards a young sailor sitting with a girl in a corner of the room. 'What about that one?'

Natasha shook her head, and scraped back her chair. She walked slowly over to the bar, and arranged herself seductively on a high, pine stool. 'A Pernod, please,' she ordered. Marc looked away from his companion and gave Georgia a warning glance.

Dominic scowled at Natasha's slim back. 'What the hell are we doing here? We've chosen ten already.' He glanced round the room. 'These men are scum.'

Georgia looked at him steadily. Dominic was making no effort to take this seriously. 'Marc came from here,' she said quietly.

'So what? He's nothing special.'

'How can you say that? Besides, we need the contrast.'

'I don't want her here.' Dominic's eyes rested on Natasha's provocative pose.

'She needs to see the men. She has to perform with them.'

'Later. She doesn't know what to do yet,' Dominic said petulantly. 'And look at her. She's behaving like a tart.'

And Georgia had to admit that Natasha seemed to know what she was doing when she curled her slim legs round the rough, wooden bar stool. One black leather shoe slipped off her foot and clattered to the floor. The girl balanced delicately on the edge of her seat stroking beads of moisture from the chilled surface of her glass of cloudy Pernod. She raised one knee provocatively and stared at the scarred man.

Georgia watched uneasily. Natasha was taking a risk by invading his territory. Without a word, the girl gestured to the barman who brought her another tall thin glass. The smoke in the bar thickened. Most of the tables were now taken, and several of the girls who had entered alone had found men to buy them drinks. One or two left after agreeing a price for their services. Many directed angry glances at the beautiful girl sitting at the bar.

Natasha sipped her second glass of Pernod. Her foot arched down to the floor. She shifted her fallen shoe, but failed to replace it on her foot. She stared hard at the dark man. Slowly he stood up and walked over to her, bent to pick up her shoe and pushed it on to her foot. He sat down on the stool next to her. She signalled for a drink to be brought to him, and when he put his hand in his pocket for money, she smiled, stroked the rough skin on the back of his hand, pushed away the coins and whispered in his ear. He stood up, knocking over his stool.

Natasha's eyes never left the young man's face. Georgia shivered. That scar dominated his face. Without it, he would have been good-looking. She looked questioningly at Marc's friend.

He shrugged. 'He's never been in any trouble here, but he must have upset someone to look like that.'

Natasha slid elegantly off her stool, slipped her hand through the sailor's arm and led him over to their table. 'Luc would like to audition for us,' she said. 'I'll go back with him to our hotel. We need one more man. That one will do.' She gestured casually across the room to the man sitting with Marc. 'You and Dominic can bring him to me. Then we'll work with both of them tonight.' She turned her back on them and walked up the stairs with Luc.

Dominic rose furiously to his feet. 'I'm going to stop her. What the hell does she think she's doing?'

Georgia held him back. 'Leave her. Let her find out for herself. She has to be allowed some freedom. And besides,' she said pointing to the doorway, 'Marc will go with her and make sure she comes to no harm.'

Dominic sat down, his face sullen, his eyes angry. 'Why don't you and I go straight to the villa tonight? Natasha can stay in Marseilles with Marc if she likes.'

'We all stay.' What was Dominic trying to do? Georgia felt hot and sticky in the airless bar. She, too, hated Marseilles and longed for the Riviera. The thought of their villa had kept her going throughout this long, hot summer. But they could not leave until their work was done.

'We need twelve men, Dominic. And we're almost there.' She drained her glass, wishing it was cold champagne. The rough wine hit the back of her throat, and the thick smoke hurt her eyes. 'Now, let's talk to Marc's young man and see if we can persuade him to come and audition tonight.'

Natasha allowed Marc to lead them through the dark streets to their hotel. She knew that she was probably not yet ready to perform, and that this evening she would be tested to her limit. Dominic had made it clear that he thought she wasn't as good as Georgia, and tonight he had had a strange look in his eyes, as if he wanted her to fail. Well, she would show him.

She glanced at Luc, nervous now of the massive frame that towered over her. Had she made a terrible mistake? Of all the men in that filthy bar, he had been the only one to look at her with a degree of warmth in his eyes. He hadn't leered or scowled at her. Now though, in the dim yellow lamplight, he looked dark and menacing.

Two men they had chosen the day before were waiting at the hotel. They looked presentable, but their eyes were wary and they seemed unsure of themselves. Marc sent them to their room to prepare for the audition.

'You need to go and get ready, too,' Marc advised her when they had gone. 'I'll explain to Luc what we're doing, and sort him out a bit.' He clapped the young man on the shoulders. 'It's the good life for you now, my friend. I wish I could start all over again, myself.'

Luc's shoulders tensed, then he took a deep breath and stared at Natasha. 'Let her come with us,' he said suddenly. 'Let her decide how I'm going to look.'

Marc opened his mouth as if to refuse, but Natasha stopped him. 'Please Marc. It's all right. Maybe he has a point.' And, she thought, perhaps it would help her to do well in the performance if Luc was on her side.

In the stark white hotel bathroom, Luc seemed even more out of place, with his straggly, thick hair, his big, rough hands and torn fingernails. And nothing had prepared her for the sight of Luc's naked body as he stripped off his shirt, exposing a muscular, tanned chest. She watched, fascinated, as his fingers tugged at the heavy, metal buckle at his waist. He held her gaze as if he dared her to lower her eyes, as if he knew that she had never seen a fully naked man.

The palms of her hands were damp with sweat, and she clenched her fists to hide her panic, thankful that her dark eyes hid her emotions. The Pernod she had drunk in the bar was doing nothing to calm her nerves. She kept telling herself that if she could only keep cool, and pretend that she had done this before, then she would be all right. She kept her eyes firmly on his face as his pants dropped to the floor and he stood aggressively naked in front of her.

She was supposed to be checking him out! Trying to appear calm, she stared at his chest, at the thickly matted hair, narrowing to a dark, furred line over his taut belly, and down lower until she was forced to look directly at his penis, at that long, thick organ hanging between his thighs. It stirred slightly as she held her gaze. Quickly she nodded to Marc as if she was satisfied, and hoped that Luc would submerge his body in the hot soapsuds awaiting him before he swelled any further.

She took a deep breath and choked back a burst of laughter. What was happening to her? This wasn't funny. But so far, she was coping all right. She wondered if it would be any easier to try to control Luc now that she had seen him naked, but she had a growing fear that it would not.

By the time he was washed, with a towel safely tied around his waist, and sitting in a chair waiting for Marc to cut his damp hair, Natasha felt more in control. 'Leave it long,' she insisted. 'Don't try to make him look like the others.'

'If that's what you want.' Marc checked the time. 'You go and change now. You need to start in ten minutes.'

They had booked a large room in which to stage the audition and Natasha went there as soon as she was ready. She wore a skin-tight white top and leggings, as Georgia had advised, but she felt quite naked. When she had looked at herself in the mirror in her bedroom, she had seen how the outfit clung to her slender body, outlining her high, pointed breasts, and the curve of her rounded buttocks.

Silently she repeated to herself Georgia's other instructions. Keep looking into their eyes to let them know you are in control. Never be cruel. Excite them, tease them, but never go too far. If one or two want to come, let them, the clients love it. But not too many, and never the ones who are booked for after a performance. Above all, remember – if you lose control you are at risk.

It had been so easy to dance for Dominic at Le Grand Marquis and, when he had joined her on the stage, she had responded instinctively to every movement of his body. She was sure he had felt the same thrill.

That night she would have done anything he wanted. She had never seen such a beautiful man, or felt anything like the surge of excitement he had instilled in her. She had scarcely listened to Raoul's words when he counselled her not to accept the job. From the first moment she saw Dominic in the night-club, she had longed to touch him, to be close to him. If she could perform well tonight, she hoped that he would want her too.

She saw Georgia and Dominic come in and sit on a couple of

armchairs in the corner of the room. Natasha felt their eyes on her, but she didn't look at them. She waited, standing quite still, until the door opened again and Marc brought in the four men, simply dressed in black cotton shirts and slacks.

Marc had achieved a great improvement in Luc's appearance already but, compared to the other three, he still looked unkempt. His hair remained long and wild, and his chin was shadowed with dark stubble.

As they had been instructed, they stood in a semicircle in front of her. She thought they were as nervous as she was, still not aware quite why they were there, or what they were expected to do, but eager to earn the money they had been promised.

As they watched, she padded over to them. She stopped in front of the first man, and ran her hands over his body, feeling a surge of pleasure as she felt him respond to her light touch. She raised her arms and waited. Not one of them moved. Her dancer's body twisted between the men, taunting them, sliding in and out of their group.

Natasha knew that Dominic and Georgia were testing her as much as the men. She had to make a success of this. More than anything else in the world she wanted Dominic to be proud of her.

She pretended that there was no light fabric covering her, and that she was naked in front of these men. Each time she raised her arms above her head, she watched their gaze fasten on her breasts. She could feel her nipples jutting out stiffly.

She thrust her hip-bones forward, drawing attention to the pronounced mound of her pubis, with its faint shadow of dark curls visible through the thin silk leggings. She turned quickly on one foot, letting them catch a glimpse of her high, taut buttocks, and the clearly defined division between them.

She saw Dominic lean forward in his chair, and she thrilled at his attention. Quickly she caught the men's eyes again, maintaining control, as she struggled to remember what she must do next. All four men were already aroused. Natasha could see the hard outlines of their swollen penises stretching their tight, black trousers.

She knew that the men were almost naked when Georgia performed with them, and that some of them touched her with total abandon. She wondered how it would be when she came to do that, and how Dominic would feel when he saw her.

Natasha had seen how it excited him to watch Georgia, and she was determined to do anything that Georgia did, anything at all that would arouse Dominic. But she could not risk taking her eyes off the men now to see how he was reacting.

Luc stared at her insolently, his black eyes glittering. The memory of his nakedness seared through her brain as she moved towards him, keeping her eyes fixed on his. She reached up and put her arms around his neck, moulding her body against him as Georgia had taught her, then she slid her right leg up and around the back of his thigh, pressing her crotch on his heavily muscled flesh. It was a delicious sensation.

She could feel his hands pulling her hard against him, and felt the swift surge of his penis rise against her hips. She wondered what it would be like to have a man inside her. Would Dominic respond like this? Would he desire her as Luc did now? She slid her leg higher over his buttocks, pushing him firmly down on to his knees, and pressed his head against her breasts, feeling his hot breath on her skin as she caressed his deeply scarred cheek.

She wanted to strip off her tight suit and free her body, but Georgia had warned her not to do anything like that at this stage. That would have to wait until they were safely at the villa, and she had more experience. It was too dangerous just yet.

Her breasts ached. She wanted to feel Dominic's lips sucking on them, and his hands stroking her thighs. Sliding down on to her knees, she straddled Luc's chest, lowering her body until she could feel the thick ridge of his strained cock between her legs. She rubbed herself on him, feeling the heat of his body throbbing against her.

She heard Luc groan as she writhed on top of him. For one moment she felt him draw back, then his huge penis sprang free from the black cloth and his hands grasped her buttocks, tearing the thin silk from between her legs as he reared up beneath her. She felt the swollen tip of his penis pushing against her soft inner lips, heard him gasp as she froze, unable to pull away.

She felt strong hands grip her shoulders, dragging her off. She threw back her hair and stared triumphantly into Dominic's eyes.

'I can tell you're going to enjoy the work,' he sneered, as he pulled her to her feet. 'Now go and change. We're leaving tonight.'

'Tonight?' she questioned eagerly. Did he really want her to be with him?

'Get rid of that man,' Dominic snarled at Marc. 'He's an animal.'

Natasha was puzzled. Had she lost Luc his job? Wasn't his performance exactly what they had asked for?

She was relieved when Georgia defended him. 'Don't be too hasty. He could be just what we want. Did you see what he did to the others? They're scared of him. There's an electricity between him and Natasha and she can learn to control it.'

She turned to Natasha, looking worried. 'Are you all right? It isn't easy. I shouldn't have let you do this, when the boys aren't trained at all.'

Natasha felt conscious of her torn clothing, and remembered the anger in Dominic's eyes; now he looked cold and indifferent again. She wanted him to feel jealous, but it seemed that he didn't care at all. She hoped things would be different once they were at the villa. Then there would be time for her to learn how to excite him.

Luc raised himself on one elbow. Natasha could see a slow smile soften his scarred mouth as he looked up at Dominic, and then he sprang lightly to his feet and stood, arrogantly erect, beside them.

Natasha heard Georgia whispering to Marc. 'Find them all some girls before you take them to the villa. They need to calm down a bit after this.'

So Marc would provide them all with women for the night, she thought. Was that how it was with all men? Could any woman satisfy them once they were aroused?

As she covered herself with a towel, she wondered what Georgia really thought of her performance, but the older woman had turned away to follow Dominic out of the room, and it was Marc who spoke to her. 'Go and change quickly, Natasha. He won't wait long.'

Georgia waited outside in the hotel's small garden. She loved these warm, balmy nights. She felt aroused by Natasha's skill, understanding how exciting her own performances must have been for her clients.

The promise that the girl had shown in Paris had been fully realised. Something seemed to happen to her on a stage, so that the demure young girl was taken over by a wild, free spirit. And Natasha had been right about Luc.

Georgia had been amazed by Natasha's action in the bar earlier in the evening, but could not fault her choice. Luc was a natural, and the contrast between his tall, swarthy hulk and Natasha's slender black and white colouring was dramatic. But it had been a mistake to let the girl practise with untried men. Georgia knew that it was her own reluctance to perform in front of Dominic that had made her agree to Natasha's suggestion. It would be a pity if they had to let Luc go, although she was sure that Dominic would insist on it.

Maybe she hadn't explained things properly to Natasha. She would have to go more carefully. With training, Natasha could learn to keep her body under control. So long as Dominic accepted the situation, they would be a great success. He had been sulking ever since they had left Paris, and now Natasha looked exhausted. So much had changed in her life in the last week.

At least they would have a few days' rest if they drove to the villa tonight; they could all relax far better there. Maybe Dominic was right to decide to leave now. It was not worth arguing about. In a way, Georgia sympathised. She, too, had had enough of hot, smelly Marseilles, with its seedy bars and airless streets.

It had been hard work putting together a team, but they had succeeded in finding twelve men who should do. They might as well go home. And if Dominic wanted to keep Natasha away from Luc for a while, he was making a wise decision.

In the meantime, Marc could look after the boys in Marseilles for a few days, kit them out with clothes and tame them a bit before they joined up at the villa. Maybe she should stay behind with them. It would be good for Natasha and Dominic to have some time alone. And the coast road was so romantic.

But Dominic refused her suggestion immediately. He jangled the car keys in front of her face. 'We all go together. You hate Marseilles. Of course you come with us now.'

It was three o'clock in the morning when the large car purred out of the lock-up garage where they had stored it for safe-keeping. The streets were dark and badly lit. Occasionally they passed a couple entwined in a back alley or doorway. Apart from them, and a few drunken brawlers on street corners, there was utter silence. Natasha slept, stretched out on the back seat. Dominic had insisted that Georgia join him in the front.

Georgia was sleepy, too. She envied Natasha her ability to drift off as soon as she closed her eyes. And yet she wanted to see the road; it was so full of memories for her. Even in the dark, she could see an occasional glimpse of the Mediterranean with its still surface illuminated by the faint light of the new moon.

'So what did you think of her performance?' Dominic's voice was curt.

Georgia glanced at the back seat. Natasha's eyes were firmly closed. 'She moves beautifully. Her body is graceful. And she's exciting.'

'She's exciting all right.'

Georgia waited for Dominic to say something about Luc. But he didn't.

'Do you think you made the right decision, Dominic?' she asked quietly. 'Are you happy with her?'

'Happy? That hardly matters. She's here to work. And she seems to have picked it up quickly. She'll do. I want to see her with you.'

'I'll show her the rest of the act, of course.' Georgia wanted to coach Natasha alone, not with Dominic looking on.

'No. I want to see the two of you together,' he said casually. 'I want her to copy exactly what you do.'

'She has her own style. I thought that's why you chose her.'

'She needs training.' He ran his fingers lightly over Georgia's thigh. 'She's out of control. I want to see you tame her.'

'Surely that's up to you?' Gently she lifted his hand off her leg. 'If you had worked with her tonight, she wouldn't have been at risk from Luc.'

'It was Natasha who encouraged him. You can show her what to do with him. He wouldn't dare go so far with you, would he?'

Georgia wondered about that. She had watched with increasing anxiety as Luc had reared up over the girl, as he had covered her with his body and torn the fabric from between her legs. If Dominic hadn't stopped them, he would have had her. And Georgia had struggled to control her own hot ache as she watched.

'We agreed that Natasha would train her own team,' she said. 'We shouldn't confuse them.'

'I thought that too. But now I'm sure she needs to see you

work with Luc. Unless you don't believe you can control him either?' His voice was light, but she saw his eyes dart towards her. 'Did he arouse you? How did you feel when you watched them?'

Georgia felt a swift surge of desire as she relived that moment. 'He showed promise,' she said, hoping that Dominic would soon change the subject.

'We'll keep Luc on one condition,' he murmured, as he caressed her knee. 'I want to see you perform with him.'

Georgia was hot and tired, and her pants felt damp and sticky. When Dominic's hand stroked her leg for the second time, she shifted uncomfortably beneath the pressure, feeling the heat rise between her thighs. She wanted to push him away, but instead she felt her back arching instinctively towards him.

Dominic pulled off the road and stopped the car. She felt him move closer and bend over her so that his lips brushed against hers. How did he always know when she was most vulnerable? His tongue flickered inside her mouth, inflaming her already feverish desire.

She was sure he knew exactly how she felt as he expertly unfastened her buttons and slid his fingers inside her blouse. She wanted him to squeeze harder, but his feather-light touch tantalised her without relieving her aching nipples. Her breasts were bare now in the moonlight, and she felt his lips close round them as his hand pressed down between her thighs, gently snaking deep into her eager sex until he found her swollen bud and stroked it.

She came immediately, and he laughed. 'Next time it'll be this.' He took her hand and laid it over his throbbing penis. 'Think about it.'

Georgia fought for breath. Her whole body was shaken by the strength of her orgasm. As she sank back on to the soft leather seat, she felt his cheek warm against her breasts, his long hair silky on her skin. She wanted to lie there and feel him holding her like this, but there was a faint movement from the back of the car.

It was a shock to remember that they were not alone. She sat up quickly and fastened the buttons on her blouse, but when she looked round, Natasha's eyes were still closed. Georgia felt ashamed at how little she had done to stop Dominic doing whatever he wanted. She had been as eager as he was.

As Dominic drove along the coast road, Georgia breathed in the cooler night air, scented with rosemary and jasmine and the dominating salt odour from the Mediterranean. He was driving too fast, but the road was deserted and Georgia did not want to risk a confrontation with him by complaining.

How triumphant she and Olivier had always felt together at this stage when the hard work of choosing the team was behind them and they could look forward to the summer. Often they had stopped on the way home, pulled off this road on to a secluded beach, swum in the sea and made love until dawn.

Occasional flashes of moonlit sea lifted her spirits, and the scent of eucalyptus as they neared Cap d'Antibes reassured her with the reminder of previous happy summers. They were only one mile from the villa now. Sand and pine needles covered the narrow dirt track as they dipped down towards the coast and saw in front of them the high, blue-washed walls of the Villa d'Essor.

Georgia stepped stiffly out of the car. Her skirt still felt moist around her legs; she hoped it would not look too obvious. They had telephoned their housekeeper, Mathilde, to expect them and she might well have waited up.

Dominic dumped their cases unceremoniously in the hall. She felt him close to her. Please don't let him touch her now, she prayed.

Georgia moved away from him as Mathilde emerged from the shadows. The old lady had looked after the villa for years and hated not to welcome their arrival. 'Everything is ready, Madame,' she said.

'Thank you. We're very tired.'

'And the young lady?' Mathilde had expressed a keen interest in meeting Dominic's new friend.

'Asleep in the car. Dominic will bring her in. You shouldn't have waited up for us, Mathilde, but it was kind of you. Go to bed now.' She called out to Dominic. 'Look after Natasha. I'll see you both when you wake up.' She had to keep out of his way; she could not be near him any longer. She knew now that she wanted him too much.

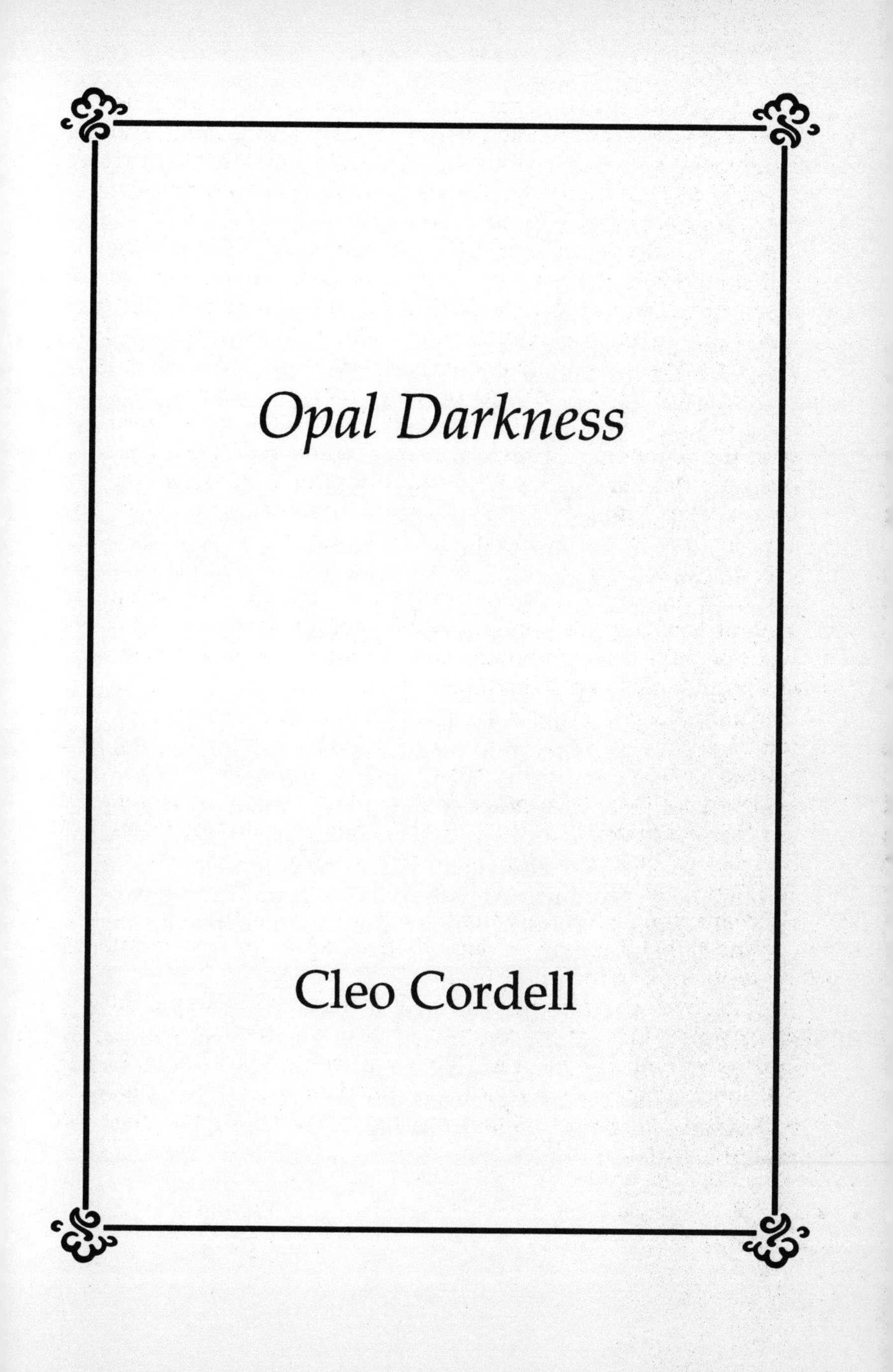

Opal Darkness

Cleo Cordell

There now follow two extracts from books by Cleo Cordell. No anthology of Black Lace historical erotic fiction would be complete without the author whose specialised area is dark, Gothic fantasy. *Opal Darkness* is set in the latter part of the nineteenth century and begins in rural Wiltshire where artistically-inclined and strikingly beautiful twins, Sidonie and Francis, live a secluded life in the care of their housekeeper and an old reverend. The twins' isolation ensures their fondness for each other – a fondness which borders on obsession. Before the twins are sent on the Grand tour, and before their forbidden love for each other is revealed, they are tutored in the arts – and in more intimate matters – by the decadent Chatham Burney, who is introduced to us in this extract. The twins also have other means of keeping themselves entertained, which involve the servants. However, their high jinks are about to come to an abrupt end.

Path of the Tiger is set in India during the early days of the Raj. Amy Spencer is obliged to spend time in the polite company of British Army wives, taking tea and playing croquet. This holds little appeal, however, for Amy has realised that far more sensual delights are on offer elsewhere. When the Maharaja's beautiful son Ravinder introduces Amy to India's sensual Tantric ways of love, she knows she will have a difficult time readjusting to stuffy Victorian morals.

Cleo Cordell's first Black Lace book was *The Captive Flesh*, which caused controversy with its harem setting and graphic description of the pleasures of sexual punishment. Its sequel is *The Senses Bejewelled*. Her other books are *Juliet Rising*, set in a strict eighteenth-century academy for ladies; *Velvet Claws*, set in Africa during the time of nineteenth century exploration; and *Crimson Buccaneer* which tells the story of a Spanish woman who turns to piracy for revenge.

Opal Darkness

As he made his way along the path which led around the back of the house to the gardens, Chatham Burney whistled merrily.

He was looking forward to meeting Sidonie and he had brought something special for her today. In the folder beneath his arm, along with his artists' materials, he had a number of drawings. He was certain that Sidonie had never seen anything like them and he anticipated her response to his gift with marked excitement.

An image of her flashed into his mind. She was so beautiful with her pale skin, unusual dark eyes, and that marvellous froth of hair. It seemed to have a life of its own, so full and vibrant it was, gleaming with tones of copper, gold and palest peach.

He chuckled. It was a good thing that she was hidden away in deepest Wiltshire in that ramshackle old barn of a house. In London she would cause a sensation. Sidonie Ryder might not be aware of the fact, but she was the epitome of the perfect Pre-Raphaelite beauty. And his friends Rossetti, Millais and the others of the Brotherhood were ever seeking a new muse.

Chatham reached the wooden gate which led into the old orchard. He pushed it and it swung open on rusty hinges. The lush green grass beneath the trees was still damp from the earlier shower and he had a sudden vision of Sidonie lying naked beneath him, her pale skin damp and fragrant.

He would love to sketch her like that, with the rain polishing her limbs and the violet shadows lying deep in the hollows of her body. Sometimes he felt guilty for awakening her to bodily pleasures, but he comforted himself with the thought that someone like Sidonie – so vibrant and eager for everything that life offered – was bound to give herself to a man at the first available opportunity.

That was true enough, but it did not explain his attachment to Francis. Chatham was not a man given to questioning his morals in any great depth. He allowed himself to be persuaded that it was Francis's uncanny resemblance to Sidonie that had captivated him. Was it *his* fault if brother and sister were so charming, so knowing, while retaining a refreshing innocence, so beautiful and so utterly captivating?

He was an artist, by God. A man who was acutely sensitive to beauty wherever he found it. How could he, a mere mortal, challenge the poetry of the flesh? Male or female, it was all one to him.

But today it was Sidonie he was meeting and all his thoughts were for her. Ah, she was waiting. He could see her there at the foot of the crumbling gazebo, her hair like a beacon shining through the trees.

She swept towards him, her shabby cloak brushing against the damp grass. Enamoured as he always was by her mere presence, he did not think to question the fact that it seemed too warm for her to be wearing the thick woollen cloak. She looked charming with her hair swept up with combs to reveal the slim column of her neck.

'Chatham! You're late,' she said reprovingly, her lower lip pushed out into a pout that made his pulses quicken.

God, just one look at her and he was so hard that it hurt.

'I apologise for my lateness. But I'm sure you'll forgive me when you know the reason why.'

'I don't know that I shall,' she said, sparkling at him. 'You had better have a good reason. I've a mind to punish you. Perhaps I'll just go indoors and forgo my art lesson today.'

'Then I must persuade you to stay,' Chatham said, reaching for her and drawing her into his embrace. 'If you must punish me, let it be with your kisses.'

She swayed against him, rotating her hips so that his erection rubbed against the base of her belly.

'Forward minx,' he murmured, then kissed her hard, pushing his tongue into her mouth, tasting and exploring her.

Sidonie made a sound deep in her throat as her tongue threshed with his. His cock pulsed in response and he put his hand down to adjust himself more comfortably.

'Let me do that,' Sidonie said, sliding her hand down between their bodies.

She rubbed her palm up and down his rigid stem, shocking him with her forwardness. Gently she squeezed him, her teeth caught in her bottom lip in a charming, childlike gesture of concentration.

When she drew away, she was breathing hard and her eyes were shining with excitement. Chatham had been going to show her the drawings as soon as they met, but now he was eager to lie with her. It was obvious that she needed no encouragement, nor did she need to look at pictures of nudes to get her into an amorous frame of mind. She had never been this demonstrative. Usually it was he who made the first approach.

Her wantonness thrilled and disconcerted him.

When he bent his head to kiss her again, Sidonie lifted her hand and placed her fingers against his mouth.

'Wait,' she breathed. 'I want to show you something.'

Taking a few steps backwards, she began to unfasten the clasp at her throat. The thick garment fell in folds to the ground. Chatham's eyes widened with surprise and pleasure.

Sidonie struck a pose. Her hand on one hip and her bent leg thrust forward.

'Would I do as a model for your London friends?' she said.

'Oh, yes,' Chatham replied, trying to take in the vision before him.

She must have spent hours making the dress, although 'dress' did not describe the garment she wore. In shape it resembled a smock, such as farmers wore. The sleeves were wide and gathered into a low neckline and the fabric was so fine that he could see the contours of her body. As she straightened up and began to walk towards him the wide neckline slipped off one shoulder, laying bare a tantalising expanse of pale skin.

Chatham's breath caught in his throat as he realised that she wore no stays or drawers beneath the dress. Such a thing would have been daring even for an experienced artist's model in London. In someone of breeding and gentle birth, brought up with no idea of the existence of the bohemian society he knew well, it was doubly shocking.

Had he really thought her an innocent?

He watched entranced as each long, rounded thigh, the curve of her hips, and the slight pout of her belly were revealed as the fabric bunched into folds with her movements.

Sidonie stopped a few paces from him and gathered the fullness of the dress in both hands. Pulling the folds tight across the front of her body, she let him see the dark shadow at her groin. The neckline slipped further and the swell of one perfect rose-tipped breast came into view.

'Would you like to paint me like this?' Sidonie asked teasingly, her sensual mouth parted to reveal even, white teeth.

Chatham groaned and stepped towards her.

'Perhaps later. First . . .'

She was as eager as he was and fell back readily on to the rug which covered the dusty stone steps of the gazebo. Twining her arms around his neck, Sidonie arched against him, her thighs falling open.

'Do it to me at once, Chatham. I want you hot and hard within me.'

Speechless with desire and almost bursting with the need to possess her, he hardly registered her words. He pulled up the dress until it was bunched in folds around her slim waist.

'God. My God,' he murmured, looking down her body to her adorable quim.

He could never get enough of that place. The fine, silky hair which covered her mound was a darker red than the hair of her head. It did not entirely mask the entrance to her body, but revealed the softly pouting lips of her vulva. He had never seen a quim more generously offered. It was as plump as a ripe fig, and the scent of it was heavenly – musky and rich, like nothing else in the world.

He opened his fly and his cock sprang free. Sidonie's hands grasped his hips, pulling him towards her centre.

'Now. Do it now. I can't wait,' she urged him.

'Oh, Christ,' he breathed as he pushed the head of his penis into the closure of her flesh.

She was tight inside, yet yielding too. Her heat and softness surrounded him, drawing him in. As he began to move, he felt the subtle pulsing of her inner membranes and tried to distance his mind. He was going to spend, he knew it, and Sidonie would be left unsatisfied.

He felt ashamed of his eagerness. Usually he was not so lacking in finesse, but Sidonie normally acted like a shy country miss – not a tavern doxy. He could not stop himself thrusting into her. The contours of her vagina slid so sweetly against his invasive maleness.

The pressure boiled within him as he moved inexorably towards his climax. And Sidonie's gasps and moans urged him nearer and nearer still.

The first tearing spurts jetted into her and he dug his fingers into the firm flesh of her buttocks, groaning deeply as he buried himself to the hilt in her moist darkness.

Serve her right. She had no business tempting him like that. A man could only stand so much.

Sidonie ground her hips against him, raising her legs and locking them behind his back. She began rubbing herself against the base of his belly, rocking back and forth, her head thrown back as her pleasure built. He felt her pubic bone digging into the base of his cock, her quim-hair mashing against him. Then she was gasping and crying out his name, her legs scissoring wildly and her vulva tipped upwards to extract the last drop of pleasure.

Chatham's rapidly shrinking cock slipped out of her, expelled by the force of her orgasm. For a second he felt affronted. By God – *she* had taken *him*. That had never happened before.

Rolling off Sidonie, Chatham took her into his arms. He did not know what to think. Should he be angry? Then he began to laugh. 'Well, it seems that the pupil has just bested the tutor,' he said. 'I must say it was a salutary experience.'

Sidonie kissed his chin.

'But you're really not sure whether you liked it or not? Let's rest for a while, shall we? Then I promise that you can roger me to your heart's delight. And, if you'd prefer it, I won't move a muscle! In fact, I promise that I won't enjoy it one little bit. It'll be all for you.'

Chatham kissed her soundly.

'Really? I've always loved women who don't keep their promises!' he said and, throwing back his head, laughed hugely.

Lying in bed later that evening, Sidonie went over the events of the afternoon.

A warm glow suffused her skin, a reminder of the potent

pleasures of love-making. She turned on to her side and placed her linked hands between her thighs, hugging to herself the knowledge that she had passed her self-imposed personal test.

Up until the past few hours she had been Chatham's willing pupil, accepting each kiss and caress with a sense of wonder. The delight in watching herself unfold had been heightened by Chatham's reactions. His artistic sensibilities had moved him to poetic speech on more than one occasion.

That was all very nice, very romantic, and she would always look on Chatham with great affection, but she knew for certain that she was ready now for earthier pleasures. If only she and Francis were not compelled to live like church mice.

How could they hope to meet anyone of note? Every garment they owned was patched, worn or woefully out of date. Not that that seemed to bother Chatham. He seemed charmed by their air of shabby gentility. He probably thought that it was romantic.

She brightened. Surely even in the depths of the Wiltshire countryside there must be opportunities for sexual adventures. She would ask Francis about that. And she would write to Father again. The first letter had produced good results. It really was time that he was reminded of his duty to his children. How much longer could he leave them buried in this place? Didn't he care that they were so poor when he was so wealthy?

Just then the bedroom door opened and a gust of wind set the flame of her bedside candle fluttering.

Sidonie sat up and folded back the bedclothes.

'Get in quickly, Francis. Before you freeze.'

Francis shrugged off his quilted robe and stepped out of his threadbare slippers, then climbed in beside his sister and snuggled up close to her. He smelt of lavender soap and clean skin. Sidonie snuggled down next to him and he took her in his arms. His familiar, long body was hard against hers and the folds of his cotton nightshirt chilled her skin even through her voluminous nightgown.

'You're certain that Smithers has retired for the night?' she said.

He nodded. 'We won't be disturbed.'

Tipping up her head to him, she kissed him passionately on the mouth. His hand cupped the back of her neck as he returned her kiss, smiling against her lips and murmuring endearments.

It was comforting, as well as exciting, to kiss Francis. She was so used to his presence, his utter devotion to her. Thrown together in their loneliness and seclusion, the boundaries of their sibling love had broadened and deepened into an almost obsessive fascination with each other.

For just a moment Sidonie imagined life without her twin and was terrified.

'What is it, sweetheart? You're trembling,' Francis whispered against her hair.

'I was just thinking how awful it would be if we were ever to be parted. Oh, Francis. I think I'd die of a broken heart. Promise me that it will never happen. No matter who you meet and fall in love with, you'll always love me best, won't you?'

'Silly goose,' he said affectionately. 'Of course. Did you need to ask? I adore you. Now, tell me how much you love me.'

She smiled at him in the darkness. The faint light of the candle picked out the planes of his face. His blue eyes were shadowed and mysterious. He has my face, but the lines of it are harder, all the angles more pronounced and more chiselled, she thought. In him she saw herself reflected. His beauty humbled her.

'Tell me,' Francis insisted, when she remained silent.

He tightened his arms around her until she whimpered with complaint. 'You're hurting me. Let me go,' she said.

His teeth flashed white when he grinned.

'I like to hurt you, but only a little,' he said huskily, bending his head to kiss her again, his firm lips moulding hers. In a moment he began kissing her cheeks, the tip of her chin and the hollow of her throat. 'There's something about you, an innocence that drives me to be cruel so that I can soothe away your hurt and kiss you better.'

Sidonie moaned as his hot mouth moved around to the back of her neck. When he bit her gently she arched her back and felt his heavy tumescence against her thigh. When Francis drew back finally she was breathless and shaking with desire for him.

'I love you, Francis. With all my heart and soul,' she said with a catch in her voice. 'No one will come between us, ever.'

Abruptly Francis rolled on to his back and lay looking up at the darkness which masked the ceiling.

'This is too dangerous, sweetheart,' he groaned. 'I think I had better go to my own room.'

Sidonie clutched at him.

'No! Don't go. I want you to stay. We can do . . . things to make ourselves feel better. Like we have in the past. Now that we are grown-up, it's so much sweeter to give pleasure to each other. It isn't a sin if no one knows what we do, is it?'

Francis chuckled and turned towards her, his chin propped on his hand.

'I doubt that the Reverend Beecham would agree with you, but I'm persuaded.' He put out a hand to stroke her face, his fingers cupping her chin. 'You've changed, Sidonie. You never used to be so bold. I suspect that Chatham had something to do with this new recklessness.'

Sliding her arms around his neck, Sidonie pulled his face down to hers.

'Why don't you tell me what you and Chatham did the last time you met,' she whispered. 'You know how I love to hear you say the words.'

'And you love me to do . . . this too, while I'm telling you every tiny detail, don't you?' Francis said, reaching down to slip his hand beneath the hem of her nightdress.

Sidonie drew in her breath as Francis's hand touched her thigh. Pleasuring each other was somehow more arousing because it was forbidden. And yet, she told herself, the fact that they never lay together skin to skin, added a strange decorum. Both of them knew that if they ever stripped naked and came together simply as a man and woman, then there would be no hope of ever controlling their passions.

There was a single, dark area of their psyche where they feared to tread. Francis cared about Sidonie too much to ever put her in danger. And if she was to bear his child, he knew that something would die between them. It was a disaster they dared not contemplate.

As Francis's slender fingers tugged gently at the curling hair on her quim, Sidonie parted her legs and hid her face in the hollow of his shoulder. She could feel the moisture gathering at the entrance to her vagina, ready to make his probing fingers wet with her silky juices.

'Tell me about you and Chatham then . . . oh,' she murmured, as he slipped a finger into the parting of her sex and began stroking her tender bud which responded by hardening until it resembled a tiny bead.

As Francis began speaking, she pushed herself towards his

hand, the low, urgent tones of his voice adding an extra dimension to her pleasure.

'I met Chatham in the old conservatory,' Francis said, a quiver in his voice. 'It had been raining earlier and his clothes were soaked. As soon as our eyes met it was obvious what was going to happen. I had brought a towel with me, thinking that he would have need of it. It was just an excuse really, as if we needed one. Anyway, I told him to strip off his wet clothes and to spread them out to dry. I said that it would be a pity if he took a chill and I'd give him a rub-down to warm him up.' He paused and looked down at Sidonie's face.

Her eyelids were fluttering and her lips were parted as she emitted soft sighs of pleasure. His fingertips slid up and down her moist folds, now and then dipping into her body and exerting a subtle pressure on the firm pad behind her pubis. He doubted whether she was actually aware of what he was saying. Just then she opened her eyes. They were drowsy, heavy with passion.

'Go on,' she whispered, sinking down on to his thrusting digit, her tongue snaking out to moisten her lips. 'Tell me what happened next.'

Smiling, he continued. 'When he had stripped off his jacket, shirt and trews and was dressed only in his under-drawers, I used the towel on his shoulders, belly and back. You know what fine, white skin he has? Well, it was buffed to a rosy hue by my ministrations and when I had finished, he was breathing hard as if he had been running. His cock was jutting straight out and he did not try to hide the fact. Instead, he took my hand and placed it on him so that I could feel the heat and the throbbing weight of it. My mouth dried as I looked at him. Before now I never desired another man. Perhaps it is because you and he are lovers – I don't know. But I felt an answering response within me. Chatham drew me to him, pressing his chest close to mine and we kissed.'

He paused, remembering. And Sidonie wriggled closer, her swollen nipples grazing his chest almost in imitation of the caress he was relating to her.

'When we broke apart,' Francis said, 'he put his hands on my shoulders and I dropped to my knees willingly. I knew what was going to happen and I was fearful and desirous at the same time. My fingers shook as I opened the buttons at his fly. His cock was thick and potent-looking, the skin covering the head of it was partly rolled back and the glans was moist and purplish.

'I could smell his arousal. It was like salt and clean sweat and there was an earthy undertone to his scent. I leant forward eagerly, my hand coming up to rest on his slim hips and I opened my lips and drew his cock into my mouth. I can't tell you how it felt. The hardness of him, the male thrusting force deep in my throat. It was intoxicating. I clutched at his buttocks, kneading the taut flesh as I sucked and pulled at his phallus.

'God, Sidonie, that such an act between men is thought to be wrong! I did not feel any shame, only a glorious sense of freedom and pride and pleasure too. It was a privilege to be able to give such delight. And, somehow, I knew just what to do. It was a little like pleasuring myself.'

Sidonie clutched at her twin, her back arched and one leg twined around his waist, giving her freedom to thrust back and forth on his fingers which were buried deeply within her. Francis flicked the pad of his thumb back and forth across the straining bud, which had thrust itself free of its tiny hood and was so hot and erect. It ticked against him, like a tiny beating heart.

'And then ... Oh, yes. Don't stop that. And then ...' Sidonie gasped.

'Then I felt his hands moving in my hair and caressing my cheeks, moving bonelessly down to my mouth and tracing my lips which were stretched open to contain his delicious flesh. I did not know that I could take so much of him in.

'But I did it. His pubic hair grazed my lips and my chin and he was moaning, his buttocks clenching and unclenching. I cupped his balls then, feeling how tight they were, ready to give up his jism. Then he spent and his seed gushed into my throat. I swallowed all of it and relished the last drops.

'When I stood up, we kissed and embraced. Chatham rubbed his tongue around the inside of my mouth, no doubt tasting the faint traces of his essence. He smiled crookedly at me then and my heart gave a great lurch, because I realised that he wanted to fellate me in turn.'

Francis paused and held her close as she climaxed, uttering sharp little cries and throwing her head from side to side.

'Oh, Sidonie, my darling.'

He pressed kisses to her throat, holding her until she was

quiet. How he loved her face when she came. It made him feel so tender and protective towards her.

They lay together, still embracing and cushioned on the pillow of Sidonie's spread hair. In a moment she adjusted her position and smiled wickedly at her twin.

'That was divine. I thought I was going to melt with pleasure. And now to attend to you. What is it that Chatham calls it – fellating? I did not know that there was a name for what I do to you.'

Francis lay on his back, his hands linked behind the back of his neck. Sidonie pushed up his nightshirt until it was raised above his waist. She studied the column of flesh, which he had various pet names for, calling it his cudgel and his pego. His cock – so hard inside, but with its velvet-soft skin – fascinated her, just as the intricate shape of her quim fascinated him. Ever since their first exploratory, childhood games, they had been charmed by the differences in their bodies.

Sidonie stroked Francis's cock lightly, her fingers moving up and down the rigid shaft. She smiled with satisfaction when it twitched and leapt in her hand. As she bent forward and gave the swollen glans a long, loving lick, she murmured, 'Oh, Francis. Whatever happens, whoever I meet, I'll always love you the best. Only you.'

Francis let out a long sigh as her hot mouth closed over his straining cock-head. The sensation was exquisite and he closed his eyes, letting the feelings wash over him. It was an effort to speak, but he just managed to get the words out.

'Me too, my pet. Never forget that I'll always care for you. We belong to each other.'

Sir James Ryder looked down at the letter in his hand and experienced an unusual flicker of conscience.

This was the second missive from Sidonie in a little over a month. Were the twins unhappy then? He had to admit that he had hardly given the matter a thought. His business commitments took up much of his time and that which was left over was filled most admirably by the company of Lady Jennifer Haversidge, wife to an aged member of Parliament and his mistress for the past two years.

Perhaps it was time he paid his children a visit. They must be thirteen, fourteen? No probably more. He realised with a sense of shock that he did not know exactly how old they were. How the years had fled since their mother died.

He had been too wrapped up in his own grief to give a thought to his children at first and then he had thrown himself into his work. London could be exhausting with its round of social engagements, but it was necessary for a man in his position to move in the right circles.

And now, of course, there was Jenny.

He liked to think that Jenny had softened him, rubbed away some of the hard edges of which he was once so proud. Sir James was a stubborn, self-made man. Everything he had achieved he had worked hard for. The twins did not know how lucky they were to be free of his worries. They were clothed decently, fed, and their time was their own.

The sound of a discreet yawn and a slight rustle of bedclothes alerted him to the fact that his mistress was awake. It was typical of Jenny that she did not fling back the counterpane, sit up and rub her knuckles in her eyes then scratch her armpits, like many a drab he had taken to his bed in the past.

His mistress was a lady of breeding and the delicacy of her manners was something he loved best about her.

'What's that you're reading, James?' she asked, the soft husky tones of her voice raising the hairs on the back of his neck.

'Just a letter from my daughter, dearest. Seems that she's set on reminding me of my fatherly duties. I have the uncomfortable feeling that I might have been remiss in leaving the twins to their own devices for so long.'

Jenny propped herself up on the pillows and patted her hair into shape. One blonde, corkscrew curl fell artlessly over one shoulder and tumbled over the exposed swell of her breasts.

'How old are the twins now?' Jenny asked.

Sir James looked shamefaced. 'Somewhere in their early teens I believe. Hardly more than children really.'

'Oh, James, you scoundrel. Don't you know how old your own children are?' Jenny chided. 'You have only one date to remember after all. I expect you've been forgetting the twins' birthday too. I see by your face that you have. This really won't do. You'll have to go and visit them. Fancy leaving them buried in the country all this time. They must be introduced to society, fitted for new clothes. Sidonie must have a coming-out ball. However else is she to meet people of breeding?'

Sir James looked worried. All this was quite beyond him. He had planned to just look in on the twins, perhaps increase their allowance a little. Jenny had made him see that there was a lot more involved.

Jenny smiled fondly at him. 'Would you like me to come to Wiltshire with you?'

He brightened. 'Oh, would you, darling? It would be a great help to me. I can handle Francis, but young women scare the daylights out of me. Perhaps if you would speak to her?'

'Of course. I'd be glad to. I'd really enjoy the change. The country air will put roses into my cheeks. And when Sidonie comes back to London with us, I'll take her to my personal dressmaker. She's just imported some dress patterns and some wonderful figured silks from Paris. Monsieur Worth, very *à la mode*, don't you know.'

Jenny struck a pose, one hand on her hip and the other in the air in imitation of a dress mannequin.

Sir James beamed at his mistress. There was nothing at all to worry about. Jenny would take Sidonie under her wing and he would see to Francis. All a young man needed to get into the right set was to join the required gentleman's club. He had plenty of influential friends and many of them would be sure to look kindly on Francis.

Yes, it was certainly high time that his son took his place in the family business. He even found himself looking forward to it.

'What would I do without you, my dear,' he said, his voice soft with affection. 'I owe you a great deal.'

Francis awoke first and looked across at the sleeping face of his twin.

Sidonie looked so childlike in sleep. Her mouth was soft and a trifle sulky in repose. There were faint violet shadows under her eyes and in the hollows of her cheekbones. The adorable dimple in her chin was not so pronounced.

He felt such a surge of affection for her that his eyes stung with emotion. His beautiful sister. His companion of eighteen years. Nothing would ever hurt her while he lived.

Suddenly he was afraid; she seemed so still. He sat up and shook her gently. She awoke with a jerk and he smiled down into her unusual brown eyes, thinking that they were the exact colour of strong coffee, rare on someone with her hair and skin.

'What? What is it?' Sidonie said. 'Why did you wake me? Did you hear the breakfast bell?'

'Oh, it's nothing. I just felt lonely,' Francis said.

She laughed softly and put her arms up to draw his head down to hers. They kissed deeply.

'How can you be lonely? We share my bed every night now. Did you remember to ruffle the bedclothes in your room? We don't want Smithers getting suspicious.'

'I remembered, but it hardly matters. No one cares what we do.'

Sidonie laughed delightedly. 'How reckless you are, Francis. I do believe that you're getting worse. Is it true what you told me last night – about the chambermaid, I mean?'

Francis looked annoyed. 'You know I never tell you lies. Other people perhaps, but I always tell you everything.'

Sidonie clasped her hands behind her head and beamed up at him.

'In that case, you won't mind proving that to me.'

'What do you mean, proving it? How can I? You can't mean ... You do! You want to watch, don't you?'

Sidonie nodded and clapped her hand to her mouth, her brown eyes dancing with amusement. When she lowered her hand her cheeks were flushed.

'Oh, Francis, you sound so shocked. What's the matter? Aren't I allowed to be a little reckless too?'

'Well, yes. But it's different for you.'

'Because I'm a girl? That's utter rot and you know it. Don't I enjoy doing all the things we do to each other as much as you do? I'm just like you, my darling brother. And don't you forget it. I shall find it very tedious if you start keeping things from me – for my own good.' She punctuated each of the last four words with a pointing finger. 'Don't you dare start treating me like you're my guardian!'

Francis's blue eyes widened with respect.

'I wouldn't dream of doing any such thing. Very well. How can I refuse? I'm meeting Clara and Rose in the old wine cellar at eight this evening.'

'Both of them!' Sidonie had the grace to look scandalised.

Francis grinned, his mouth curving with unashamed pride.

'Oh, yes. They like it better that way. One likes to watch while I do her friend. Sometimes I watch them stroke each other.'

'Two women, together? I had not thought it could happen. But I didn't know that men pleasured each other until you told me about Chatham. How fascinating. There's so much to find out, isn't there? I shall go to the cellar early and hide. I cannot wait! Be sure to take enough candles with you. I want to see absolutely everything.'

Francis swung his legs over the side of the bed, then jerked the bedclothes off Sidonie.

'You're a monster, do you know that? Now out you come. That *was* the breakfast bell. I had better go to my room before Rose brings my hot shaving water and Clara comes in here to help you dress.' He saw the gleam in his sister's eye and grasped the tops of her arms. 'Don't you dare say a word to Clara or the whole thing's off! Understand?'

'Very well,' Sidonie said sulkily, rubbing her arms.

Really, Francis did not know his own strength sometimes. At her next words her voice took on an edge of sarcasm.

'I can't think why you're worried that I'll tell. After all, I have the whole day studying the Greek classics with that old fool Reverend Beecham to look forward to. I'm sure that I can hardly concentrate on anything else at all!'

As Francis walked quickly across the room, his muffled laughter floated back to her.

'Don't ever change, Sidonie,' he said, having to almost choke out the words. 'You're priceless.'

While Sidonie read through the passages set by the Reverend, she thought of her last meeting with Chatham. Strangely it was not the erotic act they had shared that stayed in her mind, although that had been satisfying to them both, it was the things he told her about his circle of friends.

How she longed to go to London and meet the poets, writers and artists he knew. Women were welcomed amongst them apparently. Chatham often praised her unusual looks, comparing her with someone called Elizabeth Siddal who was a favourite model of the artist he admired most, Dante Gabriel Rosetti.

Sidonie felt that it was probably vain of her, but she loved to hear Chatham's compliments. There was no one, other than Francis, to notice how she looked. And he looked too much like her himself to be overly impressed. It was not that he did not think her beautiful, it was just that he saw her every day. He was accustomed to her in a way that Chatham was not.

She hoped it was not disloyal of her to long for male company. It was different for Francis; he had his own private appreciation society in the form of Clara and Rose. Then there was Smithers, who sometimes had a twinkle in her eye when Francis was around, despite her sharp tongue.

Well, there were compensations for having such a wicked self-indulgent brother; she smiled as she thought of what she was to witness in the old wine cellar. If she had not been so certain of her place in Francis's affections she might have given way to pangs of jealousy. But that would be absurd. Both she and her twin had an unspoken rule about each of them taking other lovers.

Their love for each other was unshakeable. Sexual dalliances were just pleasant diversions to be shared, examined and used as a spur for their personal satisfaction.

She gave a little shiver as she remembered the caresses she and Francis had exchanged last night. He was becoming quite expert in arousing her. Sometimes it seemed as if he knew her body as well she did. And now she knew why. Whilst he had been pleasuring Clara *and* Rose, he had no doubt been learning new techniques as well as furthering his studies of intimate female architecture.

Goodness, Francis was turning into quite a rake. No matter, as long as *she* reaped the benefits. Given the opportunity she might have followed suit. But the only other males she came into contact with, besides Francis and Chatham, were Hodgkins the gardener and Tillworth the coachman, both of whom were grizzled, stoop-shouldered and positively ancient.

One day, she promised herself, she would have more lovers than she could cope with. And she would treat them with haughty disdain, accepting their slavish attentions as no more than her due.

Was there a female equivalent for 'rake'? She did not think so, at least nothing that sounded pleasant. Perhaps she would make up a name for herself.

A woman of pleasure, she thought, that's what I'll become. A worthy she-rake – even better. Liking the sound of the phrase she consigned it to her memory then, opening the book on her lap, turned her attention to her Greek studies.

The day passed slowly. After a break for a luncheon of cold roast beef, followed by apple pie and cheese, which she took with Francis in the dining room, she was obliged to go over the following week's menus with Smithers.

The ritual was a formality only as it was obvious to everyone who was the real mistress of the house. Smithers ran things in her own way and the household tasks were accomplished with the regularity and smoothness of a well-oiled machine. All Sidonie had to do was to approve the dishes, then listen and nod sagely, while Smithers discussed the range of produce which was in season and could therefore be purchased most cheaply from the suppliers.

Smithers seemed in a hurry to get the meeting over with, which suited Sidonie. She wondered idly why Smithers was in such a flap. Already the woman was stuffing her notebook into the capacious pocket of her apron and hurrying from the parlour as if she had a hundred and one tasks to perform before dinner.

She shrugged, forgetting about Smithers' agitation almost at once. The housekeeper's problems did not concern her.

It was a relief to go up to her room to wash and change before dinner. Clara brought clean towels and a jug of hot water, which she tipped into the china washing bowl on the dresser.

Sidonie looked at Clara from the tail of her eye, seeing anew her buxom, freckled good looks. The dark, high-collared dress and snowy white apron did nothing to disguise Clara's rich curves. At the thought of watching Francis thrusting into the housemaid's willing body, while Clara sighed and surged against him, Sidonie felt quite weak at the knees.

'Thank you, Clara. Be so good as to come back in ten minutes to help me dress,' she said, surprised to find that her voice was steady.

'Yes, ma'am,' Clara said, her eyelids lowered respectfully as she dropped a curtsy before leaving the room.

Sidonie was bursting to ask her questions: How many times have you lain with my brother? How does it feel when you stroke Rose? And, most importantly, tell me what it feels like when you spend?

As she stripped and washed herself all over with a piece of

flannel and some rose-scented soap, she thought how she had never discussed such things with another woman.

Francis was her confidant, her only other source of information. Did other women get a warm, tingly sensation in the base of their bellies when they experienced their peak of pleasure, as she did? She had never thought to ask him about such things.

Tonight she would watch closely while Francis had Clara and Rose and observe all of the subtle signs of the women's enjoyment.

The inside of the coach smelt strongly of leather and more subtly of Lady Jenny Haversidge's perfume – Lotion de Guerlain, which was redolent with the scents of *chypre* and patchouli.

Jenny adjusted her position. Her back was aching and the whalebone ribs of her corset were pinching unpleasantly. She would be glad when they reached the house. The journey had been long and tedious. And they had been held up on two occasions: once by a fallen tree and once when one of the horses had become lame.

The light was failing now and the coach lamps cast a faint golden glow outside the window, obscuring the view of the Wiltshire downs. The sound of hooves on the road and the squeaking of the coach-springs was grating on her nerves. All she could think of was a soft bed and a hot drink. It was typical of her that she did not give vent to her irritation, but said only, 'It's getting rather late to arrive without notice, Jimmy. Nothing will have been prepared. Shouldn't you have warned Smithers that we were coming?'

Sir James smiled and patted the back of her elegant, gloved hand.

'Don't worry, m'dear. Smithers is expecting us. I instructed her to get the west wing ready, but to be discreet about it and tell no one that we are coming – not even the maids. I want to surprise Sidonie and Francis.'

'Won't they hear the carriage arrive?'

'Not if we alight at the gatekeeper's lodge and walk up to the house. Do you mind, dearest? It's a fine night.'

'Of course not,' Jenny said, thinking that it would be a mercy to stretch her legs and rather romantic to walk along the tree-lined drive with the moonlight shining down through the branches.

She squeezed Sir James's hand, knowing how nervous he was about facing his children. Well, she was here to help him.

'I'm so looking forward to meeting the twins. I'm sure that Sidonie and I shall be the greatest of friends.'

Sir James smiled worriedly and peered out of the carriage window.

'Ah, here's the gatehouse now,' he said.

Jenny drew her full, silk skirts together and reached for her reticule as the coach drew up in a flurry of chinking harnesses and stamping horses. Quickly she checked her appearance, wanting the twins' first sight of her to be favourable. After all, they were not aware of her existence. It would no doubt be something of a shock for them to discover that their father had a gentlewoman companion.

By the time they reached the main house, both Lady Jenny and Sir James were a little out of breath. Smithers had been keeping a look-out and opened the front door before they had a chance to lift the lion-headed, brass knocker.

'Good evening, Sir James. Your ladyship,' she said. 'I have your rooms ready. Please come this way.'

Jenny stripped off her gloves and hat as she entered the suite in the west wing. She saw that there was a fire burning in the grate and the fresh smell of lavender polish filled the air.

'Her ladyship is rather tired from the journey. Bring her some tea, will you, Smithers?' said Sir James.

'Yes, sir. And something for you? A hot toddy?'

'Nothing at the moment. I want to speak to the twins if they have not retired yet. You didn't tell them that I was coming?'

Smithers rose up to her full height and said, a trifle indignantly, 'I did as I was told.'

'Very good. Now, you attend to her ladyship. I'll go and find the twins.'

From her vantage point in the cellar behind the racks of wine, Sidonie watched the tableau unfold, her knuckles pressed to her mouth to hold in her murmurs of surprise.

In the wildest flights of her imagination she had not pictured such a scene of wantonness. Francis was plainly the worse for drink and surely Clara and Rose had been allowed to drink from the same bottle.

Both women were partly clothed, their hair awry and their cheeks flushed with colour. Two bottles of wine, in fact, lay on their sides on the floor, the last of the red liquid seeping out on to the flagstones. Sidonie gave a muffled, scandalised giggle. It was a good thing that the cellar walls were thick; there was no likelihood of anyone upstairs hearing the sounds of enjoyment.

'Come on then, Clara. It's your turn to go first,' Rose slurred, pulling at the remaining hooks on the back of Clara's gaping dress.

Clara, who had been dancing in circles, her breasts bobbing and her skirts raised up to expose her sturdy knees and calves, spun around and knocked Rose's hands away.

'Leave off, you,' she said, squirming out of Rose's grasp. 'It's Francis who says what's to do. In't that right, sir?'

Francis grinned and caught her around the waist.

'That's the way of it, Clara. But I've a strong mind to have you first. Have you any objections?'

Clara clamped both hands to his cheeks and kissed him soundly.

'I'll take that as a no shall I?' Francis said, grinning when she drew back.

Clara pushed the flat of her hand against his chest. 'Ooooh, you're sharp, you are. Mind you don't cut yerself.'

She began pulling down the bodice of her dress and freeing her arms. Rose helped her disrobe and soon Clara was dressed only in a knee-length chemise and a stout cotton corset. Her big round breasts jiggled under the chemise as she moved, the prominent nipples making little peaks in the fabric. She faced Francis with her hands on her hips, her bottom lip stuck out in a pout.

'Well? How d'you want me?'

'You're frisky tonight, Clara,' Francis said with mock disapproval. 'What shall we do with her, Rose?'

Rose's thin face lit up with a crafty smile. Flicking back a lock of dark hair, she said, 'I think she ought to be punished for her cheek, sir.'

'I quite agree, Rose. Capital idea. Come here, Clara, and lean over this bench.'

Clara sidled over to him, pushing back a strand of straw-coloured hair which had flopped into her eyes. Holding eye contact with him, she bent forward and pressed her belly to the rough wood. The curves of her broad behind became visible as the chemise was pulled tight.

While Francis looked on, Rose began rolling up the chemise until it lay in a sausage shape in the small of Clara's back. The full globes of her buttocks and her shapely thighs were laid bare. Clara giggled and waggled her bottom, parting her legs a little to expose the pouting, split-fruit shape of her quim.

Sidonie watched in fascination. She had never seen a woman undressed like that. Clara had a lot of hair between her legs. The cleft between her buttocks looked deep and the skin there was a darker, pinkish colour.

'How many slaps do you think, Rose?' Francis said. 'Tell you what, I'll leave that to you.'

Rose flashed him a lecherous grin, her eyes fastening on his fingers which were unbuttoning the fly of his trousers. Stepping out of them, Francis cast them aside and put his hand down to pull up the tail of his shirt. His cock stood out like a poker, red and potent-looking.

'Ooooh, sir,' Rose whispered. 'You is ready now. Are you goin' to do her while I spank her?'

Francis squeezed himself, running his cupped hand along the shaft of his member. As he smoothed back the skin from the purplish tip, a tiny drop of clear fluid appeared from the slitted mouth.

'I might just do that, Rose. Get started, will you? I'm a bit quick on the trigger tonight. Must be the blasted wine.'

Rose set to with a will, slapping Clara's broad white backside while Clara squealed theatrically and called out protests. 'Ow! That one hurt! You don't have to be so rough, you girt lummox!'

Sidonie was spellbound. Clara was obviously enjoying the spanking, even if it was somewhat painful. Her back was arched so that her bottom was pushed out towards Rose's hand. In a moment she began weaving her hips back and forth, bending her knees and thrusting forward to rub her pubis on the overhang of the wooden bench.

'Oh, look, sir. She's being ever so lewd,' Rose said, giggling.

Francis swore softly. He was breathing hard when he took up position between Clara's spread thighs. He placed both hands on her reddened cheeks and circled the firm, dimpled flesh. Then he slid his hands in towards the moist cleft and eased the heavy globes apart exposing the generous quim and the tight, wrinkled opening of her anus.

'Fore or aft,' he said jauntily. 'What's it to be, Clara?'

'Oh, Gawd. Do me up the back-end, sir. But rub me with your fingers too. Oh, I can hardly stand it, I'm so near to spending.'

Francis dipped his fingers into her wet folds and smeared the pearly juices around the head of his cock. Easing the swollen glans towards her anus, he pressed forward gently until the tight ring of muscle gave. Clara gasped and jerked as he slid more deeply into her and began to move slowly.

Watching, Sidonie bit her lip. She was so aroused that she had to squeeze her thighs together to try to still the pulse which was beating in her quim. But that only made the feeling worse. Her dew was seeping out of her, soaking the folds of her chemise. Lord, she had not known that there could be such pleasure in watching others doing it.

Francis reached underneath Clara's body and began moving his arm back and forth as he thrust more strongly between the fat, pink cheeks.

'Oh, my. Oh, lawks,' Clara squealed, her voice rising ever higher as she pushed her hips backwards towards Francis's flat belly. 'Do me hard, sir. Oh, my. I'm spending!'

Francis threw back his head and went rigid. His buttocks were taut and his cock buried to the hilt within Clara's body. Gritting his teeth he gave out a low satisfied moan.

At the exact moment that Clara and Francis reached a mutual climax, Rose cried out too. But her cry was one of shocked surprise.

'What the devil is going on here!' called out a strident male voice. 'Francis! Explain yourself at once.'

Sidonie almost fainted with horror. And Francis, already withdrawing from Clara and wiping himself on his shirt tail, turned around to meet the furious countenance of his father.

Path of the Tiger

Cleo Cordell

Path of the Tiger

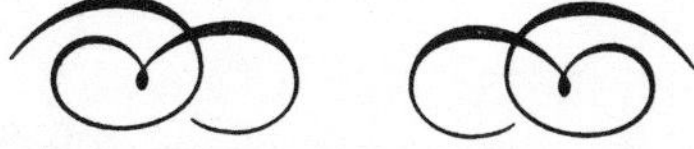

It was cool inside the elephant house after the brightness of the morning. Ravinder took Amy's hand to lead her inside.

He felt how her fingers trembled in his and he smiled to himself. Soon they would enjoy each other. What a feast that would be. He had been longing to put his hands on her since the moment they met under the tree at Government House.

But first, he had promised to show her something.

'You remember that I had to leave the party early, last night? There is the reason why. Can you see her in the darkness? I have named her Ayesha.'

He was pleased to see the look of wonder and delight on Amy's face as she peered into the stall at the baby elephant.

'Oh Ravinder. She's beautiful. I've never seen anything so sweet. Do all new-born elephants have fuzzy heads like that and smooth skins?'

He smiled and slipped his arm around her waist. 'Yes, they do. I'm glad you like her. You must come and see her again, when she has grown a little. Come, we should go now. I do not want to alarm the mother.'

Amy leant into him as they walked down the central aisle. He was conscious of the slight weight of her against his side and something inside him gave way. Pulling her into a cleaned empty stall he pushed her up against the wall and began kissing her.

She opened her mouth under his lips and he pushed his tongue inside, tasting and savouring her. His lingam was strongly erect and he pushed it against her, half-expecting her to pull away or exclaim in disgust.

She did neither. She made a little sound of eagerness in her throat and he wrapped his arms around her neck.

Ravinder wanted to show how much he could please her, teasing the responses from her body, while her sighs made music for his ears. But he was hot and ready for her now and he couldn't wait. He knew that she felt the same. So be it then. There would be time enough for gentleness later.

Moving his hands down her body, he began to lift her skirts.

Amy slid down into the clean straw with Ravinder's body half covering her own. Her topi came off and rolled into the corner, but she paid it no heed.

The tide of lust was rising within her. All she could think about was uncovering herself, so that he could push his hard cock into her body. She had thought of nothing else for hours and she knew that her quim was awash, the lips hugely swollen and her pleasure bud pushed out into an aching little knot.

She had not wanted to lie with him in a stable, but that didn't matter now. The only thing that did matter was that he did it to her.

'Yes. Oh yes . . .' she whispered, as he pushed aside the open crotch of her drawers and thrust his hand inside.

She opened her legs, shuddering as his long fingers slid up the furrow of her engorged sex. He grunted as he discovered how wet and ready she was and Amy pushed herself against his hand. His thumb was pressing on her bud, stroking and circling and she gave a little sob of wanting.

Never had she felt so desperate for easement. When he said to her, 'Uncover your breasts. Give them to me,' she tore at her blouse buttons, already anticipating the hot wet mouth that would suckle her.

She couldn't think, she could only feel, only obey him as he urged her to hold her breasts up to him. Oh God, he had pushed his fingers into her and was circling them and she was thrusting herself towards him, impaling herself on his hand. Tearing open her blouse and hearing a button pop free, she struggled to loosen the neckline of her chemise. The ribbon slackened and she cupped her breasts.

'Hold them. Yes. Squeeze them,' Ravinder murmured as he used his free hand to loosen his trousers.

Amy held her breasts up for him, pushing them together so that the nipples were side by side, her cleavage high and deep. Ravinder gave a groan and bent his head to mouth her nipples, lipping them and grazing them with his teeth. His fingers, buried inside her, thrust and pressed on the sensitive pad behind her pubic bone. The joint pleasure flowed together, became one tingling, soaring ache. Amy arched her back and climaxed, feeling her flesh convulse around his fingers.

Ravinder smiled down at her and removed his hand. She felt the hot, blunt head of his cock. He did not thrust at her, but pressed down a little so that he was collared by her puffed-up sex-lips.

'Do you want my lingam inside you?' he said, his voice harsh and breathless. 'Your yoni is tight and wet. Very wet. She weeps for love of my lingam.'

Amy lifted her legs and let them fall open. She loved the feeling of the big, ridged cock-head lodged just inside her vagina. Reaching up she placed her hands on Ravinder's smooth golden jaw and drew his mouth down to her. How she loved his lips. She wanted to have his tongue inside her mouth, to be doubly pierced by him when he entered her quim – or her yoni. She liked the way he said that.

She gave a muffled whimper when he slid smoothly into her. Her womb fluttered as Ravinder butted against it and she cried out at the visceral pleasure as he churned against her. His heavy balls brushed against her upturned buttocks and she rose to meet him, thrust for thrust.

Her tongue duelled with his and she felt straw prickling her legs and bare shoulders, but she ignored the discomfort, wholly absorbed in the strong, rhythmic plunges of his lingam. Ravinder's hands found her breasts and he palmed them, rubbing them together as he thrust hard and deep.

Amy let her head fall back and felt him mouthing her neck. He was near now, she sensed it and she too was on the brink of another orgasm.

'Tell me when you do it . . .' Ravinder groaned.

She realised that he was holding back, waiting for her to crest with him.

As he pushed into her slowly, with great control, the ripples of pleasure built to a peak.

'I'm ... spending ...' she gasped. 'Oh God. I'm doing it – now.'

With a groan Ravinder surged against her, his lingam buried inside her to the hilt. At the last moment he drew out of her and spilt himself on her petticoats. She felt the way he thrashed and grunted and was surprised by the strength of his reactions.

After a while, he propped himself on his elbow and looked at her. Stroking her cheek with one finger, he smiled.

'This was not how I imagined it for you. I apologise for the roughness of our couch.'

She laughed. 'I did not notice. My need for you was too great. All I could think of was having you inside me.'

'You're an unusual woman, Amy. Fascinating as well as beautiful. Come. Let me help you up. We'll go into my private pavilion and I'll have my women attend you. Then I'll show you that I'm not always such a brutish lover.'

'You mean ... we can do this again?'

'Why not? Don't you want to.'

Amy linked her arms around his neck. She knew now that Ravinder was her nemesis and she could no more resist him than stop breathing. Perhaps she ought not to let him know this. But it was already too late to be anything but honest. For good or ill, she was under his spell.

'There's nothing I'd rather do,' she said against his mouth.

The pavilion Ravinder spoke of was a domed building of white marble set in an expanse of lush greenery. It was placed some way from the main building of the palace and connected to it by a path made of many small glittering tiles.

Ravinder led Amy through an archway and into a spacious domed room, where women lay around on low couches, talking excitedly. Carved ivory tables held dishes of sweetmeats and hookah pipes. Amy had the feeling that she was the main topic of conversation and her fears were confirmed when all eyes turned towards her and the women fell silent.

'It is your beauty which dazzles them,' Ravinder whispered in her ear. 'The news of my interest in you has travelled fast. Do not be alarmed. They might view you as a rival for my affections, but no one will dare to risk offending you.'

Amy braved a smile, although she felt under dressed and horribly conspicuous in her skirt and blouse. The scene before her was like something out of the *Arabian Nights*, a picture book which she had loved as a child.

All the women were beautifully groomed, their hair gleaming and gold jewellery flashing from necks and wrists. They wore saris of red and orange silk or loose tunics and trousers in vivid blues and greens. Their garments were sewn with beads which shimmered as they moved.

Amy saw Madeline and tried to catch her friend's eye. Madeline was reclining on a bed which was swaying gently, little bells tinkling on its chains. She looked completely at ease and was deep in conversation with a slightly-built woman wearing red, who had her back turned to Amy.

'Come,' Ravinder said, 'I want you to meet my sister, Shalini.'

As Ravinder led Amy across the room, the soft buzz of conversation was resumed. Madeline looked up as Amy approached and smiled, but there was something odd in her expression. Then, as the slender woman in red turned, Amy saw the reason for Madeline's consternation.

She hardly heard Ravinder introducing her. Her eyes were riveted on the strikingly lovely woman who was regarding her with huge dark eyes.

Shalini was the woman she had seen Ravinder making love to in the temple.

'Will you come this way,' Shalini said to Amy when Ravinder had left the room, having promised to come to her when she had bathed and rested. 'I will entertain you and your friend in my private apartments.'

Amy flashed a quizzical look at Madeline. She was horrified by her new knowledge. It seemed that the stories about Ravinder were true. He obeyed no laws but his own. To be having sexual relations with his own sister – it was too awful. Part of her wanted to run away and never return. But she was aware that her desire for him was not diminished and her fascination was, if anything, even stronger.

When Madeline stood up and linked arms with her, Amy allowed her friend to lead her through an archway after Shalini. Shalini's ankle bracelets clashed together as she moved across the smooth marble floor. She walked with a gliding motion which was both graceful and languid.

'Madeline, wait,' Amy whispered. 'You know who this woman is?'

Madeline patted her arm. 'It is not quite what you think. Shalini is Ravinder's half-sister. They had different mothers – something which is common amongst princes. They were educated separately and lived in different areas of the palace. They never met until they were adults.'

'Even so . . . It's not right, is it?'

'Who can say? Their lives are their own. What harm are they doing? Are you revolted by the thought of Ravinder and Shalini being lovers?'

'Yes. No. I'm not sure . . .'

Madeline laughed softly. 'Look into your heart, Amy. Your British blood is colouring your judgement. Why do you care what Ravinder and Shalini do together? Is it possible that your emotions are clouded by something other than moral indignation?'

As they travelled down cool marble-lined corridors, Amy mulled over Madeline's words. Her friend was very astute. She realised that she was less censorious than jealous. Yes, that was it. She could not rid her mind of the images of Ravinder and Shalini in the temple.

A male servant pulled aside the dampened vetiver screens which hung across the doorway to Shalini's rooms. A waft of jasmine met them as they stepped inside. Amy's first impression was of fabulous colours. The walls were covered with tiles depicting extracts from Hindu myths. Huge metal containers held palms and flowering shrubs. Every surface seemed to be gilded and glowing with precious gems. More male servants moved silently through the room, passing by on some task or other.

Amy was captivated by the opulence all around. Through another archway, she glimpsed the still, greenish surface of an indoor pool. From this room, four handsome young men, dressed only in loose, white silk trousers and broad leather belts, appeared. They pressed their palms together and bowed to Shalini.

'Bring food and drink for my guests,' Shalini said imperiously. 'We will eat in my chamber. After we have taken our ease you will attend us. My guests shall benefit from your . . . singular expertise.'

Amy realised that they hadn't seen a single woman since they stepped into Shalini's private rooms. It seemed that Shalini chose to be waited on by male servants entirely. She hid her shock. But surely Shalini must have women to attend to her clothes, dress her hair, and perform the many intimate tasks which an ayah would do for a lady. It was unthinkable that men should help Shalini disrobe or worse – bathe.

Shalini seemed aware of Amy's curiosity. Her dark eyes sparkled with amusement. She turned to Amy and Madeline, flashing them a brilliant smile.

'This way, if you please.'

The octagonal chamber they stepped into was filled with a diffuse, golden-green light. The afternoon sun blazed through pierced window screens, fracturing in geometric shadows on to the green malachite floor. Brass bowls were filled with smoking incense; pungent and scented with otto of roses. There was the sound of running water. Amy saw that silver peacocks spouted jets of water into marble basins.

As she took her place on a cushioned dais, Amy felt her stomach tighten with excitement. This place was so opulent, so arousing to all her senses. The heavy perfume, the veil of blue-tinged smoke that hung low over the carved wooden tables, the exquisite gold statues of various gods and goddesses, these things were so pleasing to her.

This was the real India, mysterious and fabulous, not the watered-down anglicised version of the army cantonment.

She was aware too that it was the peerless beauty of Ravinder's half-sister which drew her fascinated gaze. Everything about Shalini, her dense dusky skin with the bloom of ripe figs; her small features; the graceful movements of her hands; the hint of promise in her words – all these things and more spoke of a deep and earthy sensuality.

Amy was finding it less incredible by the minute that Ravinder had fallen under his half-sister's spell.

'It seems that you have caught my brother's eye,' Shalini said, breaking into her thoughts. 'It is most unusual for Ravinder to invite a British woman to this house or to take her to the elephant house. Those animals are his prized possessions.'

Amy looked for any trace of malice on Shalini's face and found none. She smiled.

'Ravinder is handsome and cultured. What woman would not be charmed by him?

Shalini seemed pleased by her answer.

'Ravinder does not give his favour lightly. Take care that you value what he offers you,' she said.

And Amy had the feeling that she was being warned not to offend Ravinder. How extraordinary. Did Shalini know what they had done in the elephant house? She seemed quite amiable about sharing her brother-lover with another woman.

They conversed amiably while they ate, Madeline adding a comment now and then. Madeline and Shalini were perfectly at ease with each other. It seemed that, while she and Ravinder had been making love in the stable, Madeline and Shalini had been forming a friendship of their own.

Shalini's almond-shaped eyes often alighted on Madeline's face and her slender fingers brushed against Madeline's arm at every opportunity. Madeline seemed to be enjoying the attention. It was not surprising that Shalini found her beautiful. The Indian woman and her brother were obviously connoisseurs of lovely things.

The handsome young men moved back and forth between the women, serving them with small dishes of spicy snacks and pouring cups of thick, sweet *lassi,* flavoured with ground almonds and cardamom and topped with squares of yoghurt cream.

Amy tried not to stare at the half-naked young men, all of whom were regular-featured and well-formed. She ate with relish, hungry after the elephant ride and the energetic coupling with Ravinder.

The bold glances of the handsome servants made her feel strange. One in particular seemed unable to keep his eyes off her. It was pleasant to be admired, but the frank sexuality in his eyes made her feel uneasy and self conscious.

After the meal they relaxed against silken cushions. Shalini passed a hookah pipe around. Amy declined, but Madeline and Shalini smoked with relish. Dipping her hand into a basket, Shalini extracted something and laid it on her lap. At first Amy thought it was a piece of jewellery, then she saw that it was a green chameleon, with a tiny gold chain around its neck.

She watched fascinated as the tiny creature seemed to bleed colour as Shalini held it. Soon the chameleon was the rich, purple-brown colour of Shalini's skin. Tiring of playing with the creature, Shalini put it back in its basket. She stretched and stood up.

'It is so hot today. I'm sure that you must be uncomfortable in all those petticoats. Take off your clothes and we will swim. My servants will attend us.'

Madeline needed no urging and began stepping out of her clothes. The bodice of her khaki riding costume fell to the floor, followed by her frilled corset cover. Two of the young men appeared silently beside her and began to gather up the garments.

Amy's hands felt stiff and cold. She did not think that she could manage to undo the many small mother-of-pearl buttons on her blouse. But she found that she didn't have to. She felt hands on her as the attentive young men began loosening her belt and removing her blouse and skirt.

She felt panicky. It seemed impossible to strip in front of all these people, but she did not know how to refuse.

The other women were already half-undressed. Shalini stood in a pool of bright silk fabric. As Amy watched, a servant unfastened the back of her short bodice and drew it down her arms. Shalini's high round breasts, peaked by large wine-red nipples, bobbed into view. An underskirt of red silk was slung low on Shalini's hips, serving to emphasise the narrowness of her waist. Her navel was deep and shadowed. A dark red jewel gleamed there, suspended from a tiny ring which pierced the tender skin.

Amy coloured and lowered her eyes, shocked by the enjoyment she gained from just looking at Shalini. She felt this way about Madeline, but to a lesser degree. It was surely natural to enjoy looking at beautiful things, but Shalini affected her strangely. Shalini was so – exotic, so sexual, and unlike any woman she had ever seen before.

Perhaps part of Shalini's charm was her blood-tie with Ravinder. Amy desired Ravinder in a way that was visceral and bone-deep. She could not help but be aware that there was a reflection of that emotion in her reactions to his sister.

Tearing her eyes away from Shalini, Amy tried to calm herself. She dreaded the moment when she would stand naked beside the others, but the moment was imminent. Efficient but gentle hands drew her white blouse down over her shoulders and urged her to step out of the crumpled folds of her skirt.

She tried not to think of the way her breasts jutted over the top of her corset, the nipples barely covered by the lace on the low neckline of her chemise. Soon she was unlaced, her corset drawn free, and her chemise was lifted over her head. Stepping free of the froth of petticoats, she felt the sweetly-perfumed air caressing her bare skin.

'Take those garments to the women for repair,' Shalini said to a servant, glancing in Amy's direction.

Amy felt her face grow hot as she realised that Shalini had seen that there were buttons missing from her blouse and a slight tear on the front. Remembering how she had torn it, she felt a tingle of latent desire. Now she was sure that Shalini *did* know that Ravinder and herself had made love.

Amy caught sight of her reflection in a panel of tooled bronze. Beside the dusky darkness of Shalini and Madeline's light brown skin, her own milk-white colour seemed startling and insipid.

She felt horribly exposed. It was impossible to ignore the presence of the hovering servants. One of them in particular was raking her body with hot eyes. Shalini too was staring at her with undisguised fascination and Amy could not stop herself blushing from her toes upwards.

Shalini laughed delightedly.

'How prettily your skin changes colour. You are like my tiny chameleon. But you have no cause to feel ashamed. You are as slender as a lotus stalk, except for the rich fruits of your breasts. And the hair on your yoni is so bright. Do you dye it with saffron?'

Hardly able to believe the intimate nature of the conversation, Amy attempted to answer without stammering.

'My colouring is natural,' she said.

'How extraordinary. I can see why Ravinder is captivated by you. My brother has an eye for beauty. He could not resist this white goddess, a pillar of marble touched by the sun.'

Shalini reached out and touched Amy's shoulder, trailing her fingertips down over the length of one arm. Then she smiled and padded into the adjoining room. Her unbound hair hung down to her hips, screening her body with silky night-black tresses.

Madeline reached for Amy's hand.

'You can swim I suppose? I never asked you.'

'I used to swim in the river on our estate in Sussex.'

'Good. Follow me. I'll race you!'

She let go of Amy's hand and ran after Shalini, her full breasts bouncing up and down. Infected by Madeline's mood Amy followed. All three women dived into the pool. Surfacing first, Amy wiped water from her eyes and laughed with delight. Shalini bobbed up next to her, her hair swept back as shiny and sleek as a seal. Silver drops ran down her flawless skin.

The water felt wonderful and Amy lost all sense of self as she swam and splashed with total abandon. Even the presence of the male servants did not deter her from floating on her back, her hair streaming out behind her and the white mounds of her breasts and her pubis pushing up through the water.

After some time, Shalini swam to the side of the pool and climbed out. She walked over to one of the low wooden couches, which were set in shallow alcoves all down one wall. Immediately one of the servants stepped forward to attend her, washing her hair and pouring hot, perfumed water over her skin.

Shalini sighed and lay face down as the young man scooped a paste made of almonds and cream from a glass jar and began to massage it into her skin.

'Lie on the couch and one of my young men will see to your needs,' Shalini said to Amy as she emerged from the pool.

Madeline was having her hair washed now and there seemed to be nothing for Amy to do but follow suit. It felt strange to have a man's strong young hands on her body. But she had to admit that it felt good. The servant rubbed her hair with perfumed soap and began massaging her scalp with his fingertips. Amy relaxed under his touch.

The servant attending her was the young man who had been eyeing her with interest from the moment she set foot in Shalini's rooms. He had smooth dark hair, light brown skin, and wonderful liquid brown eyes. His lashes were as long and dark as a girl's.

'What is your name?' she asked him.

She sensed his surprise in the altered pressure against her scalp. Was she not supposed to pay any attention to servants? He hesitated before replying, then said quietly.

'Jalsa, *memsahib*.'

'You have a light touch, Jalsa,' she said.

'I am happy to serve you,' he said, his voice pleasant and with only a trace of an accent. 'I give you much more pleasure. You will see.'

Amy closed her eyes as Jalsa rinsed her hair and body, then bade her lie on her stomach. He began massaging her skin with a creamy paste, followed by a jasmine scented cream. Lulled into a trance by the rhythmic movements, Amy gave herself up to the pleasant sensations.

Jalsa moved his palms across her shoulders and down the sides of her waist. He stroked downwards over the small of her back and kneaded her buttocks. As he lifted the firm flesh and rolled it under his palms, she felt him drawing her sex upwards. As he exerted pressure downwards her buttocks parted, giving him a clear view of the shadowed valley between them.

She tried not to think of what he must be able to see, but was horribly aware that the tight pink rose of her anus was exposed and forced to gape a little each time he rolled her buttocks apart. If he squeezed and pressed lower down, at the underswell of her bottom, he would be able to glimpse her vagina as her sex-lips were pulled open by the rolling motion of his thumbs.

She sensed that each of his movements were deliberate and calculated to build the sexual tension within her. And indeed, she found herself longing for him to handle her ever more intimately.

It was possible to lie still and pretend that this was just a relaxing massage and allow the sensations to creep up on her. Jalsa was patient and did not seek to hurry her, rather he seemed set on prolonging her enjoyment.

'Does the *memsahib* wish me to proceeed?' Jalsa said, his voice soft and deferential.

'Mmmm,' she murmured, turning her cheek and resting it on the back of her hand. 'Do whatever you think necessary.'

'As you wish.'

Spreading his fingers he stroked the firm swell of her flesh, somehow palpating the skin so that tiny tremors spread right through to her belly. Amy sighed with pleasure. The almost casual, expert handling of her buttocks was very arousing. And now the subtle, referred pressure began to awaken her sex.

Each time he leant into her, pressing gently downwards, her pubis was pushed against the wood of the bench. Her sex was tightly closed, but inside its fleshy prison her bud began to swell and throb. The familiar heat and tension gathered strength and she felt herself growing moist and receptive.

At first she tried to hide the signs of her arousal, but Shalini's soft groans and Madeline's sighs told her that the other women were receiving the same treatment. Shalini seemed to have no such inhibitions at all.

Amy chanced a quick look sideways and saw that the Indian woman was arching her back and thrusting her buttocks wantonly towards her servant. The young man attending her had one hand buried between Shalini's parted thighs and was moving it back and forth.

'You like to watch while my mistress and your friend are pleasured?' Jalsa said obligingly.

Amy jumped guiltily. The denial rose to her lips, but Jalsa sounded so matter of fact, that she found herself nodding. Jalsa moved the wooden bench so that she had a clear view of the other women, both of whom seemed oblivious to anything but their own pleasure.

Shalini had turned on to her back and one of the handsome young man was pressing her knees in towards her chest. Her upturned sex looked shockingly red and swollen. She emitted a series of hoarse little grunts as a second servant dipped his fingers into a jar of sticky paste and rubbed it all over her pouting sex-lips.

Amy could see how the stickiness caused the delicate skin to drag a little as if it clung to the servants' fingers. Shalini closed her eyes in ecstasy as the servant tapped her stiffly protruding bud with the pad of one finger.

'Both of you – now,' Shalini breathed and moaned softly when one of the servants slipped two fingers inside her.

The other pinched and rolled her erect pleasure bud between finger and thumb, while slapping her upturned buttocks in a measured rhythm.

The sound of a palm hitting flesh was loud and shocking. Amy pressed her hand to her mouth to hold back a little moan of her own, as Jalsa parted her thighs and slipped his hand between her legs. Although perturbed by this new intimacy, she did not resist him. It was a relief to have his clever fingers parting her moist folds and seeking out the throbbing little pad in its hood of flesh.

Shalini's sharp cries of pleasure were a spur to Amy's aroused senses and she no longer tried to hold back. She began panting and arching her back, rubbing her pubis against the wooden couch as Jalsa slid his fingers up and down the slippery groove of her sex.

As he continued to move his hand, Jalsa knelt on the couch between her parted thighs, nudging her legs more widely apart. Amy didn't care now that the whole of her sex and parted flesh-valley were on show to him. Her one thought was her quest for release. She loved the feeling of being opened, her buttocks spread apart and the split pink plum of her sex hanging down moistly between them.

She felt the pad of Jalsa's thumb stroking across her anus and her quim trembled and pulsed. She tensed, thinking that he would penetrate that secret place, but he did not. His fingers slid inside her vagina and she gave an uncontrolled groan of pleasure. Her breasts were squashed almost flat against the wooden couch and her nipples yearned to be stimulated. She moved from side to side, rubbing the aching peaks against the smooth wood as Jalsa turned his fingers stroking her inner flesh walls and exerting a gentle pressure on her womb.

Shalini's buttocks glowed a dull dark red now. The sticky paste on her sex had liquefied and it ran down her buttocks in dark oily streaks.

'Hit me harder,' she screamed. 'That's it. I want to sting and burn. Ah . . . penetrate me more deeply . . .'

Madeline gave a little sob as the servant attending her began to slap her bottom gently. She writhed as the fingers which penetrated her were worked slickly in and out.

Amy was fast approaching a climax. Jalsa moved his fingers in and out of her and just at the moment when her pleasure crested and broke, he slapped her buttocks with his free hand. One, two, three blows crashed on to her bottom. Following on swiftly from the sharpness of pain came a tingling heat.

'Oh . . . oh . . . stop . . .' Amy whimpered, tipped over into a realm of sensation as yet unexplored.

Jalsa obeyed, running gentle fingers over the swell of her reddening bottom, his other hand still at work inside her. Amy sobbed as she came, her whole body shuddering and trembling.

After she had recovered somewhat, Jalsa completed her body massage. He was deft and efficient and there was once again the invisible barrier of mistress and servant between them. At length he said, 'Would you rise please, *memsahib*? There is refreshment in the adjoining room.'

Amy sat upright, her damp red hair cascading around her shoulders and down her back. Her skin glowed softly like a pearl. She stretched feeling completely relaxed and sated.

'Thank you, Jalsa,' she said and he flashed her a surprised grin.

'It was a pleasure to serve you, *memsahib*. I hope that I have the honour of doing so again.' With a small bow, he backed away.

Amy followed Shalini and Madeline, who were making their way back to the adjoining room. The marble floor felt cool under her bare feet. She was aware that she was swinging her hips as she walked. The massage and sexual pleasure had made her aware of every inch of her skin. She felt vital and very much a woman.

She saw that Madeline and Shalini felt the same. The two women walked side by side and, as Amy watched, Shalini slipped her arm around Madeline's waist.

The prickle of jealousy surprised Amy. Madeline was her best friend. She did not like the thought of Shalini trying to usurp Madeline's affections. Then she realised that Madeline was leaning in towards Shalini, her hand coming up to rest lightly on the curve of the other woman's hip.

The gesture was no longer simply one of friendship, it was heavy with erotic possibilities.

Gold Fever

Louisa Francis

Gold Fever was the first Black Lace book to be written by an Australian author and is set in that country. It's a fascinating and exciting story of one woman's battle with changing fortunes in the 1860s – a time when a woman's opinion counted for little. Ginny Leigh's marriage to a man much older than herself has brought her security, wealth and status, but also boredom and an unrewarding sex life. When Ginny begins to indulge in illicit pleasure, her course of desire leads her to someone who will shadow her life for longer than just a brief encounter. The following pages describe their first clandestine, but intense, tryst.

Louisa Francis has written one other Black Lace book. It is called *Desire Under Capricorn* and, like *Gold Fever,* is set in nineteenth-century Australia and follows the fortunes of a spirited young woman who refuses to conform to what is expected of her.

Gold Fever

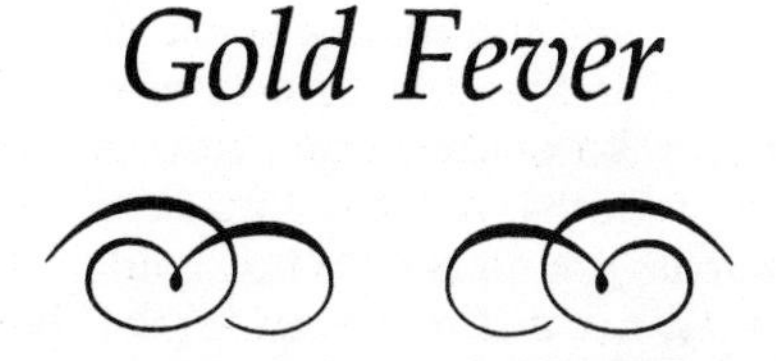

Ginny picked up the crystal goblet, sipped the golden wine, and pretended an interest in the pontifications of the elderly gentleman seated on her left. She glanced along the table taking little note of the expensive silverware, glittering crystal, fine china and delicate hothouse flowers which sat upon the perfectly starched, snowy damask cloth. From the other end her wealthy, estimable husband gave her a faint nod of smiling approval. With a barely suppressed sigh Ginny took another sip of the imported German wine and told herself she should be content.

Everleigh was one of the grandest mansions in Melbourne and its owner, William Leigh, had taken Ginny for his wife some four months earlier. His position in colonial society was of the highest standing, and Ginny's life was a pleasant succession of dinner parties, balls, theatre outings and all the other activities deemed entertaining and suitable for the elite and wealthy. She wore gowns of the latest fashion and jewels of considerable value, yet she was becoming increasingly restless and discontented.

William Leigh was an impressive figure of a man. Tall, well built, with only the slightest of paunches, his thick grey hair enhanced his distinguished features. His appearance gave the impression of a man barely fifty rather than one rapidly approaching his sixty-sixth birthday. Just six months after her arrival in the colony, Ginny had exchanged her vows with her husband, for it had taken very little time to bring him to that stage once she decided he would be able to give her everything, and she meant everything, she wanted.

Unfortunately his manly shaft did not match the rest of his splendid physique and the fact his heart, in spite of his virile appearance, was less than strong, rendered him disinclined to engage in any strenuous bedroom capers. On the few occasions he came to his wife's bed it was for a quick coupling in the dark, which left Ginny aroused and totally unsatisfied.

At least he was a kind and generous husband and if it were possible for her to take a lover, or preferably lovers, then she would find no complaints with her life. Ginny knew there were many among their acquaintances who would be only too eager to satisfy her sexual needs except, without it being in any way obvious, her husband managed to keep her under close and jealous surveillance.

The conversation at the table had drifted to politics. Totally bored by a subject about which she knew little and cared less, Ginny allowed her gaze to rove over their guests. Playing an amusing little mind game she tried to imagine how each would act in the bedroom. All of the women, she decided, were so corseted and correct they were probably, without exception, relieved if all they were forced to endure were quick copulations beneath the blankets in the dark.

Of the ten male guests, four could be deemed too old to have either interest or ability in the act and the priest could definitely be discounted. Ginny was positive no licentious thought ever crossed that pious man's mind. The doctor was too fat and she rather imagined the thin, effeminate-looking man talking to him held little interest in women. That left three.

The number conjured erotic memories of her wonderful last night aboard ship. As clearly as if it had been yesterday, she recalled how Johnny and the second officer held her legs high and wide, opening her up for the steward. She remembered how he had rubbed the head of his organ against her slit then pressed it against her until she was at the throbbing threshold of a climax. So vivid were the memories she realised she was becoming rather wet between the thighs.

'They say it will be a hot summer again, Mrs Leigh. What do you think?'

'It – I – oh yes.' Ginny brought her attention back to the table to smile at the man who addressed her. 'Oh yes, Mr James, a very hot summer indeed,' she agreed, with a direct stare of open-eyed innocence which brought a quirky smile to the corners of his mouth.

After dinner the guests adjourned to the drawing room where most soon became engaged in various card games. Seeing that her husband was thus occupied, Ginny turned to Mr James who, with the doctor, had declined to play. 'I believe you have an interest in rare books, Mr James. Perhaps you would be interested in seeing my husband's collection. You too, doctor,' she added with perfect propriety.

'No, no,' declined the doctor, 'too replete to get up.' He accepted another glass of port from a servant. 'You two go along, I don't mind.'

Walking sedately Ginny led the way out of the drawing room and down the hall to the library, her companion following silently behind. Inside she lit a single lamp and turned to smile at him. 'It is unfortunate, Mr James, but we must be quick.'

'I understand, Mrs Leigh. If you would be so good as to bend over the desk.'

Ginny obliged.

Mr James deftly lifted her skirts, spread the seam of her pantaloons and inserted his finger, not surprised to find she was already dripping wet and becoming wetter with every stroke he made.

'Oh do hurry,' Ginny begged, impatient to have a decent shaft inside her, fearful they might be discovered.

Mr James withdrew his finger, and a few moments later a gasp of pure pleasure left her lips when she felt his warm shaft slide into her pulsing sex. Oh God! It was heaven! He was big and hard, thrusting into her to stroke places which had been deprived of stimulation during all the months of her marriage. It was too much. She came quickly, violently, biting her knuckles to prevent herself from crying out loud her excitement at both her wonderful orgasm and the magnificent feel of his eager shaft sliding in and out of her long-deprived channel.

In less than ten minutes they were on their way back to the drawing room. Outside the door he paused and raised her hand to his lips. 'You have done me a great honour, Mrs Leigh. It is a pity I leave Melbourne tomorrow for I would have liked to have had the opportunity to become better acquainted.'

* * *

The greater pity, Ginny mused several weeks later, was that such brief encounters only exacerbated her dissatisfaction with her sex-starved life and heightened her longing for something more exciting. As she had done when an unawakened virgin, she resumed the habit of using her own fingers, except now she knew how to rub and stimulate herself to achieve a climax. It afforded her some relief even if it was not the same as having a man.

Thus it was she lay one afternoon resting on the *chaise longue* in her private sitting room, thinking of the dinner party they were giving that evening. Which of the guests she wondered, giving them a mental review, might be interested in being shown the library. The afternoon was hot and she was clad only in a robe, her near nakedness and erotic imaginings stimulating an awareness within her sex place. She opened her robe, fondled her breasts with one hand and positioned the other between her legs.

Resting her head back she closed her eyes, relaxed in the enjoyment she was giving herself. In no hurry to climax she stroked languidly, soothingly, almost lulling herself into a half sleep. In that state she did not hear the light knock on her door and was unaware her maid, Tessa, had entered the room until the girl spoke.

'Would you like me to help you, ma'am?'

Ginny's eyes sprang open and with a gasp she hurriedly removed her hand and attempted to close her robe. The maid, however, had already sunk to her knees and rapidly inserted her fingers in place of Ginny's. Her actions were so perfect the protest Ginny had been on the point of making was immediately forgotten. She closed her eyes again and gave herself up to the maid's expert ministrations.

Tessa removed her fingers, lifted one of Ginny's legs over the back of the *chaise longue,* spread her thighs wide, and applied her tongue in the same manner as she had applied her finger. Shivers of satisfaction ran through Ginny's body. She would never have believed she would enjoy having another woman do such things to her, but enjoy it she did. Oh, how adroitly the girl stroked, licked and tickled her clitoris.

Ginny felt the quickening deep down, the flow of warmth inside. She writhed and twisted, jerking herself against the skilful tongue until her juices seared forth in a tiny flood which the maid licked and sucked until Ginny's twitching ceased and she relaxed. The girl rose to her feet, wiped her mouth on her apron and looked down at Ginny with an insolent smirk.

'I can solve your problem, ma'am. You have need of a lover and I know my brother is eager to have you.'

Ginny had pulled herself to a sitting position and gathered her robe over her nakedness. Something in the way the maid was watching her filled her with unease. Instantly she regretted what had just taken place for she realised the girl intended to use it to whatever advantage she could.

'You are being presumptuous,' she stated, in her haughtiest voice, 'to even make such a suggestion. You will forget – completely – everything which happened in the last few minutes or you will be dismissed.'

The girl gave a slight shrug, the insolence remaining in her expression. 'Dismiss me, ma'am, and Melbourne society will have much to talk about. And you would not want the master to learn just how you show your guests the library.'

Ginny's gasp was a mixture of outrage and shock. For how long, she wondered, had the girl been spying on her? There was no doubt her threats were very real. Ginny shuddered; not only at the thought of becoming a social outcast, the laughing stock of Melbourne, but with the knowledge of how such disclosures would humiliate and hurt her good, kind husband.

'Very well – ' she sighed, 'what is it you want?'

'I want my brother to have what he desires. I will tell him to be waiting for you tonight, after the guests have left.'

It was blackmail! Straight out blackmail. Any intention of resting for the remainder of the afternoon now totally abandoned, Ginny paced her room, her emotions fluctuating between regret at what had occured, anger at her maid for taking advantage, and an uneasy fatalism. She was aware Logan wanted her, but she had never meant him to have her.

When she first laid eyes on her husband's stablehand, Ginny had known a stirring of interest. There was a certain indefinable something about his dark features, and a strange intensity in the depths of the black eyes; piercing black eyes which seemed to challenge her. A familiar quivering had shivered from Ginny's stomach to down between her legs. Quite casually she allowed the back of her hand to brush across the front of his trousers when he was assisting her to mount.

Looking down at him from the height of her horse's back, she pursed her lips in amusement at how easily he had been aroused. Then she looked into his eyes and what she saw there faded her smile. A small jolt of fear hit her stomach and she urged her horse forward, aware he stood watching her. From then it seemed he was always watching her, with a brooding sentience which stimulated her sexual awareness of him yet filled her with unease. Even though her body told her he would be able to carry her to the heights of passion she treated him with disdain. Some deep instinct told her he was a dangerous man, a man to whom she must never give in.

Now, because of a moment of weakness, it appeared Ginny had no choice but to go to him, and in spite of her chagrin the prospect induced a warm tingling reaction in the place where their bodies would be joined. But she determined she would make it very plain to Logan she was condescending to do him a favour. He would be left in no doubt she viewed him simply as the instrument of her pleasure.

It was midnight before the guests had departed and Ginny and her husband retired to their respective bedrooms. By that time she was in a state of highly aroused anticipation. With only a robe to cover her nakedness she crept cautiously downstairs. True to her word, Tessa was waiting to open the back door for her, though Ginny did not like the way she said, 'I will be here to let you back in when Logan has finished with you.'

Then Ginny was outside in the cool night air. The blue light of a full moon enabled her to easily see her way to cross the yard to the stables. A steep, external flight of stairs led to Logan's quarters above, and Ginny's legs were trembling almost too much to carry her to the top. The door was opened just as she reached the landing, and Logan stood staring at her with a dark brooding expression.

'So you came,' he said and drew her into the room, shutting the door behind her.

Ginny glanced curiously around. There was not much furniture in the room. A chest of drawers, a small table and chair, a washstand and narrow iron bed. That was all she had time to notice.

Logan twisted one hand cruelly in her hair and pulled her to him. His mouth closed savagely over hers, possessing rather than kissing. The other hand gripped her buttocks to press her hard against his body, against the rigid evidence of how much he wanted her. The brutality of his actions angered Ginny and she began to struggle; a futile effort which only caused her greater discomfort when the hand in her hair twisted the strands more savagely.

'You have played with me long enough,' he said. 'Now it is my turn. I am going to watch you squirm and make you beg.' He released her and stepped back. 'Take off your robe, I want to see you naked.'

A little frightened by the cold deliberation of his words and hint of malice in his voice, Ginny did as she was told. With his eyes narrowed to black slits, Logan exhaled his breath through his teeth in a slight whistle. 'By God, you are something. You have a body designed to drive men wild, but you know that, don't you?' He was walking slowly around her, inspecting her from every angle. Ginny could almost feel his gaze caressing the most intimate parts of her body. Certainly she felt the dampness between her legs.

When he again stood in front of her he reached his hands to her breasts and began to fondle them. Ginny sucked in her breath. It felt good, so good. His hands were instruments of exquisite pleasure as they kneaded, squeezed and rolled her breasts. The pads of his thumbs stroked delicate circles over her hardened nipples. With a soft moan Ginny closed her eyes and gave herself up to the marvellous sensuality. Gradually the pressure increased and pleasure metamorphosed into pain. She opened her eyes with a cry of protest when her nipples were viciously pinched, and saw he was watching her with his lips thinned in a sadistic smile.

'You bastard,' she spat, and turned to pick up her robe. There was no way she was going to tolerate being hurt.

His movement was quicker; he grabbed her and threw her backwards on the bed, kneeling astride her to prevent her escaping. When he drew some rope from his pocket, Ginny realised his intention and cried out in protest, swearing at him, as she twisted and turned in an endeavour to free her body.

Her futile efforts appeared only to amuse him and with slow, deliberate movements he tied both her wrists to the bedhead. His mouth remained thinned in the same hard line and there was a gleam of cruelty in the jet black of his eyes. Ignoring the oaths she screamed at him, he stood up to shed his shirt and trousers.

Ginny ceased her struggles to look at him. Her mouth went so dry she found it necessary to wet her lips with her tongue. He was impressive to look at – God no – he was beautiful. The darkness of his skin enhanced the sinewy muscularity of his body. His hips were slim, his legs long, and where they met, his rampant manhood drew her admiring gaze. Her insides lurched and she experienced a sharp stab of longing between her thighs. To hell with the fact he had her tied to the bed, she wanted him to take her, wanted his magnificent shaft thrust deep inside her.

Then he straddled her chest so that the proud organ was close to her face. She raised her eyes in question only to be captured by the mesmeric intensity in his. Placing both hands behind her head he pulled her forward. 'Suck me,' he ordered, thrusting his shaft into her mouth before she could object.

He worked her backwards and forwards, encouraging her to slide her mouth up and down his shaft. Realising he was doing this to prove his domination, Ginny rebelled and brought her teeth sharply down.

Her triumph at his cry of pain was short-lived. A vicious slap across the face knocked her sideways and she recoiled beneath the black malignancy of his expression. He wrenched her legs apart and jabbed two fingers inside her. Ginny cried her protest at the manner in which they pushed, twisted, tweaked and pinched her, then gasped because they were inflicting just sufficient pain to stimulate her nerve ends and stoke the flames of desire. Relentlessly they worked to bring her burningly close to an orgasm. His fingers were removed.

There was nothing.

Her nerve ends were screaming; she was hanging on the edge of a chasm – and he simply sat there watching her. On the verge of begging him to give her release she recalled his words and clamped her mouth shut. The glint of battle entered her eyes. There was no way she was going to give him that satisfaction.

A grim smile twisted his lips in acknowledgement of her silent challenge. Her eyes were telling him that no matter what he did he would never hear her beg. He leant forward to mould and squeeze her breasts again. His head came down and he suckled first one breast then the other, sucking up and dragging the nipple through his teeth with just enough pressure to hurt, then gentling the aching tip with his lips.

The eroticism was too much. Ginny moaned and lifted her hips upwards, twisting and gyrating them to indicate her readiness to have him inside her.

Again he sat back – and waited. Ginny almost screamed in frustration. She knew exactly what he was doing. Quite sadistically and deliberately he was drawing her to the very edge of an orgasm then removing the stimulation to watch her writhe.

'Bastard!' she swore at him.

He shrugged his shoulders as if it was no concern how many names she called him. Going across to the table he picked up a bottle and poured some type of strong spirit into a mug. Returning to the bed he lifted her head, held the mug against her lips, and commanded her to drink. Ginny was forced to swallow, gasping and choking on the fiery liquid. Whatever it was it sent a sensual warmth flooding through her veins. A warmth heightened by the light caress of his fingers as they trailed over her body, teasing her nipples before carving a sensuous path over the flat of her stomach, down between her legs then back up again. It was a butterfly touch, so light, yet so, so – dear God! She was nearly ready again.

Logan walked back across the room, drank the remaining spirit in the mug and watched her with that darkly mesmeric, taunting gaze which was sapping her will. Angrily she closed her eyes to break the spell and turned her head away, twisting on her side and pressing her legs together to ease the terrible ache in the core of her being.

Her thighs were pulled open, spread wide apart. His fingers parted her sex lips to give his tongue easy access. It was an exquisite tease. It licked and darted, tickled her special spot, worked quickly then slowly, then quickly again, driving her into a crying, gasping frenzy. Surely this time.

But it was not so. For the third time he deprived her. Her plea was uttered with a sob. 'Do it, damn you, do it.'

He eyed her with mocking satisfaction. 'Are you begging me?'

'Yes, you bastard,' Ginny cried, the tears spilling down her cheeks, 'I'm begging.'

He straddled her; rammed hard into her, each controlled, forceful thrust banging into the very depths of her. She came immediately, the release more violent for having been so long denied. Her tears flowed rapidly, precipitated by the exquisite, searing agony of her orgasm. She felt as though she was in some strange netherworld. There was no reality except for the magnificence of Logan moving within her and the warm surge of love juices which spilled in crashing waves from her body.

When he pulled away she was bereft, crying a protest. He lay down beside her, lifted her leg over his hip, re-entered her, so she again felt complete. From that position, somewhere between the side and the back, he worked her expertly, reaching over her body to finger her clitoris at the same time. Ginny burned from the fires flaring within, cried his name, 'Logan! Logan!' and he increased the rapidity of movement both with his shaft and his finger to bring her to a second climax.

Again he withdrew. Realising he still had not come she marvelled at his supreme control. This time he untied her wrists, rolled her on to her stomach and, lifting her hips, drew them back towards the edge of the bed so that her knees were bent under her and her face was down on the mattress.

Standing next to the bed he thrust into her from behind, viciously pinching her buttocks at the same time. He thrust and pinched again and again, the pain which made Ginny flinch increasing her awareness of the hard organ that was pleasuring her. Then he held her by the hips and, remaining perfectly motionless, moved them in circular fashion, rotating her love tunnel around his shaft.

Even though Ginny understood the manner of his handling was intended to underline his assertion she was simply a tool for his pleasure, her own enjoyment was indescribable. Every nerve in her body was vibrantly alive. Dear God! It was superlative. She was coming again! At that moment he pulled her buttocks back hard against his body and began slamming vigorously in and out, his movements increasing in speed and force. With his name a sob on her lips she felt the rush of his fluid and knew, that time, he too had climaxed.

But even then he was not finished. He turned her on to her back, pushing and twisting his shaft inside her until it finally began to relax. Dormant within her he kissed her savagely on the mouth. When he lifted his head, his dark eyes gleamed down at her. 'This is how it will always be, Ginny. You are mine now and will always be mine to have as I will. Every time I want you, any time I want you, you will come to me. And you will come', he assured her, 'because your body will know it can not be otherwise.'

Ginny was too distraught – and too sore – to get out of bed the next day. Upset and confused by the way her mind and body conflicted with each other, she dreaded the coming night. If he intended to use her in such a manner every night her body would soon be worn out. Yet just thinking of him set her afire with remembrance of the heavenly heights – or was it hellish depths – to which he had taken her.

He did not send for her that night, nor for the next week. Although initially relieved, Ginny soon began to wonder why. With a little flare of triumph she hoped he had discarded his threat to use her as he would; then she despaired that it might be so. The need within her was like a creeping malaise, increasing with each night she was left to ache and toss alone.

If Logan had changed his mind so had she. Ginny wanted him, more than she had ever wanted any man before. Inventing whatever excuses she could for going to the stables, she suffered the chagrin and humiliation of having him ignore her presence, while the cynical twist to his mouth told her he was well aware of her reason for being there.

When his summons did come, anger consumed her. With heightened colour and flaming eyes she informed Tessa she could tell her brother to go to the devil – if the devil was willing to take him. But the hours of darkness slowly wove their spell. At midnight, convinced Logan was the very devil himself, she took her throbbing, eager body to his room.

Logan was a master in the art of sadistic pleasure. The skilfully inflicted pain heightened her sexual arousal, drove her into a frenzy of desire. He used her, abused her, and his powerful shaft carried her away to hitherto unknown realms of erotism. She was enslaved. Her body belonged to him in a way it could never belong to any other man. The enormity of her need frightened her more than the power he wielded. It was as if he held her in a thrall from which she was unable to break.

Tessa held her with blackmail. Ginny was forced to part with both money and jewellery to ensure Melbourne society did not learn the truth about Mrs William Leigh.

* * *

Three months passed in that manner. Three months during which she felt as if she was two different people. One was the charming social beauty, wife of William Leigh. The other belonged to Logan, became whole only when her body was joined with his. How easy it was to believe his declaration she had belonged to him in a previous life, that she would belong to him again in the next. She did not love him, she was closer to hating him, but he was a part of her and she of him. In an endeavour to regain some control of her life, Ginny determined she would, for once, decide when and where she would give herself to Logan.

Everleigh was set in several acres of parkland which blended into the virgin bush that clothed the foothills of the ranges. One of Ginny's greatest enjoyments was the rides she took into that bush; rides on which she was always accompanied by the elderly groom for her husband felt even that activity to be too strenuous for his heart. On her chosen day she contrived for it to be Logan who was her escort.

They rode beyond the parkland and up into the foothills with Ginny leading the way. When they reached a grassy clearing beside a tiny moss-lined stream she called a halt. She announced her intention of remaining there awhile, dismounted, and ordered Logan to secure the horses. By the time he had done so she had discarded her hat and gloves and was in the process of removing her riding habit.

His dark eyes observed her actions yet he said nothing. With a haughty tilt of her chin she demanded that he undress. 'For once you will do what I want and I want you now.' When he did nothing except stand staring at her with a cynical twist to his lips she lost her temper and struck him across the cheek with the leather strap of her riding crop. Although he flinched and his eyes smouldered with rage he did not even lift a hand to the reddening welt. Using deliberate movements he began to unbutton his shirt. A triumphant smile curving her own lips, Ginny continued to undress. Naked, they stood facing each other.

'Touch me,' she ordered, taking his hand to guide it between her legs, exhaling a deep breath when he slipped a finger inside her and began to leisurely stroke and caress. Dear Lord, but he was incomparable; knew just when to cease pushing in and out; when to begin stroking her externally; how much stimulation her special spot could take. Her nerves tingled. She felt wet, warm and so wonderfully aroused she was becoming weak-kneed from pleasure. It became necessary for her to clasp his shoulders to keep herself upright. Her voice came as a husky plea. 'I want you to suck me, to lick me and suck me until I come.'

He removed his finger, pulled away from her, and stared at her with cold black eyes. 'And if I refuse?'

She hit him hard across the chest with the riding crop. His breath sucked in with the pain and something menacing flared in his eyes again. 'I see,' was all he said.

'I'm glad you do.' Ginny lay down on her discarded clothing, bent her knees, and spread them wide in readiness. Her complacency vanished when Logan bent forward, grasped her knees and pulled sharply upwards. In that position he held her, upside down, with only her head and shoulders on the ground.

His mouth lunged at her moist sex lips, nibbling and sucking hard. When his tongue began to lick back and forth between her folds Ginny stretched herself up towards him, thrilled by the shameful display of her inverted position. With her hips so raised and her sex place opened wide to him she was doubly sensitive. She wriggled her hips, pushing her slit against his tongue, crying out her delight when the fiery quickening told her she was about to come.

Her legs were dropped. At first she was startled then, believing he intended to mount her so she could climax with his shaft inside her, she spread her legs and smiled eagerly up at him. She did not care how he gave her the ultimate satisfaction, as long as he did. To her utter astonishment he turned away and picked up his shirt. Ginny shot to a sitting position. 'What are you doing?'

'Getting dressed. You thought you could force me to your will, but you cannot. I give you your pleasure only when, and if, I am prepared to give it to you.'

'You bastard,' Ginny cried, scrambling to her feet and going for him with the riding crop raised in her hand.

This time he caught her wrist and twisted the crop out of her grasp. Keeping both her wrists captured in the vice-like grip of one hand he hit her sharply across the buttocks with the leather strap; a stinging slap which brought tears to her eyes. Then he turned the crop in his hand and pushed it down between her legs to rub the rounded heel of the metal head against her sex.

At the cold touch of metal Ginny gasped, then moaned, the carnal contact making her sag at the knees.

'Are you ready to beg?' Logan asked.

Ginny raised her eyes and stared defiantly into his cruel black ones. He twisted the crop and she felt the hammer head push inside her. 'Beg,' he ordered, circling the head of the crop inside her with the shaft tilted so that it pressed against her clitoris and seared her with sexual fire. 'Beg me, Ginny.'

'God damn you! I hate you, Logan,' panted Ginny, going almost wild from the immensely erotic experience of being invaded and stroked by cold metal instead of warm flesh.

He pushed her away, down on to all fours, dropped to his knees behind her and pulled her back on to his shaft. At her cry of fulfilment he gave a cruel laugh. 'Is this what you wanted me to do, Ginny?' he asked, easing back and slamming savagely into her. 'And this?' reaching around her body to roll and squeeze her nipples with a measured brutality, which inflamed her already vibrant response to his deeply embedded shaft.

When he clasped her hips to rotate her around that shaft, she almost swooned from the sheer intensity of sensation. Taking control she moved her hips herself, grinding over him, wanting more and more. The stinging slap on her buttocks made her jerk. With one hand grasping her hips, he forced her to continue her movements; slapped her repeatedly with the other hand; pushed and worked his shaft to the depths of her gyrating sex.

Sobbing his name and panting her need, she jerked at every stinging slap, grinding frantically against him. He bent over her, kneading her breasts. When a finger moved down to stroke her clitoris Ginny cried out in wild delight, working herself feverishly over him to induce waves and waves of rapture.

Then he lifted her away and rolled her on to her back. Still kneeling he raised her hips and plunged into her. 'You see, Ginny,' he said, 'you must always do what I want you to do.' And he slammed vigorously in and out of her until he achieved his climax.

That he should order her to come to him that night surprised her, for he derived sadistic pleasure from leaving her alone until she was going almost mad from need of him. Sore and bruised from the things he had done to her that afternoon, she obeyed his command. And, although she swore at him and told him how much she hated him she was aroused by his delicate torture.

Frenzied with desire, she begged him to fill her with all his hard muscle and make her complete.

Just one week later William Leigh sat down at his dining table, clutched frantically at his chest, and died.

La Basquaise

Angel Strand

The scene is 1920s Biarritz. Oruela is a modern young woman who desires the company of artists, hedonists and intellectuals. Jean is her seemingly devoted lover who will help her realise her wildest dreams. Jean keeps some shady company, however, and the following extract finds him at Madame Rosa's salon about to purchase a most unusual gift for the discerning Oruela. But all is not well. Oruela's complicated home life is about to take an unexpected turn. Very soon, both their lives will be thrown into turmoil as Oruela is accused of a serious crime.

Angel Strand is an original writer of erotic fiction whose surreal imagery lends a unique quality to her work. Her one other Black Lace novel, *The Big Class,* follows the fortunes of an Anglo-Italian woman who finds love is a tricky business in a climate of impending war.

La Basquaise

'*Attention, s'il vous plaît!*' Madame Rosa had a voice that was rich, throaty and created for talking dirty. She moved like a liner coming into port, her dress floating around her in a rosy pink wash.

The salon of La Maison Rose grew quiet. There were about fifteen well-heeled men in the room attended by beautiful, semi-naked women who came to rest like butterflies on laps, on cushions, on the thread-flowers of the whorehouse chintz.

A couple of young men sitting on the soft green velvet couch exchanged a conspiratorial smile. Jean Raffoler was twenty-four and in the peak of masculine health. He had long, dark, curly hair and light brown skin. His body was big and strong under expensively-cut evening clothes. He had loosened his black tie and he sat with his legs apart, confidently.

Paul Phare was in his early thirties and had a rebellious lock of sandy blond hair that wandered into his smoky green eyes. He was in his shirt sleeves, his cravat was awry and a day's growth of beard showed on his fine chin. A young woman in a chemise sat on the floor at Paul's feet, resting her head on his long, lazily crossed legs. He stroked her curly ginger hair with a tender, masculine hand.

'The moment for which you have been waiting has come,' trilled Rosa. 'My dear baron has returned from his travels at long last, from the far-flung corners of the world, and he has brought with him some very charming erotica.'

She sailed across the room, a pair of naked young males

bobbing in her wake, and stopped in front of red velvet curtains. She nodded to the boys. They clasped the curtains and drew them back. In the small room beyond stood a squat male figure carved out of opaque yellow stone. Its *pièce de résistance* was a huge, erect phallus, the head of which gleamed softly in the light from two thick, long beeswax candles.

The baron stepped out from the shadows. He was squat too and he glowed with perspiration. His smile was accentuated by a long scar on one pale cheek and seemed to spread to his ear. He flicked his pudgy fingers at the boys and they each lit a flame from the candles. They fired a pair of silver incense burners with movements graceful as swans. The room began to fill with plumes of heady scent.

'Gentlemen,' said the baron. 'The following performance is based on a rite over five thousand years old. This figure was found in the tomb of a queen. Around the walls of the tomb paintings depicted the dance that you are about to witness. It is re-created faithfully and lovingly for your enjoyment by a descendant of this ancient and beautiful queen.'

The boys began a soft roll on little drums as a tall, black girl, her hair cropped closely to her head, writhed out from behind the curtains. She wore nothing but charms and shells and beautiful bells. Every graceful movement she made was accompanied by the music of trinkets. From her earlobes hung huge silver hoops bearing little bells in their centres. Round her neck and clicking between her handsome breasts were hundreds of glass beads. At her waist a thousand tiny sparkling gems made a fine girdle and around her left thigh some kind of reptile had given his skin for a thong.

She shimmied, rooted to the spot like a tree in a breeze, stretching her arms up as if to the goddess of the dance. The men in the room grew still. When she could feel the whole room in her power she began to move.

Slowly she gyrated her hips, in half-moon shapes, to the drums. Her hands cut through the air like the blades of knives. She parted them at her navel and rested them on her thighs and then, suddenly, she thrust her hips forward, opened her legs and showed off her best jewel. The movement was like that of a magician who shows off the beautiful girl he is about to saw in half. Her sex was beautiful. A mature rose. Someone in the audience growled with desire.

She turned her back on them and mounted the dais, taking some oil on her fingertips from a silver tray as she went. Slowly she oiled the head of the huge phallus. As she worked she spoke in some unknown language and her words became a strange, lilting song that twisted around the room like a rope.

The men were spellbound as she violated the statue, her body glistening with the exertion, her strong thighs rippling as her movements up and down the phallus gathered momentum. She built up to a crescendo and climaxed with a wild call that silenced the catcalls of the loutish element in the crowd, piercing everyone to the core.

Paul Phare reached for a cloak that was behind him and with one adept movement he covered himself and the girl who rose from the floor into his arms.

Jean Raffoler sat still as a bird entranced by a cobra.

But the show was not over. The baron was announcing in his thin weedy voice that the girl would tell them a story. Hardly two minutes passed before she re-entered the room and, sitting in a big red plush wing chair, she began:

'My people,' she said in accented French, 'believe that if a marriage is not right then it will bring misfortune on the whole people. So the ancient ritual of the lizard is always observed. On the Day of the Marriages a very special lizard is pressed into service by each couple who wants to be married. It will take the first juices from the man's penis and take them into the woman's vagina. If the lizard refuses at any stage in the ritual it is taken as a sign that the couple must not marry. No one has ever dared go against the rule because to do so would mean living as an outcast.

'To guard against the chances of a refusal, each spring the young women who want to, go with more experienced women to the high ground where this lizard has his habitat. Once there they set about capturing and training as many as they need.

'The young women are shown how to hunt down the creatures by way of calls and beautiful songs. They beat the ground, make thunder with their fists until the lizards are drawn, compulsively, to the camp. Then the women decorate their bodies. They paint circles around each others' nipples with the juice of many different and beautiful coloured berries, till the nipples seem so huge that they almost cover the whole breast. Then they plait soft hair from female animals into their own pubic hairs and bead it so that it falls around their thighs. They make the lips of their vulvae red with the leaves of a sacred plant and paint a great area around in beautiful colours, so that the whole sex seems to reach out across their thighs. Lastly, their eyes and their lips are adorned with the brightest colours in nature and they drench themselves in the perfumes of the orange flower, jonquil and jessamine.

'At length they dance. They dance morning, noon and night; wild, sensual dances that become more and more frenzied until it seems that the camp is filled with huge nipples and whirling vaginas.

'The lizards grow mad with what they see and smell and hear and many of them die in the rush into captivity. But the dances don't end until the women are exhausted. And then they sleep where they drop. Their colours smear and run in a crazy mess and everyone revels in it.

'When enough lizards are captured we gather roots that are shaped like the male organ; mandrakes they're called in Europe. It's easy to train the lizard to lick the root because if his reward is to snuggle between the legs of a woman, this animal will do anything.

'Within seven or eight days each woman will have her own, trained lizard. She decorates him with precious stones and gems. She carves pieces out of his very thick skin and embeds her mother's own jewels that are handed down, right into it. The skin grows back to hold the gems in place. The lizards have short lives. They live while the marriage is young and produces children – and then they die. We keep their skeletons and use them as charms to bring our lovers to our beds.'

'See,' said the baron, stepping forward. He grinned as he held out his podgy palm. In the middle of it sat a tiny white skeleton. 'There were no more female children in this family and I was given it by an ancient who knew she was near to death. I paid handsomely for it.'

With the story at its end the dancer rose and, virtually unnoticed, she left the room. Virtually, but not completely. Jean rose and followed her.

Evidently he was not successful. He came back into the salon a moment later. He approached the group talking with the baron and hovered. A butterfly, with straps falling off her rounded, peachy shoulders, came up to him and entwined her fingers lovingly in his long, curly hair. But he brushed her off gently. Finally he butted in.

'I'd like to talk to the dancer,' he said to the baron.

The baron performed an obsequious little bow. 'I'm sorry, monsieur, but she is mine.'

'I sincerely beg your pardon. But I really do just want to talk to her,' said Jean firmly.

The baron touched him on the arm. 'But everything has its price, monsieur.'

A note of distaste crept into Jean's voice. 'Let me be clear. It is the lizard that interests me. Might I be able to buy one? A live one?'

The baron drew in a breath between his teeth, making a hiss like a plumber. 'Well, I don't know,' he said. He stroked his chin.

'Everything has its price?' mocked Jean.

'It may be arranged,' smiled the baron. 'Your name, monsieur. I should like to know with whom I am dealing.'

'An unusual request, monsieur, in such a place. If you want credentials, I suggest you speak to Rosa. She knows me well and knows that I have money enough.'

'No, monsieur, you don't understand. Your name would be, how shall I say, a gesture.' He grinned. 'I am very discreet.'

'Impossible. Either speak to Rosa or I'm afraid . . .' said Jean.

'Very well,' said the baron.

When Jean returned to the green velvet couch Paul was stroking the chin of his girl.

'You have the jawline of a goddess,' Paul was saying.

'Oh, you!' she giggled. 'You bloody artists are all the same. Goddesses, mices.'

'Muses, darling, muses,' said Paul.

'Whatever they are, I'm a real woman and I want you upstairs where I can fuck you.'

Paul threw back his head and laughed. 'Sounds wonderful but you'd better not let Rosa hear that. I can't afford you.' He turned to Jean. 'Can he get it?'

Jean sneered. 'He's a cad. He tried to sell me his girl.'

But their conversation was cut short. Rosa was bearing down on them, observing Paul with open hostility. Paul rose from the couch. He was tall, slender. He picked up his cloak. He had pushed his luck by staying for the baron's presentation. Rosa let him spend his afternoons taking photographs of the girls and didn't charge him for their time. At present he was experimenting with movement. The girls seemed to enjoy themselves rolling around on the Persian rug while he captured them on film. He did it with love and, of all the people he knew, they were the only ones who seemed to believe there was something fine in what he was doing. They dreamt together that the pictures would hang in Paris galleries and capture the attention of the whole world. Besides, he always gave them proper portraits if they wanted them and some of these sold on the seafront as postcards. Perhaps Rosa resented the fact that this money all went to the girls, without a cut for her.

Jean asked him to stay, but he refused. 'I want to develop some work,' he said.

Rosa brushed the seat he had vacated before she sat on it. 'Now, Jean, tell me everything, dear,' she said.

'I want one of those lizards.'

'Well, you know the baron's a crook, dear. I wouldn't trust him as far as I could throw him. But, as I always say, if you want something badly enough in this world, you have to take risks.'

'Rosa, come on. You know I can't get my family name mixed up in anything dubious.'

'I know, I know. What is it you have in mind? You want me to act as a go-between? For a small consideration, dear, I shall be pleased to. That will sort things out nicely, won't it? And then even if he cuts up rough I would deny any involvement on your part.'

'Thank you, Rosa!' said Jean eagerly.

'I can't guarantee your money, my love, but your reputation is safe, and that of whoever you want to share your little whim with.' Rosa's eyes twinkled and her gaze strayed to his well-formed thigh. 'Now let me send one of the girls over to soothe away your worries while I deal with the baron. Can't have any of my gentlemen solitary now, can I?'

'Send me Annette,' said Jean, stretching his arms.

'Here you are, dear,' said the tiny, red-haired, haberdasher. She took a key from under the counter and gave it to Oruela Bruyere with a wistful little smile. 'You are a lovely girl, my dear. A lovely, sad girl.'

'I don't know what you mean. I'm not sad,' said Oruela. She

was feeling wonderful. Every cell in her body was looking forward to the touch of love.

'Mmmm,' said the little woman, wistfully.

Oruela went up the concealed staircase that rose secretly from the midst of silks and stockings. What a funny woman, she thought. The haberdasher was the aunt of her maid, Michelle, who said she was as good as a mother. Oruela had opened up to her a bit once and ever since, the woman had seemed to pity her. It was ridiculous.

The stairs continued up past one landing and a long narrow window that looked out seawards across the rooftops opposite. She came to a halt at the very top in front of a door and put the key in the lock. The door opened into an apartment in the roof.

She dropped her green kidskin purse and a pair of driving goggles on a glass-topped side table. A small glass-fronted stove in the fireplace heated the room against the unusually chilly spring day. That was thoughtful, she thought.

Heavy velvet curtains were tied back from the face of the small window. The room was never particularly light, even in the afternoon. She turned on a single standard lamp in the corner.

She removed her green gloves and then, carefully, a cream leather hat. She had flawless olive skin and soft brown eyes. Her glossy crown of deep brown, almost black hair fell into place. It was shingled at the back and swept behind her ears. She smoothed it in the mirror. Her figure was slender and she was tall. Her stylish driving coat of pale cream raw silk was buttoned diagonally from hem to shoulder and trimmed with creamy fur. She bent down to the hem where the fur caressed her pale, stockinged legs and slipped the first button free. One by one she widened the aperture as if rehearsing a scene. Underneath, her dress was a sumptuous hand-made peach mousseline. She tossed the coat on a chair as if it were no more than a bath towel.

A single string of pearls hung at her neck and cascaded over her breast to her waist. Following the fashion, the bodice of her dress was cut to disguise the curve of her waist and it fell straight to her hips where a sash was loosely tied. Her thighs suggested themselves to the eye as long and shapely; certainly, if her calves were anything to go by, her legs were a real asset. Her shoes were creamy, with kitten heels and a satin strap at the front.

She left the mirror and walked into the bedroom. The room was windowless. The only light was from a small skylight. Its patch of blue was turning misty violet as the evening drew in. Beside the big bed was a lamp made from the carved figure of a naked, plump cupid, his hands reaching up to hold the bulb. She turned him on and the soft light that filtered through the fringed shade shed itself on the sea-green counterpane. A fire burned in the small grate. She warmed her hands by it and the firelight leapt about her face and body. A secret smile danced in her eyes.

Back in the sitting-room, she took a bottle of cognac from a low cabinet next to the table. She poured herself one and, glass in hand, she nestled into the big sofa, her legs underneath her, a hint of lace peeking from under the hem of her dress. She seemed to survey the tall palm standing in a pot in the opposite corner of the room. The door of the bedroom behind her stood slightly ajar.

She was too young to marry. That was the excuse she was currently giving her guardian who acted like he was fending off suitors left, right and centre. There had been two, as far as she could gather. She found the whole business of them asking *him* ridiculous. For the moment at least the excuse seemed acceptable, but she was on shaky ground. Apart from the fact that she was pushing twenty-five and wasn't anything like too young, although she felt it, her girlfriends were marrying all around her. There was a whole rash of weddings to be attended this spring.

Her friends were very practical. Of course they would take lovers, they said. Marriage was the only freedom that a girl could get. This wasn't Paris and even though Biarritz had its fashionable visitors, a single girl just didn't have the chance to explore love. Marriage therefore was a business arrangement, best got over with so that fun could start.

The truth was that Oruela wanted something different, something more. She didn't exactly know what, but she wanted to explore life. If she married it would be for love. Her guardians' marriage was like that of two stuffed dummies. Horrible! She would have something better. Besides, she had another, secret ambition which had nothing to do with marriage. She wanted to go to Paris, to the Sorbonne.

She didn't really have an academic mind but she had a romantic one and she had a vision of herself at Henri Bergson's philosophical classes, being noticed by artists and intellectuals for her beauty and brilliance. She hadn't articulated her brilliance yet but it was there, in embryo. She had a kind of confidence in it, even if others only described her as wilful.

The sound of a key turning in the lock shook her from her reverie. In whirled Jean looking more decidedly handsome and more in love than ever.

He immediately rushed to Oruela's knees and covered her hands with kisses. She laughed and pushed his chilly outside clothes away. He jumped up and unbuttoned his overcoat, flinging it on the chair and his hat flying after it.

'Oruela, Oruela!' he moaned.

This time she made no attempt to push him away. She stroked his long glossy hair and kissed his nose.

He touched her face and sighed; he ran his finger down her neck and sighed; he cupped her lovely shoulder in his hand, sighing all the while. 'I have something for you, my darling! Something so special you will hardly believe it! I wanted you to have this as soon as I heard about it. It's taken a whole year to get!' He reached for a package wrapped in brown paper, placed it in Oruela's lap, and fixed his eyes on her face.

'How was Paris?' she asked, not quite nonchalantly.

'Paris? Open your present!'

'I shan't until you tell me at least one word about Paris,' she said.

Jean laughed. 'Paris was Paris! It was beautiful! It was busy! Open your present.'

'Did it come from Paris?'

'It came *via* Paris,' he said enigmatically.

'It's got little holes in it . . .' She began unwrapping the parcel, under Jean's adoring gaze.

The tiny, ornate silver cage that emerged contained a greenish lizard. She couldn't help but shriek. The lizard stilled itself completely, trying to merge into the grass that lined the floor of its dwelling. But the ruby embedded in its forehead, and the cluster of sapphires at its neck shone and sparkled in the twin suns of the lamp and the firelight, preventing its camouflage tactics.

Jean laughed. 'Don't be frightened.' He got up and refilled her brandy glass, pouring a generous measure of the delicious amber liquid for himself.

Together they sat in the gathering twilight and he told her the story he had heard about the lizard's role in life at La Maison Rose.

Oruela found herself aroused by the thought of the women decorating their bodies, and by the dancing. 'Do you mean you think we ... What if he refuses? I haven't trained him!' she whispered, barely trusting herself to speak.

'Oruela, my darling, don't be silly. We don't need to bother with the meaning of the thing. It's an adventure. Besides, why should he? We're perfect for each other.'

'Should we ... should we do it?' she asked again.

'Do you want to?' he asked.

She could only nod her head. Her voice was too heavy with wicked excitement to speak.

Jean kissed the rustling fabric at her breast and her skin responded to the touch of him, gradually pushing away thoughts that had no place in this moment. The silence was broken only by the crackle of the coals in the fire. The lizard moved and sent ripples into her lap.

'My darling!' crooned Jean. 'Nothing will part us, I swear,' and he raised her chin gently.

She looked at him. I could be happy with him, she thought, I could really ...

'What do you say?' he whispered.

A wicked grin suddenly lit up her face. 'What the hell! If he refuses, he refuses! There are plenty more where you came from!'

'Minx!' cried Jean, gripping her arm.

She wriggled herself free, sending the little lizard's cage rolling on to the couch as she climbed on top of Jean. The lizard darted furiously about in his cage as she slid the delicate fabric of her dress up her thighs, showing off the tops of pale silk stockings. Jean grew hard as she pushed her sex at him. He laughed, a little nervously.

She straightened her back, pushing out her breasts. They ached for kisses and the feel of his lips was heaven. His hands were strong and his touch a little rough. She pulled his hair gently as he slid her dress further up her body. Her knickers were mere wisps of silk that were tied on the inner leg with tiny ribbons. His fingers searched her sex through the fabric, rolling her swollen labia. She covered his face and hair with soft crooning kisses.

Jean rose, carrying her with him. He kicked open the bedroom door. The lamp sent wriggling shadows dancing over their bodies as they fell into the soft pillows.

'Turn over,' begged Jean. 'Let me undo your buttons.'

She rolled slowly over and lay still, sinking into the darkness as his hands discovered the lovely shape of her back, button by button, tie by tie. When she felt it bare, she raised her arse and slid out from her chrysalis and turned to him. Her bare breasts were beautiful, with lustrous dark nipples, her belly a little rounded, her dark triangle of hair waiting to be discovered.

'You're a work of art,' groaned Jean and he took her breasts once more in his mouth to suck. She loved the sight of his head bent at her breasts, his shoulders bowed at her service. A suggestion of expensive hair oil rose from his head. She wanted to see his body. She pulled at the shoulder of his shirt, and reached for his waistband. 'Undress,' she said. 'Undress.' And he was forced to leave his worship of her to undress.

He hadn't an ounce of fat on him. He moved around the room like a young lion. His skin was just a touch paler than her own, the kind that goes honey-coloured in the sun. Even in his nakedness everything about him suggested wealth and the confidence that goes with it. He had just the right amount of hair on his chest. It trickled down darkly to his thick straight prick.

'Wait!' he cried and sprang out of the room. His arse was a delight to behold.

'As if I wouldn't,' she breathed.

He returned with the little silver cage and lay down next to her, resting on one elbow.

He lifted the latch.

The lizard darted out and stopped still on the counterpane. It stayed absolutely still for half a minute. Oruela watched it with a mixture of mounting apprehension and excitement.

It moved so suddenly it made her shudder.

It scampered on to his long thigh and jumped lightly from there into his lush pubic hair. It stopped, then it darted on to his cock and he groaned, falling back into the pillows helplessly. The lizard ran around his cock, up, down, across his balls. It ran into the crevice underneath and his legs fell apart. It ran under him to his arsehole and back up again. It circled his hard sex. With an effort Jean raised his head to watch.

Oruela suddenly thought, Hickory Dickory Dock, the lizard ran round his cock, and she began to giggle. But then it jumped.

It was on her hand. It ran fast up her arm, over her shoulder and down across one breast, flicking its tail at her hard nipple as it went. The sensation made her serious. Her whole body tensed. The lizard ran across the smooth plain of her belly, its jewels gleaming. It dived into her soft pubic hair. She bit her fist.

The little green reptile slid down into the folds of her vulva and pitter-pattered around at the opening, relaxing her, like adept fingers, gently. She began to open. She began to want it inside. She wanted it so much. Yes. She could feel the little creature begin to squeeze itself inside her.

At that precise moment Jean's fascination turned to rabid jealousy. He tore the lizard away from her and claimed her as his own. Yes, this was what she really wanted. His prick replaced the animal and he moved with a passion so complete it was everything. His hair in her face, his breath on her hair. She ground against him, massaging her clitoris. There was no return from here. He was hers. The power of him made her gasp. Everything else was irrelevant. He gave one long moan as he came and she was taken along with him, into the best of all possible worlds.

Sometime later she opened her eyes and he was lying close.

She said his name.

'Let's get married,' he said, raising himself on one arm. The way his torso curved into his hip was lovely. It was perfect.

'What!' she said.

'Let's get married soon?'

'Oh!' she said.

'What does that mean?' he asked, sounding a little peeved.

She raised herself. 'I'm surprised, that's all.'

'I want you. I want you to be mine for ever,' he said, and kissed her bruised nipple.

'But I've told everyone I don't believe in it!' she said. 'Besides – don't laugh at me – but I want to go to Paris. I want to go to the Sorbonne and meet bohemians and intellectuals and go to salons and live outrageously!' There! It was out.

Jean smiled and kissed her lips lightly. 'As my wife you can do all the things you want to. Of course you'll go to Paris and meet the people I like.'

'Will I like them too?'

'Of course. And they will love you. Nothing you could do would displease me, Oruela. I love you so much.'

She reached for him and kissed his mouth, lovingly. There was a whole world in his kiss.

'Apparently, people are beginning to talk about us, did you know?' she asked after a moment.

'What? Who? How? I haven't heard anything,' said Jean.

'People meaning my father really. He says you won't suffer. It's me that's supposedly in the wrong.' She hadn't told Jean she was an orphan, looked after by guardians. She didn't know why.

'There isn't any wrong,' he cried. 'Oh, Oruela, what does this mean? Why are you telling me this. Is it an excuse for not getting married. Don't . . .'

'Perhaps it's an excuse *for* getting married!' she said.

'Yes. Yes. Yes!' cried Jean and leapt up as if he'd just scored a winning goal. 'Oh, my darling. Come here.' And he came back to her and before the first sex had grown cold they were making more. The stars began to peek through the patch of indigo sky in the skylight above them.

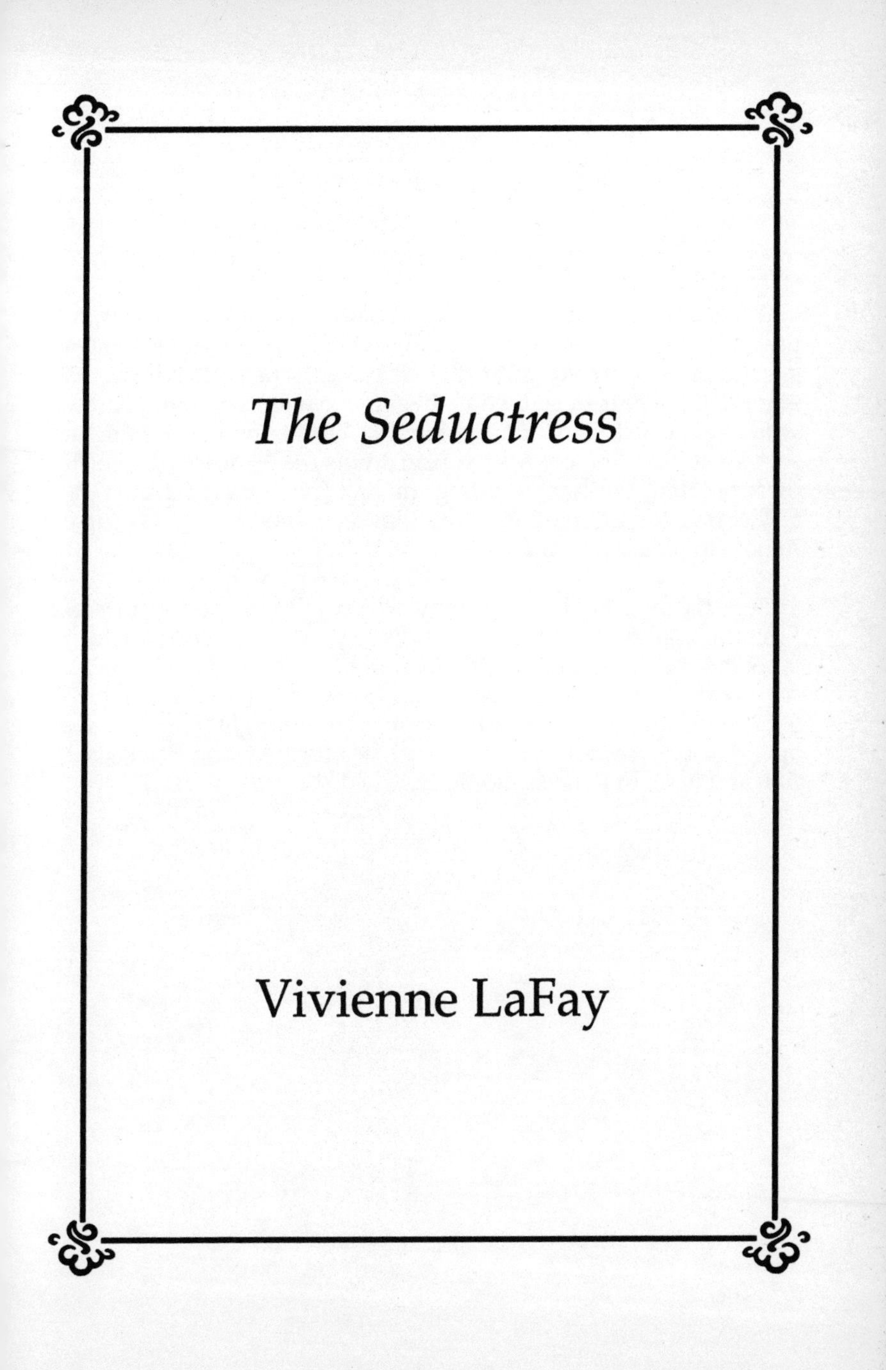

The Seductress

Vivienne LaFay

Lady Emma Longmore has been found physically unable to produce an heir for her husband and they have agreed on a separation – a rare thing in the 1890s. This has left her free to embark on a tour of seduction, beginning with the young curate who is expected to ask for the hand of her young cousin. Emma sees to it that her beloved cousin Louisa will not find herself disappointed on her wedding night. This excerpt from *The Seductress* sees Emma giving the innocent Robert a crash course in how to please a woman.

This is the first book of a trilogy which follows the fortunes of Emma Longmore and her friends. Its sequel is *The Mistress* which is set against the changing tide of social history in the time of the suffragettes, and the series concludes with *The Actress,* which focuses on the adventures of Emma's god-daughter in the jazz age. *Artistic Licence* is Vivienne La Fay's forthcoming Black Lace title and is set in Renaissance Italy.

The Seductress

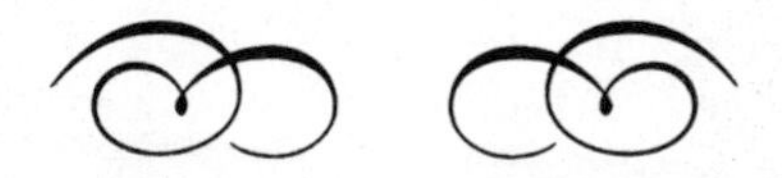

Cousin Anne lived with her husband, two young sons and her eighteen-year-old sister, Louisa, in a pleasant old house near Chichester. She greeted Emma warmly, since the two women had known each other from their childhood and had many shared memories. They took tea in the drawing-room then Anne showed Emma to her quarters herself.

As Kitty unpacked her mistress's clothes in the pretty guest room she said amiably, 'This is what you've been needing, Miss Emma, if you don't mind me saying so. A nice holiday. The change of scene will do you good, I'm sure.'

Emma sighed, gazing out over lawns in which the first daffodils were appearing. She knew now was the time to break the news to her maid. 'I needed more than a change of scene, Kitty. Henry and I have agreed to part, and I have left home for good. I intend to go abroad for a while, passing as a widow. If you wish me to find you another post, I shall – '

'Oh no, ma'am!' Kitty's face was filled with horror. 'I want to stay with you. If you want me to, of course.'

Emma gave her maid a warm hug. 'Thank you for being so loyal, Kitty dear. Well, it is only right that you should know of my plans. I thought we would stay here a week or so, then go on to Dover where we shall take the ferry to Paris. I should like so much to see France.'

'Oh, ma'am!' Kitty's eyes were bright as she clapped her hands together in delight.

Yet Emma was secretly afraid that her plans might come to

nought if Henry did not keep his side of the bargain. Before she'd left Mottisham Hall, Emma had persuaded him to send an allowance to her, care of banks in Paris and Montreux. In return he had insisted, tight-lipped, that their marriage should be declared null and void.

'Doctor Fielding will declare that our marriage was unconsummated,' he'd told her.

'But he has examined me!' Emma had gasped, blushing as she remembered how well she had demonstrated her sexual experience to the good doctor.

Sir Henry had given a wry smile. 'True, but he owes me a large favour for getting him out of some gambling debts that I always knew would come in handy some day.'

Emma had quickly agreed to his plan. Ludicrous as the deception was, she would be far away from Mottisham by the time the annulment was granted. Soon after that, she imagined, Henry would take the widowed Catherine to be his wife and start his wretched dynasty in earnest. Emma knew she would not feel completely free until the whole matter was behind her.

By the time she descended for dinner, Emma was in a carefree mood. Anne had invited several local people to join them in her cousin's honour. At first glance, the men and women were not a very prepossessing bunch, but then she spied a young man loitering gauchely on the edge of the company. His face was handsome, despite its diffident expression, with clear blue eyes, a long straight nose and a wide, sensual mouth. Emma also liked the look of his dark brown hair, which curled most attractively about his ears.

'Ah yes, that is Robert Earnshaw, our local curate,' Anne smiled, drawing her cousin aside. 'He is interested in our Louisa, and we're hoping to be able to make an announcement soon.'

She took Emma over to him. 'Robert, may I present my dear cousin Emma?'

After his perfunctory bow, the curate eyed her nervously. The lad looked hardly more than twenty, and it was clear that he was unused to female company so he would be a totally inept lover. Poor Louisa! Surely that spirited young woman deserved better?

Emma decided that she must act quickly. If she were the first to pluck the sweet flower of his virginity, Louisa would be assured of a more satisfactory wedding night. She would be doing her young relative a favour and enjoying herself at the same time.

'Have you been at Arnford long?' she began, gazing into his eyes with mesmeric intensity.

Er . . . no, Miss . . . er . . . Mrs . . .'

'Just call me Emma,' she smiled. 'And I hope I may call you Robert?'

'Oh, well . . . Emma . . . I have been at Arnford for approximately six months now.'

'Tell me, Robert, are there any pleasant walks hereabouts? I do so like exploring the countryside, don't you?'

'There is an agreeable walk by the river,' he volunteered. 'When it has not been raining, of course.'

'And has it been raining lately?'

Emma was enjoying the faint flush of embarrassment that was colouring the young man's cheeks. Her supposition had been correct – he was clearly unused to conversing with women, let alone having any other form of intercourse with them.

'Not of late, M . . . Emma. I think it would be quite dry. Providing it does not rain overnight, of course.'

'In that case, I wonder whether you would escort me tomorrow afternoon, Robert? If you have no other business to attend to, I should be most grateful.'

His blushes deepened, and Emma noticed with satisfaction that he was afraid to look at her. 'If you wish Miss . . . ah . . . Emma. Shall I call for you here at three?'

'That will suit me very well,' she smiled, as the dinner gong sounded.

Next morning Emma bore her cousin's trivial conversation as best she could, but her mind was elsewhere. When Robert finally appeared, punctually at three, it was hard for her to hide her excitement. She was wearing a pretty blue cape and bonnet, and knew she looked her best, as Robert's admiring gaze proved.

'Will you be back for tea?' Anne enquired.

Robert coughed, turned crimson and shuffled his feet. 'Er . . . I should like to invite Emma to take tea at the vicarage,' he mumbled.

Soon the pair were walking along the river bank, admiring the wild flowers that were raising their timid heads to the spring sunshine.

'That bank of daffodils over there reminds me of William Wordsworth's lyric,' Emma said. 'Do you read poetry, Robert?'

He shook his head. 'To me, the finest poetry is to be found in the good book, Miss Emma. The psalms, for instance.'

Emma smiled. 'Or the "Song of Solomon", perhaps: "Let him kiss me with the kisses of his mouth, for thy love is better than wine".'

Robert cleared his throat and stared hard at the path. 'Yes, quite. The poem is an allegory of spiritual love, of course.'

'Is it?' Emma feigned surprise. 'I had always thought of it literally, as a beautiful tribute of a lover to his beloved.'

'Of course physical love may be beautiful,' Robert went on, pompously, 'provided it is pure and holy, sanctified by the sacrament of marriage.'

'Ah yes! My late husband and I greatly enjoyed celebrating that sacrament over and over again. I was fortunate that my husband was experienced in the ways of love, since he had made love to many women before he met me.'

Robert's eyes widened in astonishment. 'Are you saying your husband was . . . a degenerate libertine?'

Emma smiled. 'No, just an experienced lover. There is a difference. A libertine cares nothing for the pleasure of women, only for his own. My Henry always made sure that his partner was as satisfied as he.'

Robert looked decidedly uneasy. His pace quickened, suggesting he wanted to get back to civilisation as soon as possible. 'I think one should not talk of such things,' he muttered.

'What, of women being satisfied? It is not fashionable, I know, to admit that women also have desires. However, I can assure you it is true. And if a man does not recognise that fact and try to please his partner, you may be sure she will find another who does.'

'I think a woman may be pleased with a virtuous and chaste husband, Miss Emma.'

'Do you intend to marry, Robert?'

'Perhaps. When I can get a living.'

Emma could feel her pulses quickening, and decided to press home her advantage. She was aware that while the curate was extremely embarrassed by her talk he was also filled with curiosity. She took his arm as they came to the bridge over the river, pressing close to his side.

'Perhaps you should start "living" a little more yourself, Robert!'

He drew back from her, his cheeks scarlet. 'I took you for a modest woman, Miss Emma, but our conversation so far has been very immodest. Shall we change the subject?'

'If you wish,' she sighed. 'What shall we talk about – the weather?'

'I fear you mock me. Perhaps we had better cut short our walk and postpone your visit to the vicarage.'

Emma sighed. 'I see that you are afraid of life, like too many of your fellow clerics.'

'Afraid of life? How absurd!'

'You fear the vital urge, Robert, that wonderful wellspring of ecstasy that is the province not only of saints but of ordinary men and women, if only they would throw off the shackles of so-called civilisation. Church doctrine has labelled sex sinful to deprive us of that right to pleasure.'

'I repeat, love is not sinful within the frame of marriage.'

Emma realised that all this argument was futile. A more direct approach was needed to break their impasse. There was a small copse nearby, and she drew him into the shade of the trees on the pretext of gathering some early bluebells.

'They wilt in a day or so,' she sighed. 'But they are so delightful while they last. Like love.'

He was watching her, obviously excited by the sight of her bending low so that her rump was thrust into the air. She knew he wanted her, but he would never make the first move. She must be bold. Bringing the flowers to him she invited him to smell their delicate scent.

'They were created for us to enjoy,' she said, smiling, 'like our bodies.'

So saying, Emma stood on tiptoe and pressed her mouth to his. She perceived that conscience and curiosity fought in him for a few seconds, but then curiosity won. Roughly he pulled her close, thrusting his mouth on to hers with a low moan, and she pushed his lips apart to allow access to her questing tongue. She could feel his soft lips tremble, fluttering like the wings of a nervous butterfly, as she ran her tongue lightly between them, tasting the violet scent of a cachou he had been chewing earlier. He did not pull away but moaned, softly, so she reached down and felt his hardness through his trousers, making him moan all the more.

'Pray stop, temptress!' he gasped at last, pulling back.

'I would not be a temptation if you did not desire me,' she murmured.

'It is true, I do desire you, wretched woman! But tempt me no more, I beg of you!'

She pushed him away from her. 'Well, that is enough for now, Robert. Perhaps we should walk on?'

Smiling to herself, and filled with elation at giving the man his first kiss, Emma let him lead her back on to the path. She knew she had him well aroused, and this delay would work to her advantage.

'I do not know what came over me,' Robert declared, in a daze, as they resumed their progress.

'It is quite natural. I think you will be more compassionate towards your fellow men and women when you understand the true nature of their desires. After all, passion and compassion are close bedfellows, are they not?'

'So are sex and sin!' he retorted.

They walked in silence until the spire of the church and the slate roof of the vicarage were in sight. Once the maidservant had left the tea things and Emma had him alone in the drawing-room, she realised that she must again make a bold approach. Ignoring his small talk she began unbuttoning her blouse, watching his flushed, stunned face all the while. Soon the naked bulge of her cleavage was clearly visible and Robert's eyes fastened on it helplessly. She knew she could take complete command of him now. He was in thrall to his own desires, forced, for the first time in his restricted life, to acknowledge that he wanted a woman. She took his hand and placed it on the cleft, murmuring encouragement.

'Feel how soft my skin is, how warm and inviting. You may kiss me there if you like.'

Impelled by sudden hunger the curate plunged his face between her breasts and began to kiss them greedily.

Emma gave a soft laugh. 'That's right, they are made for your delight. And oh, how delightful it feels to me, to have your sweet lips upon them. This is your first lesson in pleasuring a woman, dear Robert. Mutual satisfaction, you see?'

Panting, Emma drew him down on to the *chaise longue*, where he knelt and grasped her bosom at once, kissing her there frantically and burying his long nose in her abundant flesh. Soon he was opening more buttons, exposing her loose-fitting camisole. Emma had purposely left off wearing her corset that day, so her heavy breasts swung free beneath the covering of white *broderie anglaise* and blue ribbons. His clumsy fingers fumbled with the drawstring until the flimsy garment was revealing almost all of her torso. Smiling, she pulled out the objects of his desire. Robert moaned at the sight of them as they spilled over the camisole, their pink nipples rearing provocatively at him.

'Oh, what beauties!' he sighed. 'I have never gazed upon a woman's nakedness before.'

'Then look your fill,' she said, smiling, but as his hands reached out for them she suddenly rose and went over to the table where the tea-tray was arranged.

'I am thirsty and this tea is going cold. Shall I be mother?'

He was on his knees still, looking up at her with an expression of adoration more appropriate to a religious painting than an erotic encounter. As Emma bent to pour the tea her breasts swung forward like a pair of ringing bells, and his eyes followed them, full of frustrated longing. She handed him a cup of tea and he took a few sips, then set it down in a daze.

After she had drunk her own tea, Emma reached out and opened one of the scones. It was filled with cream and jam. Smiling seductively at him she smeared a finger with the sweet mixture and wiped it on each of her turgid nipples, then returned to lie in a languid pose upon the chaise longue. Sticking her finger into her mouth she licked off all the residue, slowly and appreciatively.

'This is excellent strawberry jam and fresh cream, Robert. Why not taste it?'

Holding up one of her breasts invitingly, Emma used the other hand to pat the velvet seat beside her. Robert needed no further encouragement. He leapt up and was soon sucking wildly on her sweet teat, groaning and rubbing his thighs together. While he suckled at her nipple and stroked her distended breast, Emma took his other hand and placed it between her legs, squeezing against it rhythmically, and giving herself some intense stimulation where it mattered most.

Suddenly Robert let out a series of gasps which Emma knew could only mean he had climaxed. She cradled his head against her sticky bosom, not wishing to embarrass him further. At last, when he had calmed down, she gently removed his head and sat up.

'More tea, Robert?' she asked, casually, as if nothing had happened.

He made an inarticulate noise which she took to be assent. On her way over to the table she tied up her camisole and buttoned up her blouse so that she was soon the very picture of a respectable woman. Robert's first lesson had been a great success, but she knew when it was time to stop. The man had been overwhelmed by his first encounter with naked, tumescent female flesh and must only be introduced to further pleasures by stages.

As they drank their tea, Emma tried to make him feel better about what had happened.

'You have nothing to be ashamed of, dear Robert,' she said. 'What has occurred between us this afternoon is our secret and shall remain so.'

'But I have sinned in the sight of God!' he moaned, rolling his eyes heavenward.

'Then you must ask his forgiveness. But I truly believe you will be more understanding of the peccadilloes of others now that you have succumbed to temptation yourself'

Cousin Anne's carriage called for Emma at six, as arranged, and by then she was more than ready to leave. The thrill she had experienced at seducing the pious curate had worn off somewhat after his guilt-ridden maundering, but she knew that for all his self-recrimination seeds had been sown that would soon clamour to be harvested.

Emma called Kitty to her room directly she returned and asked the maid to run her a bath. As she did so Kitty enquired about her visit to the vicarage, and Emma had a sudden urge to tell her the truth. 'What do you think of young Master Robert?' she enquired.

'I think he is most handsome, but a little shy.'

Emma let Kitty undo her buttons and remove her blouse, relishing the light touch of the girl's fingers on her naked skin. Her breasts still smelt faintly of strawberries. She stepped out of her skirt then removed her petticoats until she stood stark naked. Kitty's eyes swept briefly over her mistress's body then looked away as she turned off the taps.

'You are right, my dear. He is certainly unused to talking with women.' Emma lowered herself into the lavender-scented water. 'But I fancy he may be a little more bold in future.'

'Why is that, ma'am?'

Kitty reached over for the loofah, then began to apply it to her mistress's back while Emma soaped her own breasts.

'I have given him a little lesson in how to please a woman.' Emma looked into Kitty's innocent eyes and saw a flicker of interest there. She smiled. 'Perhaps he will not be so quick to condemn other men's desires, now I have acquainted him more thoroughly with his own.'

Faint alarm showed in the girl's eyes. 'What are you saying, ma'am?'

Emma let her slippery hands move over her stomach and down to her thighs, enjoying the warm thrills produced by the combination of hot water, sensual massage and wicked confession.

'I am saying that I let him kiss me, Kitty. A true lover's kiss, such as he had never experienced before.'

'Oh, Miss Emma! I should not have believed it of a man so . . . upright.'

'He is a man like any other, and with normal instincts. Put him in the company of any attractive woman for half an hour or so and he will lust after her. Give him the opportunity, and he will act on it.'

'And you gave him that opportunity?' Kitty's eyes were alight with wonder, and she could not resist a giggle as she added, 'Shame on you, ma'am!'

Emma laughed too. Kitty's amusement showed that she had distinct possibilities. The girl was proving to be a very promising confidante.

'It is true, believe me. It is the sweetest thing, my dear, to introduce an innocent man to the pleasures of the flesh. I hope you may enjoy a similar experience one day.'

Emma dismissed her maid with a smile, and set about pleasuring herself with a soapy finger. As she worked herself up into a fine lather, she began to plan what she would do at her next encounter with the naive curate.

On Sunday Emma insisted on going to church, much to Anne's chagrin.

'Oh Lord, the sermons are so dreary, especially when poor Mr

Earnshaw is in the pulpit. That man is so nervous he stutters and stammers his way through what is always an indifferent sermon, making it ten times more tedious!'

'And is it his turn this Sunday?'

'Yes. Would you think me terribly impolite if I excused myself with a headache? You may go with Louisa, if you wish.'

So at ten o'clock Emma and Louisa were driven to church in Anne's carriage. They sat in the second row of pews, where Emma could get a good view of the pulpit. Robert had not expected to see her in church and when his eye lighted on her he gave a sudden start and blushed scarlet. She smiled pleasantly at him, enjoying his discomfort.

When the time came for him to mount the steps of the pulpit Emma could tell that he was really anxious. He rubbed his sweaty palms on his cassock, and ran a finger around his dog collar in a vain attempt to loosen it. When he began to speak he studiously avoided her eye.

'My t ... text t ... today is taken from the gospel of St Matthew, verse 46: "For if you love them which love you, what reward have you?"' Robert cleared his throat and launched into his sermon, although his face was a bright pink. 'How easy it is for us to love ... to love our f ... friends and family ...'

His theme was the familiar Christian doctrine of 'Love Thine Enemy' but he made heavy weather of it, and Emma preferred to think of love in the carnal sense. To love one's enemy was to wallow in one's own humiliation, as she had read some women liked to do. The time Henry had always spent in preparing her for the act of love had been almost as satisfying as the act itself. To be forcibly taken, to submit to love from a man one disliked, could surely not be pleasant.

Yet the idea had an odd fascination for her. Sometimes, in the dreamy state before sleep, she had imagined being ravished by some strong and handsome warrior and had become so aroused that she was obliged to pleasure herself before she could rest. Even now the thought of a man's hard tool being thrust straight into her, without preliminaries, was causing her private parts to throb and moisten, so that she wriggled a little against the hard wooden pew.

'So, my friends, n ... next time you make an enemy of s ... someone, consider your r ... reward. Are you h ... harvesting hatred, or love?'

As the sermon wound painfully to its conclusion, Emma grew excited at the prospect of carrying out her plan, and her thighs shifted restlessly on her seat until they had to kneel and pray.

When the last blessing had been uttered and the congregation began to file out, Emma turned to Louisa. 'Would you mind going back in the carriage by yourself, my dear? I wish to speak with Mr Earnshaw about a spiritual matter.'

At the mention of the curate, the young girl's eyes widened. 'But how shall you get home, Emma?'

'I shall walk. It is a fine spring day.'

Louisa was reluctant and Emma suspected she had been hoping for an encounter with the curate herself. But she was an obedient girl and went off in the carriage without demur. When the last few loiterers had left, Emma approached Robert at the church door.

'May I congratulate you on your sermon?' she began. 'It caused me to reflect on the nature of love, and there is something I would like to discuss with you in private. I thought we might retire to the vestry for a few moments.'

It was obvious that he was both fascinated and repelled by the idea of being alone with Emma once again. As he stood there gaping like a stranded fish, she added, 'My soul is troubled and I need guidance.'

So Robert had no option but to follow Emma down the aisle. She entered the musty-smelling vestry and looked about her. The vicar's robes were already hanging on their peg, and there were a few spare chairs and a *prie-Dieu*, facing a table on which a simple wooden cross was arranged. The place seemed perfectly suited to her purposes.

'What do you want of me?' Robert asked, once he had closed the heavy door behind him and drawn the baize curtain across.

There was a note of desperation in his voice so Emma tried to put him at ease. 'Just a few moments of your time. Shall we sit down?'

He drew out a couple of chairs. Emma sat facing him, aware that she was looking her Sunday best. His eyes skimmed her torso in the figure-hugging dress. 'You m... mentioned something in my sermon...?'

'Ah, yes, the question of love's reward. I was reminded that the chief reward of love, as we ordinary mortals know it, is pleasure. And yet the church seems to frown on the pleasures of love. Surely there is an inconsistency there?'

Robert frowned. 'As I mentioned before, love sanctified by marriage . . .'

'But how can you say that, when the average husband has no idea how to express his love by giving pleasure to his wife? And, likewise, the average wife has no idea how to pleasure her husband.'

'I know not what you mean.'

'I am concerned only for you, Robert, and for any future wife you might have. I am aware that you are interested in my cousin Louisa, and I would not wish her to remain ignorant of the joys of love for the rest of her life.'

'Whatever affection is between myself and Miss Louisa is pure and unsullied,' he said, haughtily.

'But she will want to serve you in any way she can. And if you do not know how a woman may serve a man, how can she oblige you?'

Emma knew she had him almost in the palm of her hand. He was backing away towards the *prie-Dieu*, looking flushed and confused. When he was standing with his behind against the little shelf designed to hold a prayer-book, she made her move.

'Allow me to show you some of the good service a wife may perform, Robert.'

Emma looked down at the plump hassock, smiling as she read the text embroidered upon it: '"The unbelieving husband is sanctified by the wife".' She knelt upon it and lifted up his black cassock. He seemed paralysed, unable to prevent her from opening up the buttons of his fly and pulling out his already stiffened member. It was long and slim, with a shiny pink bulb on the end. When Emma gripped it the shaft jerked in her hand and Robert gave a groan of mingled shame and desire.

'Such a fine member!' she murmured, taking its tip between her lips. She felt eager hands clutch at her bonnet as she worked her mouth slowly down the rigid shaft. Robert's breath was coming in loud pants, his hips writhing as she reached in and felt the loose sac that contained his seed. She continued to play gently with his scrotum while she licked and sucked, lightly tickling the hairy skin with her nails the way Henry had liked her to do.

'Witch! Demoness!' she heard him moan, as she accelerated

her efforts and felt the balls tautening ready to shoot their load. At last the hot stream seared its way down her throat and she gulped appreciatively. It was so long since she had tasted sperm and Robert's was fresh and copious, the sweet sacrament of carnal love.

'God forgive me!' Robert gasped, turning to the small altar and flinging himself on to his knees.

'What for?' Emma asked, softly. 'For being a man, with a man's desires?'

'Get you behind me, creature of Satan!' he snarled.

Emma decided to leave him to his self-abasement. After wiping her lips with her lace handkerchief she stepped out of the vestry and, enjoying the spring sunshine, began to walk back to cousin Anne's house.

Next morning Emma found Louisa alone in the drawing-room and decided to take the bull by the horns. She noticed that her young cousin seemed somewhat wan, almost lovesick, and guessed at the reason. She entered quickly, closing the door behind her.

'Louisa dear, what is the matter? A young woman like you should be full of the joys of spring!'

'Oh Emma, indeed I should be if only I were safely betrothed. In two weeks' time I shall be nineteen, and practically on the shelf!'

Emma laughed. 'Nonsense! I was twenty-one before I married. And at your age I had no one in mind.'

'But I *do* have someone in mind. The trouble is, I am not at all sure if he and I are of the same mind.'

'You speak of Robert Earnshaw, do you not?' Louisa smiled shyly. 'I am quite sure he looks upon you favourably, Louisa. I have mentioned your name in conversation several times and he has always showed, both by looks and words, that he regards you most highly.'

'Then why does he not come forward?'

'He is a reticent man, a little shy of women I feel. Besides, he probably thinks he should be made vicar of a parish before he proposes marriage.'

'There is no need. Papa will see that we are comfortably off until he has a good enough income. Oh, I am so tired of living here Emma! Anne is very good to me, but it is not like having a home of your own, is it?'

Emma looked thoughtful. 'I think we may be able to make him realise how strong your feelings are. Perhaps I could deliver some little *billet doux*? Nothing too forward, of course. I will help you write it.'

'Oh Emma, would you? You're such a dear!'

At once Louisa's face took on a lively aspect as she hunted out pen and paper. Emma racked her brains for a suitable approach, then began her dictation. 'Dear Robert . . .'

'Is that not too familiar, Emma?'

'Not at all. The intimacy is appropriate in the circumstances, I am sure. "Dear Robert, I hope you will not think me too forward for writing to you, but I should like to congratulate you on your sermon last Sunday. I found the section on the rewards of loving most apposite. I have often reflected that in my heart there is an abundance of love, but few people to share it. Perhaps you may advise me on how this might be remedied? Yours affectionately . . ."'

'Are you sure he will take this well?' Louisa asked, doubtfully.

'Quite sure, providing you will let me deliver it. Then, if there are any misunderstandings I can rectify them directly.'

Emma took the letter to the vicarage that afternoon. She found Robert alone, it being the servant's afternoon off, which suited her purposes perfectly. However, he did not invite her in straight away but looked decidedly mistrustful.

'I have come with a letter from Louisa,' she began.

Stiffly he held out his hand for it, but she shook her head. 'Will you not ask me in?'

The curate frowned. 'For a few moments only, then. It is not seemly for me to be entertaining you unchaperoned.'

Emma almost laughed aloud. It was rather late to be concerned about proprieties! He led the way into the hall and would have asked for the letter there, but Emma boldly went up to the drawing-room door and opened it. Only when they were both inside the room with the door shut would she produce the missive.

'Emma, give me the letter,' Robert said, crossly.

She eyed him saucily then undid some buttons and placed the folded paper in her cleavage. 'Come and get it, Robert dear!'

'Do not play games with me, I have not the patience.'

'Then come, take it, and be done with it.'

He tried to snatch it out of her bosom, but she caught his wrist and kissed it, making him stroke her bare breast. The curate groaned, allowing the letter to fall to the floor as he came under her spell once again. Crushing her lips with his, he proceeded to lift up her skirt until his fingers were feeling the warm flesh of her naked thigh, above her stocking tops.

'Vixen! I have had no sleep since last I saw you! You have me on fire and I know not how to extinguish the flames of my desire. They consume me, night and day!'

'Tut, tut Robert! You know very well how such fire may be dealt with. Put your hand higher up between my legs and you shall feel another conflagration raging. Shall we not fight fire with fire?'

His fingers were creeping beneath her beribboned petticoats, reaching the soft petals of her sex, and his groans increased in volume. Emma put her hand down and felt his hard member struggling within its tight confines.

'One moment, Robert,' she whispered, moving away from him just long enough to remove her skirt and hooped petticoat, so that her body was more accessible to him.

Robert threw himself down on to his knees and buried his face in the soft cotton of her undergarments. Emma knew that the musky scent she was emitting would be inflaming his already overheated desire, and she wriggled her buttocks beneath his clasping hands so that her pubis was thrust into his face. Her fingers fumbled with the ribbons of her chemise and soon she had pulled out one ripe breast, fondling the nipple to a long, stiff peak.

'Come, Robert, let us lie down,' she urged him, throwing some cushions on to the Persian carpet and settling back with her body seductively displayed. It was too much for the curate. Furiously he struggled with his trousers until he had pulled them down and his tumid organ sprang to attention. Emma smiled, but slapped his wrist when he tried to fumble with her most intimate place.

'Not so fast, Robert! Pretend I am your blushing bride and this is our wedding night. You would not wish to cause a poor virgin pain when deflowering her, would you?'

He swallowed and shook his head then muttered, hoarsely, 'Tell me what I must do.'

'That's better. First you may kiss and stroke my breasts, which helps to get me wet down below.'

He obeyed with relish, and was soon rolling her nipple confidently between his finger and thumb while he planted soft kisses all round. Emma encouraged him with sighs and murmurs, then directed him to remove her under-petticoat gently. He gasped when he saw the tightly-curled hairs that hid her private place, and declared he had never seen anything so exquisite.

'M . . . may I see what lies within?' he faltered.

Chuckling softly, Emma opened her thighs wide and spread her labia apart with her fingers. Robert gave it an earnest perusal, his face flushed and his breathing heavy.

'You may touch it, if you like,' she encouraged him. 'But be gentle.'

Tentatively the curate stretched out a hand and probed her folds with his forefinger. Emma felt her wetness increase as he found her hole and penetrated to the depth of half an inch or so. He pulled his finger out and licked it, wonderingly.

'If you like the taste you may suck at my parts directly,' she told him.

Robert knelt down on all fours and put his lips to her privates. At first he was cautious, licking her very gently, but he soon acquired a taste for it and began gobbling away at her, so hard that the sensitive tip of her clitoris began to be sore.

'Wait! Let me show you something.' Emma sat up and pointed to the tiny erect bud at the top of her labia. 'This small knob is the source of a woman's greatest pleasure, but it must be treated with care. Do not rub it directly, but just above. Then it will cause a woman to become very wet and aroused. Try it with your tongue or finger, and see what happens. I shall tell you if you are too rough.'

Robert proved a quick learner and soon had Emma dancing on the edge of orgasm. But she didn't want to come yet. Taking his slender tool in one hand she softly squeezed his balls with the other until she felt them tighten.

'Now, Robert, this is the moment of penetration. It requires great self-control if you are not to tear the woman's delicate membrane and cause her pain. Place the tip of your member at the entrance to my cunny, and let my juices bathe you awhile.'

He did as he was told, but was clearly impatient to thrust into the warm, wet chasm. Emma caressed his glans with her inner lips then bade him slowly enter, an inch at a time. He did his best to hold back, but when he was about halfway in he was overcome by fierce lust and pierced her mercilessly, up to the hilt. Emma gave a cry of joy and clasped him with her internal walls. It seemed an age since she'd had a man probing deep inside her and, even though Robert's organ did not fill her as well as Henry's shorter, thicker one, she revelled in the intimate mingling of his flesh with hers.

Fearing that he might eject his sperm too soon, Emma held him immobile for a while then began to move her vagina slowly up and down his shaft, urging him to do likewise. They soon had a gentle rhythm going, despite Robert's urge to plunder her treasures with wild abandon, for as soon as he tried to speed up she whispered notes of caution in his ear. 'Make it last, Robert dear. Easy does it! That's the way.'

But eventually not even her mild admonitions had any effect. The curate's fire began raging and he pinned down her arms, put his mouth greedily to her nipple and thrust away like fury until all the hot seed had been spilt from his taut, aching balls. Feeling the delicious fountain springing up inside her, Emma also climaxed with a long satisfying series of pulsations that left her spent and breathless.

'Dear God, if I am to be damned, let me be damned for such a sin as this!' he sighed, resting his head on her breast.

They lay for a while then Emma gently removed his head and sat up.

'I must be getting back, or they will be wondering what has become of me. Read the letter from Louisa, Robert, and tell me if there is to be a reply.'

'Louisa?' Robert said, vaguely, as if there could be no other woman in the world for him right then.

'Yes. The poor girl is in love with you, did you not know it? She longs to know your mind.'

Dazed, Robert picked up the discarded letter and read it. He stared at Emma in disbelief. 'She wishes to lavish her affection on me?'

Emma smiled, buttoning up her blouse. 'Yes, and I am sure she could find no worthier object of her devotion.'

'Yet I am not in a position to make an honest woman of her. Please advise me, Emma. You have opened my eyes to a whole new world, one which I long to explore more thoroughly, but I cannot make Louisa my wife. Not until I am well established in my profession.'

'Nonsense! If you are sincere in wanting to wed her I am sure her father will help you financially. He may even be able to secure a living for you, since he is a man of influence. Now, dress yourself and come over to the davenport. I shall tell you what to write to poor Louisa that will set her mind at rest.'

It pleased Emma to dictate the reply that would seal her young cousin's fate. Now that her own desires had been satisfied, and she was sure that Robert would be a considerate husband, she was content to move on to pastures new.

Handmaiden of Palmyra

Fleur Reynolds

Many earthy pleasures were to be found in the third century. As the title suggests, Syria is the setting for this tale of adventure and decadence which features the inquisitve and sensual Samoya. She is expecting to take her place as a trainee priestess in the temple of Antioch. The lascivious and powerful Prince Alif has other ideas, though, and sends his scheming sister, Bernice, to bring her back to his palace. The chosen extract finds Bernice testing Samoya's suitability as a wife and sister-in-law.

Fleur's first book for Black Lace was *Odalisque,* set against a backdrop of jet-setting sophistication and family rivalry. She went on to write *The House in New Orleans,* set in contemporary America, and *Conquered,* the tale of an Inca princess. The sequel to *Odalisque, Bonded,* is due for publication in September 1997.

Handmaiden of Palmyra

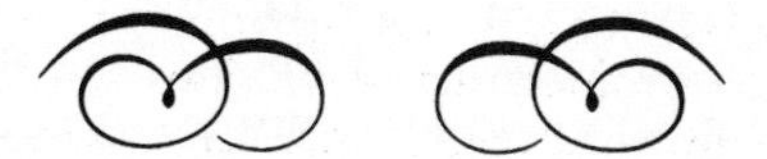

'You must submit willingly,' said the voluptuous Princess Bernice, who, enveloped in a golden cape, was sucking on a juicy quince.

'Yes, your Highness,' replied Samoya, instinctively keeping her beautiful face bland, not allowing her true thoughts to be betrayed by the slightest flicker of emotion.

Samoya, like everyone else in Antioch, knew Princess Bernice was procuress for her decadent brother, King Hairan.

It was two hours before dawn and the darkest part of the night. The great bedroom, held up by pillars and decorated with murals, was lit by candles. Samoya was feeling put out. Too late to visit Zenobia she had come back from rehearsals at the temple and found Princess Bernice and her entourage waiting for her. And the only thing Samoya was really interested in doing was taking a nap before her initiation ceremony. With the unexpected, and unwanted, arrival of the Palmyrene princess this was denied her.

Samoya was furious the Palmyrene was in her house. There was nothing she could do about it, except be polite and hope the princess would go away convinced that Samoya was unsuitable for any role at court. For, before the day was out, one of the fathers in the city would lose a daughter. Of course that father would be told it was an honour; that his daughter had been chosen for her beauty, elegance and good breeding and that he and his family would be serving the Palmyrene Empire. But every father knew it wasn't just the Empire his daughter would be serving.

Samoya wondered who had told the princess about her. Perhaps it was one of her father's business rivals not wanting one of his own daughters to be picked. Samoya desperately hoped she would not be chosen. That would throw her plans for her future in complete disarray. Nevertheless, Samoya had to play hostess and etiquette demanded that she had to comply with the princess's requests.

'Loosen her hair,' Princess Bernice commanded a buxom bare-breasted female slave, who immediatley set to work to release Lady Samoya's luscious red-gold tresses from their tight silken bindings, allowing her crowning glory to cascade sensually over her shoulders.

'That's much better,' said Bernice, dismissing the female slave.

'Do you know why I'm here?' asked Bernice imperiously.

The King's sister was sitting on an ornately carved, sweet-smelling cedar wood chair and staring lasciviously at the lithe, barefoot, young woman in front of her who was clothed in a creamy-white linen shift, encircled at the waist with a belt of plaited gold.

'No, your Highness,' lied Lady Samoya as she watched the Palmyrene princess begin to strip herself of her ornaments.

She slid gold bracelets down her full rounded arms, took off her gold anklets and her many necklaces which were made from a variety of precious stones interlaced with gold. Bernice tossed them carelessly into her jewel-box then she clapped her hands. From a far corner of the room two huge Nubians, wearing the briefest of tunics, stepped forward. One was carrying an alabaster bowl, the other a pitcher.

'Undress me,' commanded the princess.

She held out her arms so the slaves could remove her golden cape, her translucent purple silk ankle-length robe, her long black silk drawers and leave her naked.

Samoya felt a wisp of envy as, mentally, she measured her own small rose-bud breasts against the ample fullness of the princess's. She gave a deep sigh. For the first time in her life Samoya wished she looked like someone else. Which was surprising because, whatever quirks of character Samoya possessed, vanity was not one of them. But, because she did not possess the standard beauty, she did not know she was beautiful and would have been genuinely amazed had anybody told her she was. Samoya thought that if she was a candidate for marriage it was due to her father's fortune not to her own physical assets.

There was no doubt about it, thought Samoya, the Palmyrene princess was stunning. She was also very sexual. Her large, round, deep brown eyes, enhanced by black kohl, were set in a large round face. Her unmarked, dark olive skin was highlighted with soft red on her cheeks; her thick sensuous lips were painted a much brighter red. Her whole body, her large breasts, her rounded arms and stomach, her curvaceous thighs and legs, oozed sexuality.

Samoya felt uncomfortable. Even in the half-light she could feel the other woman giving her an odd stare.

Bernice was sizing up Samoya. The more Bernice looked at her, the more she thought that she was the one who seemed to have the right possibilities. However, Bernice knew she had to tread carefully. The girl's father was a problem. He had told her that unless his daughter was willing to be married and go to Palmyra he would not give his permission. His lack of desire to see his daughter married increased Bernice's determination to see that she was. And to her kinsman, Prince Alif. It was Bernice's job to make sure the girl agreed to her proposal.

'Now take off my hair clips,' ordered Bernice.

The handsome young Nubians obediently began the intricate task of extricating Princess Bernice's delicate pure gold decorations from her mass of softly waving black hair.

'So, you don't know why I'm here?'

'No, your Highness, I don't,' replied Lady Samoya.

'I will tell you,' said Bernice, as the slaves finished brushing her hair. Bernice rose up from her chair and walked naked and with the liquid grace of a large, sensual feline towards a mountain of fabulously embroidered silk cushions. She lay down on them like a panther waiting to strike at its prey. She sighed provocatively then spread her legs wide and stuck her feet out towards her slaves.

Samoya's eyes followed her every movement. She wondered why the slaves should have left the strange long thin leather belt tied around the princess's waist. Samoya gazed at it carefully. It did not end with the usual floppy flat tassels; instead it had been thickened, moulded and stiffened. It seemed to her as if the

Palmyrene princess had two huge leather truncheons dangling between her legs.

Bowing low the two Nubians set the bowl on the floor in front of the King's sister. They poured soothing, warmed, aromatic oils from the pitcher into the bowl. Then each slave took one of their mistress's feet, lowered it into the bowl and slowly and rhythmically began to massage Bernice's ankles, moving along her calves and up her thighs.

'Our kinsman, Prince Alif, needs a wife,' Princess Bernice stated baldly. 'And one family in Antioch will be honoured by my choice. Now, what do you think of that?'

'I think it is no business of mine for it is too great an honour for our simple family,' whispered Samoya, sweetly, with downcast eyes. The fragility of the girl excited Bernice.

She felt a rush of licentiousness. She wanted to touch Samoya, feel her soft, pale skin, her legs, her breasts, her lips. She wouldn't do it yet. There was pleasure in waiting. She would enjoy the sensation of anticipation. To assuage her immediate desire Bernice began to run her hands sexily along the thick well-muscled legs of her two black slaves.

Enjoying the feel of their skin, Bernice looked up slyly at Samoya. The girl's figure was almost boyish, her small breasts did not have the full bloom of womanhood. Her violet blue, slightly almond-shaped eyes, would make a pleasant change from the endless brown and black ones usually seen at court. Her short, straight typically Palmyrene nose and her red-blonde hair meant she was of good old stock. Although Samoya and her father, Pernel, lived in Antioch, they both had the shapes and colouring that were special to Palmyra and that part of Syria. Bernice liked what she saw and, fully aware of his inclinations, she knew her brother would, too. In that instant she decided she would take the Lady Samoya to court. Bernice had no doubt whatsoever that the King and Prince Alif would be very pleased with her choice.

Samoya stood silently by, watching the princess's slaves perform their duties. Nobody would have guessed that she was intensely wary of the older woman and that she realised she was in a difficult situation. She did not want to be married. But if Princess Bernice chose her as Prince Alif's wife what could she do? How could she refuse?

Samoya reasoned that to be turned down by the Royal household would do little for her future marriage prospects, and that did have to be taken into consideration. But to be chosen meant living a life of virtual prostitution. At least, that was the rumour in parochial Antioch where scurrilous stories of life at court in Palmyra were a constant source of gossip for its inhabitants. Samoya suddenly realised how she could escape from her predicament. The demands of the Great Goddess took precedence over those of the King. She would ask Priestess Verenia to take her as a novitiate into the temple. Samoya tried not to look crestfallen as she remembered she would be unable to talk to the priestess that night. The King's sister was exercising her royal prerogative to attend the special initiation rite at dawn. And the next few days would be filled with various temple ceremonies, so Verenia would have no time to see her. Samoya mentally stamped her foot with impatience. Instinctively she knew that time was of the essence. A wave of irritation flooded through her, knowing she had no alternative but to wait.

Samoya looked towards the two black slaves who were bending over their mistress massaging oils into every part of her body. Samoya felt a tingling in her body and her face suffuse with blushes. The tingling was familiar. Samoya remembered how recently she had gone to bed and had let her hands glide down her lithe body, exciting herself. As her fingers had roamed, exploring past her fair red-gold mound to the fleshy lips beyond, her hidden sex had grown softer, more pliant and wetter with her every languid stroke. She had fantasised about ordering Irene to put her head between her outstretched legs and lick her hidden opening. But she hadn't done it. Instead her slave, lying beside her, had realised what she had wanted and had stretched out her hand. She had gently stroked Samoya's buttocks then pushed her fingers round finding Samoya's wet sex and had rubbed gently on her virgin lips. She had continued to play with her until an exquisite sensation had forced its way down and out through her body in a great shudder. She had been left with a feeling of contentment and had slept a deep, deep sleep.

Samoya watched the princess roll over squirming as the slaves' big hands fondled her full breasts, stroked the black curly mound between her legs and her big fleshy bottom.

'A moist, tingling pussy is one of life's greatest pleasures,' said Bernice, 'and I have one now. You two know what to do.'

Samoya was mesmerised by the woman's words. She felt a

thrill pass through her body as one of the men nestled between Bernice's thighs and let his tongue travel between his mistress's legs, pushing slowly at her secret lips until his tongue was darting at her clitoris. Bernice began to sway and moan and lift her hips. The other slave stayed caressing her breasts. 'Deeper. Go deeper,' commanded Bernice hoarsely as she writhed with pleasure. 'Do as I say or I'll have you whipped.' The slave buried his tongue deeper and moved it faster inside the Princess's sex.

Samoya was quite amazed. She was a mass of contradictory emotions. She was repelled and excited. It seemed to Samoya as if she was opening and swelling. She felt a tremendous desire to be touched. She forced her hands to stay by her side, although, almost of their own accord, they kept wandering over her thighs. She found her mouth had gone dry. Her throat was constricting. She licked her lips and swallowed hard trying to increase her own saliva. Her breasts were aching. She tensed the muscles in her buttocks.

As she watched the slaves obey their mistress and fondle and suck Bernice, Samoya gave tiny wiggles of her hips and clenched her fists in an effort to stop herself lifting her dress and touching herself.

Watching the Palmyrene princess gliding on the silken cushions, moving with her eyes closed as the men continued to caress every part of her full, rounded nakedness, Samoya thought perhaps she would be able to inch her way from the other woman's presence without Bernice being aware of her departure.

'Stay exactly where you are,' commanded Bernice to Samoya. 'I might need you.'

As she said that the princess untied her belt and handed one of the thick phallus-shaped ends to the slave who was sucking her.

'Be a man,' she ordered. Only then did Samoya realise that the slave was a eunuch. The slave positioned his knees between Bernice's thighs, tied the belt around his waist, held the object poised at the entrance to Bernice's sex and waited.

'Now, enter me,' said Bernice, seconds later.

Samoya watched transfixed as the slave gradually pushed the thick long leather truncheon into Bernice's wet sex. He moved his body backwards and forwards as if the object was attached to him and let it plunge deeper into Bernice's warm swollen pussy. Before she realised what she was doing, Samoya found herself moving her hips in rhythm to the slave's thrusting. Tensing and untensing her buttocks, her breath, like Bernice's, issued in short sharp bursts.

'Are you wet between your legs?' Bernice asked.

'I don't know,' replied Samoya haltingly.

'You don't know!' said Bernice between gasps as the slave continued to penetrate her. 'Then stand beside me. I will feel you and I will tell you if you are.'

Trembling, Samoya slowly walked over to where Princess Bernice was lying. Bernice reached out a hand and gently began to stroke Samoya's ankles. Samoya's whole body shook at the woman's touch. Bernice's hands went higher and higher under the creamy white linen robe. Samoya held her breath as the princess's fingers started to caress the soft fleshy lips at the top of her thighs. Samoya could feel her wetness exuding and her nipples had hardened. Samoya wanted them touched.

'Do you like that?' asked Bernice, softly rubbing Samoya's juicy, wet and open sex.

'Yes,' replied Samoya, hoarsely. The touch of Bernice's finger gliding backwards and forwards was making waves of delicious tingling flow through her body; from her throat and neck to her breasts, to her belly and her womb then down; down to change from a sensation that she could barely hold to a lubrication that she could feel. And with that feeling the whole cycle was reproduced again but taking her higher and higher as the wetter she became the more Bernice's fingers were able to invade her, push upwards and stimulate her. As she watched the slave eunuch pretending to be a man and piercing Bernice with the leather dildo and the other fondling her breasts, squeezing their large brown nipples between his fingers, Samoya wanted to feel more hands straying on to her body. Bernice suddenly stopped stroking Samoya's sex, and hauled her down on the cushions beside her. Still jerking to the slave's rhythm, Bernice pulled up Samoya's robe, encircled her rose-bud breasts and teased her erect, dark pink nipples.

'Remove your robe,' commanded Bernice.

Samoya obeyed. 'Now, give me your mouth and open your legs wide.'

Samoya turned her full pouting mouth towards the Princess who began to trace its outline with her tongue before bringing her lips down hard on Samoya's.

Samoya closed her eyes and gave herself up to the touch of Bernice's mouth on her mouth, tongue on her tongue and her plump exploring hands on her breasts. Samoya began to writhe.

Moments later Samoya felt another body over hers and then a newer, stranger, more wonderful diversion as something small and warm, wet and thick, began to trace the edges of her swollen labia. She opened her eyes to find that the huge black eunuch who had been caressing Bernice's breasts was now upturned beside her. He had his head between her legs. It was his thick tongue which was searching out, exciting and thrilling Samoya's open wet sex. Then he touched her clitoris. That touch was so potent, so enthralling, that Samoya instantly let out a great gasp of pleasure and rolled and writhed and swayed. And she continued to do this until every ounce of energy inside her contracted to her belly. With her body rigid and arched she suddenly shook with the delirium of ecstasy. Then a great rush of fervour balled up inside her and was expelled in a massive explosion.

Samoya lay back exhausted and overwhelmed by varying emotions. She glanced at Bernice whose thighs were quivering as the slave with the dildo continued to pound into her. She was rolling and moaning then she arched, went rigid, and with a long shriek of gratification suddenly collapsed and fell back on the cushions. Bernice took Samoya gently in her arms and kissed her cheek.

'My dear you enjoyed that, didn't you?' said Princess Bernice.

'Yes,' replied Samoya in a whisper.

'Would you like it to happen again?' asked the seductive older woman, softly caressing Samoya's breasts and nibbling her ear.

'Yes.'

'And you can, if you agree to marry Prince Alif. You see the Prince has some very interesting habits and desires,' said Bernice, smiling cat-like as she remembered some of his more perverted antics. 'And one of them is that he enjoys watching women make love. He would love to see you with your legs stretched far apart and me fingering your lovely sweet little virginal delights. And I would suck you and I would teach you to suck me. After all, you enjoyed that slave putting his tongue between your legs, didn't you?'

'Oh yes,' Samoya replied enthusiastically.

'I will get him to show you how it's done,' said Bernice, picking up her truncheons. 'And these.'

Bernice began to run them along Samoya's thighs, 'Feel the softness of the leather, open your legs a moment.'

Samoya did as she was told and Bernice began to trail the thick object along the girl's sex and, despite her recent orgasm, Samoya reacted by opening her legs further.

'Ah, so you'd like to have it stuck in you would you? You'd like to be penetrated by my handsome treasure. Well, you will, but not now. Another day I will show you how to get pleasure whenever you want it. I will have one made especially for you. Now all you have to do is say you'll come to Palmyra and marry Prince Alif. Will you do that?'

Bernice kissed Samoya's soft yielding lips and caressed her breasts whilst leaving the dildo poking very slightly at the girl's entrance.

'Yes. Oh yes,' said Samoya. The awakening had begun. She had discovered her body and its potential for pleasure.

'Good. Then that is settled and I will talk to your father. Now we must hurry,' said Bernice. 'The Goddess waits.'

Bernice turned to her slaves and told them to dress her and then dress Samoya. Whilst the purple silk robe was once more wrapped around her ample form, the leather thong belt re-tied around her waist and the fine spun gold cape was draped over her shoulders, Bernice gazed at the girl lying on the cushions. She was perfect. A beautiful face, a superb body and, from the intensity of her reactions, obviously very highly sexed. Bernice had confirmed her original estimate. Samoya was the choice and the King would be thrilled. She had a lot to learn but, Princess Bernice licked her lips at the thought, she would be easy to teach. And Prince Alif would have a most submissive wife.

The two slaves gently roused Samoya from the sleep she had drifted into. They rubbed her body with fresh aromatic oils, paying special attention to her nipples and between her legs. Samoya had thought that after the violent explosion she would never want to be touched down there again. Much to her surprise she discovered that far from not wanting it she had been sensitised. Her whole body was alive, her secret opening was still open, pulsating and enjoying their soft caressing hands. She wanted more. Lazily and sensuously she writhed backwards and forwards, up and down as the two eunuchs coated every inch of her so that she was again sexually heightened and glistening. Then the two Nubians covered Samoya's body with her fine linen robe.

'We'll do it again soon,' said Princess Bernice, gently touching the girl's hard nipples, then running her hands up her legs and giving Samoya's sex a final thrust with her fingers. 'That's to remember me by. Oh and Samoya . . .'

'Yes, your Highness?' said Samoya trembling at the woman's expert touch.

'I suggest you do some practising on your slaves. Line them up, make them open their legs, suck them, find out which ones you like best, who responds and opens fastest to your tongue. Then open your legs, make them bury their heads between your legs and suck you. You've been felt by experts, you know now what you should feel, so tell them exactly what you want, make them do it. But don't allow yourself the real thing. That pleasure is for another time and place. And my dear, after you've tested them, bring the best, the sexiest ones with you to Palmyra.'

Listening silently to their mistress with a secret smile upon their faces, the two Nubians tied the gold belt around Samoya's waist, put a garland of bay and asparagus leaves on her head, gave her her empty clay cup and her ceremonial flute. There was still an hour before dawn but Samoya was ready for the Goddess with Many Names.

Princess Bernice clapped her hands and the doors of the great bedroom opened into the black night and the courtyard. Irene and the other female slaves appeared with candles. Slowly, they walked in procession out of Pernel's mansion and into the dark freshly swept streets. As they wound their way towards the temple other friends and acquaintances joined them. Everyone walked barefoot except Princess Bernice who was borne along in a litter. Normally her eunuchs would have carried her but no male was allowed anywhere near the temple at the time of the rite, especially the important rite of initiation.

It was as Samoya put her foot on the first step leading up to the great gaping stone vulva that was the entrance to the temple that a shiver of fear blew over Samoya's body. In the heat of extreme sexual excitement she had agreed to marry the Palmyrene Prince Alif. Somehow the marriage had to be stopped. But who would help her? With each step she took Samoya prayed fervently to the Goddess to send her a saviour.

* * *

Over the next few weeks very few of Samoya's arrangements went according to plan.

Princess Bernice stayed on at the mansion making it impossible for Samoya to get away and see Zenobia. She had wanted to tell her friend about her meeting with the old crone at the city gates and what she had said about her and Irene's futures.

She had also wanted to tell her about Princess Bernice. How that decadent woman had spread her own legs wide, allowed her slaves to part the lips of her sex, and thrust their fingers and their tongue into her hidden place and how watching this had excited Samoya. And seeing this had sent a raging hunger storming through her body so that when the debauched Princess had told her to stand beside her and had stroked her thighs and found Samoya's sex, it had opened willingly to her touch. She wanted to tell Zenobia how unexpected and thrilling it was to feel the other woman's fingers exploring her. How her inner parts seemed to be made purely for pleasure and Princess Bernice had shown her how those parts could be aroused. She also wanted to tell her friend how one of Bernice's beautiful black eunuchs had put his body over hers, his head between her legs and had sucked at her open wanton place flooding it with desire. And how he had found a spot, a point within her, that when touched by his tongue covered her in waves of licentiousness that were so delicious that she had writhed and squirmed, never wanting it to stop. And how she had been overwhelmed by erotic dreams of total abandonment.

And that, whilst her body was being subjected to such pleasures, she had imagined men putting their sex into her mouth. Ordering her to suck it, lick it, tease it with her tongue until the sap was released. And then she had imagined being bound hand and foot and gagged. She wanted to tell Zenobia all these things and also how under the influence of extreme sexual pleasure she had agreed to marry Prince Alif.

Samoya was unable to do it because Bernice seldom let her out of her sight. She felt she was watched and spied upon all the time. And much to her chagrin her father ordered Irene to sleep with the rest of the slaves. She was unable to confide in her and had to sleep alone. When the princess wasn't beside her, her eunuchs were dogging her footsteps. Even when Bernice was actively bargaining with Pernel over the size of Samoya's dowry she kept Samoya by her side. Bernice played with her like a cat with a mouse. This annoyed Samoya on many levels. Uppermost because she was in a permanent state of sexual arousal and frustration. She wanted to be touched by the princess again. Wanted her eunuchs to stroke their hands over her body. She was denied this at every juncture. She kept hoping the princess would call her into her bedroom, but she did not. Samoya had then decided she would play sex games with Irene but her father's dictum made sure she couldn't do that either.

Late one morning, a week after her induction, Samoya managed to evade everybody, her father, her slaves, even Irene, but most of all she managed to get away from the oppressively sexual presence of Princess Bernice and her mainly male entourage.

In a quiet corner of the large and carefully designed courtyard, surrounded by tamarind and fig trees, Samoya sat by herself. She gave a sigh of relief, adjusted the many layers of her long, blue, floral patterned silk robes and stared contentedly at the fountains and the flowers, the myrtle hedges and the birds. The garden always soothed her. When she was agitated it calmed her. When she was moody and melancholy its symmetry of line, its combination of metals and stone, its colours: the cool blue and green tiles in the covered walkways and the vibrancy of the reds and yellows in the flowerbeds, the honeysuckle, jasmine and roses, and the brightly coloured flitting butterflies, made her spirits rise, gave her peace of mind and left her serene. She closed her eyes and sat quite still, unaware of anything except the sweet smell of roses and the buzzing of the bees.

'Stand.' The suddenness of Princess Bernice's order broke through her contentment.

Without thinking, Samoya stood to attention. Bernice lifted the back of Samoya's skirts revealing her neat bare buttocks.

'Hold that up,' said the voluptuous princess.

Bernice was carrying a small cushion on a long golden cord. She placed it on the cedar bench where Samoya's buttocks had been moments before. Then she put her hand, palm uppermost and her fingers sticking towards the bright blue sky on the cushion and told Samoya to sit down again, making sure her sex was arranged so that Bernice's fingers had instant access to her.

'Tell me, which season do you like best?' Bernice asked, as she eased her fingers along Samoya's hovering labia.

'Spring,' Samoya replied, and the touch of Bernice's cool

fingertips on her soft warm sex caused her juices to flow. Samoya rolled her hips and took more and more of Bernice's invading fingers.

'You must not squirm,' Bernice hissed. 'You must not let anyone guess what I am doing to you. You must learn to enjoy this without betraying pleasure. And you must learn to use your muscles. They must grip my fingers.'

'My muscles!' exclaimed Samoya, bemused.

'Your love-muscles. Squeeze my fingers with your love-muscles. Now do it,' she ordered. 'Grip and talk to me as if nothing was happening. We don't want your father realising his sweet virginal little daughter is having her most intimate parts played with.'

Bernice's words made Samoya wetter. She tensed her buttocks then flexed her inner muscles and gripped Bernice's fingers.

'Good,' said Bernice with approval. 'Continue to do that whilst pointing out to me the flowers in the garden. That way your father can know what you are saying but will have no idea what I am doing. He will think you are teaching me the joys of gardening; we will know I am teaching you the joys of sex.'

Samoya sat beside Bernice, her back upright, her nipples stiff and poking hard against the soft silk of her bodice and told Bernice which plants were what. Whilst Samoya spoke in a loud voice and loosed and unloosed her inner muscles around Bernice's ever thrusting fingers, Bernice continued to play with her and whisper in her ear.

'Your nipples are stiff. Would you like me to touch them. Don't stop talking, just nod your head.' Samoya nodded her head. 'Tonight I will have dinner in my bedroom and I want you as my guest. Do you understand . . .?'

'But my father . . .'

'I will tell your father I have to teach you court etiquette, which of course I do – and I am. I want you to come to my bedroom, but before you do I want you to cut a hole in this bodice so that those delightful nipples of yours are exposed and touchable and I want you to slit all your skirts from waist to floor. From now on you are to be accessible at all times.'

'At all times!' exclaimed Samoya.

'Yes, from now on at all times you are to be accessible to me and anybody else that I say may have access to you. Is that understood? Carry on talking, just nod your head.'

Samoya, excited by Bernice's suggestion, nodded her head vigorously. There was something so blatantly sexual in the thought that Bernice or one of her slaves could bend her over and stroke her whenever they pleased. In anticipation and muted excitement Samoya squeezed her muscles harder around Bernice's fingers.

'All your trousseau will be made in this way. I will leave you two of my slaves. They are fine dressmakers. They will help yours to make everything according to my instructions.'

'Who?' asked Samoya.

'Two girls, Phyllis and Hermione. They are excellent. Their needlework is the finest. Oh and tonight, Samoya, I want you blindfolded.'

'Blindfolded! Why?' asked Samoya.

'For my pleasure. You have to understand, Samoya, everything is done for my pleasure. Even teaching you is done for my pleasure,' said Bernice, withdrawing her fingers from Samoya's sex. 'I want you to go now. I want you to rest, sleep. It will be a long night tonight. Besides it's almost noon and it's getting too hot even for playing.'

Samoya left the princess and went to her cool marble-floored room to obey her commands. She was thoroughly aroused, her sex was open, full, swollen and frustrated. She wanted and needed it touched and stroked. It was only noon. How could she last until the evening in her heightened state of sexual awareness? She undressed and sitting on a number of silk cushions arranged against the marble wall, slit her skirts from top to bottom. Samoya was sitting naked, cutting small holes in her bodice when Irene came in unannounced. Since Princess Bernice's arrival she had seen very little of Samoya and had been acutely jealous. Her lips pouted sexily as she looked at her mistress.

'Why are you cutting up your beautiful clothes?' Irene asked.

Samoya looked up at her blonde slave. She wondered whether to tell her the truth or not. She stared at Irene's wide lips, her large breasts, their prominent nipples skimpily covered by a thin strip of black material, and her long thighs loosely encased in black diaphanous silk and thought how she would miss her if she went to Palmyra without her. Then she remembered Princess Bernice's instruction before her initiation. Test your slaves. Find out which are sexually interesting. Perhaps this was the time to see if she would take Irene to Palmyra with her.

'You ask too many questions,' said Samoya witheringly, adding, 'sit down on my bed.'

Irene was bemused by Samoya's tone. She had never talked to her like a slave. She had always been a friend. She didn't understand this new person who was going to marry a prince of the Royal household. Irene bowed and sat on Samoya's large bed.

Having cut two perfect holes Samoya put the pale green bodice back on, making sure the nipples stuck through enticingly. She chose a couple of her newly-slit fine transparent skirts, one in fiery red, the other in muted yellow and put them on over her bare skin. She tied a long thin leather cord many times around her waist and left her feet without slippers. She twirled around the room noticing how the skirts flared wide showing off her buttocks and her neat red-gold mound. And Irene sat watching her, excited, desperately wanting to touch Samoya's protruding nipples and the secret place at the top of her thighs. The place that was hers whenever they slept together. Samoya danced over to where Irene was sitting and bent her body offering her breasts to her slave.

'This is why I cut my bodice,' she said boldly. Irene did not touch Samoya, but stayed still, her eyes downcast. She didn't know what to do, what was expected of her.

'Touch my nipples,' Samoya ordered.

Tentatively Irene put out a hand and took the tiny red buds between her fingers and squeezed.

'Kiss them, suck them,' commanded Samoya. Irene did as she was told, then suddenly Samoya pushed her slave back on to the bed so that she lay flat. Then Samoya knelt, her knees either side of her slave's head, her sex hovering over Irene's mouth.

'I want you to put your tongue here,' commanded Samoya holding her secret lips apart so that her slave could see every hidden curl and crevice within. 'I want you to kiss me and lick me and find my special spot.'

Irene was shaking. For weeks she had wanted to bury her head between her mistress's thighs and now, in an unemotional, unloving way she was being ordered to do it. She wondered why. What had changed Samoya? When they slept together there had been a sweetness between them; when they had stroked one another there had been a gentleness, a lovingness. But now she was being commanded to do it and she didn't want to. Irene turned her head away. Samoya was furious. All her pent up frustration spilled out in a spoilt child's rage.

'You're being disobedient,' she roared. 'I will whip you for that. You're a slave, only a slave, my slave. Remember that and bend over.' Swiftly Samoya untied the leather around her waist, tore Irene's skirt from her body and made her part her legs. She stroked and teased her slave's bare buttocks with the thin leather strip, dragging it backwards and forwards over Irene's full rounded pink skin. Then she stepped back and the leather whistled through the air and landed on Irene's flesh with a sizzle. The girl jumped with the pain. Samoya did it again and again, finding increasing sexual excitement with each stroke and at the sight of the livid marks on her slave's pale flanks. Irene was hers to do with as she wanted, and the power she felt as she whipped the prostrate girl overwhelmed her, adding further impetus to her desires. Irene's body jumped and curled, writhed and hurled as the leather flashed down on her naked buttocks. Samoya began to stroke herself between each lash. Her sex had opened wider with the thrill, her juices were oozing out of her and she needed Irene's tongue to start licking her.

'Now you will suck me,' said Samoya, 'but first you will thank me for whipping you.'

'Thank you, mistress,' said Irene, sliding off the bed and kneeling before Samoya in a state of supplication.

In the distance Samoya was suddenly aware of voices. Her father and the bishop were returning. She covered herself hurriedly and decorously.

Her father hurried into the room closely followed by the bishop. He seemed agitated.

'Where's the princess?' he asked.

'In her room,' replied Samoya.

'We've just had a messenger from Palmyra. She's wanted back there immediately,' said Pernel, noticing Irene on the floor beside his daughter. 'You, go and tell Her Royal Highness.'

When Irene arrived in the opulent room and gave Princess Bernice the message that she was urgently needed back in Palmyra the princess immediately threw herself into a simmering rage. Bernice had been looking forward to an evening and night of debauchery. She had planned a variety of lessons for Samoya and her slave. And punishments.

Bernice watched her two eunuchs pack away her special playthings and sighed with anger. A great opportunity had been lost. There were times when she regarded her brother the King as a nuisance. But his word was law. She had to obey and return immediately. A pity. Bernice looked across at Irene who was standing still and silently waiting to be dismissed. Well she would have to defer Samoya's lessons in obedience until she arrived in Palmyra but she could punish the two of them in a minor way now. She would take Irene with her.

Samoya was devastated when Princess Bernice announced her intention. By the time she stood on the steps of her father's mansion to wave them goodbye Samoya was a ball of pent up fury. She kissed Irene with tears streaming down her face. But it was all she could do to say a civil word to the princess.

Before climbing on to her seated camel Bernice beckoned Samoya over. She parted her cloak and tweaked her nipples, reiterating her command that every bodice must have holes for her nipples, every skirt must be slit from top to toe, and that she was to wear these things at all times. If decorum was needed she could cover up with a black or a white flowing robe. But no matter what, she must remain accessible. Bernice then gave orders for Samoya's arrival in Palmyra. She was to wear white and gold. She must be perfumed and oiled and arrive completely shaved.

'Prince Alif likes a naked mound,' she said. Then the camel driver hauled the camel up and Bernice rode leisurely away.

Samoya was standing by herself when she felt eyes boring into her. She turned to see the Princess's two enormous charioteers leering at her. Samoya stared back at them. There was something about them that made her shiver. They approached her menacingly. Samoya refused to budge. She was not going to back down or show fear, especially on the steps of her own home. They put their hands under their tunics, and brought out their massive cocks. Samoya held her breath.

'One day, lady,' they said, 'one day we're going to have you.'

'Never,' she said and spat at them.

'Oh we will and we'll make you pay for that.'

'Amos, Aaaron,' called the Princess Bernice. The two charioteers dropped their tunics hiding their huge members. They bowed insolently to Samoya, turned on their heels and joined their mistress. And then the princess, her caravan and Irene were gone.

BLACK LACE NEW BOOKS

Published in April

PALAZZO
Jan Smith

Disenchanted following her divorce, Claire Savage, a successful young advertising executive, finds her sexuality reawakened by the mysterious Stuart MacIntosh, whom she meets on a holiday in Venice. Stuart encourages her to explore the darkest reaches of erotic experience but, at the same time, draws her into a sensual intrigue involving one of his rich clients and Claire's best friend, the feisty Cherry. To complicate matters, Claire's ex-husband appears on the scene, leaving Claire not knowing who to trust.

ISBN 0 352 33156 9

THE GALLERY
Fredrica Alleyn

Jaded with her dull but secure relationship, WPC Cressida Farleigh agrees to take part in the undercover investigation of a series of art frauds which will separate her from her long-term boyfriend. The chief suspect is the darkly attractive owner of a London art gallery, and Cressida must use her powers of seduction in order to find out the truth. She encounters a variety of fascinating people, including a charming artist specialising in bizarre, erotic subject matter, and is forced to face up to the truth about her innermost desires.

ISBN 0 352 33148 8

Published in May

AVENGING ANGELS
Roxanne Carr

Disillusioned by the chauvinistic attitude of men in the idyllic summer resort of Tierra del Sol, tour guide Karen puts her fledgling skills as a dominatrix to the test. Pleasantly surprised by the results, Karen opens a bar – Angels – where women can realise their most erotic fantasies. However, the one man Karen really wants – Ricardo Baddeiras – the owner of a rival bar and brother of her business partner Maria, refuses to be drawn into her web of submission. Quite clearly, Karen will have to fine-tune her skills.

ISBN 0 352 33147 X

THE LION LOVER

Mercedes Kelly

It's the 1920s. When young doctor Mathilde Valentine becomes a medic in a mission in Kenya she soon finds out all is not what it seems. For one thing, McKinnon, the handsome missionary, has been married twice – and both of his wives have mysteriously disappeared. Mathilde falls for a rugged game warden but ignores his warnings that she might be in danger. Abducted and sold into slavery, she finds herself in the weird and wonderful harem of an Arabian sultan and discovers the truth about the two Mrs McKinnons. Will she regain her freedom?

ISBN 0 352 33162 3

PAST PASSIONS

An Anthology of Erotic Writing by Women
Edited by Kerri Sharp
£6.99

This is the second of the two larger format Black Lace anthologies – *Modern Love* being the first. While *Modern Love* is a selection of extracts from contemporary Black Lace novels, *Past Passions* is an inspired collection of excerpts taken from tales set in a variety of countries, cultures and centuries giving the reader the added pleasure of detail essential in the creating of historical settings.

ISBN 0 352 33159 3

To be published in June

JASMINE BLOSSOMS

Sylvie Ouellette

When Joanna is sent on a business trip to Japan, she expects nothing unusual. She soon finds that her sensuality is put to the test as enigmatic messages are followed by singular encounters with strangers who seem to know her every desire. She is constantly aroused but never entirely sated. As she gradually gives in to the magic of Japan – its people and its ways – she learns that she is becoming involved in a case of mistaken identity, erotic intrigue and mysterious seduction.

ISBN 0 352 33157 7

PANDORA'S BOX 2
An Anthology of Erotic Writing by Women
Edited by Kerri Sharp
£5.99

This is the second of the Pandora's Box anthologies of erotic writing by women. The book includes extracts from the best-selling and most popular titles of the Black Lace series, as well as four completely new stories. *Pandora's Box 2* is a celebration of four years of this revolutionary imprint. The diversity of the material is a testament to the many facets of the female imagination. This is unashamed erotic indulgence for women.

ISBN 0 352 33151 8

If you would like a complete list of plot summaries of Black Lace titles, please fill out the questionnaire overleaf or send a stamped addressed envelope to:-

Black Lace, 332 Ladbroke Grove, London W10 5AH

BLACK LACE BACKLIST

All books are priced £4.99 unless another price is given.

BLUE HOTEL	Cherri Pickford	ISBN 0 352 32858 4	☐
CASSANDRA'S CONFLICT	Fredrica Alleyn	ISBN 0 352 32859 2	☐
THE CAPTIVE FLESH	Cleo Cordell	ISBN 0 352 32872 X	☐
PLEASURE HUNT	Sophie Danson	ISBN 0 352 32880 0	☐
OUTLANDIA	Georgia Angelis	ISBN 0 352 32883 5	☐
BLACK ORCHID	Roxanne Carr	ISBN 0 352 32888 6	☐
ODALISQUE	Fleur Reynolds	ISBN 0 352 32887 8	☐
THE SENSES BEJEWELLED	Cleo Cordell	ISBN 0 352 32904 1	☐
VIRTUOSO	Katrina Vincenzi	ISBN 0 352 32907 6	☐
FIONA'S FATE	Fredrica Alleyn	ISBN 0 352 32913 0	☐
HANDMAIDEN OF PALMYRA	Fleur Reynolds	ISBN 0 352 32919 X	☐
THE SILKEN CAGE	Sophie Danson	ISBN 0 352 32928 9	☐
THE GIFT OF SHAME	Sarah Hope-Walker	ISBN 0 352 32935 1	☐
SUMMER OF ENLIGHTENMENT	Cheryl Mildenhall	ISBN 0 352 32937 8	☐
A BOUQUET OF BLACK ORCHIDS	Roxanne Carr	ISBN 0 352 32939 4	☐
JULIET RISING	Cleo Cordell	ISBN 0 352 32938 6	☐
DEBORAH'S DISCOVERY	Fredrica Alleyn	ISBN 0 352 32945 9	☐

THE TUTOR	Portia Da Costa ISBN 0 352 32946 7	☐
THE HOUSE IN NEW ORLEANS	Fleur Reynolds ISBN 0 352 32951 3	☐
ELENA'S CONQUEST	Lisette Allen ISBN 0 352 32950 5	☐
CASSANDRA'S CHATEAU	Fredrica Alleyn ISBN 0 352 32955 6	☐
WICKED WORK	Pamela Kyle ISBN 0 352 32958 0	☐
DREAM LOVER	Katrina Vincenzi ISBN 0 352 32956 4	☐
PATH OF THE TIGER	Cleo Cordell ISBN 0 352 32959 9	☐
BELLA'S BLADE	Georgia Angelis ISBN 0 352 32965 3	☐
THE DEVIL AND THE DEEP BLUE SEA	Cheryl Mildenhall ISBN 0 352 32966 1	☐
WESTERN STAR	Roxanne Carr ISBN 0 352 32969 6	☐
A PRIVATE COLLECTION	Sarah Fisher ISBN 0 352 32970 X	☐
NICOLE'S REVENGE	Lisette Allen ISBN 0 352 32984 X	☐
UNFINISHED BUSINESS	Sarah Hope-Walker ISBN 0 352 32983 1	☐
CRIMSON BUCCANEER	Cleo Cordell ISBN 0 352 32987 4	☐
LA BASQUAISE	Angel Strand ISBN 0 352 32988 2	☐
THE LURE OF SATYRIA	Cheryl Mildenhall ISBN 0 352 32994 7	☐
THE DEVIL INSIDE	Portia Da Costa ISBN 0 352 32993 9	☐
HEALING PASSION	Sylvie Ouellette ISBN 0 352 32998 X	☐
THE SEDUCTRESS	Vivienne LaFay ISBN 0 352 32997 1	☐
THE STALLION	Georgina Brown ISBN 0 352 33005 8	☐
CRASH COURSE	Juliet Hastings ISBN 0 352 33018 X	☐
THE INTIMATE EYE	Georgia Angelis ISBN 0 352 33004 X	☐

THE AMULET	Lisette Allen ISBN 0 352 33019 8	☐
CONQUERED	Fleur Reynolds ISBN 0 352 33025 2	☐
DARK OBSESSION	Fredrica Alleyn ISBN 0 352 33026 0	☐
LED ON BY COMPULSION	Leila James ISBN 0 352 33032 5	☐
OPAL DARKNESS	Cleo Cordell ISBN 0 352 33033 3	☐
JEWEL OF XANADU	Roxanne Carr ISBN 0 352 33037 6	☐
RUDE AWAKENING	Pamela Kyle ISBN 0 352 33036 8	☐
GOLD FEVER	Louisa Francis ISBN 0 352 33043 0	☐
EYE OF THE STORM	Georgina Brown ISBN 0 352 33044 9	☐
WHITE ROSE ENSNARED	Juliet Hastings ISBN 0 352 33052 X	☐
A SENSE OF ENTITLEMENT	Cheryl Mildenhall ISBN 0 352 33053 8	☐
ARIA APPASSIONATA	Juliet Hastings ISBN 0 352 33056 2	☐
THE MISTRESS	Vivienne LaFay ISBN 0 352 33057 0	☐
ACE OF HEARTS	Lisette Allen ISBN 0 352 33059 7	☐
DREAMERS IN TIME	Sarah Copeland ISBN 0 352 33064 3	☐
GOTHIC BLUE	Portia Da Costa ISBN 0 352 33075 9	☐
THE HOUSE OF GABRIEL	Rafaella ISBN 0 352 33063 5	☐
PANDORA'S BOX	ed. Kerri Sharp ISBN 0 352 33074 0	☐
THE NINETY DAYS OF GENEVIEVE	Lucinda Carrington ISBN 0 352 33070 8	☐
GEMINI HEAT	Portia Da Costa ISBN 0 352 32912 2	☐
THE BIG CLASS	Angel Strand ISBN 0 352 33076 7	☐
THE BLACK ORCHID HOTEL	Roxanne Carr ISBN 0 352 33060 0	☐

LORD WRAXALL'S FANCY	Anna Lieff Saxby ISBN 0 352 33080 5	☐
FORBIDDEN CRUSADE	Juliet Hastings ISBN 0 352 33079 1	☐
THE HOUSESHARE	Pat O'Brien ISBN 0 352 33094 5	☐
THE KING'S GIRL	Sylvie Ouellette ISBN 0 352 33095 3	☐
TO TAKE A QUEEN	Jan Smith ISBN 0 352 33098 8	☐
DANCE OF OBSESSION	Olivia Christie ISBN 0 352 33101 1	☐
THE BRACELET	Fredrica Alleyn ISBN 0 352 33110 0	☐
RUNNERS AND RIDERS	Georgina Brown ISBN 0 352 33117 8	☐
PASSION FLOWERS	Celia Parker ISBN 0 352 33118 6	☐
ODYSSEY	Katrina Vincenzi-Thyne ISBN 0 352 33111 9	☐
CONTINUUM	Portia Da Costa ISBN 0 352 33120 8	☐
THE ACTRESS	Vivienne LaFay ISBN 0 352 33119 4	☐
ÎLE DE PARADIS	Mercedes Kelly ISBN 0 352 33121 6	☐
NADYA'S QUEST	Lisette Allen ISBN 0 352 33135 6	☐
DESIRE UNDER CAPRICORN	Louisa Francis ISBN 0 352 33136 4	☐
PULLING POWER	Cheryl Mildenhall ISBN 0 352 33139 9	☐
THE MASTER OF SHILDEN	Lucinda Carrington ISBN 0 352 33140 2	☐
MODERN LOVE	Edited by Kerri Sharp ISBN 0 352 33158 5	☐
SILKEN CHAINS	Jodi Nicol ISBN 0 352 33143 7	☐
THE HAND OF AMUN	Juliet Hastings ISBN 0 352 33144 5	☐

------✂--------------------

Please send me the books I have ticked above.

Name ....

Address ....

....

....

.... Post Code ....

Send to: **Cash Sales, Black Lace Books, 332 Ladbroke Grove, London W10 5AH.**

Please enclose a cheque or postal order, made payable to **Virgin Publishing Ltd**, to the value of the books you have ordered plus postage and packing costs as follows:

UK and BFPO – £1.00 for the first book, 50p for each subsequent book.

Overseas (including Republic of Ireland) – £2.00 for the first book, £1.00 each subsequent book.

If you would prefer to pay by VISA or ACCESS/MASTERCARD, please write your card number and expiry date here:

....

Please allow up to 28 days for delivery.

Signature ....

------✂--------------------

WE NEED YOUR HELP . . .

to plan the future of women's erotic fiction –

– and no stamp required!

Yours are the only opinions that matter.

Black Lace is the first series of books devoted to erotic fiction by women for women.

We intend to keep providing the best-written, sexiest books you can buy. And we'd appreciate your help and valued opinion of the books so far. Tell us what you want to read.

THE BLACK LACE QUESTIONNAIRE

SECTION ONE: ABOUT YOU

1.1 Sex (*we presume you are female, but so as not to discriminate*)
Are you?

Male	☐
Female	☐

1.2 Age

under 21	☐	21–30	☐
31–40	☐	41–50	☐
51–60	☐	over 60	☐

1.3 At what age did you leave full-time education?

still in education	☐	16 or younger	☐
17–19	☐	20 or older	☐

1.4 Occupation ______________________________

1.5 Annual household income

under £10,000	☐	£10–£20,000	☐
£20–£30,000	☐	£30–£40,000	☐
over £40,000	☐		

1.6 We are perfectly happy for you to remain anonymous; but if you would like to receive information on other publications available, please insert your name and address

____

____

____

____

SECTION TWO: ABOUT BUYING BLACK LACE BOOKS

2.1 How did you acquire this copy of *Past Passions*?

I bought it myself	☐	My partner bought it	☐
I borrowed/found it	☐		

2.2 How did you find out about Black Lace books?

I saw them in a shop ☐
I saw them advertised in a magazine ☐
I saw the London Underground posters ☐
I read about them in ____________________
Other ____________________

2.3 Please tick the following statements you agree with:

I would be less embarrassed about buying Black Lace books if the cover pictures were less explicit ☐
I think that in general the pictures on Black Lace books are about right ☐
I think Black Lace cover pictures should be as explicit as possible ☐

2.4 Would you read a Black Lace book in a public place – on a train for instance?

Yes	☐	No	☐

SECTION THREE: ABOUT THIS BLACK LACE BOOK

3.1 Do you think the sex content in this book is:

Too much	☐	About right	☐
Not enough	☐		

3.2 Do you think the writing style in this book is:

Too unreal/escapist	☐	About right	☐
Too down to earth	☐		

3.3 Do you think the story in this book is:

Too complicated	☐	About right	☐
Too boring/simple	☐		

3.4 Do you think the cover of this book is:

Too explicit	☐	About right	☐
Not explicit enough	☐		

Here's a space for any other comments:

SECTION FOUR: ABOUT OTHER BLACK LACE BOOKS

4.1 How many Black Lace books have you read? ☐

4.2 If more than one, which one did you prefer?

____

4.3 Why?

SECTION FIVE: ABOUT YOUR IDEAL EROTIC NOVEL

We want to publish the books you want to read – so this is your chance to tell us exactly what your ideal erotic novel would be like.

5.1 Using a scale of 1 to 5 (1 = no interest at all, 5 = your ideal), please rate the following possible settings for an erotic novel:

- Medieval/barbarian/sword 'n' sorcery ☐
- Renaissance/Elizabethan/Restoration ☐
- Victorian/Edwardian ☐
- 1920s & 1930s – the Jazz Age ☐
- Present day ☐
- Future/Science Fiction ☐

5.2 Using the same scale of 1 to 5, please rate the following themes you may find in an erotic novel:

- Submissive male/dominant female ☐
- Submissive female/dominant male ☐
- Lesbianism ☐
- Bondage/fetishism ☐
- Romantic love ☐
- Experimental sex e.g. anal/watersports/sex toys ☐
- Gay male sex ☐
- Group sex ☐

Using the same scale of 1 to 5, please rate the following styles in which an erotic novel could be written:

- Realistic, down to earth, set in real life ☐
- Escapist fantasy, but just about believable ☐
- Completely unreal, impressionistic, dreamlike ☐

5.3 Would you prefer your ideal erotic novel to be written from the viewpoint of the main male characters or the main female characters?

Male ☐ Female ☐
Both ☐

5.4 What would your ideal Black Lace heroine be like? Tick as many as you like:

Dominant	☐	Glamorous	☐
Extroverted	☐	Contemporary	☐
Independent	☐	Bisexual	☐
Adventurous	☐	Naïve	☐
Intellectual	☐	Introverted	☐
Professional	☐	Kinky	☐
Submissive	☐	Anything else?	☐
Ordinary	☐	______________	

5.5 What would your ideal male lead character be like? Again, tick as many as you like:

Rugged	☐		
Athletic	☐	Caring	☐
Sophisticated	☐	Cruel	☐
Retiring	☐	Debonair	☐
Outdoor-type	☐	Naïve	☐
Executive-type	☐	Intellectual	☐
Ordinary	☐	Professional	☐
Kinky	☐	Romantic	☐
Hunky	☐		
Sexually dominant	☐	Anything else?	☐
Sexually submissive	☐	______________	

5.6 Is there one particular setting or subject matter that your ideal erotic novel would contain?

____

SECTION SIX: LAST WORDS

6.1 What do you like best about Black Lace books?

____

6.2 What do you most dislike about Black Lace books?

____

6.3 In what way, if any, would you like to change Black Lace covers?

____

6.4 Here's a space for any other comments:

____

____

____

____

Thank you for completing this questionnaire. Now tear it out of the book – carefully! – put it in an envelope and send it to:

Black Lace
FREEPOST
London
W10 5BR

No stamp is required if you are resident in the U.K.